Hic est sacerdos quem coronavit Dominus

THE MASS OF BROTHER MICHEL

The

MASS

of

BROTHER
MICHEL

MICHAEL KENT

Foreword by
Peter Kwasniewski

 Angelico Press

Angelico Press reprint edition, 2017
This Angelico edition is a republication
of the work originally published by
The Bruce Publishing Company, Milwaukee, 1942
Foreword © Peter Kwasniewski 2017

For information, address:
Angelico Press
4709 Briar Knoll Dr.
Kettering, OH 45429
info@angelicopress.com

978-1-62138-290-4 (pb)
978-1-62138-291-1 (cloth)

Cover Design: Michael Schrauzer
Photo Credit: Crucifix and Manuscript at Silverstream Priory,
County Meath, Ireland, by Dom Benedict Andersen, O.S.B.

CONTENTS

Foreword

Peter A. Kwasniewski

Like countless novels, *The Mass of Brother Michel* is a romance based
on the all-consuming love of a man and a woman for each other.
After this, however, the resemblance to most other novels ends. The
conventional "happy ending" is here the point of departure, and the
shattering of it is only the first step in a labyrinthine plot that culmi-
nates in a scene one could never have predicted and will never forget.
It is a story that begins in innocent vanity and ends in the terrible
beauty of self-sacrifice, a story that stretches from love to love, as
"deep calleth on deep" (Ps 41[42]:8)—the human love of parent and
child, lover and beloved, brother and sister; the divine love that
irrupts into our now-orderly, now-chaotic lives; and the transfigura-
tion of the one by the other, until God is "all in all" (1 Cor 15:28).

God created the world for Himself, to reflect His beauty and give
glory to His Name. God created the world also for man's sake—male
and female He created them, to behold that beauty and participate
in that glory. There is a tight connection between these two truths.
Man cannot find himself, cannot be happy, cannot finally benefit
from God's gift of reality, unless he reaches past himself and the
world to seek God in Himself and to embrace Him for His own sake.
The condition for seeing reality truthfully is self-abnegation, the will
to order oneself and all things to their Maker. The sweetest fruit of

love hangs from the tree of the Cross; other fruits are cloying, empty, even poisonous. This is no less true about the relationship of man and woman. Ever since the curving inward of Adam and Eve, human beings have striven to find their meaning, worth, identity, happiness, in the relationship of the sexes. Whether this relationship takes on the grasping form of *eros* or the noble self-giving of friendship, it cannot avoid being inadequate and even destructive when cut off from the love of God, of which it was always meant to be the dynamic sign, a universal novitiate for the consecrated life of the world to come.

It was a priest (now a monk) who gave a copy of this obscure novel to my wife, who was delighted to discover what appears to be the only Catholic historical novel in English that is set in the context of the continental Reformation.[1] She read it with mounting amazement, and then handed it to our son. When he finished, he said to me: "We *have* to read this book out loud together." Since reading aloud is a favorite pastime in our family (and just about the only way I ever manage to read fiction), I gladly obliged—not at all prepared for the exhilarating shock, the overwhelming satisfaction, of *The Mass of Brother Michel.* It is quite simply one of the most powerful books I have ever read, not only for the fascinating characters embroiled in an accurately rendered historical narrative full of surprises, but also for its fearless probing of massive existential questions that go the heart of who and what we are as fallen and redeemed creatures, as Christians who live from and for the holy sacrifice of Christ. It is a book of searing intensity that addresses with unflinching candor the power of romantic love to cripple its subject and deform its object, the power of suffering to undermine illusions and induce the labor of self-discovery, the power of prayer to reassemble the shards of the shattered image of God in the soul, and the power of the priest as the privileged instrument by which the divine Physician probes and heals man's grievous wounds, meet-

---

[1] Thanks to Msgr. Robert Hugh Benson and other English writers, the English Reformation period is extremely well covered, but the messy situation on the continent—such as the Huguenot violence in France, which is the setting for *The Mass of Brother Michel*—has suffered neglect in our language.

ing his hunger and thirst with the infinite hunger and thirst of a God who, being All and lacking nothing, nevertheless longs to take complete possession of the noble, fragile creature made unto His image and likeness.

At the center of the novel is the sovereign mystery of the Mass. No book of which I am aware comes close to this one for its ecstatic hymn of praise to the Cross planted in our midst, a prose-poem offered up like incense before the altar of sacrifice. Through the author's contemplative gaze, one is given new eyes with which to see the Church's most precious and most potent treasure. One of the many virtues of this remarkable book is the way it gives sublime narrative expression to the peculiar tranquility of the Low Mass and the uplifting majesty of the High Mass, the one as a "still, small voice" (1 Kgs 19:12), the other "more glorious than the surgings of the sea" (Ps 92[93]:4).[2] Never has a novel conveyed more powerfully the mysticism of the Roman Catholic Mass in its authentic traditional form. "Gradually, as the sacred liturgy progressed, he became aware of a presence, intangible but real. . . . This reality pierced his insensibility, summoned him with insistence, demanded that he recognize it and give it a name. Something within him stirred and woke; he was in the midst of Beauty, and he knew it." That such an evocative novel could never have been written about the reformed liturgy of the 1960s, newly fashioned for Modern Man, is a poignant sign of the woes from which the Church is suffering today, and to which the only solution will be a reawakening, recentering, and transformation as radical as the one experienced by the story's protagonist. Thus, while a new edition of *The Mass of Brother Michel* needs no other justification than the inherent excellence of a gripping story of a man and a woman and their toilsome pilgrimage to the heavenly Jerusalem, it also becomes for readers today—in a way the author could never have intended in 1942—a parable of the postconciliar

---

[2] As phrased in the Grail translation of Psalm 93. See my chapter "The Peace of Low Mass and the Glory of High Mass" in *Noble Beauty, Transcendent Holiness: Why the Modern Age Needs the Mass of Ages* (Kettering, OH: Angelico Press, 2017), 235–55.

Church in desperate need of renewal from the forgotten wellsprings of her life.

When Pope Benedict XVI wrote, concerning the traditional Latin Mass, that "it has clearly been demonstrated that young persons too have discovered this liturgical form, felt its attraction, and found in it a form of encounter with the Mystery of the Most Holy Eucharist, particularly suited to them,"[3] he might well have been writing a description of the journey of Brother Michel, as you, fortunate reader, will discover in these pages. But that is because there will always be Michels in this world; there will always be those who are yearning for more, for divine Beauty, for the eternal God; there will always be those for whom God Himself yearns. These He will call to Himself, as lovers, as virgins, as victims, as monks or nuns or priests, as His own possession in whatever ways He will arrange and accomplish. Like Daniel the prophet, Michel is that "man of desires" (Dan 9:23) to whom the Lord will show visions and give understanding. May this book make such a man of desires out of each one who reads it.

---

[3] Letter to Bishops *Con grande fiducia*, July 7, 2007.

Dedication

Every priest who opens this book may consider it as dedicated to himself.

For it is dedicated to the great High Priest, and all who are priests in Him.

Since it is impossible to mention, individually and by name, all who are included in this dedication — to whom, after Him, this work is humbly offered, in grateful recognition of their response to His choice and of all that it entails — each must read his own name, written here surely if invisibly, for himself.

Three, however, may be mentioned as representative of all: Rev. James M. Gillis, C.S.P., Rev. John A. Silvia, and Rev. Daniel E. Carey; for without the help, encouragement, and inspiration of these three, it is certain there would be no

BROTHER MICHEL

PART ONE

THE NIGHT OF MICHEL

Pretiosa in conspectu Domini
*mors sanctorum ejus**

1. Death of a Saint

i

In her great room overlooking the gardens of the Château, the vineyards and olive trees beyond, and the brilliant ribbon of the Mediterranean flashing in the sunlit distance, the Comtesse de Guillemont lay dying.

About this fact there was nothing remarkable. It was bound to happen sooner or later to the Comtesse de Guillemont as to other women of greater and less degree. That it occurred in this instance soon rather than late was regarded as a grave misfortune by all save the Countess herself, who was inclined to look on the event with relief rather than otherwise. In fact, the circumstance was attended in her estimation with only one matter for serious regret, which, however, her continued existence could have done nothing to remedy.

It was a perfect day on which to die, if one believed death to be a birth and a beginning, a reward and a release. The air was a crystal transparency, charged with a magic that sharpened the edges and heightened the colors of all things. The cloudless sky was no mere emptiness, but an inverted sea, a swimming blue depth and intensity, in which the birds, plunging upward, were lost in flight, and which poured its superabundant riches of color into the waters of the Mediterranean, spread to the horizon to

---

* The English translation of passages in Latin will be found on page 271 listed in the order of the pages whereon the Latin appears.

3

receive this largess. Across these waters the path of the sun traced a blinding and jeweled brilliance. A green mist shimmered in the air, woven of the young foliage of fruit and olive trees, and punctuated at intervals by the dark and pointed silhouettes of cypress, standing singly or in groups.

The village of Guillemont, crowning the summit of a steep hill, was a patchwork of cream-colored walls and mossy tiled roofs, weathered to a rich depth and softness of hue, and compactly fitted into the stone girdle of the wall encircling it. Between the village and the sea, the Château de Guillemont presided over its outlying buildings, its vineyards and groves, its pools and statues and gardens, a shining splendor in the sunlight.

To all this beauty the dying woman who had been its mistress for more than a score of years now lay blind and indifferent. The curtains at her windows were tightly drawn, shutting out the view, and concealing also the rich furnishings and hangings of the chamber, notably the celebrated tapestries depicting the travels of Ulysses which the Count had ordered woven at Arras as a wedding gift for his bride. The one passion of Madame being her faith, which she practiced with ardor and devotion, it was the habit of Monseigneur to show his regard for her with frequent gifts — a tapestry, a carving, a miniature — representing some hero of classical mythology, some episode memorable in pagan lore.

Adélaïde de Guillemont was but little over forty. Since the age of eighteen she had been the wife of Henri, Comte de Guillemont, and this cross she had borne with a fortitude and resignation truly remarkable in view of the fact that she lacked neither intelligence nor spirit. Only one extremely dull, or utterly wanting in sensibility, could have endured for so long the Count's vagaries and malice without the loss of health, or reason, or both. No specific name, such as cholera, or typhus, or the stone, could be given by the attending physicians to the malady from which it was now clear that she would not recover. They bled her, and leeched her, and starved her; but none of these remedies being of any avail, her death was now only a question of time. She lay in the center of the great bed from which the heavy curtains had been drawn back, her face hardly distinguishable from the linen pillows on which it rested. Always a slight figure, she resembled now a very little girl who was also very old. The dying, the aged, and children, have this in common, that while still on this earth, they are closer than others to eternity.

The day previously she had rallied somewhat; and it was decided to bleed her again in the hope of postponing, if possible, the inevitable. This measure had an effect precisely the reverse of what it was intended to produce. Death, who had stood within sight but motionless, like a vessel becalmed, instead of withdrawing still further, approached in a stride and claimed her. Immediately following the bleeding, she appeared to dissolve before the eyes of those in attendance; she became, as they watched, transparent, substance turning to shadow, sound fading into silence. This was the more unfortunate in that her son, Michel, who had not left the estate for a week, had taken advantage of her slight improvement and the physicians' solemn assurance that she would linger for some days, and was off for the day on urgent business of his own, at a distance where he could not be reached.

The Abbé Courtot was summoned with all haste, though it was doubtful that she would find strength to make her last confession, if indeed she lived till he arrived. But that, the weeping servants reminded each other, could hardly matter: what had Madame to confess? On earth she had been an angel; in heaven she would be a saint.

Madame, as it happened, had a great sorrow, a cruel disappointment, to confess. Her need to do so gave her strength sufficient for the task. The Abbé Courtot had been for many years confessor to the family, and tutor to her sons; but this was the only time she mentioned this sorrow to him or anyone.

The room being emptied of all save the priest, Madame opened her eyes. These were a clear and livid blue, of an astonishing depth and brilliance. Life still burned in them from the white and shrunken mask of her face.

She raised her eyes now to the face of the Abbé, which, in repose, wore the look of one who has but recently suffered a great grief. This mark had been graven on it slowly, through the years; it was the fruit, not of his own personal sorrows, but of those born of his calling. For it was the lot of the Abbé Courtot to exercise his ministry among a callous and indifferent aristocracy, where he encountered such hypocrisy and contempt of religion, and wore himself out in such fruitless expenditure of toil, as no shepherd of the poor and oppressed can ever know.

Beyond its habitual look of sorrow, the face of the Abbé gave no further hint of the pain which the performance of his duty in the case of Adélaïde de Guillemont now cost him. He had given her the last rites before, but each time with the conviction that she would recover, as she had indeed done, to the surprise of all save himself. But now he knew that she was beyond hope; when these brilliant eyes closed again, they would not open till the resurrection. She had bequeathed their exact replica to her son Michel, of whose future the Abbé dreamed dreams which he had disclosed to no one but his Maker; but should this secret hope be realized, it would bring such a reward and justification of his labor as the aging priest hardly dared look for on this earth.

It would also be some consolation in the deep personal sorrow which the death of the Countess meant for him. If she had drawn strength from his counsel, he had taken courage from the mere fact of her existence: from the knowledge that in the decadent society where his ministry lay, God had placed one soul of such radiance and purity that to think of it was to feel increase of faith and hope. To lose this soul from among those entrusted to him was the chalice he had prayed might pass from him; until now that prayer had been granted. But this time his hour was come. The chalice would not pass; he must drink it, and show nothing of what he felt.

The Countess made her confession in a whisper, very faint, with long pauses between the words, but distinct.

"I accuse myself — of rebellion against the will of God."

"Who of us could not do likewise, my daughter? Perfect submission to God's holy will was practiced only by One. Our hearts are naturally rebellious, or there would be no virtue in obedience."

She made a sign of negation, weak but positive.

"I have asked a favor of God, a holy gift. I have offered all the sorrows of my life for this grace. And He has refused. This seems to me a cruelty, *mon père*. I cannot accept it. All else, yes. But not this."

"What is it you have asked, my child?"

"That one of my sons might be a priest of God."

The Abbé paused, astonished at hearing from the dying woman the precise statement of his own hope. But of this, also, he gave no sign.

"My daughter, it is not too late. Have you not two sons living? God may still grant your request, especially when you shall entreat Him face to face in heaven."

Again she shook her head.

"Paul has not the desire, nor Michel. André — yes. But André is dead. Jean or Pierre, perhaps. But they, too, are dead. In this I see God's judgment on me, *mon père*. I wished — long ago — to enter religion. I believed that God called me to do so. But I did not obey. I yielded to the will of my parents. I married instead."

"But has not all your married life been a penance, my child, which you may offer to God in reparation for that disobedience — if disobedience it was? Of that, God alone can be the judge, who knows the circumstances to which you refer."

She trembled, like a flower held in a palsied hand.

"But yes, *mon père*. A penance — a purgatory. I have made it an offering — a prayer — that the service I refused to God, a son of mine might give Him in my stead." She moved her head on the pillow; her voice grew stronger. "Oh, *mon père,* the desire has been a pain — a long and cruel pain — for a son to be ordained, to stand before the altar, to offer the Holy Sacrifice of Mass, to be a priest on earth and in heaven, forever. And it can never be. Three might have done so, and they are dead. Michel and Paul remain, but with them it is not possible."

"With God all things are possible. He asks you only to keep faith in His goodness to the end. With Paul it is not likely, I will grant. With Michel — I will say for your comfort, my daughter, that I believe Michel to have the vocation, but he does not know it yet."

The eyelids of the Countess fluttered. The effort she had made exhausted her, and she struggled to speak, summoning all her strength, and a strength beyond hers, for the words she still wished to say.

"But Michel — will marry. I have never seen one — so deep — in love —"

"We may neither force God to do our wills, nor compel another to do the will of God. But if Michel wears the sign of the priesthood in the sight of God, as I firmly believe he does, God will make it clear to him, in His own time and manner. And those who love most truly with the love of earth, are capable of loving most deeply with the love of heaven."

"You believe — in truth — it may yet be —?"

"I believe that with God all things are possible. In heaven you will pray that if God calls Michel to His service as priest, he may hear, and hearing, he may not resist. It may indeed be for this reason that God gave you the desire to enter religion, but did not permit the fulfillment of that desire, that you might give Him a priest in Michel. If Michel accepts the call — for I have little doubt that sooner or later he will hear it — he will make such a priest as the world has desperate need of now. I will add my poor prayers to yours, my child, and I believe that it shall be as you desire."

She received the last sacraments and died, apparently in peace. Whether she was convinced by the Abbé's words, it was impossible to say. In any case she could hardly have guessed the truth: that although her opinion and that of the Abbé contradicted each other, both were to be proved correct.

ii

Appearances, however, favored the verdict of the Countess rather than that of the Abbé in this matter.

Michel showed no sign of a vocation to the priesthood or to the religious state.

In fact, at the time of his mother's last confession, he was bent only on making the attainment of that state impossible for himself.

That is to say, he was on his way to the Château de Cançonnet, having risen before daybreak that no time might be lost in the accomplishment of his errand. His mother's improvement, though slight, was reassuring; he had the promise of the physicians that he might safely absent himself from Guillemont for the day; no hope was held out for her recovery, but she was sure to linger for some days, perhaps even weeks. And the emergency which had arisen in his own life was such that delay would prove fatal; it must be dealt with firmly, and at once. He bade his mother good night the previous evening, told her where he was going but not why, since the reason for his journey would have caused her great distress, and set off at dawn, confident of finding her at least no worse on his return, and of settling the business in hand to his satisfaction.

For the heart of Michel was lost in the depths of a pair of smoky eyes, shot through with flashes of fire, that smoldered in a clear young face framed in a mass of burnished curls. Nor was this any new infatuation; into this beauty the threads of Michel's life were tightly woven, and had been so woven since childhood, the two forming one fabric, one design. To destroy this fabric it would be necessary to unravel the threads, pulling them apart one by one: an undertaking manifestly impossible. But now an intruder was embarked on this destruction, expertly engaged in separating the warp and weft, with intent to weave the latter into a new pattern to his own liking.

The horror was that he who attempted this desecration was Michel's brother, Paul. After a moody boyhood and petulant youth, Paul had been shipped to Italy with a tutor to see what travel could do to polish him into assured manhood. The experiment succeeded, in one respect at least, beyond all expectation: Paul returned expert in the unraveling of tapestries.

Michel knew that Paul had called at Cançonnet, as was but fitting; he did not know that Paul had returned daily ever since, until informed of it by a groom who had Michel's interest at heart, and to whom this information had been relayed by a succession of tongues set going by a *femme de chambre* at Cançonnet, whose interest in the affair was not Michel, but gossip. But though the report of Paul's visits at Cançonnet, and their obvious purpose, came to Michel's ears by this devious and generally unreliable route, there was no doubt of its truth: all knew of it, apparently, save the one whom it directly concerned. Thus, Paul had made headway in his destructions before Michel suspected that he had so much as undertaken them. To stop him and to repair the damage was now of first necessity. Michel saddled his horse Roland — who resembled the Paladin, his master boasted, in all respects except that he could not sing — and rode off with all hope.

Cançonnet lay some twenty-five miles to the north of Guillemont, in higher country bordering the foothills of the Alps. About this region there was a character rugged and desolate, contrasting strongly with the gentle slopes, the sun-drenched fields and vineyards of Guillemont, and appealing to Michel's imagination. The way thither lay through a forest to enter which was an enchantment. Here silence and beauty were enclosed and concentrated; never did he set foot in the forest, but they laid an instant spell on him. He was impelled to go softly, almost to uncover, as in church. Even in the urgency of his present errand, he slowed his pace, restrained by a deep wonder and delight. Here the coolness of the night still lingered. The early light seeped through the foliage and spread within the forest a veiled brightness. Sounds inseparable from the wood — that ensemble of rustlings and whisperings compounded of the sighing of the wind in the tree, the scurrying of rabbits, the chattering of squirrels, the fluttering and calling of birds — these accompanied the silence, but did not break it. Even the hoofbeats of his horse on the mossy path added rhythm to the stillness without disturbing it.

Emerging from the forest, Michel saw far ahead the Château de Cançonnet, a creamy patch glowing in the sunlight against the dark evergreens banked on the hill behind it. The sight effectively broke for him the spell of the forest. He urged his horse to a gallop: *Dépêche-toi, Roland, mon vieux!* An hour later he clattered noisily into the kitchen court of Cançonnet, where Baptiste, the fat manservant whom he remembered from childhood, was ensconced with brushes and a box, cleaning shoes. The polished leather flashed in the sunlight beneath the brush of Baptiste. Michel dismounted and approached.

"Good morning, Baptiste! Your mistress — is she at home?"

Baptiste looked up, the buckled shoe on one hand, his brush in the other. His round pink face shone with fine drops of moisture, a peculiarity which never varied, winter or summer. As a boy Michel used to wonder why this moisture did not freeze in cold weather and encase the rosy countenance of Baptiste in a film of ice, like a peach under glass. Baptiste had never been known to hurry; not even a conflagration, it was agreed, could have induced him to quicken his movements. He put down his shoe and brush now with his customary deliberation, wiped his hands carefully on the leather apron drawn tight across his paunch, and looked up, squinting in the sunlight.

At the sight of Michel, his heart gave a skip of pleasure: it was the young Seigneur, not Monsieur Paul. Baptiste greatly preferred the young Seigneur to his brother. The former dealt with him as if he, Baptiste, had been a seigneur also, whereas the manner of the other indicated that he was no better than a worm or a bug, if indeed he had any existence at all. Baptiste relished the jests of the young Seigneur, though failing often to comprehend them. He had been greatly troubled by the recent absence of the young Seigneur and the frequent visits of his brother, who had laid an injunction on Baptiste to say nothing of these visits to Monsieur Michel when he should again appear. Baptiste therefore found himself in a quandary, but he was pleased to see the young Seigneur, none the less.

"Ah, Monsieur Michel! *Bon jour, bon jour!* My mistress?" His frown deepened. "Monsieur Michel speaks of Mademoiselle Louise, not of Madame la Marquise, is it not so?"

Michel smiled. "Time has not lessened your powers of penetration, Baptiste. They are as keen as ever. Yes, it is Mademoiselle Louise I wish to see, if she is agreeable — or if she isn't, for the matter of that. At this hour she will surely be at home?"

"Yes — that is — " Baptiste hesitated in sudden embarrassment: "Truly, Monsieur Michel, I do not know."

"You do not *know?*" Michel raised his brows. "Well, then my brother Paul, he has been here, has he not? Yesterday, and the day before, and the day before that?"

Baptiste lowered his eyes to the toe of his shoe which, as was to be expected in the case of one who polished the shoes of others, was scuffed and gray with dust.

"Of a truth, Monsieur Michel, I do not know that, either."

Michel sighed. "Baptiste, as a liar, you are no better than myself. I advise you to stick to the truth, for to lie with skill and conviction is a gift, and we to whom the devil has not given it, can never learn it. Roland here is consumed with thirst" — he laid his hand on the shining flank of his horse — "as I am with the desire to see your mistress. Roland will thank you for water, and I for informing Mademoiselle Louise that I am here. Please say that I will wait for her in the garden, by the statue of Diana."

It was on the tip of his tongue to say Venus, but he decided otherwise. It was sufficiently incongruous to be compelled to send his message by the squat and unromantic person of Baptiste, without subjecting it to further desecration by stipulating the goddess of Love herself as the place of tryst. So he said Diana instead, as being, if not more appropriate, at least more discreet, although he had no hope that Baptiste would so far recall the message as to mention the statue of any goddess whatever. Louise, when she did come, would just walk up and down the garden till she found him.

Baptiste waddled off to the stables with Roland. Michel strolled into the garden to wait for Louise, who was asleep and dreaming of Paul.

It was a bad dream, a very nightmare, and it awakened her.

iii

What in sleep had filled her with terror, appeared on awakening to be merely grotesque: ludicrous, in fact, and she began to laugh. It was an immense relief to discover that Paul was not cutting her head off with an ax, chopping at her neck as a woodsman chops a tree, while Michel stood by with his back to her and paid no attention to her cries for help. But it was also ridiculous that in her dreams Paul should appear as her executioner, who the evening before had filled her with compliments and protestations of love; and the very height of absurdity was the method he chose to effect her decapitation. She put her hands around her throat; why, she could encircle it easily with her thumbs and forefingers, and Paul with his ax had been chopping as viciously and with as slight effect as if her neck had been a granite shaft. Michel did nothing to help her. She could not see him, because her head lay on a block and was turned the other way, but she knew that he was there and paid no heed to her distress. It was the most absurd dream she had ever had. Freed from its terror, she could not check her laughter.

Rising, she threw open the tall doors giving onto the balcony which extended the length of the Château, and overlooked the modest but beautiful gardens that were her father's delight. These gardens had not the splendor and magnificence of those of Guillemont; they were intimate and charming, with their trimmed box hedges bordering the flower beds, and the shining pool descending the slope of the grounds in a series of shallow steps over which the smooth water flowed like silk. Aisles intercepting the flower beds at regular intervals extended beyond them, and terminated in hidden alcoves or recesses, about which evergreens formed miniature groves. In each of these recesses stood the statue of an antique deity, recently imported from Italy, and beneath it a stone bench with carved back, of classical design and proportions.

At the far end of the garden Louise observed her father. He was walking up and down with an open book, reading. She wondered if Paul had spoken to him the night before, as she had told him to do, and if so, what her father had said. She would dress and go down to the garden. If Paul had approached him, her father, she knew, would tell her.

But whatever he reported, nothing would thereby be settled. Her dilemma would remain; the final decision in any case would rest with herself. Her parents had always been firm with her, but never harsh; in the matter of marriage above all, they would not compel her, but leave her free to choose.

Till now the question had been simplicity itself. With Michel she had played as a child, the families being close friends, and visits on both sides being exchanged with great frequency; with Michel she had grown up; with Michel she expected to spend the rest of her life, because it was inconceivable that this should not be so. There had been as yet no formal betrothal, but marriage between them was none the less inevitable. She took it for granted, as did Michel and everyone else. The long and serious illness of the mother of Michel had resulted in the post-ponement of what otherwise might have been openly settled long since; the festivities incident on the betrothal would now be gravely out of place. And what need was there for haste in a matter already certain? It never occurred to her that a doubt might arise, or another possibility present itself.

Now such a doubt had risen, and in the order of her soul chaos reigned as a result.

The brother of Michel, who had been traveling in Italy, had returned to Guillemont but ten days ago, summoned by news of his mother's illness, which had been late in reaching him. As a matter of course he rode over to pay his respects at Cançonnet. On this occasion he made a series of discoveries which surprised him greatly. He observed that his brother's little playmate, whom he had hitherto ignored as beneath notice, was grown up. He saw further that she was exceedingly beautiful and quite unaware of it, which added immensely to her charm. He decided all in a moment that he loved her and wished to marry her; he deter-mined, in fact, that he would marry her, and nothing short of death should prevent. He told her as much while she was show-ing him the improvements that had been made in the gardens during his absence; and the declaration threw her into a state in which the complexity of her emotions made it impossible for her to think clearly or to reply.

She could not marry him; she belonged to Michel; but did she? Michel had never addressed her thus in his life. Nor had Paul any right to do so; but why had he not? He was bound by no engagement, and her relationship with Michel, although a tacit acceptance, was not yet an avowed betrothal. She was vexed that Paul approached her in Michel's absence; but the fact remained that Michel was absent, whereas Paul was not, which would argue a certain laxity of devotion on Michel's part, and a cor-responding ardor on Paul's. If Michel had in truth a prior claim on her, let him appear to defend it; meanwhile, in the absence of a formal engagement, Paul had full right to present his suit, to hope for its success, to take all possible means to achieve that success. Thus he argued, and she could not deny that it was so.

He opened his campaign with a question already classic in antiquity: had no one ever told her how beautiful she was? No one had; and his astonishment at this reply created in her a disturbance for which she was wholly unprepared. It argued either a singular obtuseness on the part of Michel in not having observed her beauty, or a singular lack of the most elementary gallantry in having failed to tell her of it. Paul proceeded to make up for Michel's deficiency in this respect. He held up to her a mirror of words in which she saw herself for the first time. He pointed out to her perfections of whose existence she had never been aware; he made known to her his own appreciation of them; he declared his need of her in whom these beauties resided. Never had she heard such talk. It roused in her a storm of feeling in which anger had no place. Confusion, doubt, dismay, even terror — she felt all these; but the anger she tried to feel, escaped her. Paul loved her. He came to her in Michel's absence, and told her so, in words such as Michel had never used. She belonged (did she not?) to Michel: she should dismiss this trespasser at once, and in fury. But she could not do so. She was frightened, confused, distressed; but she was not angry.

During the whole week Michel did not appear, whereas Paul returned every day, and every day pressed her further. Last night he asked her for the tenth time to marry him. When she hesitated he seized her and kissed her, as she had not yet been kissed by Michel or anyone. With the strength of desperation she freed herself from him and stood trembling, her face in her hands. The summer night was heavy with sweetness; the moon was a white shimmer on the silken pool.

"Oh, go!" she gasped. "Please go! I cannot answer you! I do not know! Ask my father, and if — he consents —"

She gave a deep sob and was gone, so quickly that Paul could not stop her, being unaware of her intention to go until he found himself alone. She fled to her room and threw herself on her bed, sobbing brokenheartedly, and for her tears she could give no reason, either then, or now.

Now she felt calmer; but still she did not by any means know what to do. To reject Paul finally, positively, would settle the matter; but this was not as simple as it appeared, in view of Paul's determination and his tactics. Besides, she was not at all sure that she wished to reject him. Until last night, when he had contrived to see her alone, someone had always been present at their meetings, though not always within earshot. His visits had nothing of the clandestine about them, and he had not offered to touch her. But what he omitted to do in fact, he did with his words, his glance, the tone of his voice, his every gesture; these drew her, entangled her, caressed her, so that she not only could not escape, she actually did not wish to free herself from this disturbing enchantment. She had always been eager and glad to see Michel; she looked forward to Paul's visits now with a queer, suffocating excitement utterly different from anything she had ever felt before. A new note had sounded in her life; had she never heard it, she would not have missed it; but having been intoxicated by its cadence, she could not bear that it should cease ringing.

And she did not in the least know what to do.

She finished dressing, and was on her way to join her father in the garden, when on the staircase she encountered Baptiste. She wished him good morning, and was passing, but he stopped.

"Mademoiselle Louise —"

"You wish to see me, Baptiste?"

"Not I, Mademoiselle, but the young Seigneur — that is, Monsieur Michel."

She gave a little gasp: "Monsieur Michel, Baptiste? You are sure — Michel?"

"But yes, Mademoiselle. He waits in the garden, by the statue of Venus."

"Thank you, Baptiste."

She ran downstairs, her heart lifting with eagerness. She was glad it was Michel. To see him now would be like stepping into cool fresh air from a room in which an excess of warmth had made one dizzy. She felt a tingling of exhilaration.

"Baptiste, of course, will be mistaken," she reflected. "I will therefore seek Michel by the statue of Diana."

This she did, and there she found him. With him she found also her father. Both men were seated on the stone bench beneath the goddess, their heads bent over the book her father had been reading. The girl recognized it: the magnificently illuminated Book of Hours her father had recently acquired after much bargaining with the Abbé of Cluny in Paris. It was filled with lines of fine and beautiful writing, and decorated with rich colors and initial letters in burnished gold. Michel was looking at it intently, turning the pages slowly and with a sort of awe.

"I suggest that you do not show this to my father, Monseigneur," he was saying as Louise approached. "If you do so, you will place your life in hazard. It is the sort of treasure he would go to any lengths to possess."

"Even to cutting my throat, eh, Michel?"

"Good day, messieurs," Louise interrupted the colloquy. "I desire to speak with you, Papa, but I see you are engaged."

The men stood up. Michel bowed.

"I was reading my Office," the Marquis explained, "when I stumbled over our friend, who has come to call. He is unconscionably early, this Michel."

"I am unconscionably eager, Monseigneur."

"Obviously. Well, let us see how this may be arranged. Michel desires to see Louise; Louise desires to speak with me; I desire to continue reading my Office. Now, I shall do as I desire, and meanwhile Michel may see Louise. When I have finished Prime and Terce, Louise may see me. This should be satisfactory to all."

He looked from one to the other. Louise nodded; Michel bowed; the Marquis resumed his reading and walked off, leaving his daughter alone with her suitor, adequately chaperoned by the stony surveillance of the goddess of the hunt.

"Papa is very religious," observed Louise, looking after him. "He reads the Divine Office every day, like a monk. Sometimes I think he should have been one."

"Decidedly, he should *not*," replied Michel with energy. "Had he been a monk, where would you be? And without you, where would I be?" He emphasized his words by pulling a branch from the boxwood hedge behind him and breaking it in small pieces. Thence he proceeded to the reason for his visit: "I hear that my brother Paul has been paying court to you. Is that true?"

"Perhaps. But I do not see that it is a reason for destroying the shrubbery of papa."

"I must destroy something," said Michel savagely. "You should be glad that it is not you. I thought it was understood, by us and by everyone, that you are to marry me."

"It seems I shall have to do so, to preserve papa's hedges."

"I care not for what reason, if only you marry me. But I would prefer it to be because you love me, as I love you. You know that, Louise. You have always known it."

"Why have you not told me so before?"

"For the love of heaven, was there any need? Must I tell you that it is summer, that the sun shines, and the sky is blue? Are there not certain things we all know, and one of them is that I am only half myself without you? In all I do, you are present. I say, 'What will Louise say to this? How will Louise like that?' It is unthinkable that anyone should try to change things between us, least of all my brother Paul. It is monstrous, it is not possible. When I heard it I did not believe it. I do not blame him for loving you. Who could help it? But it is wicked and wrong of him to pay court to you, using the arts and flattery he learned in Italy, of which I know nothing, and would not use with you if I did. Tell me, Louise: you have not really listened to him. Have you?"

She had kept her eyes on his; these had the color and brilliance of his mother's, and in them burned the same life and fire. Never before had she feared to meet them for any reason, but now suddenly she could endure their penetration no longer. She lowered hers, and did not answer.

Michel took a deep breath. He pulled another branch from the hedge, all but uprooting the shrub with it. Louise did not protest the depredation, not seeing it.

"I must not stay longer," Michel went on. "Our mother is very ill. I doubt if I should have come at all. But I must settle this. I must have your word that you will marry me, and that you will refuse the advances of my brother Paul. I cannot continue in doubt. Till now I did not think there could be any doubt. Tell me that you will marry me, and then I will go."

"Did you —" her words came haltingly "— did you speak of this to my father?"

"Yes."

"What — did he say?"

"That if you marry me, it will be with his blessing and consent."

"Oh, Michel —" Still she could not meet his eyes. She was trembling furiously, and although she tried to speak naturally, her voice shook also: "Michel, I cannot tell you. I cannot promise. I — I cannot."

"You cannot?" Michel echoed in astonishment. "Do you mean — you do not love me, Louise?"

"No, no!" she gasped. "I love you — of course."

"Then you mean, you love also my brother Paul?"

She covered her face with her hands: "Oh, Michel!"

"Better than you love me?"

She shook her head. "No, Michel! Not better — not —"

"But at least as well."

She did not answer.

There was, indeed, nothing more to say. Michel returned to Guillemont without obtaining the promise he had come to seek. On his arrival he was met with the news that during his absence Madame his mother had died.

Et concupiscet Rex
decorem tuum . . .

2. *"Thy King Desires . . ."*

"Requiem aeternam dona eis, Domine, et lux perpetua luceat eis."

At the funeral of his mother, Michel found himself unable to pray for her soul, convinced that she was already in heaven and therefore did not need his prayers. But he needed hers, and desperately. He therefore prayed to her rather than for her, and entrusted to her the success of his cause with Louise.

"For Paul there may be others," he whispered, kneeling in the chapel. "For me there can be only Louise. *Prie donc pour moi, ma mère,* for if I lose her, I am lost as well."

As on earth the Countess had been able to penetrate the surliest moods of the Count, his father, and obtain for her sons favors which they as children dared not ask, so Michel did not doubt that her prayers in heaven would have weight with the Divine Majesty, where his alone might fail. And apart from the decision of heaven, he had, he knew, no chance of success. To attempt to outwit Paul in this game was the limit of folly; he could not rely on his own subtleties, for he had none. In these matters Paul, though two years his junior, had been born old; Michel, however long he lived, would die young.

He knew that women could be won by the arts Paul practiced so expertly, but for these arts Michel had no taste and less skill. He dealt with all people, including women, with simplicity and directness, being unable to do otherwise. From others he expected only directness in return. That love spoke another language than honesty he was fully aware, but it was a language he did not understand and could not hope to learn. It had never occurred to him that Louise might understand it, but suddenly she seemed to do so, and even to prefer it. If he could not hold her except by becoming expert in this game of innuendo and flattery, all hope for him was lost, for learn it he never could.

But he did not believe all hope was lost. The possibility of her final preference for Paul he refused even to consider seriously. There are things too terrible to be, and this was one of them. Louise was as necessary to him as sunlight, food, the very air he breathed. Without her he would starve and suffocate; he could not live. That he would continue to live, he was reasonably sure. Therefore, ultimately Louise must decide in his favor. Heaven, logic, necessity, all indicated this as the only possible outcome of the affair. He was surprised, therefore, not that it happened, but that it happened as soon as it did.

He attributed this wholly to the prayers of his mother in heaven. He did not know that he had also the very considerable support of the mother of Louise on earth. The Marquise was a handsome, black-haired woman, just stout enough to have great dignity and a slight shortness of breath. For this reason, although she showed no sign of age whatever, having sound teeth and a firm clear skin, it was impossible to imagine that she had ever been really young. She was a woman not of imagination, but of resource; because she greatly preferred Michel to Paul as a husband for her daughter, she took matters into her plump and competent hands, employing in his behalf the subtleties he was unable to use for himself.

The Marquise was working at her embroidery frame and she asked Louise to sort and arrange a box of silken skeins which had become snarled.

"See, what a beautiful color, *Maman.*" Louise held up her fingers from which cascaded a shimmer of cerulean silk. "It is like the robe of Our Lady in the window of the chapel at Guillemont when the sun is shining."

The Marquise suggested another comparison: "It is also precisely the color of those extraordinary eyes of your Michel. Or perhaps," she added meaningly, "I should no longer say, *your* Michel."

Louise, who was busy searching in the blue tangle for the end of the skein, looked up. "Why not then, *Maman?*"

"Have you not transferred your affections to Paul? Certainly it would appear so."

Louise lowered her eyes in confusion. "No — no, I have not, *Maman.* That is to say, not altogether."

"Then I advise you to complete the transfer as soon as possible, so that Michel may be free to —" The Marquise appeared to hesitate.

"To what, *Maman?*"

"To do what I believe he was intended to do by heaven."

Louise put down her skeins and regarded her mother in alarm. "What are you talking about, *Maman?* What do you mean?"

"Michel is like your father, Louise. I believe neither of them belongs in this world. Your father would have made an excellent priest, and I am sure the same is true of Michel."

"Michel!" gasped Louise. "A priest!"

"Do not look so horrified, my child. What then do you expect him to do, if you do not marry him? Certainly he will not spend the rest of his life adoring you from afar, when you are married to his brother. I am equally certain that he will marry no one else. Clearly, if you marry Paul, Michel will become a priest. You will do well to decide quickly, so that, if you choose Paul, Michel may be released for the higher life without delay. The Church has need of good priests."

"But, *Maman!*" Louise protested vehemently. "I do not want Michel to be a priest! I do not want to marry Paul! I do not care if I ever see Paul again! It is Michel I want — not Paul! If — if Michel becomes a priest —" Her eyes filled and her lips quivered suddenly: "I cannot bear it! I shall die!"

And she put her face in her hands and burst into tears.

The Marquise raised her straight, black brows. "So? In that case, I suggest that you inform Michel of your sentiments, and at once."

Henri, Comte de Guillemont, was busy at his favorite occupation of planning an improvement in his estate. In this alone did he take satisfaction, or find what came as near to happiness as he was capable of experiencing. The fierce and despotic old man had suffered all his life from an ailment of the chest, an asthma, which had warped his spirit and stunted his growth. Hampered thus by ill-health, he devoted himself exclusively to cultivation of his property. It was his career; nay, more, his other self. He watched it expand and grow beneath his care as he might have done had nature dealt less harshly with him. He exacted from it the utmost in revenue; he improved and enlarged the Château, laid out gardens, cultivated vineyards, collected books, miniatures, priceless illuminations, treasures of art of all kinds. The original gloomy pile, the foundations of which dated from Roman times, became during his lifetime a gracious vision of creamy stone and rose-colored brick, beautiful without and filled with beauty within. This would be remembered as the work of Henri, Comte de Guillemont, by those who would forget that the Comte himself was a stunted apology of a man who could not draw one full breath. This beauty, this length and breadth of magnificence, this living stone, would to future generations represent, and in a sense become, himself. Thus, he was always eager to seize any excuse which might serve as a reason for extending or altering the gardens of the Château.

The reason at present was Madame his wife, whom he had made miserable while she lived, but whom he wished to honor with some signal mark of devotion now that she was dead. He planned a grove of trees, enclosing a miniature temple in the antique manner, which should enshrine the memory of Madame. Michel being at Cançonnet, Monseigneur de Guillemont summoned Paul to consult with him on this matter, not because he desired the advice or even the opinion of his son, but because he wished to clarify and emphasize his own ideas by explaining them in detail to someone else. He showed Paul the sketches he had made.

"Observe," he said, "The temple will appear the same from all sides. However it is approached, it will seem as if one entered it from the front. Walks will lead to it through the grove, over which the branches of the trees will form natural arches. Or perhaps there should be no walks, but one should come upon the temple suddenly, not suspecting it to be there. In this case it may be built upon a little rise, and the ground around it cleared. We should in some way arrange a vista, and yet I prefer that the temple should not be seen too soon. How does it seem to you?"

Paul looked quickly at the sketches his father handed him, then tossed them on the table.

"Why do you ask *my* opinion?" He made no attempt to disguise the bitterness in his voice. "You know I have no interest in the estate. Why should I, since after your death it will fall to Michel, not to me?"

"Ah?" The Count gathered up his sketches with great deliberation. "And you have likewise no interest in honoring the memory of your mother?"

"Michel was her favorite, as he is yours, and everyone's, it would seem."

"I comprehend." The older man nodded slowly. "You refuse to give me your opinion regarding a building to honor the memory of your mother because you are jealous that you did not succeed in seducing the affections of the fiancée of Michel."

Paul flushed. "That is not true," he said furiously. "You have no right to use such words. She is not the fiancée of Michel, nor did I attempt to seduce her."

"Not her person, perhaps, but her affections, certainly. And she is as good as affianced to Michel, as you are fully aware. But she is not the only woman in France, or even in Guillemont, for that matter. Instead of nursing your anger that you did not succeed with her, why do you not seek consolation elsewhere?"

"Excellent advice, *mon père,* but unnecessary. I have already undertaken to carry it into effect. But, like yourself, in all things I seek only the best. I shall find nothing here or anywhere to compare with the little Cançonnet. Her hair is fire, her eyes are the night itself, her lips are wine. She is wasted on Michel — utterly wasted," he added scornfully. "I wager the fool half believes she is a boy."

"Paul!" cried the Count harshly. "However little you may regard the merits of your brother in other respects you will at least have the goodness to remember that he is a man."

Paul bowed. He did not trust himself to pursue the subject further. "Since I appear to be of so little use to you architecturally, Monseigneur, I have your permission to depart?"

"By all means."

Paul took himself and his anger into the garden, where he walked up and down in a fury. Perceiving Michel's red setter asleep in the sunshine at the end of one of the transverse walks, he threw a stone at the animal. This relieved his feelings somewhat, though he regretted that the target was merely the dog and not its owner.

"Though my father pretends such regard for Michel," he reflected angrily, "it is not Michel he loves, but himself. In Michel he sees himself as he would like to be. And truly Michel is a handsome devil — or rather, a handsome fool, for he has not wit enough to be a devil. It is not surprising that a sickly, wheezing, pasty-faced, evil-tempered dwarf of a man like my honored father, full of asthma and the rheum, should elevate on a pedestal a long-limbed agile young colt like Michel, forgetting that he is only a colt, or rather, an ass in the form of a colt. Unfortunately, Michel does not resemble an ass, and for that reason my father and others are deceived."

In this Paul was not wholly wrong: the Count did indeed see in Michel all he himself was not but wished to be. And since Michel was truly his son, the fruit of his loins, since he had actually encompassed this masterpiece in spite of the many afflictions of his miserable physique, to him Michel seemed not so much another person as a prolongation, in happier form, of himself. All the physical grace and charm that nature had denied to him, the father, she had held in reserve, as it were, that she might bestow it with a doubly lavish hand on the son. Michel was precisely what he would have chosen to be had God Almighty called him aside and permitted him to select the pattern according to which he should be made, as one selects from the architect's plans those best suited to one's taste. Paul was right to this extent: in Michel the Count loved not his son, but himself.

Nor had any of his other sons appeared to him in this light. Three of them, indeed, disappointed him by dying before they reached maturity. This was a weakness in them which he could not forgive. Himself frail in health and all but dwarfed in body, he regarded nothing with such contempt as weakness or deformity in others. About him, in persons and things, he wished to see only strength and beauty. When André, Jean, and Pierre sickened in turn and died, he felt rage and bitterness rather than grief; he regarded death in each case as an insult rather than a loss. For Paul he had a certain regard; Paul at least had had the grace to live, though he had been delicate in childhood and still retained a sallow complexion and a tendency to cough. Michel, however, made up for everything. Michel was his desire made flesh and blood, living and moving and acting. All things had in some way failed and disappointed him save two: Michel and his estate. In these his embittered manhood found its freedom and lived on, incarnate.

Paul's understanding of the cause of his father's preference for Michel did not help him to endure that preference without rancor. Rather, it increased it. He considered his father's bias to be grievously unjust, based as it was on a trick of nature, and not on values that mattered more than well-set shoulders and a lithe body. His father refused to see that Michel was simply a fool, and that in his hands the estate would go to wrack and ruin after his death. Michel had no mind for affairs, whereas he, Paul, knew how to drive a bargain, to cultivate the land to its limit of productiveness, to exact the utmost in labor from those who worked it. Michel was admittedly ornamental, but otherwise useless. Because he was ornamental, his father forgave him everything. Paul could only nurse his wrath in silence.

He might have endured being set aside by his father had he not now been set aside also by Louise, and in favor of the same fool who had no more of an eye for women than he had a head for business, who knew even less how to manage them than he did the estate. Pressure had been applied to Louise from another source, Paul was sure; Michel, left to himself, could hold no woman against him. For the time being, Paul must appear to acquiesce in this decision which seemed to give so much satisfaction to everyone, but he reserved the right to regard himself as temporarily outmaneuvered, but by no means defeated. Michel was at Cançonnet, summoned to dine by invitation of the Marquise, brought to Guillemont by the perspiring Baptiste. From it all mention of Paul was pointedly omitted. The latter could only walk up and down the gardens of Guillemont, thinking of the opportunities which his brother Michel was at this moment undoubtedly wasting, and shy pebbles at Michel's dog to give vent to his disappointment and rage.

The business had thus all the appearance of finality, but Paul swore to himself that it should not be final. He had determined when he first saw her on his return from Italy that the enchanting daughter of Cançonnet should belong to him. What he had told his father was true: neither in Guillemont nor anywhere could he find another to compare with her, and, like his father, he was not to be put off with inferior goods. He might seek temporary consolation elsewhere, but what he had made up his mind to possess, that he would ultimately possess.

The end, therefore, was not yet. Regardless of how matters stood officially, he could still win Louise from Michel, given an opportunity to do so.

And if no opportunity presented itself?

In that case he would make one, and nothing should prevent.

iii

"Michel —?"

"Louise."

"One thing frightens me, Michel."

"What is that *ma mie?*"

"One of us must die before the other. What if it should be you? I should go mad. I cannot live without you."

They were again in the gardens, seated on the bench beneath the statue of Diana. The air was brilliant and golden with sunlight, and filled with the hum of locusts, the chirp of crickets, the tang of wood smoke rising from the nearby fields, and other signs indicating the approach of autumn. Michel sat with his legs crossed, his arm outstretched along the back of the stone seat, his eyes fixed on the satin waters of the pool, which seemed all burning and golden in the sunlight, as did the air about him, and all of heaven and earth besides. Louise, with a sigh, leaned back and rested her head against his arm. He dropped his hand from the back of the bench so that his fingers touched her shoulder; she raised her hand and clasped his. Otherwise they did not move.

"Nor I without you. It is truly a thought to terrify," Michel agreed. "I can think of but one remedy. Let us both ask my mother, who is now in heaven, to pray for us, that neither of us may outlive the other, but that we may die together."

Louise looked up hopefully. "You believe it can be arranged, Michel?"

"If my mother asks it, yes. Did she not arrange this?" His fingers tightened on her hand. "Is it true, Louise? I am not dreaming? You have decided? You will marry me?"

"But of course, Michel."

"And this because you love me, and not merely to preserve the shrubbery of Monseigneur your father? For I warn you, if you change your mind again, I shall go through the gardens like a marauding army, and spare none of them."

"Well — of course, I love the gardens of papa very much. But I think I love you a little more, Michel."

"And more than Paul?"

"Oh, much more than Paul! In fact, I do not love Paul at all."

"And when did you arrive at that satisfactory conclusion?"

"When I saw that, if I married Paul, I could not also marry you."

"But obviously."

"But I am so stupid, Michel. I do not always see what is obvious. I believed that I could marry Paul and at the same time you would always be here, too. You must forgive me, if you can, Michel, for I cannot forgive myself. Paul flattered me; I had never been flattered before. It — it was pleasant to be courted by him, and I played with the idea of marrying him, simply to prolong it, not realizing that to marry him meant also losing you. When I saw that, I knew I had no choice. I could not endure to lose you."

"Paul is master of a very ancient art and I am not even a novice. What made you decide?"

"*Maman* said if I married Paul, you would become a priest."

"A priest?" echoed Michel. "But I have never thought of such a thing!"

"Then please do not think of it now. It is simply what *Maman* said. I am glad she did so, because it served to awaken me. Paul had put me to sleep."

"And how did it wake you?"

"Why, that is easy. If you should become a priest, I could not marry you. I did not want you to become a priest, because I wanted to marry you. But, if I married Paul, also I could not marry you. Therefore, I did not want to marry Paul."

Michel stared at her a moment, then laughed outright. "And they say women have not the gift of logic! Well, since that is settled, perhaps you can also solve another problem which has been occupying me while we have been talking."

"What is that?"

"Your hair, I cannot decide what color it is."

"My hair!" Louise sat upright and turned and stared at him. "But I did not think you had observed that I had any hair!"

"I have observed in passing that you are not bald."

"I am glad of that." She leaned back again. "Yes, I can tell you the color of my hair, because Paul told me. It is golden."

"Paul is wrong," said Michel with emphasis. "If it were golden, there would be no problem. Nor would it be as beautiful as it is. It is not golden, being too red. It is not red, being too brown. It is not brown, being too golden. So you see how difficult it is."

"I thought you did not know how to flatter."

"That is not flattery, it is the truth. At least, it is an attempt to arrive at the truth, which so far as the color of your hair is concerned, eludes me."

"But can you not flatter and tell the truth at the same time?"

"It is a question of motive, Louise. One does not flatter, except to obtain something from the flattered. See now: Paul tells you that you are beautiful. It is the truth, but he does it in order to commend himself to your good graces, and for that reason it is also flattery. If I should tell a snaggle-toothed, bleary-eyed old hag with a wig and a fortune that she has eyes like stars and hair like spun gold, in the hope that she will bequeath her fortune to me, it is an outrageous lie, and it is also flattery. But I seek from you, Louise, only your love, which you tell me I already have. Therefore, when I tell you that you are beautiful, it is not flattery. It is only the truth — nothing more."

"I hope that you will continue to tell me the truth as long as it is true. When it is no longer true, I hope that you will flatter me a little. It would be dreadful if one day you should say, 'You used to have lovely hair, Louise, but now you are quite bald.'"

"But that would be a great rudeness. To be rude is worse than to flatter. Therefore, of two evils, I should choose the less."

"Michel, I wish we could be married at once."

"While I, of course, am perfectly content to wait."

"*Maman* says that we must wait until after Easter, at the very least, since you are in mourning. Just think — seven, eight months." She shivered: "All sorts of terrible things can happen before then."

"*Par exemple — ?*"

"You might fall in love with someone else."

"I shall try to avoid temptation, Louise."

"But if temptation should not avoid you — temptation with golden hair and blue eyes?"

"That will make everything easy. I do not care for blue eyes."

"No? I thought no man could resist them."

"Look at me, Louise." She did so. "Now, I will describe to you the eyes I like. They are soft as smoke, and dark as night. They have the look of the forest at dusk, when the trees are all in shadow, and filled with mysterious colors that have no name. They glow always with a deep and hidden light. There is only one pair of such eyes in the world, and for that reason I am in no danger of meeting any others like them."

"For my part, Michel, I do not like mysterious colors that shift and change and are neither one thing nor the other. I like eyes that are honest brown, or gray, or best of all, blue: so deep and clear that you seem to be looking not at them, but through them, at the very sky beyond, and on such a day as this."

"I might approve your taste, did such color exist. But I have never seen it, and I never shall."

"Is it possible" — the eyes Michel had described widened in

astonishment — "that the Château of Monseigneur your father, otherwise so sumptuously furnished, contains no mirrors?"

"Louise! You have been taking lessons from Paul. I will not have it."

"Not from Paul, but from you. Paul flatters; you tell the truth. And, Michel — " Reaching over, she seized his hand which rested on his knee: "I love your hands also. How slim they are, and yet strong, as if you could do anything you wish. Paul has not such hands, Michel. Have you ever observed?"

"No, I have not." Michel withdrew them abruptly and thrust them behind him. "And now please do not tell me that you love the right ear or the left foot of Michel, but rather himself, all of him. That is the only truth I care to hear."

Dispossessed of his hands, she threw her arms around his neck. "I do, Michel. I love you."

"And you will not change your mind? You will love me always?"

"Always."

"Forever, Louise?"

"Forever, Michel. Forever, and forever."

Michel, riding home, emerged from the forest as the sun was setting, a disk of fire in the crystal silence of the sky. On a whim, he turned Roland off the road, and struck into a little-used path that went round to Guillemont by a much longer way, passing, not far from the forest, the Monastery of Our Lady of the Meadows. He could not have explained, to himself or anyone, why he did this, except that it had something to do with that extraordinary statement of the mother of Louise, that in the event of her daughter's marrying Paul, Michel would become a priest. He frowned in bewilderment: what could have put such a fantastic thought into the exceedingly practical head of Madame la Marquise? It was the next to the last thing he ever would have thought of, and the very last thing he wished to do. Knowing him as she did, the Marquise should certainly have known that.

But if Louise had chosen Paul?

He shook the thought from him, refusing even to consider its possibilities and its implications. All alternatives were excluded, all doubts removed. Louise had not chosen Paul, but him. He knew beforehand that it must be so, and it was so. His heart sang within him at the memory of the day just ended, at the thought of days still to come; and he turned toward the buildings of the monastery, visible in the distance, a look of compassion and of joy: compassion for those shut up in its dreary solitude, many of them young men, no different from himself, and joy for his own extraordinary good fortune. He was sorry for all enclosed in those distant walls: not one of them could marry Louise. By the same token, he was sorry for everybody in the world, excepting only himself.

The sun was gone now; night would soon come. For a brief interlude, the sky was filled with a golden pallor, and a late glow hung over all the fields. Overhead the radiance faded quickly into darkness, but along the horizon light still lingered, and the far-off trees and buildings of the monastery stood black and distinct against it. In all this solitude nothing moved, nothing lived, except himself. The heart of Michel lifted with joy as he rode on into the twilight, and silence, and peace.

De profundis clamavi
ad Te, Domine

3. Out of the Depths

i

Paul opened his eyes, dragged from sleep by a shrill harassing sound that penetrated the surface of his unconsciousness and continued to irritate him until it brought him fully awake. He lay for a moment, confused; then jumped out of bed, roused by a burst of anger. The devil take Michel! Was it not enough that he should be afflicted by a mania for early rising, without insisting that all about him should share his vagaries, whether they wished or not? Paul decidedly did not wish; but with Michel whistling in the next room loud enough to wake the dead, he had no choice. Michel was already dressing, though it was bitterly cold and dark as pitch; it could not yet be five o'clock.

He was about to make known his indignation by pounding on the wall, when suddenly he recalled what day it was, and a measure of his anger abated. Michel was justified in rising early, and in announcing the fact by whistling if he chose, at least today. For this was the day of the boar hunt, which was to begin with a breakfast at Guillemont, and end with a banquet at Cançonnet. The presence of boars made riding through the forest of Cançonnet dangerous in winter; the purpose of the hunt was to lessen this hazard. The banquet was to be the occasion for announcing publicly the betrothal of Louise and Michel.

It was likewise the birthday of Michel; he was twenty-one.

Paul's anger subsided, but his irritation remained. Shivering, he began to dress. He objected to rising at this hour, whatever the season, and in winter it was an outrage. The hunt, however, was to assemble before dawn, and Paul wished especially not to miss it. There was a trophy offered for killing a boar. Not that Paul had any hope of winning it; that glory, he supposed, would fall to Michel. To the good fortune enjoyed by Michel, which he did nothing whatever to merit, there appeared to be no end.

"The boar will no doubt approach Michel and humbly beg for the honor of being killed by him," Paul reflected, as he dressed rapidly in the cold. "Why things do not occasionally go ill with Michel, I fail to comprehend. It is to be foreseen that he will return with the trophy for killing the boar. Why does not someone offer the boar a trophy for killing Michel? That at least would be a novelty in boar hunts, or perhaps not altogether a novelty, for many have been killed in that disagreeable fashion, but I have never heard of the boar being rewarded for it, though no doubt he has often deserved it, as he would in the present instance."

Examining his conscience later (or being examined by it, for the last thing he desired was to subject himself to the torture of self-scrutiny in this matter), Paul was unable to determine to what extent this trivial fancy influenced his conduct when the crisis arose. What he had conceived as a sort of bitter jest he had no expectation of seeing enacted before his eyes in grim truth. He alone, of all those present, perceived that Michel was in danger; he knew, with an instant flash of knowledge, that he could save him; but the coincidence of the situation with his reflection of the morning held him paralyzed, and he did nothing.

Dawn was breaking in the forest when the party sighted the boar: a winter dawn, icy, remote, hung with clouds which held back the reluctant daylight, permitting it to find its way with difficulty through the crowded columns of the trees. It was, as Paul had foreseen, Michel who started the quarry; it was Michel who was first in pursuit. Suddenly the boar resorted to one of those tricks of which only the desperately hunted are capable; as if by magic, he disappeared. Michel, losing sight of him, reined his horse short. The boar doubled back on his tracks and came at Michel through a thicket, unseen by any but Paul.

A shout rose in Paul's throat, but died unuttered. The exactness with which the event reproduced his anticipation stunned him. He made no move to prevent what must happen. In that second's hesitation Michel was lost. The horse Roland went down, pinning his rider beneath him. The boar had both at his mercy before anyone but Paul knew what threatened.

The brittle winter daylight brightened on a terrible scene.

The actual disaster broke the spell of Paul's inaction and he set on the boar with a shout. There was a grim struggle before the animal was killed. When they dragged the carcass of the boar away, it was thought his victims also were dead. But the horse, in his death agony, still lived. Michel, held face downward by the writhing animal, was a mass of wounds. On investigation it was found that he had been injured in no vital spot: he also lived.

The horse was summarily dispatched to put him out of his agony. Michel was carried back to the Château where it was expected that nature would soon perform for him a similar service.

But nature showed no such consideration. Michel proved to be incredibly tough. His back was severely lacerated; one thigh was injured; his left hand was gone and the other mangled so that the amputation of two fingers was necessary; but none of these wounds was fatal. Cautery and bleeding saved him from the fever. Ultimately it became apparent that he would live, and, as far as was possible for him, recover.

During the long illness of Michel, Paul showed the utmost consideration for those most intimately concerned with the tragedy: for his brother, for the agonized old man his father, and especially for Louise, in the midst of whose romance so harsh a note had sounded without warning. Paul tried deftly to turn his father's thoughts from his grief to that which had always been able to interest and occupy him: his estate. He was full of plans for the future; he informed himself concerning innovations which, tried elsewhere, had resulted in improved produce and increased revenue. The Count was delighted by this display of proprietary interest and insight on the part of his younger son and began to turn to him for companionship and, occasionally, for advice.

The winter was long and cold. Days of low and sullen clouds, of bleak, raw winds, of everything but sunlight, succeeded days of driving rain, sleet, and even snow. When the weather permitted,

Paul rode to Cançonnet to carry to Louise news of Michel. Louise was not permitted to travel to Guillemont because she had caught a cold early in the winter from which she did not wholly recover. By Paul, however, she dispatched to Michel letters filled with tenderness and with prayers for his recovery; from Paul she learned that Michel was improving rapidly and that there was no cause for alarm. The full extent of Michel's injuries Paul concealed from her, as he concealed her letters from Michel. She was deeply appreciative of Paul's kindness in playing courier, of his solicitude in her behalf of Michel's, especially since now he could hope to gain nothing by it. Paul's manner toward her was one of complete detachment and of concern only for herself. As time went on, she failed to understand why Michel, now greatly improved, neglected to answer a single one of her letters.

Michel, meanwhile, lay in the midst of fire, in a very well of flame which he believed would have no end. He remembered nothing before it; he looked forward to nothing ahead, but only to a continuation of this present, which thus became for him eternity. It threw about him a wall he could never scale. It surrounded him with a sea which had no shore. Time ceased. There were no longer hours or minutes or days by virtue of which change succeeded change in the lives of men. There was only one fact, one reality, in the midst of which he was held fixed and suspended, and would be so held forever, and the name of this reality was Pain.

But within this permanence there were variations, and these he soon learned to recognize. Sometimes the sea on which he lay was a deep blackness, which beat against him in an interminable succession of waves, each rimmed with fire. Sometimes he opened his eyes to daylight, but the light was darkness, a thick purple mist, in which infinitesimal sparks spun and whirled, like snowflakes in a driving storm. All objects seen through this haze lost their depth and became two-dimensional, sharp, and thin as if cut from paper. Nothing was real save this one fact which stole reality from all else, this infinity and eternity, this pain.

Nor could he hope that it would end, for in it there was no room for hope, nor for anything save itself.

At length, however, the waves of the black sea began to subside. They beat with less violence, and the intervals between them grew longer. The objects in his chamber began to resume their proper form and color. When he moved, he was reminded of what had been; but to lie utterly still was to be immersed in that incredible sweetness which is the cessation of pain. He began to recall a past when it had been permanently absent. He could anticipate a future in which he might again be rid of this companion whose presence had demanded his total allegiance, his complete surrender.

But, jealous lest he forget her too soon, she left behind on departing certain tokens which would insure his recollection of her as long as he should live. Nor did she, indeed, leave him altogether, but withdrew rather to a certain distance and there stood, like a mother watchful of a child or a lover jealous of his mistress, returning swiftly, frequently, demanding all his attention and receiving it, lest he grow careless in her absence and forget her, as he was in no danger whatever of doing. For when the shreds of him grew together, and he was able to crawl about again, it was evident that the Michel that had been was gone forever. His head and shoulders had escaped injury, so that in repose this mutilation was not apparent; but the swiftness with which he had formerly moved, seeming to cover the ground without touching it, the grace which had been his father's especial delight, were destroyed beyond all hope of repair, replaced by a gait not so much tragic as grotesque. He could not be said to limp; he hobbled. His whole person was warped and twisted, and bore an unmistakable and ugly stamp, that of cripple. He resembled the ruin of a magnificent building that can never be restored.

No man lives or dies, suffers or rejoices, alone. This disaster of which Michel was the heart and center, radiated outward from him, and its shadow fell on all who stood within its circumference. Chief of these was his father.

The anguish of the old man was unspeakable, seeing that its object was not Michel but himself. The mutilation of Michel was the mutilation of his pride in the stronghold where it had hitherto dwelt. Had Michel had the grace to die, the loss, however grievous, would have been endurable; the son would have lived in his father's memory with his magnificence intact, and with this memory the old man could still have identified himself.

He watched Michel drag himself from chair to chair, resting after every few steps to gather strength, his face white almost to transparency, and covered with beads of moisture from weakness and from the exertion demanded by this superhuman task of learning to walk again with the limited equipment for that purpose which remained to him. The soul of the old man was filled not with pity, but with revulsion and disgust. His son had ridden away one morning in full youth and beauty, and that son had never returned. In his place stood now a hopeless cripple whom the old man could not bear to acknowledge as his son. The love he had lavished on Michel, being not love but pride, shriveled at the sight of this wrecked body which had usurped Michel's place, and became what such love becomes in the face of disappointment: hatred. He could no longer endure the presence of Michel; the pain to himself was too great.

Accordingly, he called his son to him and ordered him from his sight.

"It does not concern me where you go or what you do; only have the kindness to spare me the necessity of looking at you again. I do not wish it to be said that I am responsible for your death. If therefore you will contrive to leave word of your whereabouts from time to time at the Château, I will see that you are provided for, and amply. For the present this will suffice." He tossed a purse, heavy with coins, on the table. "As long as you are a man, however little you may resemble one," he continued, "you will always find women to console you. You will need consolation. Take what you can get, but do not give your children our name. You may indeed consider yourself as no longer entitled to that name. As for Louise, she and Paul seemed to find comfort in each other, while you were in bed, like a sick baby. I desire that she shall be the mother of my grandsons. I shall have no difficulty in arranging it. Now go!"

ii

It was market day at Guillemont.

To the village, from the neighboring countryside, came folk

laden with produce for the market: fruits and vegetables, bread and pastries, chickens and geese, goats and pigs — all things that were edible or that could, with the exercise of a little Gallic ingenuity, be made so. They set up their stalls in the cobbled square at the top of the hill, where stood the Hôtel de Ville and the church. From earliest dawn on market days the square reverberated with the hum of activity and with sounds of strife. The atmosphere vibrated with the altercations of bargaining peasantry. From these clashes the victor, triumphing by a single sou, would emerge flushed with conquest, to proclaim to all the measure of his shrewdness, but for which he would have been irreparably ruined by the thieving knavery of Jean Martin, who sold meat under the very doors of the church, and should have been impelled by the ecclesiastical atmosphere to a holier way of life. Mingled with the insults and vituperations of the bargainers, the shrill protests of Provençal tongues, were other protests which, though sufficiently raucous, nevertheless passed unheeded because those who aired their grievances could do nothing to obtain redress. These were the pigs, the chickens, the geese, and other members of the humbler creation, destined for the spits and soup kettles of those who contested their possession so bitterly over their unfortunate heads.

There was one who took no part in this commercial strife, and at whose appearance in the square the squabbling promptly diminished and all but ceased. This was Father André, who came from the Monastery of Our Lady of the Meadows, accompanied by Marceline the little gray ass, bearing in her panniers a quantity of sweetly smelling loaves fresh baked in the monastic ovens. This bread was of a flavor, a crispness, a lightness that no baker in Provence could rival; there was constant demand for it at the market. Father André had a word for all, and commanded from all both affection and respect. While he was present, peace reigned. But it was an armistice merely; no sooner had he quitted the square than strife broke loose again.

The baskets of Marceline being now empty, Father André turned the little ass toward home. It was an early summer day of such sweetness that it cost no effort to believe in the love of God for all things. The sun was bright but not yet too hot; the fresh breeze bore with it the intoxicating scent of newly turned earth and growing things; a green haze shimmered in the air from the young leaves of the vines and trees. As he struck into the road that wound from the back of the village across the fields to the monastery — a distance of some five miles — he began to whistle the *Salve Regina* with all blitheness. Marceline twitched her ears, evidently in annoyance. Observing his companion's displeasure, Father André was moved to protest.

"*Eh bien,* my music does not please thee, little one? How often can I say the same of thine, but customarily refrain, from consideration of thy feelings. But if my execution is at fault, my intention is not, for that is solely to give honor to Our Blessed Lady, without whose gracious favor — But in the name of heaven, what is this? What have we here?" he cried in sudden astonishment.

He came to a halt just in time to avoid stumbling over the figure of a young man lying face down in the dust and gravel of the road.

Evidently here was one in sore need of help, perhaps even of the last rites. He knelt by the prone figure and shook it. To his surprise, the body was not supine, but rigid. It stiffened yet more beneath his hand, and with a jerk the young man raised his head. The monk found himself confronted with a pair of blazing eyes, from which anger and pain looked forth with such fierceness that he was momentarily taken aback, not being prepared for it.

These eyes, moreover, were set in a face of extreme whiteness, with a look on it which Father André recognized. The black garments of the young man, though gray with dust from the road, accented the crystal pallor of the face. The monk knew what hand had left its mark on that face, though ignorant of the tools that had been used.

"My son, what is it?" he asked. "What is the matter?"

"Who are you?" the young man asked rudely.

"I am Father André from the monastery yonder." He nodded across the sunlit fields. "I take our bread to the market at Guillemont on market days — or rather, my friend Marceline" — he indicated the ass, who had taken advantage of the halt to refresh herself with a nap — "she carries the bread, I but negotiate the affairs. Business is over for the day, we are on our way back to Our Lady of the Meadows, when behold, we discover you at our feet. Are you in trouble, my son? Are you ill?"

"In trouble! Ill!" the young man echoed, catching his breath in a deep gasp.

"And what is the name of your trouble, my son?" the priest asked gently.

Deliberately, passionately, the young man answered, *"Louise."*

"Oh! I see." Father André nodded slowly, as one who compassionates an ill, though he has ceased to share it. To himself he added, "There is more here than woman's work. No woman of herself alone did this." The young man looked away, and beat with his clenched fist on the gravel of the road. The priest seized the wrist; observing the hand, his eyes filled with pity. The first two fingers were missing. The scar was a fresh one, the wound evidently but newly healed.

"Oh, my son! How did this happen?"

"That?" The young man answered with fierce contempt. He tried to jerk his hand away, but Father André held the wrist tight. "That is nothing. Nothing at all. See — " He extended the other arm, which he had kept hidden behind him. The sleeve fell over the wrist, the cuff hanging empty. "And I am crippled so that I shall never walk, except like a hunchback lame from birth," he added with great bitterness.

The monk was silent. He permitted only his eyes to make comment. "And who is this Louise?" he asked at length.

"She was to have been my wife. My brother will have her now. It is my father's decision — and mine too. Did he think I would thrust myself upon her as I am, as I shall always be? She is spring, light, heaven, everything, and I — "

The monk's fingers tightened on the young man's wrist, which they had not relinquished. He permitted himself the shadow of a smile.

"No, no, my son. Only God Almighty can be all that. You and Louise, and your father and brother, and my poor self — yes, and little Marceline here, the ass — we all belong to Him, and to His love. I should say, my son," he added very gently, almost as if to himself, and looking on the young man with great kindness, "that He loves you especially; more perhaps than the rest of us."

"Love?" The word burst from the young man, a cry of torment. "Is this the way He shows His love? And you — what do you know — ?" He was going on scornfully, but suddenly recollected himself. His white face colored, and he lowered his eyes. "Pardon me, Father. I did not mean — "

"It is the way He showed His love for us." Father André ignored the apology. "What is your name, my son?"

"Michel, *mon père.*"

"And how came you by these injuries, Michel?"

"At a hunt, in honor of — of my betrothal, *mon père.*"

"And what do you here on the road?"

"I am dismissed by my father, *mon père.* He will no longer suffer me in his presence, seeing I am a cripple and an offense to his sight."

"An offense? You? But that is truly extraordinary. Look up, my son. Look at me." Michel obeyed. The monk held his eyes for a few moments in a searching gaze. Then he nodded slowly and rose to his feet. "It is as I thought. I see what I see. Now, my son, will you come with me?"

"With you?" Michel asked suspiciously. "Where? Why?"

"To the monastery, to be our guest, till you recover from your trouble and — "

"I shall never recover," Michel declared with passionate finality.

"Very well, then: till you die of it, and we can give you Christian burial. But in either case," the priest added reasonably, "for the present you must go somewhere. Is it not so?"

"But the way is long. I can scarcely walk at all, let alone so far."

"Marceline is here for that very reason. See how sweetly God disposes all things. The bread is delivered and the baskets empty. I shall carry them, and Marceline shall carry you."

Thus it was arranged; and thus Michel, escorted by Father André, arrived at the monastery of Notre Dame des Prés on the back of Marceline the ass. When or under what circumstances he should leave, God alone knew, and Michel did not care.

Lux in tenebris lucet,
et tenebrae eam
non comprehenderunt

4. Light in Darkness

i

What the priest had seen and recognized blazing in the eyes of Michel was a thirst, a capacity, for love, which would never be filled or satisfied by any love on this earth, but only by the love of God.

Of this Michel had not the least suspicion. He did not know that the love which tortured and consumed him, raging in him like a fire that will not be quenched, was but the starting point of a love as utterly surpassing it as the light of the sun surpasses the flame of a candle, and in which his first love would burn on, transformed and absorbed, but not extinguished.

He did not know this love because it is arrived at only by experience. Heaven is filled with its witnesses, and how many on earth give testimony to it can never at any time be known. Those who know it are willing to declare it, but keep silence because one does not play music to the deaf or show color to the blind. What surgery in each case is necessary to open the heart to its reception depends on the nature of the lesser love that would lock it out; but surgery there must be, and therefore it can never be taught by word of mouth, or learned by hearing only. To talk is of no avail except to those who listen with understanding and interest, and these are the fruits, not the cause, of experience.

Arrived at the monastery with Father André and Marceline

the ass, Michel had but one thought: there was no hope for him in life, and no cure for him but to die. To Father André he had spoken what reason showed to be only the truth, when he declared that he would not recover. For, to recover, he must either cease to love, or attain the object of his love. Both were alike impossible. There was plainly but one remedy: death.

But he did not attempt to inflict this remedy on himself, considering that it was, in a sense, already effected. His body retained its limited capacity for movement, his lungs filled and emptied themselves, his heart kept up a meaningless ticking in his chest; but what did these things signify? Had the boar succeeded in putting an end to any of these vital functions, Michel could not be more thoroughly dead. It even gave him a sort of bitter pleasure to wonder how long his wreck of a body would continue to convey to others the appearance and semblance of life, while he himself lay within it, as in his grave.

Nothing had any power to rouse him from this death. Indifference possessed him now, as, so short a time ago, pain, its opposite, had done. Not that this companion had quitted him wholly; for this, Michel was now persuaded, she would never do. She returned after periods of absence, and held him straitly in close embrace, as before; and when she was present all was living fire, and he could do nothing but give himself in complete surrender until she let him go; and although he dreaded her approaches, by a strange contradiction he also welcomed them; for only when she was present did he know he lived. She alone had power to quicken and rouse him; to all else he was insensible and wholly dead. All things which had formerly stirred his interest and delight now produced no response in his soul, beyond a desolate wonder that this should be so.

"I am no longer Michel," he thought. "But what am I, and who am I become? To Michel all things were in their measure beautiful, and to live in a world so beautiful was joy. Here is the same beauty — I know it with my mind — but it falls on my eyes as on the stone eyes of a statue, and I see it not. I tell myself that this is beautiful, and that, but my heart does not agree. To live like this is an abomination. Pain — yes, pain is better. When I have pain, I know I live. At other times I am a stone, a lump of clay, a stick. I differ from other stones, and sticks, and lumps of clay only in that I know that I am one, whereas they do not. To know this is a terrible bitterness, and it is the only emotion I can feel."

Apart from the weight of this bitterness that oppressed him, the thought of Louise now gave him no added sorrow. This surprised him, and filled him also with regret. He would have preferred the continual sharp thrust, the pain constantly renewed, reminding him that his love lived and would always live, though he himself had died. He wanted to suffer through eternity in proof of the ardor and permanence of his love.

But he could not do so; everything in him was dead, even this. He forced himself to think of Louise — and how extraordinary, that unless he deliberately recalled her, she was so much absent from his thoughts; he pictured her in all her captivating grace; he purposely set his mind on the progress of his brother's suit, as one might thrust a sharp instrument into a paralyzed limb, hoping for the stab of anguish in proof that the nerves still lived. But it was of no use. He felt no jealousy, no anger, no pain of a positive character, but only weight and oppression, weariness and deadness. A storm had swept his soul, leaving wreckage in its wake. Looking over the scene of its passage, he expected to find the high tower of his love standing impregnable, where everything else lay waste, but not even this had been spared. All was desolation — ruin and emptiness and death — to the very horizon of his soul, and beyond.

Meanwhile, the life of the Community flowed about him but did not include him, as the waters of a busy stream flow about a branch caught and held immovable in its center. Michel was free to do what he wished and to go where he pleased; he hovered about the cloisters and the chapel, the common room and the gardens, because here haven had been offered him, and he felt a sort of weary gratitude for it, which was as near as he could come to feeling anything. He would go into the chapel when the monks assembled for choir; he would listen while they chanted the Office; he would remain in the silence that followed their departure, not because he particularly wished to do this, but because he desired to do nothing else.

It did not yet occur to him to seek life from the Life that waited, beneath the same roof with him, his discovery of It. He was a corpse, kept in motion by some unnatural agency; a ghost, moving among the living, but having no contact with them, and desiring none. To the monks and brothers who were his only associates, to their comings and goings, he paid no heed, and they as little to him, preferring to leave to the Divine Hand the task of rebuilding the ruined castle of his soul. This was by order of Father André, who made it plain from the start what their attitude toward their guest must be.

"He has suffered as have few of us," Father André told the Community on the evening of Michel's arrival. "Nor has he our consolations in his sorrow. It must be the hope and prayer of all of us that he will find them. When the devil discovers a soul in torment, he redoubles his efforts to possess himself of it, and with some hope of success, because it is then more susceptible to his advances, especially if he beguiles it with the promise of release from its pain. I doubt if our friend can be enticed by the ordinary allurements of sin: he has a look which is not seen apart from great purity of heart; but he is in grave danger of falling through bitterness into despair, and thus the devil may have his way with him. A soul wounded as deeply as his must either live in Christ, or curse God and die. For such a soul there is no middle road. I believe God sent him to us that he may live. If the waters of bitterness are not to overwhelm him, if he is to find life, not death, we must help him. We can do this in two ways, of which the second — note this, my brothers; the second is to *leave him alone.* We must show him friendliness but no curiosity; above all, we must give him no counsel he does not seek. God will prompt him to ask for all the help he needs, and anything beyond that will increase the hurt rather than cure it. That is the second way in which we may help him. The first, I should not need to tell you, is to pray."

This injunction which Father André laid upon his fellow Religious was not entirely superfluous; for there will always be those, in religious communities as out of them, who believe that they know best what is good for everyone, and who will be at no loss to convey this knowledge to any whom they perceive to stand in need of it. This conviction of superior wisdom does not exist apart from curiosity concerning the affairs of those destined to be the recipients of unsought counsel; and from the disastrous attentions of such benefactors Father André was determined to shield his protégé. Thus, the Community were constrained not to question or instruct Michel; to treat him as nearly as possible as one of themselves, or at least as one to whom nothing extraordinary had befallen; and to pray for him without ceasing.

It is evident that curative measures of such admirable wisdom could not fail of their effect.

ii

Michel limped around the wing of the main building which housed the refectory and kitchens. A wide veranda of flagstones bordered the end of the wing; over it extended a trellis from which clusters of grapes hung ripening in the hot sun. Beside a door which gave access to the kitchens, a wooden bench stood against the wall. Here Michel now seated himself.

On the low step at the end of the flagging sat Brother Joseph, scrubbing pots and cutlery with sand, and singing loudly off key. The sunlight falling through the vines on the trellis threw patches of light and shade on the flagstones, on the broad back of Brother Joseph, and on Cendrillon the cat, who suckled an assorted brood of kittens nearby. From his bench Michel looked out over a wide stretch of fields and vineyards silvered in the white heat of the midsummer sun. Far beyond, the trees of the forest of Cançonnet, drenched with the same light, shone and rippled in the wind. Through the fields curved a narrow thread of road, along which diminutive figures passed: peasants accompanied by laden donkeys, or carrying baskets on their heads. The air quivered in the August heat. A drowsy silence hung over everything, broken only by the singing of Brother Joseph.

Michel leaned back against the wall and drew a deep sigh. The tranquillity of the scene filled him with contentment. The peace was somewhat disturbed by the vocalizations of Brother Joseph, in which there was more good will than art; an even better will, thought Michel, would have prompted him to keep silence altogether. The musical aberrations of the Brother were such that Michel could not identify his song, beyond recognizing that it was of a devotional character.

"I can endure," said Michel to himself, "some things, seeing there is no escape. But the singing of Brother Joseph is not one of these."

He was about to rise and depart when the Brother spared him the necessity. Terminating both his scouring and his song, he piled his kettles and utensils together with a great clatter, and trudged back into the kitchen, beaming at Michel as he passed. Michel smiled quickly in return. His heart smote him that he should have thought so hardly of one from whose countenance only goodness shone, but the fact remained that although the virtues of Brother Joseph were manifestly many — "far beyond any I might ever hope to attain," Michel told himself — the music of Brother Joseph was atrocious.

Michel settled himself to enjoy the peace which, following the departure of Brother Joseph, was now complete. Hearing a step, he looked up. Father André stood before him. Michel made a move to rise, but the priest put a hand on his shoulder.

"Do not stand, Michel. I will share your bench with you."

He seated himself beside Michel, who felt at this encounter a quick stir of joy. Recently he had begun to entertain for the priest who had befriended him a reverence and regard beyond the respect demanded by the dignity of his office. This dated from a certain morning some two weeks ago, when Michel wandered into the chapel at High Mass, and knelt down, not from devotion, but from want of anything else to do. Gradually, as the sacred liturgy progressed, he became aware of a presence, intangible but real, familiar enough to him in days past, but now long ignored. This reality pierced his insensibility, summoned him with insistence, demanded that he recognize it and give it a name. Something within him stirred and woke; he was in the midst of Beauty, and he knew it.

"Pater noster, qui es in coelis — Sanctificetur nomen tuum — Adveniat regnum tuum — "

The chant, rising from the altar, flooded the chapel and poured into the empty soul of Michel its serene and austere beauty. He listened, enraptured. The majestic syllables proceeded, rich with a meaning to which his heart and ears were now suddenly opened: *"Fiat voluntas tua —"*

"This is Mass. How beautiful it is — how beautiful. All my life I have heard Mass. Why have I never seen how beautiful it is before?"

The celebrant was Father André. Michel recognized his benefactor with pride. He told himself that this was folly; for to the beauty of Father André's singing he had contributed nothing; but he felt himself bound to the priest almost by ties of kinship, as if Father André, in rescuing him, had taken the place of his own father, who had cast him out. For this reason he was entitled to take in the attainments of Father André a just and secret pride.

After Mass Michel did not leave the chapel. He remained kneeling, seized and held by a presence as compelling as that of the companion to whose embrace he was now so used, but of how different an aspect! For this presence was beauty: a beauty heightened and glorified, transcending any he had ever known. The fire of dawn in the sky, the benediction of twilight on the fields, the shadowed silence of the forest, the joy and the promise of love — these had captured and filled his heart to the brim, but they had not overflowed it as this beauty now did, surrounding it and pouring from it, as the waters of a pool overflow and surrounded a vessel deeply immersed in them. That beauty he could understand; this surpassed his comprehension. That could be held and borne within the heart; this was akin to pain, and hardly to be endured.

After some moments he raised his head and looked about him. This presence, this beauty, which had laid hold on his heart, entering it through the chanting of Father André and the beauty of Mass, now made itself known to his sight as well. He was as one to whom vision is restored after long blindness. The carvings on the choir stalls; the jeweled windows through which the sunlight poured in slanting shafts; the colored brilliance patching the gray stone floor: all sang, and his heart sang, in answer.

All was filled with radiance; all was made new. For a moment he could almost believe that the past had been a dream, a nightmare from which he had just wakened, shaking off the hideous spell that had held him in sleep: but he knew immediately, and with no diminution of joy, that this was not so. He was in the chapel, not of Guillemont, but Notre Dame des Prés, and the reason for his being there was no dream, but the truth. He glanced down, as if to verify this fact; his left cuff still hung empty, his right hand was still maimed; when he rose to leave the chapel, he would limp, he knew, as before; but what did these things matter? Incurable as his infirmities were, suddenly they seemed no longer a part of him; they affected him essentially no more than torn garments could alter his appearance; and although he must wear them till he died, they were matter for neither sorrow nor regret. On the contrary: except for them, he would not now be here. Except for them, he would not this morning have been quickened and roused and stirred by a beauty greater than he had ever known in his life before.

Thus, in the dead heart of Michel, a bird awoke and began to sing.

All day this wonder went with him. He lay down with it at night. He awakened to it at daybreak. It reached even into his sleep, so that he was aware of its warmth and joy before he was fully awake. He lay, staring at the rough white wall before him, delaying to move lest he shatter and dispel this radiance in which he was immersed. For in all his life he had felt nothing comparable to it, except the first lifting of pain at Guillemont, when he would lie hardly daring to draw breath, for the slightest motion would break the frail peace which enveloped him, and invite a raging onslaught of pain. But he arose now; he dressed; he went into the chapel for Mass. The presence did not vanish. The shining remained; the joy endured.

Thereafter Michel attended High Mass each morning. Here was a net which ensnared his feet; it drew him to the chapel at the hour of Mass inevitably, irresistibly; it entangled his soul and held it, so that he could withdraw neither his presence nor his attention; and the cords of this net were Beauty.

From the end of one Mass, he looked forward all day to the next, anticipating it with eagerness and joy. He soon learned to distinguish the characteristics of each priest, as they celebrated in turn. He realized with added joy that his admiration had not been misplaced. Whoever the celebrant, Mass was always Mass, and therefore always beautiful; but Father André brought to the celebration of the sacred mysteries a dignity truly conspicuous. At the Masses of Father André in particular Michel felt his soul possessed with beauty, pierced and flooded with delight.

As it was Father André who had salvaged his wrecked body from the roadside, so it was Father André who performed a like service for his heart and soul, rousing the love of beauty which slept there, and quickening it to life. Michel loved Mass; he loved Father André; he saw, heard, felt; he was not dead; he lived.

And he would continue to live. For this joy was no interlude, but a permanence and a possession. Not even pain could darken this light, or dispel this beauty. For some days he remained free from pain; he felt a physical lightness and well-being, as if his injuries had been fully healed, and he would never suffer from them again; but a few mornings later, as he knelt in the chapel after Mass, he was aware of the approach of the companion so familiar to him. She came quickly; she knelt with him; she seized and clasped him in her fiery embrace. He felt the moisture start out on his forehead, he set his teeth against the shock and ardor of her greeting. He yielded to her, as he must perforce do; but although she withdrew him, as always, from the knowledge of all things but herself, she could not withdraw him now from beauty or from joy. For beauty had returned to his heart and possessed it, as this returning pain possessed his body. Each held its separate territory, and neither excluded the other. He had been swept into a flood of beauty. Pain joined him here, but she did not take him from it.

And he knew that it was not her purpose to do so. Closely as she held him, it seemed to him also that she stood apart from him, and addressed him, and he listened, willingly:

"Michel, I am she whom you know so well. Men hate me, and fear me, above all others on earth. My countenance affrights them and my touch appals them. They turn from me with cursing and reviling, and for this reason they do not learn the truth. I am not hideous, Michel, but beautiful. I come laden with rich treasure, but men flee at my approach. They will not wait to receive my gift from my hands.

"I courted you: you did not shrink from me. I embraced you: you suffered it. Therefore I will reward you beyond all your expectation. I will lead you to great beauty and deep joy, of which this joy you now feel is but a taste. Only make room for me in your heart. When you feel me coming, stand to meet me: do not flee. I will come to you in many forms, but whatever guise I wear, greet me as your chosen friend. Make me your bride. For I was the companion of Him whose beauty you have seen in Mass. Give me your hand without fear. Yield yourself with confidence to me. I will lead you to His beauty, and to Him."

"Make me your bride."

What strange summons, what dark invitation, was this? Had not holy St. Francis chosen a bride equally despised by men? Had he not loved and courted Lady Poverty, and wedded her, and kept faith with her, living in gladness with her all his life?

She who courted Michel, holding him now in close and burning grasp, was she not sister to holy Poverty? And as St. Francis had chosen the one sister, would he not choose the other? He had not courted her: it was she who had wooed him. She had waited in the forest of Cançonnet on a black winter morning, to keep tryst with him, who was on his way to keep tryst with another; she had seized him, and made herself known to him, with violence; she had returned with him to Guillemont, and remained with him in closest union; nor had she quitted him since.

And now she demanded his choice of her, his fidelity and allegiance, as long as he should live. What were the words which above all others had arrested his attention at Mass? *Fiat voluntas tua.* She came to Michel as the emissary of Him who first spoke those words, bidding His followers repeat them after Him. For this reason Michel would accept her suit; he would not withhold himself; he would give all she asked.

His bride — how different from her he had chosen, but not unlovely after all. This rude and unwelcome comrade, whom others drove from them, he would wed, as St. Francis had wedded Lady Poverty. He would walk her way, he would follow where she led, he would not turn from her; and though his flesh cried out against her coming, in his heart he would welcome her, and love her, and make room for her, whenever she desired it. He would not seek to part from her, until she chose to part from him. Neither would he go in search of her, but he would send his heart to meet her when she came, he would yield himself willingly to her embrace.

Thus Michel plighted his troth in the chapel of Notre Dame des Prés to this companion who knelt with him, this sister of St. Francis' chosen bride. She remained with him for some time longer, tightening her embrace till he thought he should cry out beneath it. Then slowly she released him, and was gone.

Of all this he said nothing to anyone. He longed to confide in Father André, to seek his understanding and his counsel. But he hesitated to address the priest, from shyness and unwillingness to intrude himself and his affairs on Father André's time and attention. He knew, however, that ultimately he must do so. And now here was Father André seated beside him, evidently in no hurry to leave, and by his presence and the friendliness of his manner inviting the confidence Michel had so far withheld.

His lean face was deeply tanned by exposure to the suns of summer and of the Midi. Fine white lines which had escaped the sun marked his forehead and radiated outward from his dark eyes. He was, perhaps, twenty years older than Michel, a fact of which these lines gave the only hint. His spare person wore a look of youth, and Michel, although sensible of his greater dignity, felt that here was one who could feel and know all that he himself did. He was conscious of no barrier between himself and the priest. His glance fell on Father André's hands, resting on his knee. They were indeed beautiful hands: strong, sensitive, slender; the hands of an artist, of a priest. Michel had a moment of bewilderment. He had remarked these hands of Father André on some previous occasion, but he could not recall where. A shock jarred him as he remembered: not the hands of Father André, but his own.

He looked up. His love for the priest dispelled the last shreds of his reserve and broke through the silence he had hitherto kept.

"How happy I am to see you, *mon père*. For a long time I have wished to speak to you, and especially to thank you for your great kindness to me. I cannot do so adequately, but that is no reason why I should not do so at all, or at least attempt it."

Father André smiled. "Do not thank us, Michel. Rather, it is we who should thank you. I believe God Almighty contrived to send you to us for our good. You are an example and an inspiration to many."

Michel stared. Observing his expression, the priest laughed.

"Does it not occur to you, Michel, that man's customary response to suffering is railing and complaint, and that those who endure it in silence are very few, and an inspiration to those about them? Brother Antoine, now, has occasionally a rheumatism of the knee. One would think to hear his groanings that he was being gored by twenty bulls. The other day in the midst of his lamentations I pointed out to him that none of us had heard so much as a murmur from you, who plainly endure more than a twinge of the knee. This consideration had a salutary effect on Brother Antoine, as on all of us. The silence that followed refreshed me exceedingly."

Seized with confusion, Michel protested. It was plainly incumbent on him to correct so grievous a misapprehension.

"If I have kept silence, *mon père,* it is not from fortitude or any other virtue whatever, but rather the contrary. I have been filled with rebellion and bitterness. I have lacked the heart even to complain. I wonder that you have endured my sullen presence so long. And now it is no virtue in me to keep silence, for I no longer have any reason to complain."

At the sound of voices, the ears of Cendrillon had begun to twitch. She got to her feet now, shaking off her reluctant kittens. Picking her way over them gingerly, as one who crosses a muddy street, she approached Michel and rubbed her head vigorously against his foot. The bewildered kittens staggered uncertainly after her; catching up with her one by one, they demanded a resumption of activities. Cendrillon resigned herself to the inevitable. She collapsed with a sigh, pillowed her head on Michel's foot, and permitted her family to continue their interrupted meal. The last kitten took a wrong turning and started off by itself into uncharted wilderness, squeaking its distress. Michel, reaching down, picked it up and restored it to those comforts essential to its happiness. He stroked the head of the mother cat, who purred loudly.

Father André watched Michel narrowly. The face before him had lost neither its pallor nor its transparency, but the look of fierce rebellion had given way to an unmistakable peace. It was such a face as must in any case be handsome, but which bitterness could have rendered harsh, or cruel, or sullen, if self-pity did not stamp it with petulance, or with an ugly and sneering defiance. This might have happened; but it had not. On the contrary: the brilliance of the eyes was unshadowed by resentment, and the mouth, firmly held, as against weakness and pain, was not on that account grim, but rather of a singular appeal. It was a face to please all eyes and to stir any heart not insensible or dead; watching it, the priest knew with gratitude and relief that disaster — the worst of all disasters — had been averted. The beauty of this face had not been marred but heightened by what must either kill beauty altogether, or greatly increase it.

He said, "Is the pain gone, my son?"

Michel looked up. "From my heart, Father — yes."

"And otherwise?"

"Otherwise?" Meeting the eyes of Father André, Michel smiled. "Did not the holy St. Francis love a lady, and her name was Poverty? Was he not wedded to her all his life? It has occurred to me, Father, that this lady has a sister, and it is this sister who has courted me. And as St. Francis was wedded to Lady Poverty, so I must be wedded to this lady, and be faithful to her, and love her, while I live. And — " he colored slightly, but did not lower his eyes " — I believe, Father, that she is the only lady I shall ever love."

"I may guess her name, Michel?"

"You may Father, if you wish."

"It is she of whom we have been speaking?"

"It is so, Father. She has not left me, nor will she leave me, altogether. Most people flee from her, believing her rude and ugly, and finding her attentions unwelcome; but they are wrong. I would have fled her, too, and gladly, but she was swifter than I. She overtook me, and remained with me, until she compelled me to look, and to see the truth. She is not ugly, Father, but very beautiful. But one must know her well to find that out."

Father André continued to regard Michel, and then he said,

"Oh, my son! This is a great and profound secret — in truth a *mysterium fidei* — which you have stated. It is possible to spend a long life, even in religion, without discovering this truth: that suffering is not necessarily an evil, and that pain may conceal great good. But it takes a valiant spirit to face this truth, and accept it, and speak it from the heart, as you have done."

The color deepened in Michel's face, and he lowered his eyes in embarrassment.

"But, Father, I did not mean — I did not intend — "

"No, Michel." Father André smiled. "I know you did not intend to lay claim to any merit in this matter, much less to reveal it to me. Shall we say, then, that this secret was forced on your attention, more or less against your will, and that your natural intelligence, for which you rightly take no credit, was sufficient to enable you to draw conclusions which are not obvious at a glance?"

Michel looked up. Meeting Father André's, eyes, he laughed.

"And I will not deceive you, Father. This lady is by no means a faithful mistress. She does not love me as she did. She is absent for long intervals, and when she returns, she soon wearies of me, and goes again. So that I am in truth greatly recovered. Surely it is time that I go, too."

"Go, Michel? Where?"

"That I do not know. But I eat your food and make no return. It is not right that I stay here always and do nothing, a burden on your hands."

"Yes, and you breathe our air also, and for that, too, you should make some accounting."

"I am not jesting, Father."

"Nor am I, Michel. If you wish to make a return for the food you consume, which amounts to hardly more than the air you breathe, you might apply to Brother Joseph. He has always too much to occupy him in the kitchen."

"Brother Joseph?" Michel swallowed. "He who sings?"

"Brother Joseph is indeed of a cheerful and devout nature. There is little one can do about it." The eyes of Father André gleamed with silent mirth. "Have you any knowledge of music, Michel?"

"Somewhat, Father. I was taught by the Abbé Courtot, who was confessor to our family, and tutor to my brother and me. I learned enough," he added quickly, "to appreciate the great beauty of your singing at Mass, *mon père.*"

"I see you at Mass each day, do I not, Michel?"

"Mon père," Michel replied earnestly, "all my life I have attended Mass, but until now I have failed to perceive how beautiful it is. I do not understand how that beauty could have so long escaped me, or how any can fail to see and be held captive by it. It was at your Mass that it first compelled my attention, and now I cannot stay away. *Mon père —"* He hesitated.

"Yes, Michel?"

"It is many months since I have received the sacraments. Every morning, when the Brothers communicate, it is a pain to me to remain in my place. I wish to receive Holy Communion. Will you hear my confession, *mon père?"*

"But assuredly, my son."

The manner of the priest gave no hint of the joy that filled him at this talk and this request. For now he knew, and beyond doubt, that what he had seen in the eyes of Michel on the occasion of their first meeting, he had not read amiss.

iii

After this the waters flowed back into the soul of Michel, as into a stream from which the floodgates are removed. Alive himself, he woke to a realization of life about him. He perceived that the life of the Community had an order, coherence, and meaning of which he had hitherto been unaware; the succession of bells that clanged their way through his days, formerly a senseless jangle, had each its separate message and command. They spoke a language, as the notes of a staff of music speak a language to those who can read it, but are without meaning to those who cannot. He wondered what that language was, what these commands entailed that demanded such unwavering obedience from the brotherhood, while leaving him always outside. He asked a question, then another and another. Each question, satisfying his curiosity on one point, increased it concerning the matters that lay beyond. He found himself in a world whose existence he had never hitherto suspected. His interest was fully aroused; he must know more and still more. His thirst for information overcame all shyness. He pursued Father André with questions. He harassed him; he gave him no peace.

"The Sacrifice of Mass is the Sacrifice of the Cross. Then it follows, Father, that to be present at Mass, is to be present, in very truth, at Calvary?"

"Precisely, Michel."

"And to absent ourselves from Mass, when nothing prevents, is to turn aside from Him on His way to the cross, with those who abandoned Him through indifference or fear?"

"Yes, Michel. You have stated one of the greatest truths and deepest mysteries of our faith: the altar and the cross are one. At the altar, time stops. At every Mass, we are present in the Upper Chamber, we are present at the cross. At each celebration of the Holy Sacrifice, He gives Himself for us, and to us, as He gave Himself to the Twelve on Holy Thursday, and on Good Friday, to the world. And it is not a second giving, for there is but one Sacrifice. Mass is Calvary continued on our altars, that we, who could not be present at the cross, may nevertheless be present at that same Sacrifice, and share in it, and unite ourselves with it, at every Mass."

Stone by stone, these questions built a new castle in the heart of Michel and this castle housed a new beauty and a new love: Holy Mass. For him Mass now took precedence over all things; he was absorbed and possessed by it; he could think of nothing else. A day which did not have its origin and center in Mass, was a day lost. More, a life which did not derive its meaning and its reason from the Holy Sacrifice, was equally lost. Here was the beginning and the end of everything, the Life of all life, the Beauty surpassing all beauty, to live without which was death indeed. The impossible had happened, the incredible was true: Madame the mother of Louise was right. With an immense and solemn joy Michel saw now what he had been too dull of heart, too slow of wit, to see before; he, no less than Father André, was called to perform this most beautiful and sacred of all acts, to be a priest, to celebrate Mass.

He went again to Father André, his heart bursting within him. "Father, I know now what I want most in the world. I desire never to leave, but to remain here always."

"You mean, you wish to enter religion, my son?"

Michel nodded, his eyes shining.

"That is my desire and my intention, *mon père.*"

"You are willing to renounce the world and its pleasures, not for a few months only, but for the rest of your life?"

"Pleasures!" Michel echoed. Then, restraining himself, he continued calmly: "I admit, *mon père,* that it will cost me an effort to renounce the pleasure of hunting boars. For that sport I have an inordinate passion. Other than that, I can think of none I would not willingly forego."

Father André smiled. "And your Louise, Michel?"

Michel took a deep breath. He held Father André's eyes with his, as if by the very intentness of his gaze to supply whatever strength or conviction might be wanting from his words, for words alone were inadequate to express what he wished to say:

"Father, how can I persuade you of the truth? I have never loved any but Louise — I could never love any but her. And now she is married to my brother: of that I am sure. I tell you this in tranquillity and peace, without pain and without regret. Not that I have ceased to love her, or even that I love her less: but I love her differently. I would not in any case marry her as I am now — but if by some miracle I should be restored, and become again as I used to be, even then I would not return to her, or to my former life. I would still come to you, as I do now. For I know that there is a greater love, and a better way, than marriage." He took another deep breath: "You have chosen it, Father. I choose it, too."

"You have no need to persuade me, Michel. You tell me only what I knew to be true of you, long before you discovered it yourself."

"And for that reason, Father," Michel pursued with great earnestness, "I rejoice with my whole heart that I am not married — to her, or to anyone. I thank God who in His mercy contrived to prevent it in time. And I am determined never to change, but to remain always as I am, if God will continue His mercy to me, if He will give me that grace. For I desire only one thing, Father; and that is to be a monk — a priest, like you."

"A — *priest,* Michel?"

"Yes, Father." He felt his knees go weak, and his throat dry. "Beyond everything in the world — beyond anything I have ever wanted in my life — *anything,* Father — I long to be a priest and to celebrate Mass."

There was a long silence.

"Oh, my son!" murmured Father André at length. *"My poor son."*

He looked steadily into the eyes of Michel, burning now, not with pain and anger, but with eagerness and hope, and with that love to which Michel had just confessed, and which Father André had foreseen that he would one day know. In his own eyes there gathered a depth of compassion such as had not been evoked by the sight of the suffering figure lying by the roadside months before, deep and genuine though his pity then had been; and Michel, gazing back, read in the priest's face what he could not bring himself to utter: that Michel, crippled as he was, with his grotesque limp and single maimed hand, could never aspire to the priesthood, could never celebrate Mass.

Before the sorrow in the priest's eyes, Michel lowered his own; and within him welled up a cruel disappointment that was akin to shame. With the pain of this rejection were mingled confusion and chagrin, the abasement of one caught reaching for forbidden fruits, a shame beneath shame. His breast heaved; his throat contracted; he did not raise his eyes; they had filled with tears. He felt them overflow and drip onto his breast. This added humiliation filled him with rage against himself, with contempt for his inability to control such weakness.

"Forgive me, Father," he gasped. "I — I forgot. You have been kind. No one observes it here. I am used to it by now. Outside I could never forget, but here — besides" — he took a deep breath — "how could I wish for it? How could I hope? I am not worthy —"

Father André laid his hand on Michel's shoulder.

"Do we not all say that? Three times at every Mass? We are all alike unworthy. None would stand before the altar of God, if it depended on worth. Your desire is very pleasing to God, my son. He has other plans for you, that is all."

Michel, his head still bowed, did not reply. Father André continued:

"If you wish to stay with us, my son — to take our vows, to share our life, as Brother, if not Priest — it might be the sacrifice God asks of you, to further some august purpose of His own. That you will decide, with the help of His grace."

In silence, without raising his eyes, Michel turned and left.

Father André watched him limp slowly out of sight. "God pity me," cried the priest in his heart, "who have had to strike him this blow! And God pity him, and strengthen him to endure it! For it is truly enough to drive him to final bitterness and despair, that he should be compelled to suffer this, who has suffered so much already. May the love and mercy of God hold him fast, for if he turns from Him now, to whom will he go, and where, except to his death?"

The priest need not have feared. The soul of Michel was now the dwelling of a Guest, who, indeed, was not absent on the occasion of the first trial, but who made His presence known to Michel in his second and deeper need, because it was to Him that Michel was led by that need. The heart of Michel had been opened to welcome and receive Him; he could turn nowhere now, he could not flee his sorrow, without finding Him.

Michel knelt in the chapel, his bent head resting on his folded arms. It was late afternoon; though still light outside, within the chapel the shadows gathered rapidly. Father Pierre, the sacristan, was busy at the altar; Brother Antoine, he of the rheumatic knee, was sweeping the chapel floor.

Father Pierre had a genius for silence and for economy of motion. He was never guilty of a superfluous gesture or an unnecessary sound. He moved before the altar now, hardly less silent than the encroaching shadows, disposing even the massive candlesticks as quietly as if they had been feathers. His genuflections before the tabernacle were exhibitions of a classic dignity and grace.

That Brother Antoine should have performed his duties simultaneously with Father Pierre was a masterpiece of celestial irony. For the mere presence of Brother Antoine was an affront to silence; at his approach, she fled, and remained in hiding until his departure. From his person, even in repose, there issued a continual creaking and groaning like that of the rigging of a ship in high wind. The beads of Brother Antoine clanked and rattled; he swished and flounced like an old lady with fifty petticoats; he was always turning and twisting, whether he knelt, or stood, or sat; his every breath was a gusty sigh, punctuated for emphasis with intermittent groans; he did not say his prayers, he whistled them. The sweeping of Brother Antoine reverberated through the chapel like the charge of a regiment of horses, and for this reason Michel customarily chose a time for his meditations when Brother Antoine and his broom were elsewhere. Today, however, it did not matter. Nothing was capable of disturbing him, not even the sweeping of Brother Antoine.

His companion, his chosen lady, had returned to him. She held him in close embrace, she demanded his entire attention. She wore a different aspect, but he knew her touch too well not to recognize her, even in this guise. She had come in accordance with her promise, and she would never again leave him. Time, that heals other pain, would not heal this, but rather increase it. There is no pain like that of love deprived of its object; and that was to be the lot of Michel while he lived.

But in this pain there was no bitterness; against this suffering he did not rebel. He accepted it; he chose it; he preferred it to any possible escape. There could, indeed, be no escape, except to follow the hideous suggestions with which his father had dismissed him from Guillemont. From these the soul of Michel did not shrink, because he did not so much as consider them. His lady had kept her word to him; he would keep his to her. He would open his heart wide to receive and embrace this pain, this deprivation, which could never be lessened, or changed, or ended; he would seek no escape, as He sought none from the cross.

Brother Antoine finished his sweeping and quitted the chapel. Following his departure, silence returned; the sanctuary lamp flickered and glowed, the only light and motion. In the darkness and silence Michel remained kneeling, alone.

Alone? — The chapel was filled with the Presence of Him who had summoned Michel so insistently to Himself, and who waited only this surrender that He might seize the heart of Michel and possess it entirely.

"I seek all those, Michel, to whom love is a suffering. Was not My love a suffering for you?"

Michel went again to Father André and told him his mind was decided. He wished to take the habit of the Order, to become a lay Brother, if God would grant him that grace. And, there being no obstacles in either his dispositions or his conduct, Brother Michel, having passed his novitiate, took his vows and was received into the Order in that capacity which God had ordained for him. And none at any time suspected, save only Father André, the cross which Our Lord had erected in the new Brother's soul: the yearning to be a priest and to celebrate Mass was a thirst which could not be slaked, but which would torment him till the day of his death.

PART TWO

THE WAY OF PEACE

Vidi impium
superexaltatum et elevatum
sicut cedros Libani

5. As the Green Bay Tree

i

A wedding was celebrated at Cançonnet with every sign of rejoicing but without joy. Since joy and grief reside in the heart only, their absence may not be detected on those occasions when they should be present but are not, if it is concealed beneath a careful display of the exterior signs proper to those emotions. The heart may wear deep mourning though the body is arrayed in white: a fact which Louise de Guillemont (née Cançonnet) very well knew.

This knowledge thrust itself on her as she dressed for her wedding. The white gown, with its pointed bodice and wide stiff skirt, embroidered all over in gold thread and seed pearls, clothed a figure so young, so full of charm and grace, that it was impossible to think of it in terms of sorrow: here, if anywhere, Joy should make her home. The radiant curls, whose color Michel had been at such a loss to describe, were gathered into a snood of pearls, over which the bridal veil hung, foaming downward in a cascade of lace. The dark eyes beneath this veil had a certain wistfulness not unbecoming in a bride. The absence of marked radiance, of effusive joy, did not so much denote sorrow as due restraint and a shyness proper to the occasion. Human flesh, otherwise so frail, resembles rock in this, that sorrow requires time to leave its imprint on the countenance, as the dropping of water on the face of a cliff.

Louise emerged from the hands of her attendants in all ways perfect. She surveyed herself in the great glass in the upper hall and her heart cried out at what she saw.

"How is this possible?" she thought in her desolation. "Why is not my face hideous and wrinkled and old, as my heart is? If it were so, if my dress were black instead of white, if I wore a mourning veil and the church were hung with crepe, then I could endure it, for it would speak the truth. Is it not a sufficient evil that I am to marry Paul? Why must this mockery of festivity be added to it? But since it is so, let the mockery be consistent. Let my whole life be a mockery from this day on."

It was the very consummation of mockery that she should be arrayed thus as befitted the bride of Michel, when within the hour she would be the wife of Paul. A knife turned in her heart; she thought she would drop from the pain of it where she stood. *Michel!* Her soul uttered one final cry of impassioned rebellion before she met it with her will, subdued it, suffocated it, silenced it utterly.

"I, Louise, take thee, Paul —"

She spoke the words very clearly and calmly, with a distinctness which permitted of no doubt that she meant them. She withheld nothing of her full consent. Deliberately she did this, marrying Paul whom she did not love and never could love, not because she was forced or persuaded against her will, but because Michel was gone and what happened to her did not matter.

Paul was under no illusions concerning the nature of her feeling for him, but he was not troubled by it. He had got what he wanted: herself. That he did not have her love also was of secondary importance.

The accident to Michel gave Paul the opportunity he awaited, to turn defeat to success. He believed that he could easily supplant his brother in Louise's heart, as he had so nearly done before; but his past triumph was not repeated. Michel persisted, in spite of the expert tactics Paul employed to dislodge him.

These tactics took the form of a feigned indifference concerning her feelings for him, and a marked demonstration of regard for her. Her comfort, her convenience, her wishes: these were his only concern; he anticipated them and carried them into effect whenever possible, with no thought of himself. Surely such disinterestedness should bear rich fruit. But Michel was now too strongly entrenched in the heart of Louise to be thus easily displaced. She was grateful to Paul for his kindness and attention, but she listened to his words with her ears only: her heart stood tiptoe, awaiting Michel.

But Michel never came. Day after day passed; he neither appeared himself, nor sent any word. During the winter she had not expected him; but now he was recovered; surely he must come. Neither she, nor anyone at Cançonnet, knew to what extent he had been hurt. The nature of his injuries was not discovered until he was taken to Guillemont and there examined, and there was none to carry the details back to Cançonnet except Paul. Those at Cançonnet therefore heard only as much as Paul wished them to hear; and they did not question the truth of what he told them, having no reason to do so.

All things conspired to aid in maintaining this deception. Rather, he did not so much deliberately foster it, as allow it to pass without correction, once the impression had been created that Michel was not seriously hurt. Gossip might well have contradicted him; rumor equally might have reached the ears of Louise, supplementing Paul's story with something more nearly approaching the truth, or going far beyond it, except that rumor and gossip both, otherwise so bold, will not travel except in human company. Due to the unusual severity of the winter, there was no one to give them transportation save Paul, who therefore had things all his own way. When spring came the accident was no longer news. The departure of Michel might have provided matter for gossip, had anyone known or suspected the reason for it, save Michel himself, and his father, and Paul. The fact that he was gone could not be concealed from Louise or from anyone; but the explanation of his going, Paul determined, should be as he decided.

Louise waited, sickened with disappointment at the prolonged silence and absence of Michel. Something was seriously amiss, of that there was no doubt; but in spite of her apprehension and bewilderment, she was not prepared for the blow which put an end to waiting and to hope.

"Louise, I have news for you. It will distress you, but it cannot be helped. Michel is gone."

"Gone?" she repeated, nonplussed. "I do not understand. What do you mean? Where is he gone? Why?"

"We do not know. He is gone, that is all. His illness affected him strangely; he is greatly altered. I shall not be surprised if he turns monk. But he did not confide in my father or in me, so I can tell you nothing more."

It will be observed that in this Paul took great care not to deviate from the truth.

Louise could not believe him. What he told her was beyond reason and beyond possibility. At the same time she could not deny that it was so. The damning facts of Michel's silence and absence proclaimed the truth of this monstrous desertion: Michel, who would love her forever, in whom she would still have believed, though everything and everyone in the world had proved false — Michel had jilted her; abandoned her; left her, without explanation and without farewell.

The life of the frantic girl resolved itself into a single question, to which there was no answer: *why?*

"But it does not astonish me in the least," said her mother. "Did I not tell you long ago that I believe God intended Michel to be a priest?"

"Why then did not God call him before this? Why did He let Michel love me, and promise himself to me? Why did God give us such happiness, if He meant only to destroy it now?"

"Perhaps God did call him, but Michel was so captivated by you that he refused to hear. Remember, you and Michel have hardly been separated for a week in your lives, until this winter. Illness gives one opportunity for serious reflection, my child; and Michel has undoubtedly decided that his duty lies where he least suspected it. As I say, I am not surprised. I regret it deeply, for your sake; but it causes me no astonishment."

"But why did Michel not let me know? Why did he not tell me he had changed his mind? Why did he go as he did, without a word?"

"I do not think he has ceased to love you — that is why. Without doubt he realized that if he was to be true to his calling, he must not see you again. Even a letter might have caused him to hesitate or to weaken. He preferred not to run the risk of writing it. I can understand that, if you cannot."

"And it was God who did this — God who took him from me?"

"It was God who called Michel, undoubtedly."

"Then," said the girl, in a cold, small voice, "I hate God."

"That is very unreasonable of you, Louise. I repeat, God may have called Michel long ago, and he refused to hear. Also, unless I mistake, you were interested in Paul some time since, almost to the exclusion of Michel. It is better to be satisfied with what you can have, than to grieve for what you cannot. Michel is gone, but Paul remains. Cannot you revive that interest?"

"But I want Michel! I love Michel!" she cried fiercely. "I do not love Paul — I can never love him!"

Nor did she; but she took her mother's advice, notwithstanding. The love of Michel had failed her, and with it all love. What happened to her now mattered less than nothing. Paul asked her to marry him, and she gave her consent.

"Ite, missa est —"

It was over. The farce of the Nuptial Mass was ended. Louise left the church on the arm of her husband, surrounded by the compliments and congratulations of those present, who were enraptured by her beauty and envious of her good fortune. All outward signs spoke of rejoicing, and effectively concealed the desolation that filled the empty vessel of her heart. She, who should have been the bride of Michel, was now the wife of Paul, and must so remain till he or she should die.

ii

The departure of Michel affected him who was responsible for it in a manner he could not have foreseen. The remnant of health still enjoyed by the old man failed completely; he took first to his room, then to his bed. His frail body had been hitherto preserved from disintegration by some agent exterior to it, as a broken object may be held together by a cord. Now the cord was cut; and the shattered fragments it had bound into a unit fell asunder.

He failed with a rapidity which caused everyone to hope that he would soon die; but he did not. The progress of his disease halted just short of death. It took from him everything except the mere fact of continued existence; having gone so far, it seemed in no hurry to proceed further. He lived on and on, changed almost beyond recognition, repulsive and detestable. He continued to dominate the Château with his influence, although he would permit no one near him but Louise.

His reason was disordered, but not dulled; in fact, quite the contrary. It now attained a perfection of malice impossible to a sound mind, however depraved. Reason serves as a check, even to vice, the limits of which are to be found in those murky regions of the mind whence reason is outcast — as Louise discovered.

Of the fastidiousness which had served as a foil to his physical defects, no vestige remained. To the ravages of disease he had formerly opposed a fierce pride in personal nicety, in being groomed to a fault; this was now degenerated into a perverted glee in being repulsive. He was unable to care for himself, and unwilling that others should do so, beyond what was of unavoidable necessity.

He would accept no attention except from his daughter-in-law, who believed that he lived now only to devise ways of making more revolting the already hideous task of caring for him. He would summon her fifty times a day, for any reason or for no reason. When she had satisfied his demands he would not let her go, but would play with her as a cat with a mouse, torturing her with the hope of release, calling her back before she was out of earshot for some whim or necessity he had overlooked. She soon discovered that her only chance of escape lay in her ability to conceal every sign of revulsion or impatience. At the least hint of these he would multiply his demands, keeping her in his presence till she was on the point of madness.

He talked continually of Michel, watching her the while with alert, malicious eyes that peered, like those of an unkempt poodle, from behind a tangle of locks, yellow and matted as dirty straw, which he would not suffer to be washed or combed. White and rigid, the girl locked her fingers together as she listened, and forced her heart to become stone, that the knives of the old man's malice might not pierce it, but rather blunt themselves on its hardness. Sometimes he sent for her only that he might have an audience for these reminiscences.

"Eh, Michel, Michel!" He ran his tongue over his sunken lips, like a gourmand recalling some favorite dish. "There was a man, my girl! This miserable Paul you have married is nothing to him. He had a gift for motion, Michel. I would rather see him walk than others dance. Tell me — you remember him — did you ever see anyone so splendid as that son of mine?"

"No, Monseigneur. Michel was indeed beautiful. You are right. There was no one like him."

"True, true." The old man nodded. His eyes filled, and tears ran down the furrows of his shriveled cheeks. "And now Michel is dead. I cannot believe that Michel is dead, and that I shall never see him walk, or ride, or swim, or play tennis again. On the tennis courts he was a bird. The heart rejoiced to watch him. You loved him, did you not, my girl? And that is the reason I love you. There is that between us, you understand: no one loved Michel as you and I. If he had not died, you would have married him, is it not so?"

"But yes, Monseigneur. That also is true. I would have married Michel."

He persisted in the delusion that Michel had died, whether because his reason was unsettled to that extent, or from deliberate self-deception, Louise did not know. He himself, however, showed no sign of doing likewise. Indeed, he gave every indication of living as he now was, Louise thought bitterly, forever.

"A hundred years from now," she told herself, "he may be alive, but I at least shall be dead. I will therefore set my mind a century ahead, for otherwise I shall not be able to endure this present. Oh, God in heaven! Why may I not die, since he will not?"

In this unending purgatory her life was now become, she had no consolations, except perhaps one, and this was not so much a consolation as the absence of an additional trial she had fully expected to be called on to endure. Time went by: month after month, a year, two, three. Fulfilling the obligations she had freely incurred when she married, she nevertheless remained childless.

At length she began to hope that this situation would not be changed; it seemed to her now that she could not endure to bear a child to Paul. It might yet be required of her, and then she would endure it indeed, as she had endured the loss of Michel, as she endured marriage with Paul, and the daily torment of caring for his father. The protest of the heart against the limits of suffering, on the plea that it "cannot endure" them, is, Louise now realized, without foundation; the heart can and does endure each new limit as it is reached, though protesting always its inability to endure those that lie beyond. While the heart lives, it can endure anything; when it reaches that limit of endurance, it dies.

But if there were such a limit, Louise thought, it would be reached for her in the discovery that she would become the mother of a child of Paul's. The indifference she felt for him at marriage, the mere absence of love, had hardened now into dislike and aversion that extended to all that had to do with him. Had she conceived soon after marriage, the necessity of occupying herself with the child would perhaps have quickened in her some positive emotion: love for the child at least, and possibly a semblance of warmth toward Paul. It would also have made impossible the old man's terrible and prolonged demands upon her. But in him she now saw Paul as he would one day be; and that she should cooperate in continuing this strain was a hideous impossibility. She could not have believed that Michel was the son of this repulsive old man, that he and Paul were brothers, except that Michel was all his mother's, as Paul was his father's likeness.

One consideration was still capable of stirring a dead sweetness in her heart, of filling her with indescribable yearning and sadness, and this was the thought of what happiness it would have been to bear a child to Michel. Any pain she would have endured — no, *welcomed* — for this joy, which, with all joy, was now barred from her life. To carry within her body such sweet burden: a child of Michel's! This would not be a trial, but a prolonged delight. She would watch the days go by with eagerness, but also with regret. The very discomfort would be happiness, considering its cause; and when her time came, with what contempt she would regard the suffering, how eagerly indeed would she welcome it, as part and proof of her love! But to bear a child from duty, to a man she did not love — from this she did indeed shrink, as from that limit of suffering which could not be endured. It had not yet been asked of her; she waited, daring finally to hope, and almost to believe, that she would be spared it entirely.

The feeble thread of the old man's life endured so long because the spool on which it was wound turned so slowly. But it must come to an end sometime, Louise reminded herself; sooner or later an instant must occur, after which he would no longer torture her with his demands and his talk of Michel.

It did so suddenly, without warning, one night when she was alone with him. There was no sign that anything was more than ordinarily amiss. She was smoothing his bed in preparation for the night when he asked, "You are my daughter? You are Louise?"

"Yes. I am Louise."

"You are the wife of Paul?"

She bowed her head, assenting.

"Why are you not the wife of Michel?"

"But Michel —" she gasped — "Michel is gone."

"Gone?" He plucked at the sheets, moving his head from side to side. His breath came whistling between his words: "Gone? Where is he gone? Why — Ah. I remember. I know. I sent him away: I. If I had not sent him away, you would be the wife of Michel. You would have children. I want grandsons. You have given me none. It is because you are the wife of Paul. With Michel — there would be children. I did not want you to have children by that — that cripple. That is why I sent him away. I wish now that I had not — I wish — I — ah."

He drifted into an incoherent mumble, plucking furiously at the bed clothing, gasping for breath. Louise had listened, stunned into silence. Now she bent over him and grasped him by the shoulder, shaking it.

"What are you saying?" she cried. "You *sent* Michel away? You sent him away — he did not go of his own will? Answer me! Oh, God in heaven! Answer me!"

She shook him furiously, but he was beyond speech. He jerked the covers up under his chin with a convulsive movement of his arms, and uttered a queer choking gasp, accompanying it with a motion of the head which might have been intended for an affirmative, and so Louise interpreted it.

"Oh, you are horrible," she cried. "Horrible! I hate you! I did not know anyone could be so wicked as you! You have ruined my life, and Michel's, and I shall never forgive you, never!"

She fled from the room.

She summoned no assistance, although she knew that he was dying. She ran into her own chamber and locked the door. She stood against it, her face in her hands, trembling. Understanding broke over her in violent waves; she stiffened against the shock of them.

Michel had not left of his own will. He had not gone because he wished to become a monk, or because he had ceased to love her. He had been sent away by that hideous old man who now lay dying unshriven, and would so die for any move she would make to prevent it. What was it he had called Michel? A cripple? She did not know what he meant, and he was beyond telling her, but it did not matter. Whatever had happened, Michel loved her. He would always love her, as she would love him. She had been deceived, lied to; she had married Paul on the strength of that lie. Her marriage was a farce; she belonged to Michel, as she had always done, now, and forever.

Standing rigid, her fists clenched, she made a vow: from this day forward she would not rest until she found Michel. Wherever he was, she would find him. She would move heaven and earth, but she would find him. When she found him, she would belong to him, and neither her marriage, nor any other obstacle whatever, should prevent.

She locked this resolution deep in the stone fortress of her heart. Then she went in search of her husband, and informed him that his father was dying.

"No," said Paul. "He is dead."

"You have seen him?"

"How would I know, otherwise?"

"He did not receive the last rites."

"The last rites!" Paul gave a little laugh. "My dear Louise, at the confession of my father, the devil would have returned to hell for very shame, thus putting an end to the evil in the world. That would be too easy a victory for the other side. No; my father will roam the world with his boon companion for some years yet, and when they retire to hell for good, they will go together. Priestly interference might have disturbed the fine balance of that friendship — though, to tell you the truth, I doubt it — and that would have been a thousand pities."

"It is evident," remarked Louise, "that you entertain for your lamented father a deep affection and respect."

"For one so evil I could hardly do otherwise. But had he been the best of men, a pillar of all the virtues like our equally lamented Michel, I still would not have summoned the priest. For I no longer believe in that office."

"Ah?" Louise raised her brows. "Now that you speak of it, I have observed that your religious practice wants something in regularity and fervor."

"And so, my dear — if I may say as much — does yours."

"You may. It is quite true. I no longer practice my religion. But that is not because I do not believe in the priesthood. I would do so except for one thing."

"And that is?"

She answered in a clear, tight voice: "I no longer believe in God."

iii

Ever since Paul's accusation that she was prejudiced in Michel's favor, Fortune had been engaged in freeing herself of the charge: and with notable success. Following the accident that coincided so disturbingly with Paul's unspoken wish, the cards had been stacked in his favor, the dice loaded to his advantage. The tide which had swept every good thing to Michel's feet was now set against the older brother and in favor of the younger. Michel was left derelict; the receding waters carried all his former goods beyond his reach and into the waiting grasp of Paul. His love and his inheritance; his father's preference and the superior physical endowments on which that preference depended: all these had been Michel's and were now Paul's. Fortune spared no pains to show that when she changed her favorites, she did so thoroughly.

But there were certain things she could not give, and of the want of these Paul became increasingly sensible as time passed. Possessions and honor she could, and did, with a turn of the wheel, transfer from Michel to him; but with them she could not give a settled mind. This lack Paul ascribed to a natural intro-spectiveness, a tendency almost to morbidity, conspicuous in his father's family and due no doubt to ill-health, which led him to exaggerate and dwell on events long past and much better forgotten.

The episode of the boar hunt rankled and festered in his mind; he could not be rid of it. Memory accused him not of what he had done, but of what he had failed to do; like a stone in his shoe, however he turned and twisted, the knowledge of that omission was always there. Because of it, all that he possessed was his dishonestly.

The cry of warning that he almost uttered, but did not, would have saved Michel. He had been impelled to utter that cry; why had he not done so? This question pursued him with a relentless-ness which gave him no course but to answer it: he kept silence because he wanted Michel out of the way. He would have pre-ferred, however, that this elimination take place through some agency other than his own. He had no desire to stand accused before the world or his own conscience of his brother's murder. There was no danger that he would have to face such a charge, since Michel had not died; and, had he died, Paul would still have had to answer no accuser but his conscience, as only him-self could have known the part he played in the event. He could not, however, escape the knowledge that he had wished Michel's death, and that, had it occurred, whether anyone knew it or not, the fault would have been his.

True, Michel had not died; but he had lost everything except his life, and Paul was now in possession of all that he had lost. This abundance, this felicity of honor and wealth, was deflected to Paul in that second when his brother's life was in danger, and he knew it and could have warned him, and failed to do so. Of what precisely was he guilty in that failure? Of the will to murder, if not the act? How far did this guilt extend? Even to the theft of his brother's wife and goods? Certainly he had coveted these things; it was that covetousness which had choked and silenced his shout of warning. This knowledge lay a grievous burden on his conscience. He tried every sort of sophistry and argument to be rid of it, but without success.

He would so far succeed as to forget it for a while, absorbed in other pursuits. He would flatter himself that he had settled the problem with some argument which minimized his guilt if it did not remove it altogether; but ultimately all his efforts were useless. He could not shake the matter from his mind. It returned again and again to torture him.

The difficulty was that in this affair he could not be his own judge. As long as he essayed to clear himself, so long must he accuse himself. He had not the power to decide the measure of his guilt, nor authority to pardon it. Only by submitting his tormenting secret to the judgment and decision of such an authority could he ever be rid of it; and this he could not bring himself to do.

Had Michel been spared the mutilation which was the cause of his dismissal, Paul would have had no difficulty in confessing his part in the accident, for in that event he would have derived no benefit from it, and judgment following his confession would have involved him in no loss. But he knew now what the sentence would be: "Find your brother and restore to him all that is his. Without restitution there can be no forgiveness."

And to do this — to admit his guilt when such admission meant the surrender of the fruits of that guilt — this was out of the question.

He had stolen from Michel once, when they were boys. A hard word, *stolen:* but in this previous case, certainly the truth. He had taken a ring their mother had given Michel on his birthday; Michel, believing it lost, was inconsolable. Paul hid it among his things; his pride got the better of his conscience, and he pretended to himself that he had "found" it, until his mother discovered it, and drew the truth from him: a type of surgery for which she had a painful aptitude. She would have attained, he often thought, just renown as a confessor. Since she could not fill that role herself, she packed him off to the Abbé Courtot, from whom he received exceedingly short shrift.

"You are to restore the ring to your brother. Do not merely put it back where you found it, but give it to Michel himself. Tell him that you took it and are sorry. When you have done this, return to me, and I will give you absolution: not before."

Would he receive other treatment in the present case, from the Abbé Courtot, or any priest to whom he made known the facts? And except he made known the facts, would he have peace of mind while he lived?

Clearly, he must either confess his sin, or forget it. The one he would not do, the other he could not. He was provoked with himself for this squeamishness: why could he not dismiss the whole affair as of no importance, accounting it among those lesser sins which there was no need to mention one by one, for no confession would ever come to an end if that were essential? He had not deliberately planned to murder Michel, to injure him, or to steal his goods; he had not even sent him away; that was his father's doing; why then would his conscience give him no rest?

He was, he told himself, unduly morbid; this was a trait inherent in the family constitution; healthier stock would have forgotten the miserable business long since. Could he have persuaded himself that a priest, too, would have explained his troubled conscience as the fruit of an inherited tendency to asthma, he might have found peace outside the confessional; but no priest living would have credited such an argument, and neither could he.

Plainly, there was no escape from this dilemma except to cease the practice of religion, and this he did. He no longer frequented the sacraments, and his attendance at Mass, which formerly had the regularity of habit, if not the fervor of devotion, was now conspicuous for its infrequency. This solution, however, did not satisfy him at all. It helped him merely to ignore his conscience; it did not lessen or remove his guilt.

In one other matter Fortune failed him: his marriage produced no children. This was a disappointment as grievous as it was unforeseen; the idea occurred to him, and persisted, that it was a judgment on him for his conduct in the affair of Michel. With all his strength he resisted this suggestion as folly and superstition, but he could not prevent its recurrence.

But in both these matters Fortune merely delayed, she did not withhold, her favor. It seemed as if she had permitted these obstacles to arise only that she might show her ingenuity in overcoming them. She offered Paul a solution of his difficulty regarding Michel in the form of a compromise to which many have had recourse in a like predicament. It enabled him to silence his conscience without confessing his guilt, or making restitution to his brother, or abandoning the practice of religion. The solution of this problem included within it the solution of the other.

Paul had now a horror of his home. For many months the Château had been filled with gloom as with a fog. Someone was always ill or dying there: first the Countess, then Michel, and now the Count, who had been in no hurry to terminate either his offensive illness or his abominable life. The pall of his presence lay on the place like a curse; he dominated it as thoroughly sick as well, and far more disagreeably. It was unfortunate that Louise should be compelled to suffer his tyranny, but that was no reason why Paul should submit himself to a like punishment, while there remained a means of escape.

Accordingly, he avoided Guillemont as much as possible. He sought and found refuge at Brissac, a village about ten miles to the northwest of Guillemont, which straggled untidily over a hill and halfway down its slopes came to an uncertain end. At the top of the hill was a draughty, dilapidated Château where the Sieur de Brissac and his family were coming to an equally uncertain end. An unsavory odor had always clung to them in the minds of the neighboring gentry. The reason for this Paul did not know, but as a result of it the de Brissac were not welcomed at Guillemont. Between the families hospitality was neither given nor received. Moved now by a sudden curiosity concerning these questionable neighbors, Paul stopped there to call one day, for no better reason than that he did not wish to return to Guillemont and did not know where else to go.

The present incumbents of Brissac were of the tail end of the nobility; just what title they claimed, Paul was not sure, and neither, he believed, were they. They had inherited their decaying manor by devious ways. It was moldy, damp, and in sad need of repair, but they accepted its shortcomings as cheerfully as they accepted their own; indeed, they seemed not to be aware that anything was lacking, in their property or in themselves. Paul found them good natured and dull; he liked them immensely. Thereafter he returned frequently to Brissac, where he soon became a constant and welcome guest.

Besides Monsieur and Madame, there was a son, Pierre, and a daughter, Anne. Pierre de Brissac was a young man in all respects Paul's inferior: short, plump, good natured, dull, he had the added advantage of playing an execrable game of tennis. On the tennis court Paul had never been able to compete with Michel, who had such long legs; but he won easily from Pierre, and for that reason he conceived for the young man a deep affection.

This affection extended to the other members of the family, and for the same reason. At Brissac no effort was required of him; there was nothing to live up to; he was conscious of no strain, but only of relaxation and comfort. At Guillemont the punctilio demanded of one was almost insufferable. However far his father may have deviated from the lofty moral ideal which was his mother's rigid code, his manners were nevertheless (until this illness) beyond reproach. Conformity to a similar etiquette was expected of everyone. Michel appeared to wear this conformity as easily as he wore his skin, but Paul chafed beneath it, as beneath a hair shirt. His least deviation brought down upon his head rebuke and censure, whereas everything Michel did was perfect. And even now there was no pleasing his father, no thawing Louise. At Brissac, on the other hand, he was made to feel a very Apollo, a criterion of excellence, the embodiment of wisdom, in all ways perfect. He knew that the de Brissac were without discrimination, and that it was no proof of excellence to be judged excellent by them; but his pride was in sore need of encouragement, and he took it where he could find it, and was grateful for it.

Anne, the sister of Pierre, was precisely the opposite of Louise, being plump, and round, and smooth, and without wit. She had black hair and wide brown eyes as lifeless as those of a doll, a short nose above a baby's mouth and chin. She resembled, indeed, a little girl or a doll, but Paul at once discovered that this resemblance went no further than appearance. Her readiness to yield to his advances proclaimed itself so obviously as to anticipate those advances, and, in fact, to demand them.

He was somewhat disconcerted by this. He preferred a skirmish at least before victory, as giving him an opportunity to display his prowess, but here there was no question of a skirmish. The keys of the city were handed him before he so much as thought of storming it. She walked demurely into the room where he was waiting for Pierre; she sat down, folded her hands, looked at him; that was all, but it was enough. He had crossed the room in a stride and she was in his arms, all soft and pliant and yielding; she resisted him no more than food resists being eaten or wine drunk. She soothed and eased him, as did everyone at Brissac; and there was no hint of accusation or blame for him, no shame or remorse for herself, when she told him not long afterward that she was to have a child.

He was amazed at the complacence with which she accepted this fact, and still more astonished that this complacence was shared by her family. They regarded him and each other with sly glances of self-congratulation; Pierre wrung his hand, clapped him on the back, called him *"Mon vieux!"* with tears in his eyes. This was all most extraordinary. Differing radically from the code by which he had been brought up, it nevertheless consoled him exceedingly.

As he grew to know them better, Paul was not surprised that the father of Anne failed to denounce him for sullying his daughter's honor. Monsieur de Brissac loved his wine and his meat and his comfort. He was burdened with fat which went all to chins and paunch. He wore an untidy gray beard and his cheeks above it were threaded with fine purple veins. He suffered acutely from gout; when in the throes of this affliction, he made no more effort to restrain his outcries than he customarily did his belchings at table. He was of a genial and easy temper and no one had anything to fear from him. Clearly one of his disposition would regard the mishap of his daughter, at worst as a matter of jest, at best as a source of revenue to the family, which sadly needed such support.

"Ah, Paul, *mon vieux!*" He rubbed his hands together, his eyes twinkling with glee. "To think my Annette should be about to give you a fat son, which that beautiful wife of yours has refused to do! *Le petit comte* should be worth something to you, both now and in the future, is it not so?" He prodded Paul in the ribs, winking. "And my Annette, you see how she is made. There should be many, very many, from so fine a heifer. You need never fear for your succession now, *mon vieux!*"

No; it was not surprising that Monsieur de Brissac should regard the matter in this light, but that Madame should agree with him was truly astonishing. For Madame was as unlike Monsieur as a razor is unlike a ball of dough. She was tall and thin, with light faded hair, and pale faded eyes. She was lost in a mist of veils and scarves, and wore such a burden of jewelry that she clanked when she moved like a gaoler with his keys. Paul at first stood in awe of her. Her thin pale presence behind its barricade of veils and chains had something austere and remote about it; it was only when she took him by both hands, and made him sit beside her in the *petit salon,* and unburdened to him her mind in the matter, that he began to comprehend why she condoned, or rather approved, his illegitimate paternity of Anne's child.

He was, indeed, enlightened concerning many things he had previously failed to comprehend. He understood now the reason for his mother's hostility toward the de Brissac. Undoubtedly some hint must have reached her of the views which Madame now made known to Paul; and the orthodoxy of his mother being beyond question, these views could only have inspired in her a horror worse than any plague.

For Madame belonged to a cult which had abandoned formal religion for the worship of God in nature. She explained this to Paul, her eyes half closed, one thin hand, covered with prominent blue veins and rings, fluttering at her throat. Only those were truly religious, she informed him, who were truly natural. The marriage convention did not bind those free souls who were joined into a mystical fellowship by the worship of God in Nature.

"But, Madame," protested the dumfounded Paul. "I do not understand. I thought — I feared —"

"That I would blame you? Ah, no, no!" She shook her head and her finger at him archly. "I see you are of those who believe in the conscience. We must emancipate you from these so archaic notions, my Paul. Put yourself in my hands, and you will know what joy it is to be gay and free as the birds and animals. Are they tortured by the conscience, *mon ami?* But no! To find our happiness, we must be as they."

Paul now discovered that the Château de Brissac was a rendezvous for those who shared the beliefs of Madame, as well as for those who, while differing from her in details, nevertheless agreed in rejecting that faith in which Paul had been brought up. Their ideas were a subject for discussion at nightly gatherings at Brissac. To their number, at the insistent invitation of Madame, Paul now added himself.

At first he felt ill at ease at these meetings, as one who, clearly, did not belong. He was conscious, too, of a strange embarrassment, almost a shame, for these people who could so freely question matters concerning which he had always held there could be no possibility of doubt. It was as if children should meet to discuss the multiplication table, and passing judgment on it as only partially correct, should solemnly decide to rewrite it, each according to his own liking, and without any sense of the absurdity of such an undertaking. But to refuse to come would be seriously to offend Madame. He was, moreover, curious in spite of his uneasiness, and he desired nothing in life so much as to be emancipated from the conscience; and here was an added excuse for absenting himself from Guillemont. He soon became a regular member of the coterie. He questioned and considered, if he did not yet believe.

These people, though agreed in certain matters, yet differed from each other radically in others. The chief subject of dispute was the Holy Eucharist. The majority held that the Eucharistic species were merely symbols of the Sacred Body and Blood, since no change took place at the Consecration; while others claimed that a change occurred, but it was only partial: Our Lord was actually present in the consecrated Species, but these remained also bread and wine.

The champion of the former and more popular opinion was a slim young man with a sparse reddish beard and equally sparse hair of the same color. Paul soon discovered that he was not prematurely bald, as at first appeared; he had until recently been a priest, a state of which this scantiness of hair, the remains of his tonsure, gave now the only hint. He had restless dark eyes and well-shaped, slender hands which reminded Paul, disconcertingly, of Michel's. He was an impassioned and eloquent speaker and won converts easily to his views.

"You do not then," asked Paul, "believe in confession?"

"Confession!" the young man echoed. "I shudder" — he did so, visibly — "to think of the souls still in bondage to that superstition, I tremble to recall that I myself was once sworn to perpetuate that deceit. Now I labor only to free those who are in the bonds of Satan, to break this strongest of all the chains which the devil has forged to drag souls after him to hell."

"But how are sins forgiven, if not by confession and absolution?"

"Is not God all about us? May we not go direct to Him? When did God say — before Satan's ministers invented this lie for their own power and put it in God's mouth — that a mere man should judge another man's guilt, or stand between anyone's conscience and Himself? Did He not say, rather, *Judge not, that ye be not judged?* Are not the merits of Christ all-sufficient to obtain mercy and pardon for the darkest sins? Shall we, who are but vile worms in the sight of God, presume to think that we can add to those merits, that we can do anything to please God that His Son has not already done? Oh, vain delusion, that has darkened the minds of men for centuries and thrust their souls into the very depths of hell! But thank God, who in His mercy has decreed that after this darkness light shall come, and show the true way to heaven to all who believe."

"And that way is — ?"

"Faith," the young man answered. "Faith in the merits of Christ as sufficient to save us all. Faith always. Faith only."

Paul listened; he pondered; the new teachings began to lose their strangeness, and he assimilated them without difficulty. Even the phraseology soon came easily to his tongue; he had no difficulty now in talking this language, at first so unfamiliar. He discovered also that these teachings were fashionable, to an extent he had not suspected; and the number of their adherents was steadily increasing, especially among the nobility. However they differed in details, the bond which united them all was rejection of the Church and her ministers; for the authority of the Church, they substituted Scripture, which each could interpret as he chose; in the place of meritorious acts, they relied on faith alone; to be saved, it was necessary only to believe.

It is obvious that in these teachings Paul found a haven into which he steered his storm-tossed conscience, and there abandoned it, with immense relief. Thus he was freed from the painful necessity of acknowledging and repairing the wrong done Michel, and of torturing himself any longer with scruples on that score. In fact, it seemed that he had done Michel no wrong; he dismissed the whole affair as a matter of no importance.

The difficulty of his conscience being thus happily resolved, his good fortune was in all ways complete. Louise continued to give him no children, but he was not on that account childless. In due course Anne presented him with the fat son her father had predicted, and he determined to adopt this child and make him legally his heir; very soon, there was promise of another. Uncertain whether the failure of his marriage to produce offspring was the fault of Louise or himself, he had feared the latter. With the happy resolution of this doubt, his self-respect was fully restored. This was followed by a marked improvement in health. He lost much of his petulance and irritability; he began, even, to put on weight.

As for Michel, Paul thought of him but seldom, and without any taint of self-reproach. His injured brother receded into the background with the three who had died in childhood and whom Paul could but dimly remember. Paul now considered himself as little to blame for Michel's fate as for theirs. What had befallen him since his departure from Guillemont, whether indeed he was still alive, Paul did not know, and had ceased to care.

Veni, Sanctificator, omnipotens, aeterne Deus,
et benedic hoc sacrificium,
Tuo sancto nomini praeparatum

6. And Bless This Sacrifice ...

i

Of all those at Notre Dame des Prés, monks and lay brothers alike, none gave evidence of such serenity, such deep interior peace, as the crippled Brother who had just taken his vows. This peace was in him no mere absence of strife; it was, rather, a presence; a possession; a radiance, passing outward from a center deep within him, and, like mirth or light, communicating itself to others also. He was a brightness and transparency, glass shining but invisible, through which streamed a light not his own. Even his slow and awkward gait did not diminish, but rather enhanced, this impression.

He himself did not suspect that he gave any such impression to anyone. Had he been told so, which he was not, he would have denied it, not from modesty but because he did not believe it. He regarded himself as a bundle of harassments and defects: full of faults, and by reason of his mutilations, of little or no use. They suffered him in the Order, he supposed, out of charity, or perhaps because it was a salutary mortification to the others, and therefore a source of merit to them, to put up with his inabilities and shortcomings.

These were a constant occasion of annoyance and embarrassment to him, and sometimes even of grief. Formerly he had moved without thinking of it; to will a thing was to do it; it was never necessary to consider what motions were involved in the act, and whether these were possible for him. Now he must pause for reflection, before he so much as crossed the room. He could do nothing spontaneously; his every act was limited and curtailed; he was like a man bound with ropes. During his long convalescence this had not troubled him as it did now. Then he had lacked the strength to act, and with it the desire; to move was pain, and he had moved as little as possible. But now his strength was returned, and although he was not wholly free from pain, the attacks were less frequent and diminished in severity. What troubled him now was his helplessness, his inadequacy to perform the simplest tasks, the fact that he could do so little, and that little so badly.

His habit disguised his defects, though it could not altogether hide them. His limp, softened by the long skirts, appeared less grotesque; and so effectively did the full sleeves conceal the loss of one hand and the mutilation of the other, that those newly arrived at the monastery often failed to observe these defects altogether, unless told of them.

Among these was Brother Etienne from Normandy, who had grown gray in the Order, and now, threatened with a consumption, was sent south to Our Lady of the Meadows in the hope of averting this disaster. But this measure, thought Brother Michel, was more like to invite than avert the catastrophe, for Brother Etienne arrived at the beginning of Lent, when the weather was at its dampest and most hostile, and half the Community sick with coughs and kindred ills. Among the indisposed was Brother Joseph; Brother Etienne was sent to replace him in the kitchen.

Here Brother Michel customarily assisted Brother Joseph, his especial duty being to chop cabbages and other vegetables for soup. In this task he had developed great facility, holding the bowl tight against his ribs with the crook of his left arm. Brother Etienne had not been informed of the handicap which made this necessary, and he failed to observe it for himself.

He had not, in fact, observed his assistant at all, until he entered the kitchen to find a young Brother, tall and very slim, standing by the table chopping cabbages in a wooden bowl and accompanying his labors with a song. It struck Brother Etienne

that there was something odd about his manner of holding the
bowl, but he did not stop to inquire into the cause of this
idiosyncrasy, being impressed by a much greater one, which he
observed at once, and with profound disapproval.

The song of the Brother who chopped cabbages was frivolous
in the extreme:

> *Savez-vous couper les choux,*
> *A la mode, à la mode,*
> *Savez-vous couper les choux,*
> *A la mode de Michel?*

The singer was fully aware of the unliturgical character of his
song, but he knew of nothing in the Rule of the Order which
would prohibit his singing it, provided only he did not do so
during the hours of silence, or in chapel. And one could not very
well be surrounded with such an infinitude of cabbage without
being reminded of these verses, which have been sung ever since
there have been cabbages to plant and children to sing. Its apt-
ness to his present occupation could hardly fail to impress him;
with but slight alteration, the verses applied perfectly. He was
smiling to himself at the folly and fitness of his version of this
classic of French childhood, when the spirit of discipline
descended on him in the person of the Brother from Normandy,
effectively quenching his unmonastic levity.

Brother Etienne had, indeed, a genius for discipline. He was
horrified at the frivolity of the song, and he determined at once
to put a stop to such goings on. If this was typical of the laxness
which prevailed in religious communities throughout the easy-
going South, small wonder holy Mother Church was in need of
reform. He crossed the kitchen with his swift, sure tread and
addressed the offending Brother in a voice frigid with disapproval:

"What nonsense is that you sing, Brother?"

The Brother at the table looked up. Brother Etienne, loaded
with rebuke like a cannon charged with shot, stopped short of
discharging his intended volley. He had not expected to be confronted with such a face as the singer now turned toward him.
Those features might have been graven on the tomb of some
young Bayard, except that they were not stone, but living flesh;

and they coincided ill, in Brother Etienne's mind, with that ridiculous childish ditty about cabbages. He could not altogether repress a sudden stirring of emotion, that prompted him to soften or omit his reprimand; but he stifled it as illogical and womanish, and armed himself against such unaccustomed and insidious weakness. Appearances are of all things the most deceitful. Discipline must not be set aside for a young Brother, of however winning a countenance, who nevertheless sang at his work flippant songs, fit only for children at play.

The young Brother lowered his eyes in confusion, the color rising in his cheeks.

"But — you observe — is it not true? I do indeed cut cabbages, after my own strange fashion."

Brother Etienne did not stop to inquire what he meant. He found it easier to administer his reprimand when the eyes of the young Brother were not fixed on his.

"For the present I will overlook the fault, but in the future you will remember that this is a religious community, not a nursery."

The young Brother, his head bowed, murmured his assent. Over the fire a kettle of soup bubbled, into the making of which had gone a legion of cabbages chopped the day previously by him. Brother Etienne indicated it now.

"When the bell rings, you will fetch the soup into the refectory for dinner."

"But, *mon frère* —"

"You will do as you are told, without question."

He departed. Everything about him bespoke relentless discipline: his rigid back, his assured tread, his square, stern shoulders; even the skirts of his habit gave forth an uncompromising, disciplined swish. Michel put down his bowl and chopped and stared after his retreating figure, full of years and dignity, in dismay. Here was a situation with which nothing had prepared him to deal. To lift the soup kettle required a firm grip; for him to attempt it was to court disaster. But he had been commanded to do so; his attempt at explanation had been cut short; there was no one at hand from whom he might ask help; he had no course but to obey.

He did not wait for the bell, but set about the business at once, as he would require more time than another. He accomplished without mishap the colossal task of getting the kettle off the crane, though he all but set his skirts on fire in the act. Then he started the precarious journey across the kitchen to the refectory, staggering under the load of the kettle. Halfway there the Nemesis he had feared overtook him: the kettle slipped from his uncertain grasp just as the door opened, and precipitated its contents in a boiling steam to the feet of Brother Etienne, who jumped aside, at some cost to his dignity, to avoid a scalding.

"In the name of heaven," cried Brother Etienne, "what do you now? Why must you be so clumsy and so careless? Do you not know that it is Lent, and there on the floor lies our only meal for today?"

If Brother Michel had colored at the first reprimand of Brother Etienne, he went white at this one. He bit his lips, determined to accept this censure without contradiction or protest, as no more than his due. There was, however, no need to remind him that this was the season of fast. Had he overlooked the fact, which he was in no danger of doing, his stomach would have corrected the oversight with its all too imperious demands. Before him now, steaming on the floor, filling the kitchen with its savory aroma, lay the single meal of the Community. For this disaster the blame was his. He should not have attempted the impossible. He should have made known to Brother Etienne his defects.

Brother Etienne continued his scolding: "Another time perhaps you will pay attention to what you are doing. How could you be so careless? What were you thinking of? How did you manage to let fall the kettle? *Dites-moi donc!*"

Commanded to answer, Brother Michel did so.

"It was the weight, *mon frère*. I could not support it in my hand."

"Your hand!" echoed Brother Etienne, "Are you then such a dunderhead? Must you be reminded to use both hands, like a child?"

The scolding of Brother Etienne came to an abrupt end as

the young Brother raised his eyes and regarded his senior directly.

"It is indeed my fault. I neglected to inform you of my infirmity. I have but one hand, *mon frère.*"

Brother Michel was never again asked to carry soup. This service took its place, along with celebrating Mass, among the things he could not hope to do.

ii

No; Brother Michel could not carry soup; he could not celebrate Mass; in his attempts to be of use he was only in the way, nor was he any too quick in getting out of it; he could engage in none of the tasks of the Community which required an able body and a full assortment of limbs and digits, and there were few tasks, he found, for which these were not essential.

There remained, however, one thing he could do, and this he could still have done, had he been deprived of sight and hearing and speech, of hands and feet, of every faculty and sense save reason: he could pray.

Here, after Mass, was now his chief joy. His time, not required elsewhere, he spent in the chapel, reluctant to leave, impatient to return. Here Love spoke to him, poured Its riches upon him, demanded his love, and received it in return. In this interchange the need for words had long since passed; his soul plunged into silence, as a diver into a deep sea, rising to the surface slowly, after a prolonged submersion so profound that all activity was stilled and even breath ceased.

The heart of this silence was a burning radiance, and the light of it went with him through the day.

"Oh, *mon père,*" he cried to Father André, "I did not know that prayer could be such joy, I did not think that one could find such happiness on earth! Why do not more know of it? Why do so few pray?"

Father André smiled at the eagerness of Brother Michel, who would introduce the whole world to the beauty he had found in prayer.

"The prayer you have described, my son, is a very great grace. God gives it to whom He wills, but only to those who are prepared for it. It does not surprise me that you have received it, but how many, think you, would walk the way you have come to find it?"

"Many," replied Michel resolutely, "could they know, or even suspect, what this joy is."

Father André shook his head.

"I think you are mistaken, Michel. I believe very few would follow you, even could you persuade them of the truth of this happiness. The greater number would not listen. They would say, simply, that you were deluded."

"But is it not, Father, as I have said?"

"Indeed, yes, Michel. You are right in comparing this prayer to a deep submersion, a dive from a great height. But there is a difference. He who has learned to live may do so at his will, but the soul may not plunge into these depths of prayer, except as God wills. Therefore, if a time comes when you can no longer dive, do not grieve, or think on that account you have ceased to pray. For God so tries us, Brother. To find yourself floundering like a beginner in shallow waters, unable to swim, and much less dive — this is a real suffering, and a test of love. When that happens, you will be tempted to fear that God has withdrawn His grace from you altogether. But it is not so. At such times love alone is sufficient, and suffering itself is prayer."

"And apart from this prayer, Father, I know of only one thing —" Michel hesitated.

"Yes, Michel?"

"— only one thing that — how shall I say it? — seizes and holds the attention to the exclusion of all else, so that no shred of it remains for any other matter."

"And what is that, my son?"

"Pain, Father," said Michel. "And may not this be," he added, "the secret of the fortitude of the martyrs, that of the two, the greater intensity is prayer?"

At length an occupation was found for him, suited to his limited capacities. He was sent to assist Father Simon, artist and scribe, who was sorely overworked, and in need of someone to help grind his colors, clean his brushes, and perform other trifling tasks which consumed too much of his time, and which would perhaps be not beyond the powers of a lay brother who could neither carry soup nor celebrate Holy Mass.

Brother Michel was delighted at this promotion, for so he regarded it. The illuminated manuscripts in his father's collections had always held a deep fascination for him, and he gazed spellbound at Father Simon's work now, with the eye of one who can tell Beauty from her counterfeit.

"This is indeed exquisite, *mon père*," he said, inspecting the page on Father Simon's writing desk. "How much I should like to write as you do. Perhaps," he added hesitantly, "it is still not too late. I believe, with practice, I could."

"*You?*" asked Father Simon, then checked himself quickly. But Brother Michel was not hurt.

"I always wrote a neat hand. I can still hold a quill, thus." He picked one up, illustrating. "It should be no more difficult for me to learn this way than any other. Suppose we had all been born with only three fingers? We should never know the loss of the other two. And to write, I need only one hand. I can manage to hold and shift the parchment somehow. Nor will my limp hinder, much."

"You are right there," agreed Father Simon gravely. "We will see what can be done to make a calligrapher of you. It will be an undertaking full of interest. And God knows there is need of good calligraphers. This devil's work of printing is ruining the art, besides filling people's heads with lies: doing with the twist of a screw the work God intended a man should do with his two hands."

"Or with one," said Brother Michel. "I hereby undertake to stop him, singlehanded. But what do you mean, filling people's heads with lies?"

"That heretical monk in Germany," replied Father Simon heatedly, "is now sending his pestiferous documents abroad by means of these same presses. But I doubt if it comes to much: there is always some crackpot leading people astray in Germany." He shrugged: "I shall not worry about holy Church until Frenchmen so far forget their logic as to give corrupt doctrine a hearing. Then truly I shall fear for the Bark of Peter, and be tempted to believe that the printing presses of the devil may in the end prevail against her. May that day never come! Grip your quill firmly, Brother, and between us we will postpone it indefinitely."

But Michel was regarding Father Simon with troubled eyes. "Heretical monk? Crackpot? Germany? What are you talking about, *mon père?*"

Father Simon was a little excitable monk with bright red hair and restless gray eyes and quick darting motions which he struggled in vain to invest with a proper monastic calm. In this conflict he was somewhat assisted by his habit, which enfolded him like a collapsed tent, and served as a check to the natural impulsiveness of his movements. He was the smallest figure of a man Brother Michel had ever seen; and whereas it was quite conceivable that no habit made would fit him properly, still it passed Brother Michel's comprehension why it had been deemed necessary to select for him a habit of gigantic proportions, fit for a champion of boxers. It was as if, thought Brother Michel, the little ass Marceline should find herself condemned to trot through life clothed in the skin of an elephant.

He sat perched on a stool before his writing desk, like a restless small bird on a stump. His skirts hung below his feet, his sleeves covered his hands; these encumbrances he kept pushing back to his elbows with quick, impatient gestures. His fingers betrayed his craft, being covered with stains, cobalt, ultramarine, vermilion; his face glistened with infinitesimal points of gold, which had become transferred to it in the process of laying and burnishing gold leaf. His writing desk — indeed, his whole cell — was to Michel a fascinating disorder of inks and paints and quills and brushes and rags and parchment and manuscripts, finished and otherwise; portfolios stood against the wall, and books overflowed their shelves and stood in piles on the floor; and this disarray was welded into a coherent whole by a smell of paint and medium, as inseparable from the workshop or cell of an artist and scribe, as the fragrance of incense from a chapel.

He banged on the slope of the writing desk with his fist, the sleeve of his habit flapping like a useless sail.

"Is it possible you have not heard," he cried, "of that mad

monk in Germany named Martin — Martin something — I have forgot — who preaches that all our good works are in vain and that all we have to do to be saved is believe?"

Michel stared. No, he had not heard. How could a monk preach that which was contrary to the faith? Why was he not excommunicated and silenced?

"Of course he is excommunicated, but not thereby silenced, this Martin. That such a pestilential traitor should have such a holy name! And he draws people by the thousands after him: all Germany is in an uproar. Let us pray only that this malignant infection stop there, for if it be not checked, it will be the death of the world. As I say, I believe it will go no further: Frenchmen are not so easily corrupted in matters of reason. But I marvel you have not heard of this before."

"I do not go into the markets like the rest of you," said Michel. "How would I hear, except someone told me, which you do now for the first time? But still I do not understand. You say this Martin leads people away from the faith — from their life, their salvation, their joy? Outside the faith we cannot breathe — we are lost, we die!"

Again Father Simon pounded the writing desk.

"But you are an innocent with your head in the clouds! Have I not told you? He persuaded people that they may do as they please and still be saved, provided only they believe!"

"But that simply is not true," declared Michel.

"Ah, but all men, my dear Michel, have not your gift of discerning truth from falsehood," observed Father Simon dryly. "That lack of discernment is a particular characteristic of the German race, from which we fortunately are exempt, but through no merit of our own, so see that you take no pride in it. See now — what logic is here! This false priest declares that monastic vows do not bind, and has so far given an example of his teaching as to quit his monastery and marry an ex-nun. Others, emancipated from the superstition that a promise is a promise, in religion or out of it, have followed his example. In fact, he dispenses with the priesthood altogether, teaching, on the one hand, that all are priests, and on the other, that the Mass is not a sacrifice and therefore there is no need of priests to offer it.

How he reconciles these two opposites is a mystery too profound for my poor powers of intellect to penetrate, and he has not deigned to explain it to me or to anyone. Indeed, my dear Michel, the mystery of the Most Blessed Trinity is simplicity itself compared with those which this Martin foists upon his followers. He cannot bring himself to deny the presence of Our Blessed Lord in the Holy Eucharist altogether, as some have done — whom, mind you, he calls heretics — but he declares that both Our Lord and bread are present together in the consecrated Host. How this is possible — whether one half the Host is changed into the Body of Christ while the other half remains mere bread, or whether each grain of wheat throughout the Host condescends to surrender half its substance to Our Lord — this difficulty, equally, he does not explain. Further, there are no sacraments save baptism and the Holy Eucharist, though how the latter can exist independently of priests and the Mass is another one of those stupendous mysteries before which my faith staggers, but not his. Authority for these extraordinary doctrines he finds in Scripture, which each may now interpret for himself, thus making Our Lord say, 'This is half My Body and half bread,' or 'This symbolizes My Body but is not really so,' or reading such meaning into His words as one will. And these doctrines, my dear Michel, are the fruit of a journey made by this holy monk to Rome, where he was so scandalized by the immorality he claimed to discover among the clergy that he now undertakes to reform the Church by denying her doctrines and to cure immorality by abolishing morals. And there is the first hint of logic I can discover, for, clearly, one cannot break vows if one does not first make them. Heaven is not to be gained by attending Mass, or confessing our sins, or overcoming our faults, or surrendering our pride and our wills, or disciplining our bodies, or keeping our vows, or by any good works whatever, but only by believing that Our Lord lived and died and that His merits are sufficient to save us all. We are saved, he claims, not by sharing Christ's sacrifice and thus becoming partakers of His merit, but by believing in it only. So you see, my dear Michel, how easy it is. Every man may believe as he pleases and do as he likes, and that is the road to heaven. Why subject ourselves to discipline which is of no avail? Why should we not all follow him?"

If Michel had not interrupted this discourse, it was because he was stricken dumb from astonishment and horror, and wholly unable to speak. In this welter of unreason his mind seized upon one fact which, if he had heard aright, lent to the whole a significance even more deep and terrible than at first appeared. He regarded Father Simon fixedly, his eyes filled with bewilderment and pain:

"And you say," he asked slowly, "that this man — this Martin — is a *priest?*"

"Yes, yes! But now excommunicated for heresy."

"He forfeited his Holy Orders deliberately, of his free will?"

"Yes — of his free will."

"And you say he" — Michel swallowed — "he married?"

"Yes, he married — if one can call it that."

"But I do not understand. He surrendered his *priesthood* simply to preach this nonsense you have described to me?"

"You do not understand!" echoed Father Simon. "Have I then been talking Greek?"

"No, I do not understand," repeated Michel. "If there were a grain of sense in any of it, I might comprehend; but there is none, and I cannot."

Father Simon threw down his quill and with both hands clutched the fringe of red hair encircling his tonsure.

"Did not our first parent, Adam, forfeit Paradise and the friendship of God, deliberately, of his free will? Did he not drag all mankind to ruin after him precisely as this Martin is dragging all Germany after him? Is there not one sin at the root of all sin, and that is pride? Think it over, my dear Brother. You will understand."

Michel thought it over; indeed, he could think of nothing else. And the more he thought, the less, in fact, he understood. It passed his comprehension utterly that a man still possessed of the use of his faculties, who had been ordained to the priesthood, should deliberately surrender, for any reason whatever, the exalted privilege that was his, of celebrating Holy Mass. The mark of the priesthood he could never erase from his soul; but this privilege, this glory that accompanied it, he could indeed forfeit. This joy, for which the heart of Michel hungered continually, was within the reach of all men not prevented by physical defect. That it should be refused by any who might enjoy it was a mystery to be explained (if not understood) by the fact that all were not called to it; that it should be surrendered by one who had been so called, who had heeded and answered the call, and had received upon his soul the eternal sign of a priest of God, was an outrage so hideous that it could not be contemplated without shrinking and sickness, without a shuddering of physical revulsion.

For Michel could no longer be said to possess the love of Mass, but rather the love of Holy Mass possessed him. At first it had risen in his heart like a little stream, clear and singing and beautiful; now it was become a torrent, sweeping him along in full flood. And as love cannot dwell in the heart without seeking to express itself in acts — as one who loves music will not be content to listen, but will learn some instrument that he may play, and thus bring what he loves into being and life — so this love of Michel's was a constant goad, urging him not only to assist at the Holy Sacrifice with his presence, but to perform the sacred Rite in all its majestic detail. He yearned to participate in this beauty to the full, uniting outward action to interior love and prayer. He thirsted to stand before the altar; to chant the appointed parts; to consecrate — at the thought of this splendor his heart grew faint — to consecrate the bread and wine, and in Communion to receive not only the sacred Host, but to drink of the Chalice also.

None of these things could he do; nor could he, by any effort or sacrifice whatever, earn the privilege of doing them as others could and did. He would, he thought, have shrunk from nothing that might win for him this privilege, not even from walking again every step of the way he had come, from the accident in the forest till now, if by so doing he might attain this grace. Hope, that most Christian virtue, in other matters enjoined on him and all men, did not apply here. He must always remain in his place, silent and motionless, while the sublime rite progressed, enacted by others and never by him. He longed to annihilate the trivial but infinite distance that lay between him and the altar, to level the frail but insurmountable barrier of the communion rail. And this flood of yearning could never find its outlet in action; the utmost he could do was transform it into prayer: "Though my body may not stand before Thy altar, let my soul stand there. Though I may not offer Thee the Host and Chalice, let me offer Thee myself instead. Though by my word I may not change the bread and wine into Thy Most Precious Body and Blood, by my love and my obedience let me be transformed into Thee. And though I may not drink at the altar of the Chalice of Thy Blood, grant that I may drink It truly, in whatever form Thou hast prepared It for me."

At first this longing appeared to him almost an ingratitude, as seeming to indicate some lack of appreciation of the high privilege he did enjoy, of assisting daily at the Holy Sacrifice, and of partaking fully of the Body and Blood of his Lord, though under the species of bread only. In receiving Him, did he not receive all things? Could any honor be added to this honor, any joy to this joy? Could priest, bishop, the pope himself, receive more than did Michel each morning, when the fragile wafer that was become the very substance of God was placed on his tongue? Never was he insensible of the wonder of this divine bestowal; his heart knelt in awe, that he should have been called to this heavenly banquet, when so many received no invitation, or, being invited, refused to come. Indeed, it was the very profundity of his appreciation for what he did have, that kindled his desire into a flame of thirst for what he could never receive. His longing for the priesthood was born of his love for Mass; the two were inseparably united; without the one, the other could not be. His desire was the fruit and outpouring of that love; had God not decreed it otherwise, the flood of this longing would have carried him with it to the altar, where only his heart now stood.

"It is as if," he told Father André, "one should chain a horse to a staple so that he could not move, and then lash him with fury to make him go. Such an action on the part of man, Father, would be cruelty and folly; but God is wise and good. He does nothing without reason; and although I do not understand His reason for this, I agree to it. I accept."

"Yes, Michel. He gives no one a longing that may not be satisfied, except that greater good may come of it than the satisfaction would bring. And in this life you may never understand, but in eternity it will be made clear. Then you will see that His plan, and your part in it, and even this deprivation that is now so cruel to bear, fulfill a purpose not only good and merciful, but beautiful as well."

Nor was it a question only of celebrating Mass. Apart from the powers it conferred, Michel desired the priesthood for its own sake. A priest newly ordained could be prevented by some disaster from exercising a single one of the functions of his office, but that office itself would not be thereby impaired; the one who had received it would possess it forever; no catastrophe could erase the mark that had been impressed on his soul. Though stricken with paralysis before he could sing his first Mass, he would be none the less a priest, and forever. He might die before the oils that had anointed him had dried; nevertheless, having received that anointing, he would wear his priesthood through eternity, as truly, as unchangeably, as one who lived to sing a thousand Masses.

For it is the soul that receives the mark, not the body. Apart from the external differences of dress, those who receive this anointing are not distinguished by any visible sign from those who do not. But between the soul of the ordained and all others — between a priest and a lay brother — what infinite distance, what tragic separation!

And it was this above all that Michel desired: ordination; the priesthood; the mark on his soul which he would carry, in heaven or in hell forever, of a priest of God.

Tu es sacerdos in aeternum. Could Michel but receive the sacrament, though he could never celebrate Mass, the very fact of his priesthood would help him to endure that deprivation. To be a priest, and prevented by some exterior cause from exercising the sacerdotal privileges, would indeed be a sorrow; but to be unable to celebrate Mass because one is not a priest and can never become one — this, truly, is grief upon grief, and for it there is no cure.

And now Father Simon told him of this outrage: of a priest

who despised his priesthood, who scorned the privilege of celebrating Mass. The hands of this priest had been anointed with the sacred oils, and his soul eternally sealed with the mark of his divine calling. These hands had consecrated the Host and Chalice at the altar, they had converted bread and wine into the very Body and Blood of Him whose Priesthood Michel so ardently desired to share; they had dispensed the sacraments to others; they still possessed this power, which nothing could take from them. But in the hands of this man, the sacred power entrusted to them now lay idle and despised. In the soul of this priest the sacerdotal character went begging.

"Oh, that I might receive Holy Orders in that man's place!" Michel leaned against the wall of his cell, torn and shaken with anguish. A strong shudder passed over him; he covered his face with his hand. "That I might take upon myself the priesthood he has renounced!" But this could not be. No such transfer of dignity was possible. One may not vicariously wear another's honor, but only his sin.

His sin. . . . The chaos of Michel's thoughts came to a sudden halt; into his understanding streamed a flood of light. In the brilliance of this illumination all that had been hidden and obscure became shining and clear, revealed to his astonished gaze in a perfection of order and meaning. He looked steadily into the pattern revealed by this light, and there was no escaping the significance of what he saw.

For all that Father Simon told him about this man, balanced and opposed the events of his own life with extraordinary fitness. In those precise matters where this German had committed grievous sin, he, Michel, had suffered equally grievous mutilation or loss. This monk, bound by vows of celibacy, had broken those vows and married; Michel, free to marry, and on the point of doing so, had been kept from that state by harsh and drastic intervention, and had now willingly and gladly embraced the state and taken the vows this other had despised. The vows of poverty and obedience also taken by this monk, had gone the way of his vow of chastity: Michel, heir of an estate, born to a title and wealth, had been cast out of his inheritance and defrauded of his name, and was now good for nothing but to do humble tasks at the bidding of others; and to this life of poverty and submission he had also bound himself willingly, by vow. Moreover, this man, possessing in his soul the mark of a priest forever, and empowered in his person to celebrate Mass, had neither respect for his office nor love for the Holy Sacrifice; he had renounced the one and despised the other. Michel, who could never be a priest, who could never celebrate Mass, was consumed and tortured with desire for the office, and with a passion of love for its most august and sacred function. The hands of this man were the anointed hands of a priest: they had consecrated the Host and Chalice, they had held the Sacred Body and Precious Blood of Our Blessed Lord, and had cast them aside in mockery; while the hands of Michel —

Could he fail to see what stood revealed in this stream of light? Was there any possibility of doubt?

"I am not dreaming, or mad? I have heard, and not misunderstood? It is indeed for this that Thou hast chosen me? Because he will not, I may not? In reparation for his most grievous offense against Thy Priesthood I may offer this mutilation which prevents me from being what he has refused to be? Thou hast given me this love, and this thirst, and prevented the satisfaction of them, that I may wipe out something of the black insult he has offered Thee?"

He waited, listening.

His cell was filled with silence, and that silence became a Voice proclaiming its meaning to the heart of Michel beyond any doubt. He fell to his knees in token of understanding and assent.

Thus, the longing of Michel for the priesthood became invested with a new purpose, a profound significance, but it was not thereby lessened. Rather, it increased in ardor and strength by reason of this meaning, like a sapling growing steadily in rich soil. For this he was glad. To accomplish the end which was the purpose of this longing, no ordinary thirst, no moderate desire, would suffice. Only a thirst comparable in its degree to that which He suffered on the cross would be a worthy sacrifice to offer in reparation for the sin of one who had held in his consecrated hands the cup of living waters — the Chalice of His Most Precious Blood — and dashed it to the ground.

In spite of the cross which was thus revealed to him as the meaning and purpose of his life, the consolations of Brother Michel were abundant. God never takes from the willing heart what He does not restore in full measure.

Michel remembered a young man who had ridden from the forest of Cançonnet on a summer night at dusk, and had looked across the fields, glimmering with twilight and peace, at the distant buildings of the monastery, and had thought with pity of those enclosed therein, and of what in his naïveté he regarded as their dismal lot. Could he have foreseen that their number would one day include a Brother with an awkward limp and single mutilated hand; had he been told that the Brother so crippled could not be persuaded to change places with him, though that exchange carried with it bodily soundness, and worldly felicity, and the final happiness of marriage with Louise; had he been further informed that the Brother in question would have refused this exchange because of his own far greater happiness, in comparison with which the benefits enjoyed by the young Seigneur de Guillemont would have meant not gain, but loss, the latter would have declared such a thing to be beyond all reason, and, in fact, impossible. But far from being impossible, it was true. Not for anything would Brother Michel have found himself again in that young Seigneur's boots, with all the exterior advantages that had been his. Now his pity was for those who were as he had then been: whom God had not deprived of well-being, that they might find joy; who, content with pleasure, would never know happiness; and who, unwilling to meet the eyes of pain in full gaze, would never look into the eyes of beauty while they lived.

For the young man who rode out of the forest knew the love of a woman, but the crippled Brother knew the love of God.

And from that love he drew the peace so conspicuous in him, by reason of which many believed that he had no yearnings which had not been satisfied, no difficulties which had not been resolved. His daily companions suspected nothing of the trials and harassments, the consolations or the deep sorrow, of his life. His longing for the priesthood was a constant pain, so intense at times as to be almost unbearable; and it was also his greatest joy. Could he have purchased relief from this pain by surrendering the desire which was the cause of it, he would have refused without hesitation such an escape. To desire the priesthood without hope of attaining it was a bitter grief; but not to desire it was unthinkable, and indeed impossible.

This longing was more essentially a part of himself than his previous love had been. In face, it *was* himself. It had lain obscured by the more obvious and natural desire until the waters of disaster had washed the latter away and revealed the former securely implanted in the depths of his soul, from which now it could never be dislodged. The loss of his first love had not changed his identity, as the loss of his hand had not altered his appearance; but he could not lose the second, and remain Michel.

By reason of this longing he stood a step nearer the altar than others who, not prevented from the priesthood by physical defect, were nevertheless kept from it by want of love and absence of desire. All over the world, and even in the monastery, were men free to become priests, who had no thought of doing so; and from these Michel was separated by a chasm yet deeper than that which lay between him and the ordained. To the latter, indeed, he was united invisibly but truly, by the bond of their mutual desire. He shared with them also the condition of life inseparable from their calling, and the vows which assured its permanence. This was much, but there was yet more: had it been permitted him to offer the Holy Sacrifice, he could stand before the altar knowing that God in His great mercy had preserved him in that state prescribed, not as essential, but as ideal, for His priests by Christ Himself. *"All men take not this saying, save those to whom it is given."* All that he had ever possessed and now possessed no longer — indeed, his very life — would be insufficient to give in token of his gratitude, his joy, his wonder that God had taken measures, however sharp, to stop him in his course, to summon him aside, and to permit him, Michel, the last and least and unworthiest of them all, to be numbered among the shining company of those to whom that grace was given.

What he had told Father André when he begged admission to the Order was more than ever true; nothing could induce him to change his state, to part with this grace which God had, all unmerited by him, bestowed upon him. What threat, what temptation could effectively weaken his will in this matter, however much it might shake him otherwise, he could not imagine; and he cried daily to God to strengthen and confirm him in this resolution which he had kept so far without difficulty, because he had kept it without compromise and with joy.

To be a priest, it was not necessary, though it was certainly desirable, that one should have lived always in perfect chastity. Married men — widowers — could and did become priests; there were priests unfortunate enough to break their vows, and this was grave scandal, but it did not impair their orders; there were others called to the priesthood only after many years of grievous sin, and among these were numbered some of the greatest of the saints. Michel himself might well have married; he might easily have fallen into sin, discovering only later where his calling lay. In either case, supposing him free to follow that calling, his past sins and mistakes would have been no hindrance; a departure from strict chastity, whether lawfully in marriage, or regrettably through sin, could not of itself have kept him from the priest-hood, had other circumstances permitted his aspiring to it.

It would, however, have effectively prevented him from filling the role for which he now knew that God had summoned and prepared him. For he was chosen for a sacrifice, a victim offered in reparation for another's sin; and that state, not essential for the priesthood, was, in a sacrificial victim, a traditional and strict requirement. And certainly it was necessary in Michel's case: for his reparation must be for the offense of one who, in sinning against chastity, had sinned grievously against religion as well. It was, moreover, the state kept in holy and unspotted purity by the Supreme Victim Himself, who had extended to Michel the exalted privilege of sharing that state, and of being offered as victim, with Him: had Michel forfeited it, though without sin, another would have been chosen for this honor in his place.

It was inconceivable now that he should ever forfeit it. He had, indeed, a firm conviction that God, who had appointed him to this part, would maintain him in the condition essential to its fulfillment, to the end.

These consolations of Brother Michel were many and real. They did not, however, slake his thirst or diminish his longing, because they could neither confer on him the priesthood nor enable him to celebrate Mass. To know the reason for his mutilations was not to cease to suffer from them; to understand why he must remain a Brother was not to kill his longing to become a priest. To remove or even to decrease that longing would be to defeat the purpose for which he must accept it, and suffer it, and rejoice in it, while he lived.

Of all this he told nothing to anyone, excepting only Father André; so that none but his confessor knew the sorrow which was the cause of his happiness, the pain which was the secret of his peace.

iv

The Community was in an uproar.

Father Prior had died, and Father Pierre, the sacristan, was now Prior in his place.

Father Pierre was known for the number and rigor of his austerities, far beyond those demanded by the Rule. Reports of his voluntary mortifications, circulated among the Brothers, filled them with awe. They took no little pride in the ascetical practices of Father Pierre, which went to heroic lengths, and shed glory on the House, and indeed on the whole Order; but this pride lasted only as long as Father Pierre limited his mortifications to his own person, and did not extend them to include his fellow Religious.

The first act of Father Pierre on becoming Prior, however, was to make it impossible in the future for his Brothers in the Community to bask in reflected glory only, without contributing to that glory a substantial share of the works which produced it.

The late Father Prior had died at an advanced age, and in recent years his duties had fallen upon Father Subprior, who was of a dreamy and impractical temper, and lenient to a fault. Life in the Community under the jurisdiction of Father Subprior was most agreeable, and had all but lost its penitential character. There was a laxness in the observance of the Rule, a letting down of discipline, which Father André, Father Pierre, and others, had long viewed with alarm, but which the lay Brothers regarded for the most part as no more than a just mitigation of requirements unnecessarily harsh, considering the labors imposed on them besides.

Accordingly, when Father Pierre, now Father Prior, declared his intention of enforcing a strict observance of the originial Rule, and proceeded at once to put this intention into effect, there was such a hue and cry as Notre Dames des Prés had not heard in the memory of any living there.

The Brothers assembled to discuss the matter. After much talk, they decided that something must be done to curb the ascetical zeal of Father Prior, who would put all men into hair shirts, or worse. This earlier rising, these more frequent vigils and fasts, these grave penalties for trivial infringements of the Rule, were beyond reason, and, in fact, an outrage. It was decided to compile a list of grievances and present them to Father Prior in writing, accompanied by an oral statement of their case.

Because he was skilled in writing, and of a ready tongue, Brother Michel was selected for the office of spokesman to Father Prior. They had neglected to include him in the discussion, since it was felt he would not wholly approve the purpose of it; but now that the matter was decided, he could hardly go against the voice of the majority, and refuse to concur in a plan manifestly for the good of all. Brother Thomas went in search of him, and the business was explained to him in detail.

Brother Michel listened to the plan of the Brothers in astonishment and horror.

Echoes of murmuring had reached his ears as he went about his tasks, but he did not suspect that the discontent had grown to any such proportion as this. He looked around the assembled Brothers now, fixing his gaze at length on Brother Thomas, who had been sent to fetch him. Brother Thomas was chief gardener, but his disposition had stolen no sweetness from his long association with flowers. He was thin and waspish, pale, and afflicted with very bad teeth. To the pain these undoubtedly caused him, Brother Michel ascribed his caustic and critical tongue.

"Do I understand aright," asked Brother Michel, speaking

with great distinctness, "that you wish me to lay before Father Prior a list of grievances, and to beg that the Rule of the House, in force since its foundation, be now set aside in favor of an easier observance?"

Brother Thomas murmured an affirmative. He lowered his eyes before the gaze of Brother Michel, and tried not to look as uncomfortable as he felt. He had been strongly of the opinion that to make Brother Michel a party to their plans was to assure the failure of those plans, but he had said nothing of that opinion, knowing also that of them all, only Brother Michel could persuade Father Prior — if he himself could be first persuaded. Brother Thomas now comprehended that this was impossible.

Brother Joseph flushed scarlet as the eyes of Brother Michel met his. Brother Michel knew that Brother Joseph was present, not from conviction, but because he was of too agreeable a disposition to refuse. Had the purpose of the discussion been to implore Father Prior to increase the strictness of the Rule even beyond reason, Brother Joseph would have concurred cheerfully in it, no less.

The embarrassment of Brother Joseph was shared in some degree by all. There was a general lowering of eyes, a sighing and fidgeting, a coughing behind hands.

"My Brothers," continued Brother Michel, "what seek we at Notre Dame des Prés? Why came we here?"

Silence answered him, and downcast eyes. He went on:

"Are we not here to seek one thing, and that the love of God? None came here for bodily ease, or to pursue at his pleasure a profitable trade. Those who live delicately are still at kings' courts, and skilled gardeners and pastry cooks may always find lucrative employment at the Châteaux of Seigneurs. No, my Brothers. If we have so far forgotten the aspirations which drew us here, as seriously to contemplate sending such a protest to Father Prior as you have described to me, then surely it is time that we search our hearts to find what love holds first place there."

Brother Michel paused. None spoke. He continued:

"It may be well for us to consider the nature of this love, and how we may arrive at it. For it is true that the love of God includes all things, but all things do not include the love of God.

The heart consists, as it were, of chambers, and in each chamber a treasure lies hid. The deeper we penetrate, the richer treasure do we find, until in the innermost chamber we come upon the richest treasure of all, which is the love of God. He who finds this, finds all. He who possesses all things else, but lacks this, possesses nothing.

"This love, my Brothers, may not be found without trial and sacrifice; but why came we here, if not to seek it? There are men who set out in ships for distant lands, in search of treasure: jewels, spices, gold; and in this quest they are willing to endure grievous hardships. They must turn their backs on home and its consolations and comforts. With them into the ship they may take neither wife nor children, house nor goods, servants nor possessions, save only what is needful to cover their nakedness, and such food and drink as will suffice, with good fortune, till they reach shore. Once embarked, they face perils unspeakable: calm and storm; hunger and thirst; shipwreck, and, it may be, torture at the hands of savages. And, if they survive these perils, my Brothers, what assurance have they of finding the riches they seek? Many hundreds have died in torment, in quest of treasure which did not exist.

"How different is the case with them who are embarked on the quest of the true treasure, which is the love of God! This love dwells sweetly in the innermost chamber of the heart; to find it, we have not to undergo perils of land and sea. We have only to press resolutely on through the several chambers, such of which would persuade us by the worth of the treasure it contains, that we have come far enough; beyond we shall find no greater riches; let us stop here, and be content.

"In the outermost chamber, my Brothers, is a stuff so mean and poor that it is not worth the name of treasure. It is as base metal to precious, as tin to gold. This is the love of self. This love resides in the antechamber of the heart; and the number of those who live and die here cannot be counted. This is a great pity and sorrow, that precious gold is within the reach of all, and thousands upon thousands, my Brothers, are content with tin.

"In the next chamber is to be found a treasure scarcely more noble and yet not so base as the love of self. This is the love of riches and of possessions. In this chamber are to be found those of whom our Lord said in sorrow, 'How hardly shall they that have riches enter into the kingdom of heaven.' For it is a wonder indeed if the heart that rests in the love of lands and houses, and beautiful and rare objects, and works of art and books, will ever quit the chamber where these riches are to be found, and penetrate beyond it to that treasure in comparison with which these riches are as brass to gold.

"He who dwells in this chamber has his eyes always on the outermost room, which is the love of self; but he who penetrates to the third chamber finds a fairer treasure, and one which looks forward to the love of God. This treasure is no longer of base metal, but of precious; it is the silver of the heart, though not the gold. It is, my friends, the love of others: of husband and wife, of kindred and friends, of parents and children. This love is truly noble, and it bears a mark by which all real treasure may be known, in that it cannot be possessed without some cost to self. For this reason the heart is easily persuaded that in this love it has found, not only real love, as indeed it has, but the highest love of all. Thus it remains satisfied with its silver — precious metal, but still silver — when close at hand lies gold.

"Between this and the innermost chamber lies yet another, and here is to be found a treasure very rich indeed; the love of wisdom and knowledge, of beauty and truth, of virtue and philosophy. This is as silver dipped in gold. By its resemblance to gold it deceives those who find it into believing that they have found all; and many a heart rests here, satisfied that this treasure is the noblest that can be possessed by man, not perceiving that it is gold without only, and still silver within.

"For there is a chamber more interior still; and here, in the very tabernacle of the heart lies this treasure, this refined and beaten gold, this perfect love of God. But though so rich, so far surpassing other treasure in beauty and in worth, so that all the riches in the world are not to be compared with it, it does not lie over mountains or beyond seas, but within the reach of every one of us — yes, even of myself. It may be had by all who will;

it is necessary only that they will, and that they be not halted by the lesser treasure they will find in the chambers through which they must pass on their way. And when with resolution they persist until they find it — oh, my Brothers, words cannot describe to you what treasure it is they have found! As gold contains within itself the worth of silver and far more, in this love they will find all that in passing through the outer chambers they were compelled to leave behind. Wisdom, virtue, beauty, kindred, friends, home, possessions, and even self — now these may be loved truly, when they are loved in God. Our Blessed Lord said that they who left these things for His sake should possess them again even in this world a hundredfold, and so it is. For the love of God is not an emptiness, but a possession; it is a treasure, not a lack. Let none persuade you that in renouncing all for this, you give and receive nothing. Oh, my Brothers! How opposite is the truth! For glass, you receive diamonds, and for tin, gold.

"How may we arrive at this innermost chamber, my Brothers? How may we find this love? I know of no way, save by prayer and obedience. Father Prior has enjoined on us a stricter observance of the Rule, not for his pleasure, but for our very great gain, that we may give more time to prayer, and that through holy obedience and surrender of the love of self, we may be led sweetly and safely to that innermost chamber where we shall find the treasure we came here to seek, the love of God which is the object of our quest."

There was a long silence. At length Brother Michel spoke again:

"It was your wish, my Brothers, that I address Father Prior. Our Lord, it seems, willed that I address you instead. If you still desire to submit to Father Prior your list of grievances, you are free to do so; I cannot prevent. I can only make sure that he who carries it shall not be myself."

The list of grievances never reached Father Prior, but a detailed report of the proceedings, including Brother Michel's words, was promptly conveyed to him. Father Prior did not indicate to Brother Michel that he knew of the affair, and of the Brother's part in it; but the circumstance was such as Father Prior was not likely to forget.

Father Simon kept his promise to instruct Brother Michel in the art of lettering; and in this task he displayed a patience Michel had not associated with the excitable little man. It was indeed a laborious business, painful for apprentice and master alike. Every day Michel was tempted to throw down his quill and not take it up again, believing that perseverance in this task would avail him nothing, since through presumption he had again undertaken the impossible. It would be the part of humility to give up before he squandered Father Simon's time and energies, if not his own.

Apart from the difficulties of the art itself, the problem of mastering his materials was almost too much for him. These exasperated him beyond measure; they were not mere inanimate objects, but alive and possessed with a demon of rebellion. Like a horse recognizing a weak hand on the reins, they defied him. The parchment twisted and slid beneath his hand; he could hit on no sure device that would hold it secure and at the same time permit him to shift it as needed; the ink clogged his quill or ran from it like water; his sleeves were forever getting in his way; these and a thousand molehills were added to the mountain of difficulty involved in the task of learning this most precise and exacting of arts. His awkward and childish efforts filled him with dismay.

"My letters limp as I do, Father," he said miserably. "That scribe did not go beyond the truth, but rather fell short of it, who wrote at the end of his work, 'Three fingers hold the pen, but the whole body toils.' And to what ill effect" — he regarded his work ruefully — "when it is the wrong three fingers."

"Courage, Brother, courage!" Father Simon did not permit him to lose heart. "One *Credo* written thus by you, is worth a thousand pamphlets filled with lies, and turned out with a twist of the screw by those presses of the devil. Moreover, the devil knows it, and that is why he strews difficulties in your way, to persuade you to abandon the fight. Today, he whispers, your writing is worse than yesterday; and yesterday worse than the day before; thus, there is no chance for improvement, and no purpose to be served in continuing. But do not believe him, for as usual he lies. At present your discrimination goes ahead of your work; persist only, and your work will catch up with it. One of these days a surprise awaits you."

"It is truly an excellent humiliation of spirit to compare my misshapen and halting letters with your beautiful and running hand," observed Michel, reflectively. "Now, I suppose our German friend would say that it is necessary for me only to believe in the art of lettering, and in you, Father, who have attained such proficiency in it, and by that act of faith in your skill, but without any practice or labor or effort on my part, I forthwith become a scribe."

"Precisely." Father Simon pounded the desk with enthusiasm. "You have but stated another instance of the working of their logic, of which I have already pointed out to you the most conspicuous examples."

"But does it not occur to them that this want of reasoning, applied to the affairs of the world, quite apart from matters of the spirit and of faith, can work only havoc and ruin?"

"Nothing occurs to them, Michel, except that it is a freeing from discipline, under which the spirit and flesh of man will always chafe. As I told you, they cannot, and will not, and do not, think."

"But, if men throw off the sweet yoke of bondage to Christ, and reject Him where He lives among us in His Church, and if everyone henceforward believes and does as he wills, without order or reason or unity, where shall we end?"

"Your question is its own answer, Brother. If this heresy should succeed in breaking the unity away from the Church by persuading them that they may abandon Christ and still remain Christians — where can we end, except in strife and division, in chaos and death?"

"It is not a happy prospect, Father."

"No, Michel. But it is all the more reason why you should continue to write your *Credos* and not despair, for a time may come when there will be great need of those who can say, I believe."

Michel strongly doubted the prognosis of Father Simon concerning the future of his work. He dared not hope that his clumsy, sprawling letters would ever show much improvement; as for the fluid beauty of Father Simon's writing, that was forever beyond him. Daily he resisted the temptation to tear up his pages, break his quill in two, hurl the ink across his cell, and be done with it; he continued, because Father Simon insisted, but for no other reason.

For practice, he used the prayers of Mass, writing them again and again.

"Though I may never celebrate Mass, I can learn it, every word. Thus in time I shall know it as thoroughly as if I were a priest. This practice will avail me for that, though it makes neither a priest nor a scribe of me."

Weeks passed; winter came, numbing his fingers, congealing his paint and ink, shortening and darkening the days so that it seemed he had but prepared his materials when he must quit work for want of light. For this reason Father Simon contrived to have him moved into a cell boasting two windows, at the end of the north wing, directly over the kitchens where a year ago he had chopped cabbages, sung childish songs to the scandal of his betters, and spilled soup. These two windows which admitted more light, admitted also more wind and more cold. The breath of Brother Michel hung in the air so that he saw his work through a cloud of mist; he knew that he held the quill, perceiving it in his hand, but he could no longer feel it. An icy numbness invaded his cell, regardless of the walls, and seizing him, made him one with the bleak and wind-swept landscape outside.

"I am more fortunate than Father Simon and other scribes," murmured Brother Michel, as he guided across his page the quill he could not feel. "They have ten fingers to freeze. I have but three."

The cold paralyzed, but it did not deafen him: from the kitchen below rose the singing of Brother Joseph, as penetrating as the wind, and even more painful; for the winter was short, and the wind sometimes ceased, but the song of Brother Joseph knew no seasons, and he was silent only in sleep — when Michel was constrained by the rule of the Community to sleep, too. And to be out of earshot of Brother Joseph was hardly a relief; for the song of the Brother, which, like creation on the first day, was without form and void, was now so firmly established in Michel's memory that, audibly or otherwise, it accompanied all his labors. The pain so inflicted is truly deep and excruciating, thought Brother Michel, though it leaves no visible scar.

A companion visited him frequently in his cell, and sat regarding his work soberly but critically, refraining the while from comment: a courtesy which he deeply appreciated. This was Cendrillon the kitchen cat, who had developed an inordinate attachment to him in the days when he chopped cabbages in her domain. Bound by no rule, and subject to no discipline, Cendrillon attempted neither to overcome her partiality nor to conceal it. She darted out of the kitchen at every opportunity, and trotting up to his cell, clawed at the door, or stood up and rattled the latch, demanding the while to be admitted, until he put down his quill and yielded to her importunities.

The vocation of Cendrillon was to supply the Community with progeny which in turn kept the premises free of mice and rats: a duty which she performed with unfaltering fidelity. She was a very Nimrod of cats, and for this reason Michel found her attachment a source of considerable embarrassment; she was not content to worship from afar, but must show her affection with positive tokens of esteem. She brought him frequent offerings of rats and mice, birds, and even snakes, over which he often stumbled when leaving or returning to his cell in the dark.

The friendship of Cendrillon was no passing fancy, but a real devotion: it persisted even into the winter. She quitted the warmth of the kitchen to follow him to his cell, where she sat at his feet, her breath a miniature cloud in the air, watching him with solemn yellow eyes, and alternately raising one forepaw and then the other from the icy floor. Michel reminded her that she could warm all her feet, and her whiskers besides, by the kitchen fire. She replied, without warning, that she preferred to do so by sitting in his lap.

His quill trailed a line of ink across the best work he had yet accomplished. He threw it down and looked at the cat, who began working her claws in and out of the thick wool of his habit, purring loudly.

AND   BLESS   THIS   SACRIFICE...   117

"You are an excellent penance, my angel, and therefore I should suffer you gladly. But you are also an occasion of sin, for at this moment you tempt me to do violence against a valuable member of the Community, and an incomparable mouser. For that reason I shall put you firmly from me."

Tucking her under his arm, he carried her to the end of the corridor, where a narrow flight of stairs led to the kitchen. Down this staircase he now thrust her.

"It is well I am not of a hasty temper, my cabbage, or you would find yourself, like the cat of la Mère Michel, translated by Brother Joseph into rabbit stew."

"Whom do you address, Brother?"

Michel turned. Behind him stood Brother Etienne, who had approached unheard, on his way to descend to the kitchen.

"I address Cendrillon," replied Michel. "She wishes to be instructed in calligraphy, but I can discover no talent. I suggested instead that she teach Brother Joseph to sing."

Michel returned to his cell to put away his materials, since it was impossible to repair the damage of Cendrillon, and too late to begin another page. Brother Etienne tramped on down to the kitchen, bristling with indignation and confirmed in an opinion he had long entertained: the flippancy of the crippled Brother was no mere superficial defect but a grave spiritual malady which, persisted in, could lead to nothing but disaster.

At long length Michel discovered that Father Simon had not spoken without reason. He regarded a finished page one day and perceived that it had order and a certain dignity. With a shock of astonishment he realized, as he studied it, that it had beauty as well. He was utterly nonplussed; it passed his comprehension how this could be, since he himself had written it. Such a result from his quill must be sheer accident; he would try again. He did so; the second page improved on the first.

He designed and wrote several pages and took them to Father Simon.

"Yes!" His master nodded approvingly. "Did I not tell you how it would be? You write a fine hand, and you have besides a feeling for the beauty of a page which many scribes lack. Now we will see what can be done about setting you to work in earnest.

Leave these samples with me; I believe something will come of it."

Michel surrendered the pages and did not think of them again, until, some weeks later, Father Simon sent for him.

"Ah, Brother! I have news for you — great news." The little monk rubbed his hands together joyfully; his eyes shone with excitement. "An extraordinary honor has been done us both. You directly, and myself only because you are my pupil." He fished into a portfolio and produced the pages of lettering Michel had given him. "His Lordship, the Bishop of Tours, wishes a Mass book for the cathedral. I showed him this lettering of yours; he praised it highly. The work is to be divided among several scribes — and you, Brother, are to do the Canon."

A shock is a shock, whether its cause be pain or joy. Michel felt himself grow hot and cold and faint from an emotion for which he had no name.

"A Mass book? To be used on the altar? At Mass?"

"That is where Mass books are customarily used, I believe."

"And you say — I am to do the Canon?"

"It is an honor truly, but hardly a matter for such great astonishment. You have worked hard and you are no dunce. You are indeed an artist in your fingers and in your soul. Nor do I see any reason for weeping in the fact that you have learned to write well enough to execute an order for His Lordship."

In this Father Simon wholly mistook the cause of the emotion of Michel, which his pupil strove in vain to conceal. It had nothing to do with the excellence of his work, or the fact that he had achieved that excellence in spite of his handicap, or that he was to have the great honor of executing a commission for the bishop. No; the emotion which seized Michel so suddenly and uncontrollably sprang from the realization that although he himself could never ascend the steps to the altar, this work of his would do precisely that. It would, indeed, share the altar with Our Lord Himself; it would play an intimate part in the enactment of the Holy Sacrifice; it would be present, in close proximity to Him, at His coming; it would say through the lips of the celebrant those very words upon which that coming depended — the words which Michel hungered and thirsted to say, and could not, but would now write for the priest to speak. He was staggered, overwhelmed. Tears sprang to his eyes and he could not hide them.

Designing his pages, Michel felt his heart stand still. How could it be that this privilege had fallen to him? For Mass is the one perfect beauty in this world, and the Canon is the most beautiful part of Mass: the exquisite and balanced setting in which the jewel of the consecration is fitted and poised. And this beauty Brother Michel, who could not aspire to be a priest, who had not dared hope to become a scribe, would now make visible, placing upon an otherwise empty and barren page these living words, these words of miracle and wonder, which, bequeathed to men by the Son of God as His parting gift, His divine legacy, assure that His presence shall remain among His people, wherever they shall be spoken at His altars, until time is ended and the need for them is past.

His preparations completed, Michel took up his quill. He regarded the smooth pages, holding his breath, hardly daring to begin. For, once done, his work could not be undone; his letters once written, could not be worked over for improvement and correction. And what if he should be unable to clothe this beauty in fitting garb? He might fail altogether in this undertaking, as, had he been permitted to aspire to the priesthood, he might have found himself rejected before ordination, numbered among those called but not chosen. The beauty of Mass is perfect and complete. Nothing can be added to it, nor, in a sense, taken from it; but because of that very perfection the best work of man is inadequate to do it honor; and how grievous an affront to show forth the divine beauty in any form less than the highest of which man's poor effort is capable, to array it in vesture slovenly or uncouth!

But, one must not refrain from effort because it is possible to fail. The quill of Michel traveled down the page, writing into the appointed spaces words already deeply written in his heart:

Te igitur, clementissime Pater —

"Why then is Mass so beautiful?" The answer was immediate: "The beauty of Mass is the beauty of Calvary, the beauty of the cross. All sacrifice is beautiful in its degree, but the beauty of that sublime surrender can never be approached by any other act: and Mass is that Sacrifice. The beauty of Mass is the beauty of Christ. It is the one perfect beauty, without spot or flaw or blemish, in this world."

Qui pridie quam pateretur —

"This beauty reached its height and summit on the cross: not even crucifixion could deface it. The sins and imperfections of men cannot mar the beauty of Mass, but they do grave dishonor to it. Grant that the defects of my work may not obscure that beauty, but let it shine forth in spite of them; and may every word, every letter that I write, be a chalice filled with my love for Thee."

Hoc est enim Corpus Meum.

"The consecration — this is the consecration. These are the words which bring Thee upon the altar. Except for them there would be no Mass. These are the words which I, Michel, may never speak —"

Hic est enim Calix Sanguinis mei —

The quill of Michel came to a halt. He held it suspended over the parchment, then very slowly laid it to one side. Again his cell was filled with silence. He listened.

"Who shares My cross, shares My Priesthood, Michel. Your love and your desire are very pleasing to Me. Accept these words as My pledge to you. If it were possible in My design, I would grant that desire. I would receive you among My ordained priests."

After a long while Michel took up his quill and resumed his work. "I would receive you among My ordained priests."

— novi et aeterni testamenti: mysterium fidei, qui pro vobis et pro multis effundetur in remissionem peccatorum.

"I would receive *you —*"

These words which Brother Michel heard, in the silence of his cell and his heart, never left him. They did not assuage his thirst; they helped him immeasurably to endure it. They returned to him again and again, in the course of his daily tasks, and in his hours of silence and prayer. In his meditations they were the steps by which he ascended to the heart of God.

"I would receive you among My ordained priests."

Quisquis non receperit
regnum Dei velut parvulus
non intrabit in illud

7. Of Such Is the Kingdom

i

It was again market day at Guillemont.

The little ass Marceline had fetched her bread from the monastery as usual, and now with her escort and her empty baskets had departed; but today her departure was not followed by the customary renewal of strife. For strife is a negation; it arises from a want of something better to do; conflict is an indulgence which those may not permit themselves whose minds are absorbed by a common interest and pointed to a common end. This interest need not be of an elevating character to produce its unifying effect; a catastrophe will serve as well as a cause, and a novelty as well as either. An angry couple will drop their quarrel equally if the house catches fire, or a child falls ill, or a parade passes by.

This is not to say that silence followed the departure of Marceline and her companion; far from it. The babel of tongues awoke indeed, but not in dissension: they had other matters to occupy them than the customary subject of whether the buyer or purchaser was the greater scoundrel and thief. The ritual of market day was as fixed as the church calendar; it was as unthinkable that Father André and Marceline should not appear as that Christmas should be transferred to June. And now such an impossibility had occurred: Marceline had arrived, escorted not by Father André, but by another.

The stir caused by this unprecedented departure from custom

was such that those who came to buy had much ado to make their wants known over the hubbub which broke forth as soon as the little ass and her escort had quitted the square.

"Là, now — là là!" Paulette Dubois clicked her tongue against her teeth and craned her neck for a last glimpse of the departing pair as they took their slow way down the hill. La Dubois sold dates and figs and other fruits in her stall, the first on the left as one entered the square. Leaning her knuckles on the counter, she stood tiptoe and peered over the brow of the hill and over the head of old Jacques Colet who was almost blind and who came from the Hôtel de Ville, where he held some insignificant post, for figs with which to supplement his noonday repast of bread and cheese and sour wine. He rapped with his sou on her counter but Paulette brushed him away as if he had been a fly. A new experience had entered the life of Paulette and had left her blinking and dazed.

Paulette resembled in appearance an apple one scrubs and polishes before giving it to a child. She had flashing black eyes of incredible boldness and her life was dominated by two passions: men and money. She cared not how she came by either so long as she had plenty of both. She drove a shrewder bargain than any in the square, and nothing gave her such pain as to part with a sou or a fig except for double their value, or more. She was unable to exercise either restraint or discrimination when confronted by something that at the moment was, or would in due course become, or had once been, a man: even old Jacques Colet, who had one eye and no teeth and the palsy, drew from her cajolery and terms of endearment. On market days she declaimed vehemently against the cruelty of that legislation which decreed that some fruits, and those the choicest, should be forever beyond her reach, for though she exercised no discrimination, she possessed it. She resembled a drunkard who, knowing good wines but unable to afford them, drinks what he can get none the less eagerly for sighing after the rarer vintages that are beyond his reach.

She had a swarm of children of uncertain paternity, to the number of which she added with extraordinary rapidity and with no apparent inconvenience to herself. One or more of these usually accompanied her to market. Jean, her oldest boy, was the first to spot Marceline, and to make known the fact that he who escorted her was not Father André.

"C'est pas le père — c'est un autre!" cried the urchin shrilly. Simultaneously with this announcement Marceline and her companion entered the square, and the child proclaimed with emphasis a fact which none could fail to perceive for himself:

"Mais vois qu'il est boîteux — he limps! See how he limps!"

"Shut your mouth! Where are your manners, imbecile?"

Paulette reached over the stall to cuff her son, whose manners had plainly been left where he found them: at home. But the chastisement was not administered. The object of the boy's comment, being abreast of Paulette's stall, interfered with a protest.

"Do not strike the child, Madame. He but speaks the truth. I limp, and with no ordinary limp, as you must see." He looked down at the boy, smiling. "Indeed, it is a very king of limps, is it not, *mon petit?* One must be blind not to observe it, and I rejoice that your son is spared that affliction, Madame."

He transferred his smile for the brief shadow of a second from the child to his mother, and with a bow to her, moved on.

She stared after him, agape. In her bosom an emotion stirred, unfamiliar and disquieting. She could not give it a name, never having felt it before, but one to whom it was familiar would have recognized it as being compounded of embarrassment and shyness, and approaching very near to shame. Suddenly she wished to hide, she did not know why; and she cast down her eyes in a strange agitation, although no one had accused her of anything.

But her son did not share her disquiet, having no cause to do so. He scampered after Marceline and her escort, and catching up with them, tugged at the sleeve of the latter. This he dropped promptly, with a little shriek:

"Oh, oh! You have no hand!"

"That is almost true, but not quite. I have not two hands, as you have, *mon petit,* nor yet a whole one, but half a one: and that, you will agree, is better than none at all. I tell you this to anticipate your discovering it for yourself, as, being a boy, you are sure to do within the next five minutes."

The child looked up at his interlocutor, his eyes solemn with awe. Suddenly his face broke into a very garden of smiles, and he gave a little skip. He plucked again at the sleeve he had dropped, and trotted along beside the stranger, wriggling like a puppy in a sudden rush of confidence.

"Who are you?" he demanded.

"My name is Frère Michel. And yours?"

"Jeannot Dubois. Where is Father André?"

"I regret to tell you, Jeannot: Father André has gone away. From now on I take his place — as best I can."

"Did you —" the boy gulped, "did you never have two hands, like me?"

"Oh, yes, Jeannot. I was born, like yourself, with the customary number of fingers — ten, if I remember correctly."

"But what happened to your hand? Where is it? What did you do with it? Why —"

"I see that you have got a matter on your mind, Jeannot, that will give you no rest until you arrive at the truth. I will therefore enlighten you briefly, and then, if you please, we will drop the matter for good. The member in question is in the forest of Cançonnet, where I left it one day in the keeping of an animal called a boar."

"But why did you do that, Frère Mich'?"

"Because *le bon Dieu* decided that I could serve Him better without it. At first I was not inclined to believe this, but now I am wholly of His way of thinking."

"But did it not hurt you very much, Frère Mich'?"

"See now, here we are at the stall of Monsieur Charles, who takes our bread. You shall help me to empty the baskets of Marceline, and afterward, if Marceline permits, you shall have a ride on her back."

The Brother and his ass had now departed, accompanied by Jeannot, who was to have his promised hide at the foot of the hill; and behind the trio comment broke out like an explosion. Who was the new Brother? Where did he hail from? How came he, with a face like that, to be a Brother? No man endowed by God with such a countenance had a right to conceal it in a monastery: why, with that face, he could pick a wife of his own choosing, rich, and of the nobility, in spite of his limp. The limp was no hindrance; it but touched the heart the more. Perhaps he was of the nobility himself; crippled though he was, he had the bearing, the manners, of a king. What in the name of a thousand names did such a one do here, carrying bread to market? Father André was of gentle birth, and a priest besides; but they were long used to him, and to according him the deference due his station; whereas this new Brother — and so young — The women blinked and clucked, shaking their heads; some of them wept; and even the men had their word to say.

At length old Jacques Colet gave up trying to attract the notice of the vendor of figs. Leaving his sou on the counter, he helped himself to her produce and made off with his spoils, unobserved. "It is an arrears that has long been due me," he muttered, patting his bulging pockets. "What has come over the Robber Dubois, that she permits justice to be done at last?"

The Brother being finally out of sight, Paulette sank back on her stool, and fetched a long sigh, as one exhausted. She pocketed the sou of Jacques Colet absently, failing to note the raid that had been made on her wares.

"Mais il est beau," she gasped, *"beau comme un ange."* It is obvious that she did not refer to Jacques Colet. "He bowed to me, as to a lady. He asked me, could he give Jeannot a ride? He said" — she blinked, gulping — "he said mine is an enviable trade, to sell figs, since Our Lord showed a liking for them."

Next to the stall of Paulette was that of *la mère* Bigotte, where vegetables of various kinds were displayed, presided over by a pyramid of cabbages. If la Dubois resembled a polished apple, la Bigotte was the stem from which it was plucked, being dried and gnarled and bent, and of a brownish and scaly appearance. She wore a quantity of rusty petticoats, and a rusty shawl folded over her head, from beneath which her sharp brown face peered out, like that of an ancient and whiskered mouse. The ends of her shawl met across a cavity where it was impossible to imagine that the heart of youth had ever beat and the fire of emotion had once stirred. But in this twig the sap of life still crawled, if it could not be said to flow. In evidence of this, a moisture appeared in her eyes, and she wiped it away with her shawl.

"*Eh, le beau gars!*" she quavered. "He is one who knows cabbages, *paraît-il!* He said it would be no penance to subsist on cabbages in Lent, if all were like mine!"

Beyond *la mère* Bigotte, Berthe Masson sold pastries and confections. Here was a round tower with a head on top, sculptured, and not very skillfully, from stone. That this ponderous bulk and undeviating contour should have met in a female form was a reversal of nature so marked as to amount almost to a miracle. It was impossible to associate the massive and granite exterior of Berthe with the delicate sugared confections displayed on her counter, but this incongruity no longer astonished any, because all were used to it. Being slow of tongue, she was judged correspondingly dull of wit. Few bothered to speak to her; one does not pass the time of day with a stone tower.

She produced a handkerchief now and blew her nose violently. That which was almost a miracle by its nature, became one in fact: the tower, hitherto unmoved and apparently immovable, heaved and shook.

"He says," she sobbed, "the Brother says I am an artist! Hear you all — I, Berthe Masson, an artist! 'Such beautiful *confiseries,* Madame could be achieved only by a great artist!' Oh, oh, oh!" She hid her face in her handkerchief and rocked back and forth in a very crisis of emotion.

"But, name of a pipe, why do you weep?" Pierre Gapin popped up from behind his counter like a jack-in-the-box, this being his habit. He sold snails, moule, crayfish, shrimp, and other aquatic curiosities which some intrepid pioneer in gourmandise once discovered to be edible, in spite of an exterior calculated, both as to substance and appearance, to preserve them safe from human assault forever. Papa Gapin was himself hardly distinguishable from his merchandise; one resisted the temptation to crack him open, dip him in melted butter, and eat him on a fork. He had beady little eyes, hard and lifeless as a lobster's; above them bristled antennae-like brows; his chin was grown over with a greenish-black beard of the texture of sea moss, and tufts of the same weed protruded from his ears.

"Pah!" he burst forth. "You women are fools! The Brother would crack the pates of all of you, did he suppose you were weeping over him! In spite of his gentleman's tongue, he has a good jaw and a fire in his eye; I would not like to be on the wrong side in a quarrel with him, cripple or no. Such sniffling would revolt him. It is enough to turn the stomach of any man!" Placing his hands to his abdomen, he indicated by an inelegant pantomime that such was the effect of their tears upon himself.

"You are right, *bonhomme*. They are fools to sniffle over him." Behind her counter of geese and chickens, live and dressed, sat the Widow Douroux, who judged persons and things with implacable severity, for their good. Her manner, her attitude, her very appearance proclaimed that that which is, is wrong. She was a tower, not of flesh, but of that respectability which in her mind passed for virtue. It was a constant pain to her that she should be forced to associate, however remotely, with one of so abandoned a life as Paulette Dubois; merely to breathe the same air with that woman was an insult to widowhood and to virtue. But being left by the inconsiderate death of her husband with a chicken farm and five children, there was no help for it; she must sell her chickens, or starve. She refrained pointedly from all intercourse with the offending Dubois, and when any of the tainted progeny of this latter approached too near her stall, she shooed them away with her apron, as if they had been hens loose in her flower beds. Pursing her lips, she passed judgment on the Brother and disposed of him for eternity, sparing the Almighty the trouble of doing it later.

"Me, I am always suspicious of a handsome face. I never knew one yet, man or woman, to come to a good end. It is a sign of weakness, you may be sure of that. Did you observe how he talked to the Dubois? He must be blind as well as lame; one can tell what that woman is at a glance. His face and his limp have deceived you; mark my words, there is a defect of character there. A habit does not make a saint. It is far more likely to hide a sinner." She nodded with grim relish. "I tell you all, that face will come to no good."

Charles Poulot, the baker, rubbed his hands together and winked over at Jean Martin, who kept the meat stall opposite him.

"So, is it? La Douroux is jealous that the handsome Brother did not bow to her, and ride her son on his ass, and remind her that Our Lord had a taste for *poulet farci?* The good widow is disconsolate that he kept his salutations for the unsavory Dubois? If we cannot be handsome, let us by all means be virtuous, but la Douroux will not have it that one can be both. And if Madame is right," he bowed in her direction, gallantly, "the virtue of Madame is beyond question, being apparent at a glance."

"And in that case," piped the inadequate treble of Jean Martin, who thrust his frightened rabbit's face, adorned with sparse and tremulous whiskers, from behind his links of sausage and sides of beef: "the new Brother is the greatest among sinners, for I never saw one so well favored, though he does walk like a ship in a gale. And he observed that I am wanting a finger —" Jean Martin displayed a loss known to all, but for which a butcher would hardly be worthy of his calling, "and he asked me how it befell. Now if he has not a good heart in spite of his handsome face, then I am a mouse and no man."

"Let us hope that the Brother's merit rests on a surer basis than the claim of this cockroach to be a man. For in that case la Douroux is right and the Brother has small chance of heaven."

Henri Thomas delivered himself of this pronouncement and retired to that state of indifference, bordering on coma, in which he customarily sat lost in meditation of his cheeses. He was as pallid and pitted with holes as one of his own Gruyères, and as bald as la Bigotte's cabbages, an affliction which he concealed with a red nightcap pulled down behind his ears, though this was more for comfort than appearance.

"Cockroach! Cockroach!" The object of this stigma leaped into the air like a bouncing ball: "You, Henri Thomas, you are a species of camel and your children are pigs!"

Henri Thomas turned aside, shrugging. If he omitted to describe the children of Jean Martin, it was not from charity, he took pains to point out, but from a reason which, succinctly stated by him, drew from the rabbit-faced little butcher a shrill scream of rage. He was about to follow it with a cleaver aimed at Henri Thomas' imperturbable head, but was stayed in this murderous intent by a customer imperiously demanding a quarter of mutton, as she had been doing, she complained, without success and for several hours.

Suddenly the square was alive with customers, protesting that they had been there since earliest dawn, their presence unheeded, their needs ignored. Among them was a fat manservant with a moist pink face who had recently entered the service of the Comtesse de Guillemont, having formerly been in that of Madame la Marquise de Cançonnet, her mother, who had had the misfortune recently to die. He had discovered that the bread baked in a nearby monastery, and sold at Guillemont on market days, was of a superlative excellence, and he had won his mistress' gratitude by introducing this bread to the family table.

With his bread, he customarily brought back to the Château what gossip he was able to cull from the newsmongers of the market square, but today he had nothing to report. A new Brother had fetched the bread from the monastery, and the people in the market were so taken up with discussing him that he, Baptiste, had great difficulty in procuring his bread at all, and was unable to gather the least morsel or crumb of gossip to season it with.

ii

It was true. Father André had quitted the Monastery of Notre Dame des Prés and would not return.

He had been called to supervise the establishment of another Community near Paris, where he would serve as Prior; and his departure left behind him a blankness and vacancy suffered in some degree by all, but which in two hearts amounted to sickness and desolation. Michel concealed his grief from human eyes, laying it on the altar where it would not be without merit in the sight of God; but Marceline was unable to hide her distress or turn it to good account. She made it plain that to lose Father André was to lose everything: never again would she leave her stall, or don her harness, or fetch her bread to the market; and the Community was in despair of persuading her otherwise, although valuable time was wasted, and energies expended, and tempers riled to an unholy degree, in an unavailing effort to achieve that end. Brother Etienne pushed; Brother Antoine pulled; Brother Thomas applied stouter chastisement, with commendable vigor; all in vain. The lamentations of Marceline at length drove her three assailants from her stall, red of face, flustered of spirit, and in fear for their hearing; and after some deliberation it was decided to put an end to Marceline's undoubted sufferings by terminating her now apparently useless life.

Brother Michel got wind of these proceedings — which could hardly be kept secret, considering the principal party involved in them — and he asked that execution of the sentence be delayed until he tried what he could do to console the victim. A reprieve was accordingly granted.

He went to the stall of Marceline, and stroking the nose of the little ass, spoke reasonably to her, as to a comrade in sorrow: "All loved him, little one, but none as much as you and I. So now that he is gone, we must comfort each other. It was by your help, as well as his, that I came here, and for that reason you serve to recall him to me. If you, too, quit us, I shall be desolate indeed."

Marceline listened to his persuasions, turned them over in her mind; and at length agreed to continue her trips to market, but only on condition that she be escorted by Michel. She was very emphatic on this point; there was no doubting her meaning or disputing her will.

Except for the extra time it would necessitate, his lameness was no hindrance to undertaking these trips; and thus Michel found himself appointed to succeed Father André in one capacity, though he could never do so in another.

He set out upon his first trip in some trepidation. Since his arrival at the monastery, he had not once returned to Guillemont. It was impossible that he should traverse the road back to the village without experiencing an emotion none the less disturbing for being free from regret. His former home had become to him less a memory than a dream, removed from his present life by more than space and time, mythical as antiquity, distant as the stars. That he could re-enter it by walking a few miles of dusty road was as unthinkable as that, by the same slight effort, he should find himself present at the fall of Troy.

He was also in some anxiety lest he meet any he had formerly known, and this more on their account than his. He was armed in advance against such a contingency; to them it could come only as a shock. It was impossible that any at Guillemont should know where he was or what he had become; no doubt they believed him dead; if he lived in the memory of any of them, it must be as a ghost — to meet whom, in broad daylight, in the habit of a Religious, on the road to Guillemont, accompanied by an ass, could not fail to be disquieting in the extreme. He had no wish to inflict such distress on anyone.

But the chances of such an encounter were slight. The road from the monastery entered the village from the rear, and was little traveled by those from the Château, which lay to the front of Guillemont. Unless he stumbled upon some former acquaintance in the village square, which was hardly possible, he was not likely to do so elsewhere.

He met, in fact, no one he knew; and his return to the village failed to jar him as he anticipated. For though the locality was familiar, the world he now entered was not. This was wholly new and strange, foreign both to his past as to his present life, and full of an interest which left him no opportunity to commune with memory and ghosts.

He would have preferred to enter it unobtrusively, but was not permitted to do so. A being full of candor and curiosity — that is to say, a boy — heralded his appearance in the square by proclaiming loudly to all his most marked personal characteristic, in case any should overlook it. This introduction, though rude, was effective: it swept away strangeness and made aloofness impossible. He could hardly thereafter assume a dignity which had been stripped from him the moment he entered the square. The child's shrill announcement of his infirmity precipitated him into the heart of this world and its inhabitants, and made him, with a word, one of them.

They were a company as assorted as the produce on their counters. An old bent twig of a woman, a grandmother of grandmothers, thrust a withered brown face out from behind a citadel of cabbages and gave him a gratuitous compliment as he passed, by way of mitigating, he supposed, the child's frankness, which had not bothered him at all, though the compliment did. He could only reciprocate by commenting on the shining splendor of her cabbages; and truly, he had never seen their like. A rabbit who had miraculously been transformed into a butcher, and had lost a finger during the process of alchemy, treated him to an account of such sanguinary details as he himself withheld from the boy trotting beside him, who insistently demanded them. A mountain of a woman, with hands like boulders, offered for sale confections of such airy delicacy that it was impossible to imagine that they were of her creating, that these spider webs had been spun by this elephant. The mother of his small escort presided over a fruit stall at the entrance to the square. She was without doubt comely, and without doubt also one for whom the Pharisees would have had only condemnation and Our Lord only kindness.

These were the souls indeed for whom, singly as well as collectively, He had endured the whole torment of His sacred Passion. Nor had He held aloof from them during His ministry, but had mingled with them, supped and lodged with them, rejoiced and sorrowed with them; He had healed their sicknesses and forgiven their sins. And they in turn had thronged and pressed upon Him; they had followed Him fasting into the wilderness; they were His, and He theirs. But for the departure of Father André and the insistence of Marceline, Michel would not now be privileged to know these, whom Our Lord had known and loved; nor could he have come among them on any such basis of intimacy had he remained Seigneur de Guillemont — an accident of birth none of them suspected, and he himself had all but forgotten.

The appointment of Brother Michel to succeed Father André was by no means unanimously approved by the Community; and loudest of the dissenting voices was that of Brother Etienne. He had come finally to the conclusion that the frivolity of the crippled brother, like his infirmities, was incurable; in spite of such grievous chastisements inflicted on him by Providence for that end, he permitted this defect to go uncorrected; he did not take with sufficient seriousness the grim business of saving his soul. On the one hand, he talked of Our Lord with unpardonable familiarity, as of one with Whom he had sat at table, or had met by chance while walking in the garden, and who had gone so far as to communicate to Brother Michel His inmost thoughts; and on the other, he addressed the animals which were a necessary part of the communal equipment as his brothers and equals, thus transforming scandal into sacrilege. True, Brother Michel had gotten the balky she-ass into harness and restored her to action where all others had failed; but the faculty of persuasion which had effected this restoration was but another manifestation of that same weakness so conspicuous in the lame Brother; and although the ass was a creature of value, and in a Community vowed to Holy Poverty nothing of value should be lightly discarded, nevertheless Brother Etienne was not at all sure that the saving of the ass by such scandalous means as wheedling and cajolery was not by way of contributing to the ultimate loss of the soul of Brother Michel.

Between the skin of an ass and the soul of a Brother was there any comparison? Let the former be sacrificed, and promptly, if it means the saving of the latter. Brother Etienne saw the soul of Brother Michel as already *in extremis:* the devils hovered about it as vultures over the body of a dying man on the field of battle, awaiting only the victim's last breath to descend upon the carcass and demolish it utterly. What little life still lingered in the soul of Brother Michel would be promptly snuffed out, Brother Etienne foresaw, if subjected to the contamination of the market place. What the crippled Brother needed was discipline, more discipline, always discipline; and instead of this, he was now to be turned loose among such temptations as only a strong and tried soul could successfully withstand: in the market place he would encounter, he would perhaps speak to (Brother Etienne shuddered) women. The countenance of Brother Michel was comely, and his manner disarming; against these deceits it was necessary always to be on one's guard. He himself had been tempted by his first sight of the young Brother to feel for him a weakness which he took in hand at once and thoroughly mastered; but all did not see the need for this as he did. To send Brother Michel back into the world, so pleasing of feature and so untried of spirit, to permit him with these defects to mingle freely with the market women, and for no better reason than because a rebellious she-ass would go with no other — this, surely, was to invite the devil to do his worst. Brother Etienne groaned inwardly and put his fingers in his ears to shut out a hideous and unmistakable sound: in his imagination he heard already the death rattle of the soul of Brother Michel.

Brother Etienne considered it his duty to make these dangers known to Father Prior, who remained as unimpressed after hearing them as before concerning the impropriety of exposing Brother Michel to the temptations thus luridly represented to him. Father Prior had himself frequent occasion to pass through Guillemont on market days; he could not altogether repress a smile at the picture evoked by the fears of Brother Etienne, of Brother Michel doing battle with temptation as loosed upon him in the persons of *la mère* Bigotte, Berthe Masson, and the widow Douroux. As for the predatory Dubois, who desired nothing so much as to prove an irresistible temptation to all, Father Prior had no fear but that Brother Michel would emerge unscathed even from this encounter. He wished, indeed, that he might be present to witness the effect upon la Dubois when the eyes of Brother Michel met hers for the first time. He was willing to wager the monastery against the market place that it would not be the Brother who would be shaken by this impact, but that Dubois would be seized with the desire to crawl behind her counter, if she did not actually do so. Father Prior made it plain to Brother Etienne that he feared no more for Brother Michel than for Father André, in the market or anywhere; and he would watch with interest the effect, not of the market people upon Brother Michel, but of Brother Michel upon the market people.

If Brother Etienne failed to impress Father Prior with his misgivings, he had more success with certain of the Community, who unfortunately had no deciding voice in the matter. It developed that several of the brotherhood had been watching Brother Michel with sorrow and suspicion, convinced that he was going sadly astray in his spiritual life. Brother Thomas, it appeared, had been troubled for some time, not by the lame Brother's levity, but by his excessive indulgence in exterior and sensible devotion. He spent altogether too much time on his knees in the chapel. Did not Our Lord Himself discourage long prayers? Had Brother Michel never heard of the evils of spiritual gluttony?

Writers on these subjects were loud in their warning against this hindrance to true spirituality, this subtle impediment with which the devil would retard the progress of those who undertake to ascend the mount of Christian perfection. To this insidious temptation Brother Michel had fallen easy prey; these external manifestations of piety, these long prayers, this communicating daily, these hours in chapel (though it was conceded he did not neglect his duties) — all were further signs of that lack of interior discipline, that weakness of character deplored by Brother Etienne, of which the frivolity of Brother Michel was but another symptom.

He received Holy Communion daily; this could not but indicate great presumption: did he suppose himself a saint, that he so freely approached this august sacrament? Here was a sacred privilege reserved only for the holiest, the few; the mortified and detached; those whose hearts had been ruthlessly emptied of all loves and devotions save one, whereas it was plain that in the heart of Brother Michel a conflict of loves ran riot. He was bound to earth by subtle attachments too numerous to count, nor did he take the proper means to break them; he practiced no notable austerities; he took inordinate pleasure in created things, in trivialities as divergent and inconsequential as the beauties of nature, the beguiling ways of animals, the deceptive allurements of music and art: all subtle means employed by the devil to wean the heart from the pure love of God. He lacked simplicity and humility; he was guilty of great pride of intellect: to hear him talk, did not one know him to be a Brother, one would suppose him a priest. To make up for this want of essential interior discipline, he indulged himself in excessive pietistic practices, in sensible devotions incompatible with true spirituality. What were his confessors thinking of, that they had not long before undertaken to correct him in these errors?

This neglect Brother Etienne took it upon himself to rectify. He gathered a bouquet of these and other criticisms, and thrust them upon Brother Michel as he was making Marceline ready for market. Brother Etienne pointed out to Brother Michel that he offered these suggestions only in the spirit of helpfulness and for his good.

Brother Michel did not answer Brother Etienne, being too stunned by the fierceness and suddenness of this attack to do so; but he talked the matter over in some detail with Marceline on their way to market.

"Observe, Marceline: Brother Etienne has been in religion for more years than you or I have lived. In such matters he should know of what he speaks. He accuses me of subtle attachment; he is right. I have an attachment to Our Lord that must be subtle indeed, since none detect it who complain that I spend too much time with Him. If any has a right to object that my visits with Him are too frequent and too long, surely it is He; when He shall say to me, 'Michel, you weary Me; begone,' then I shall quit Him, but not before.

"But is it not worthy of note, Marceline, that His great courtesy forbids Him to complain that I fatigue Him, as I must often do with my dullness and importunities and distractions? Do we not find in His dealings with us a supreme example of *noblesse oblige,* which we would do well to imitate in our dealings with each other? Between Him and the holiest of men, what infinite distance intervenes, in comparison with which the distance separating the best and the worst of us is as nothing! And yet He, who has all right to scold and rebuke us in scathing terms for our good, speaks to us words only of kindness. Oh, Marceline, what sublime courtesy is here! None of us has attained so high a degree of spiritual perfection that we can afford to treat others with less consideration than He shows to us, who are all alike infinitely beneath Him.

"It appears also, *ma petite,* that we are not mortified and detached, and that we make no effort to correct this fault by the practice of salutary austerities. This criticism is justified; we are indeed far from the heroic asceticism practiced by some, for these extremes are quite beyond our attainments and even our aspiration. Here is a dark, dark road, Marceline; having trod it once, I freely own that I cannot of my own power retrace those steps. It may be the Brother has not walked this path, or that he is of stouter fiber than myself, as I willingly grant to be the case. But for me, Marceline, when I shall walk that way again, as I have little doubt but that I must, for it should be the prayer of all of us that He will raise His chalice to our lips, though we be unworthy of so great an honor — when that day comes, it must be for His glory, not my own; the manner therefore must be of His choosing, and not mine. And since it will be according to His will, then He will give me grace according to my need.

"Meanwhile, if we cannot be heroic, we can at least be courteous; if we may not aspire to be saints, let us be content to be gentlemen. Every gentleman is by no means a saint, but every saint must first be a gentleman. To discipline the tongue is an essential of Christian perfection; without it sanctity is not possible; and it is also, Marceline, the first rule of courtesy.

"But these are trivial matters compared with the grave peril in which we stand: the women of the market place, it seems, are likely to prove a source of fatal danger to us. Only the saints could face with impunity such temptations; we, who stand at the beginning of the spiritual way, should not be allowed to run these risks. Such is the opinion of the Brother.

"It has no doubt been your experience, Marceline, that life is not so much an interminable battle over a single issue as a series of tasks: we finish one that we may undertake another; we learn one lesson that we may proceed to the next. Our weakness does not permit us to accomplish these tasks to perfection; the best pages I have written are full of flaws, which it is not possible to eliminate altogether. Nevertheless, a craft once learned, as long as it is used, is not forgotten; a skill once acquired, while practiced, is not lost.

"It was formerly my privilege to love and to be loved by one so fair that I did not see how the Queen of Heaven herself could be more beautiful. To learn to live without her was like learning the art of lettering with the meager equipment at my disposal. Both I would have declared impossible; both, with the help of God, have been accomplished. And both are behind me, Marceline; I need not learn them, having once done so, a second time.

"It is not that I have ceased to love this lady: I would need to be a very monster, and inhuman, to lose or kill my love for one so lovable. I shall love her till I die — yes, and through eternity, because the love I have for her is of that sort which God not only permits, but enjoins upon us, and wills shall last forever. It is a love which is all joy and peace; which desires only her good and her happiness wherever God decrees that she shall find it. I remember her without pain, and with the deepest gratitude that my recollection of her is wholly beautiful, and free from any matter for regret; and should it be a part of God's merciful design that I see and speak to her again in this life, I have no doubt but that I would do so with joy only, and without fear. Could the Brother hear us say this, he would cry presumption; but God, who has wrought this miracle, knows that I speak the truth.

"But the Brother is hardly to be blamed for thinking us in this danger, Marceline. Since he could not know the lady of whom I speak, he is not aware that all others are to her as dried plums to a nectarine. When one has been so fed on the fruit of heaven that one has ceased to desire nectarines, it is not possible that one should fall upon and devour dried plums.

"And one must be very hungry indeed, or of a perverted palate, to relish dried plums in any case. It is a common belief that we in religion suffer continually this hunger; those who subscribe to this belief will not be persuaded otherwise. They are right to this extent: the hunger of the heart is truly for love; but they do not know that the love of heaven — the love of God — stays this hunger as no love on earth can do. Why else do we seek it, since none compels us, except for a joy and beauty that are not to be found elsewhere? By this love the heart is more than satisfied: it is sated; it is filled so to overflowing that it can hardly endure the burden of this weight of love thrust upon it, beneath which it all but bursts asunder.

"For the heart is a vessel of finite capacity, and this love is infinite. Poured into the heart, it floods and overflows it as the sea overflows a hole dug in the sand; and the heart so filled regrets only its own smallness, its own poor capacity to receive; it longs to become a greater vessel, a deeper want and emptiness, that it may contain more of this flood of beauty, of passion, that engulfs it. I say passion, Marceline, because *passion* is suffering; and this love is a suffering indeed, from our very inability to receive it in all its entirety. But how different from the passion of the love of earth! This pain is wholly beautiful; it is the burning of a white radiance and flame, a thousand times more consuming and intense than the others, which is but an angry smoldering compared with it. The heart filled with this love desires no other; it has room for no other; henceforward all loves exist in it, and by it are transfigured and exalted.

"Of himself, none has the power to acquire this love and to forego the other. It is not our virtue, but the gift of God; and should He for any reason withdraw it, I tremble to think in what dire case we should be. Then indeed the Brother would have good cause to fear. There are some who by nature are able to subsist on a meager diet of dried plums, and be content; there are others in whom this hunger for love is so deep and fierce that they must feast at a banquet, or fall into madness and vice. For such as these dried plums will never suffice; and if so be they are sworn to stay their hunger with the love of heaven alone, it is they above all others who most need the gift of God.

"For while it is true beyond question that this love of heaven rewards and satisfies the heart, filling it with riches of joy and beauty and delight as no love of earth can ever do, it is likewise true that this love may not be enjoyed without cost: for so God has ordered it. But the cost, far from tempting us to part with it, convinces us rather of its exalted worth. A man will permit trash to be stolen from him without a struggle, but a treasure beyond price he will defend with his life. And if he must fight to keep it, and is wounded in the encounter, he regards his hurts as of little moment, provided only he has beaten off the thief, and preserved his treasure from harm.

"So it is with this heavenly treasure, this gift of love, which God has given us: how little would we esteem it, if to keep it cost us nothing! Because of the cost, we know that it is not our virtue, but His gift; because of the cost, we are reminded into how hideous a state we should fall, did He withdraw it from us; because of the cost, we are on our knees daily, beseeching Him for grace to preserve and defend it to the end; because of the cost, we value it and cherish it the more.

"The Brother says that it is a presumption in us to communicate daily; but did we not do so, his fears for us in this regard might well be justified. For this sweet privilege is not so much a reward as a necessary help. All may not need this help as we do, Marceline; but without it, I fail to see how we could hope to preserve this treasure of which I have been speaking. But with this grace continually renewed, the defense is more than adequate to the danger: the Brother need not fear that we shall light a candle in full day.

"In these many strokes laid on us by the good Brother's tongue, there was one which took the sting out of all the rest. I do not believe that the Brother meant that it should do so, but intended it rather as a rebuke to our pride. It seems that we concern ourselves with matters above our station. The Brother said — did you hear, Marceline? — that if he did not know otherwise, from our manner and speech, he would suppose us to be a priest.

"Now here are words to cherish and to carry in the heart! Though all else he said was bitter, this was sweet. Like honey in a strong brew, it made palatable the whole."

iii

Brother Michel indulged himself in another devotional extravagance which would have caused Brother Etienne an apoplexy had he known of it: as Brother Michel took good care he should not. There was no way, indeed, in which Brother Etienne could have discovered it, unless Marceline had advised him of her companion's aberration, or Michel himself had made a confidant of Brother Etienne, both of which were alike impossible. Had Brother Etienne got wind of it, he would no longer have feared the worst: he would have been convinced that Brother Michel's presumption had handed his soul over to the devil at last, and now there was no getting it back.

For Brother Michel, on his way to market, sang Mass.

Unable to sing it at the altar, he did so here instead. What was there to prevent? One need not be an ordained priest to learn the prayers of Mass, as, indeed, he had already done; there was no rule of Canon Law to prevent his reciting or chanting them, did opportunity permit; and here on the road to Guillemont was opportunity ready made. He chanted the parts appointed and recited the rest, as for High Mass, supplying his own responses, since his only companion was unable to cooperate with him in this respect; and when he reached the consecration, he would stand for some moments in silent adoration, uniting himself in spirit with the Holy Sacrifice, wherever at that moment it was being offered, before proceeding on his way. He made Father André the model of his chanting, and strove always for greater perfection, that his offering, poor substitute though it was, might none the less be for the honor and glory of God.

Thus Michel put into effect his self-imposed task of learning Mass as thoroughly as if he had been a priest.

Marceline displayed a discretion unusual in women: she kept silence concerning this practice of her escort, which, had it reached certain ears, would have brought a new burst of criticism upon his head. Not that Marceline was always silent; but however loud and prolonged her vociferations in other matters, she did not betray the secret of Brother Michel.

She had, indeed, a grievance which she by no means kept to herself: she decided as winter approached that she no longer wished to go to market, with Michel or anyone. When he went to her stall to make her ready, she undertook to persuade him, with that eloquence for which her kind are notorious, that today was not the day for taking bread to market: tomorrow — the day after — next week — any day, Marceline insisted, but not today. There was a terrible rumpus and to-do; her protestations shook the stable like an earthquake; fifty donkeys, all suffering the extremes of torture, could hardly have produced such racket. Then suddenly the uproar would subside, and Michel and Marceline would emerge in all tranquillity, the latter innocent of mien and swinging her panniers with a docility truly flirtatious.

They halted at the kitchen for the bread, which was loaded into the panniers of Marceline by Brother Joseph and Brother Etienne.

"How is it you work such miracles?" asked Brother Joseph. The remonstrances of Marceline had not failed to reach his ears, as they must have reached all ears, thought Michel, in heaven and on earth. "This time it seemed certain she must win. I did not look for you to appear at all."

Brother Etienne said nothing. He dumped his armful of loaves into the basket with a thud, and dusted his hands vigorously, although on the glazed surfaces of the bread there was no trace of flour. Turning on his heel, he tramped back toward the kitchen. He took pains to avoid the glance of Brother Michel, who addressed his reply to the rigid back of Brother Etienne, no less than to Brother Joseph.

"Marceline has discovered a truth all do not know, though I fail to see how it can escape them: I am an ass in monk's clothing. For this reason she is unable to deceive me. A man might be taken in by her subtleties, but not another donkey. Is it not so, my little one?"

The door of the kitchen shut behind Brother Etienne with an unmonastic bang. Accompanying this reverberation, Michel detected the echo of a snort. Marceline agreed that it was so, and they set out, surrounded by a cloud of that delectable and pungent fragrance peculiar to freshly baked loaves, which rose and hung over the panniers of Marceline like incense.

Out of sight of the monastery, Michel began his Mass:

"In nomine Patris, et Filii, et Spiritus Sancti. Amen."

It was a bleak, raw day. A hard wind drove up from the sea, relentless and penetrating. It whipped his skirts about him and sent sand and dust from the road stinging against his face. The sky was dark with clouds; they lay heaped against each other in blue-black ridges and mounds, and concealed a hidden brilliance which streamed from behind them in pale ribbons to the slate-gray surface of the water. Charging up the hill of Guillemont like a troop of horses, this wind would make sport of the market people, though it could not dislodge them. The cheeks of Paulette Dubois would be more than ever like scrubbed apples; the nose of *la mère* Bigotte would be a pinched redness in the sere brown parchment of her face; from that of the little butcher a drop of moisture would hang trembling, and water gathering in his eyes reddened by the smart of the wind, would stream down his pallid cheeks; the mammoth pastry vendor would be so wrapped in petticoats and shawls that what little resemblance she had ever borne to a woman would be lost in this mountain of upholstery; and each would have his brazier of glowing charcoal, at which to warm his frozen hands and feet. Only the children would be unaffected by the wind, regarding it rather as a comrade and ally in sport than an enemy.

On each trip, Michel was greeted by fresh cohorts of these. Where there had originally been but a single free lance, there was now an army. Jeannot made known his discovery to all the Dubois, who were a regiment in themselves; and the story of the lame Brother, who had been deprived of his hand by a wicked boar, was carried like blown seeds in all directions, and lodged simultaneously in the hearts of children for miles around.

They reminded each other: "See, now, it is the day of Frère Mich'." They gathered to watch for him from a chosen point in the road; at sight of him they set up a shout, and raced to meet him in a body. On the first of these occasions, Michel, Marceline, and the bread were all but tumbled together in the dust of the road by the fury of this onslaught.

"A ride, Frère Mich'! A ride, a ride! I shall have first turn! — No, me! I saw him first! — Me, me! I was here first! — it is my turn first! I knew him before any of you! — No, mine! — Mine! — Mine!"

"None shall ride, if you behave thus like wolves and tigers. Marceline loves children, as do I; but we have no love for wild beasts, who were intended by God to be boys and girls, but have permitted themselves to be changed by some wicked sorcerer into savage animals. I see one who resembles a boy, and perhaps he is one in truth, for he has not shouted and demanded to ride first, and for that reason he shall do so. And the rest of you shall follow in turn, if you show me by your manners that you are not beasts from the forest, but truly boys and girls."

On the edge of the crowd stood a towheaded waif in a soiled blue shift. His eyes were solemn and his face incredibly dirty and his nose needed an attention which neither he nor anyone else thought to give it. Michel lifted the child onto the back of Marceline and paused to repair this oversight. He realized, however, that he would not be able to perform a like service impartially for all who required it, or he should never arrive at market.

"*Voilà.* So we go!" He roused Marceline from the nap to

which she considered herself entitled at every interruption, and they continued on their way. Jeannot clung to Michel's sleeve, as one who had a prior claim on him, and the others trotted alongside in a swarm. Michel addressed them collectively: "Our Lord was once a child, like all of you. None could have told Him from other children, except we may be sure He was always gentle of speech and courteous to all. If He had desired to ride on Marceline, how, think you, would He have asked it? You shall tell me, and who answers most nearly as He might have done, shall have the next ride."

The invasion had grown more orderly of late, but nothing could subdue the shrill insistence of their greeting.

"A ride, Frère Mich'! *S'il vous plaît,* Frère Mich'! A ride, a ride!"

They clustered round him, jumping up and down in their eagerness; they hugged his knees and clung to his skirts. Jeannot possessed himself of the sleeve which he now regarded as his property, and which was already worn thin by so much clutching.

"A ride, *mes petits choux?*" Michel looked into the faces turned up to him, which indeed resembled the cabbages of *la mère* Bigotte, come to life and filled with anticipation and eagerness. He effected to consider, as if hearing the request for the first time: "A ride? Is it possible that you desire a ride? Well — perhaps it may be arranged. Which do you prefer, the lame donkey or the sound one?"

There was a shrill burst of mirth at this, as if Michel had delivered himself of the witticism of the ages. The stipulation had become necessary, however: the number of passengers had so increased that there was no longer any chance of accommodating them all before reaching the village. This difficulty he solved by apportioning the burden both to himself and Marceline; and thus all were satisfied.

Usually the procession of Brother, children, and donkey continued tranquilly along the road and up the hill, meeting none but villagers and peasantry on their way to market or to work in the vineyard and fields, accompanied by the usual assortment of donkeys, geese, and goats; but today there was a ruder interruption. Michel was about to lift Marceline's first passenger onto her back, when a group on horseback was upon them.

It was a hunt, bound for the forest, both men and women. They came at a gallop, paying no heed to the children in their way. These Michel herded off the road barely in time to save himself and them from injury. The slumbering Marceline remained where she was, immovable; the riders swerved and divided, not without hostile comment, to avoid piling up over the imperturbable beast, planted with her baskets like a monument to Humility in their path. Half of them galloped by so close to Michel that he and the children were in danger from the horses' hoofs. Enraged by this carelessness, he looked up in fury, and directly into a face he had formerly known well.

He bowed gravely. The hunt galloped past, and was soon a cloud of dust in the distance, leaving himself, and the children, and Marceline with her bread sleeping in the middle of the road, unmoved by the disturbance. The encounter, however, had not passed unnoticed by his companions, who were of that species of animal that can be relied on to notice everything.

"What a beautiful lady, Frère Mich'."

"Yes. Was she not?"

"You bowed to her, Frère Mich'. Do you know her?"

"I bowed to her as befitting her rank. Surely she is a Countess, at the very least."

"But, Frère Mich', she knows you! She smiled at you!"

"Oh, I think not."

"But yes, Frère Mich' — I saw! We all saw!"

"If she smiled, it is because I am a funny Brother, and you are all my little ones. She loves children, I am sure, and perhaps has many of her own. Let us hope so. There is another Lady, even more beautiful, and all the children in the world are hers, great and small, and she will always smile at us, and we must never forget her. She rode once, not on a fine horse, but on a little ass like Marceline — as you shall ride now, if Marceline can be roused from her dreams. Toto shall ride first, since he has been sick, and this is his first ride in many days."

Michel was guilty of a slight equivocation in his reply to the children: she had indeed bowed to him, and there was no mistaking the recognition that flamed in her face. And not recognition only, but more, very much more.

His glance had rested on hers for the briefest possible moment, but long enough to show him what filled him with dismay: a fierce want and hunger, a craving unsatisfied, an emptiness and longing, transformed instantly at sight of him to astonished eagerness, to rapture and delight.

Bene fundata est
supra firmam petram

8. Sand and Rock

i

Paul was in a quandary.

Fortune, in her dealings with him, was showing herself perverse. If she did not turn her back on him to the extent of withdrawing her favors altogether, she plagued him by adding such a complication of difficulties as prevented him from enjoying her benefits in peace.

He found himself much in the position of a man who has married two wives, and must keep each wife secret from the other and himself beyond the reach of the law: a situation, in short, not without its embarrassments.

Anne demanded that he install her, her children, and her parents at Guillemont. To consent to this demand was out of the question; but he was so deeply involved with her that to refuse it was likewise impossible.

Anne was no longer merely plump; she had grown decidedly stout. This tendency, inherited from her father, had overtaken her all at once. With him she shared another attribute even less pleasing: she was untidy to a degree a daughter of the soil could hardly have equaled. Her shortcomings in this respect caused her no uneasiness or shame, and for that reason she made no effort to correct them. This was all part of the informality which had first attracted Paul to Brissac, but he began to perceive that it could be carried too far.

Anne, in a perpetual *déshabille,* her bodice undone and her hair in disarray, heavy-eyed and disheveled at noon, dandling a baby that reeked of sour milk, was neither attractive nor inspiring. At Brissac, however, she was in harmony with her surroundings, and therefore tolerable. But at Guillemont — !

The imagination of Paul quailed before the impossible task of representing Anne as sharing with Louise the post of mistress of his father's magnificent estate.

Nor was it Anne's desire that he should tax his imagination to this extent? Had she not given him two fat sons already? And now a third was on the way. She had all the burdens of motherhood but none of the privileges of a wife. She had borne the burdens uncomplainingly and now surely it was time that she enjoy the position to which her motherhood entitled her, which was no more than her due. Let Paul divorce his wife and marry her.

"It was my impression," said Paul, "that you did not believe in marriage."

"Ah, but" — she nestled up to him, sighing, "to be Comtesse de Guillemont! And our sons! Is it not right, my Paulot, that they should have a real father?"

"I have told you a hundred times," said Paul, "that I will adopt them. There is plenty of time."

"And Louise is always in love with your brother. If you divorce her, she can marry him. Then Armand Pitou can marry us, and I shall be Madame la Comtesse."

"Louise does not know where my brother is. Nor do I. Nor does anyone."

Anne shrugged: "Once she is free, she will find him, soon enough. It may be she knows, and has not told you." She snuggled yet closer to him. "Soon there will be another *bébé,* Paul, and I would like this *accouchement* to be at the Château. For this time it will be winter, and you see how cold and wretched it is here, with the windows gone and the hangings full of holes."

The dilemma of Paul was very serious indeed, for both women were essential to him, and each was a thorn in his flesh. Dull, common, even offensive as she sometimes was, Anne nevertheless satisfied him as no woman had ever done. He was bored with her; he despised her; but emotionally and physically he needed her, as, socially, and for the sake of his pride, he needed Louise.

Since the death of his father, Louise had grown into her position rapidly; she filled it now with ease and brilliance. The Château, for so long a tomb, had become the scene of unending festivities, presided over by a mistress who shone and sparkled like highly polished metal. Madame la Comtesse extended to her guests a hospitality lavish but exclusive: sumptuous, elegant, in perfect taste. There were banquets; there were balls; there were hunts. The affairs of the Château were conducted with faultless economy, for Paul had the gift of management, as had Louise. The tradition of Monseigneur the late Count was continued. Guillemont shone with a splendor which shed glory on its incumbents, the young Count and his brilliant and beautiful wife.

All this was necessary to his self-respect, as Anne was necessary to his comfort. He needed ease, relaxation, a letting down of restraints; and he found them at Brissac. But he also needed something to be proud of; and here he looked to his wife and estate. They made for his honor in the sight of others, and his esteem in his own eyes; without them, he would have fallen to the level of a de Brissac; and although the prospect of such a deterioration appalled him, he realized that of himself he would have been incapable of avoiding it. Lacking the brilliance of Louise and the magnificence of his property to minister to his satisfaction and feed his pride, he would have found himself all too readily in Papa Brissac's spotted dressing gown and run-down shoes, encased in lard, and suffering continually from gas and the gout.

He had, in fact, put on weight alarmingly: his jaw line was no longer visible and there was a roll of flesh at the back of his neck. He noticed also a coarsening of the skin, an increasing scantiness of hair, which filled him with dismay. These were signs of middle age, and Paul was not yet thirty. Such unwelcome manifestations goaded him also in the direction of greater fastidiousness. He knew that Louise regarded with amused contempt his efforts to disguise his increasing girth, while pretending that there was no increase to conceal.

It was thus manifestly impossible to install Anne and her children at Guillemont, even had there been question only of these; but with Anne, he would have to take also Mama and Papa, Armand Pitou the ex-priest, and the whole company of hangers-on in whose doctrines he had found relief, but with whom he did not propose to be identified, much less burdened, for the rest of his life.

Anne wheedled and cajoled; she nagged and scolded; she wept and stormed; she threatened violence to Paul and to herself; she predicted her death in her approaching confinement, and this would be the fault of Paul, who forced her to undergo the ordeal in this barn, this stable, fit only for cows and pigs. But Paul remained unimpressed by her cajoleries and tears, her threats and predictions of disaster, especially since she had undergone the ordeal on the previous occasions with such ease as to deprive these prophecies of their weight. In other matters perhaps too amenable to persuasion, Paul here remained adamant: he could not and would not have her and hers at Guillemont.

In the end, however, she had her way. She was moved to Guillemont with her parents, her children, Armand Pitou, and the rest. They took over a wing of the Château and there established themselves, in ample time to assure Anne's safety in her confinement, and their comfort through the winter. The crumbling manor at Brissac was abandoned to bats, wind, and decay.

Paul in his turn raged and stormed, but he could do nothing to prevent; for this transmigration was effected, at the insistence not of Anne, but of Louise.

Paul had an uneasy suspicion that Louise contrived this *déménagement* — this farce, this burlesque — for his humiliation, to make him appear ludicrous in the eyes of those whose good opinion he valued, and strove to retain at all costs; and he was right.

It was her purpose to wound Paul as deeply as possible in his most vulnerable spot, his vanity. To this end she sharpened on the whetstone of malice a wit and a tongue already sufficiently keen. She seized every possible opportunity to taunt and annoy him, and these opportunities increased as his hair thinned and his waistline thickened. From these encounters he emerged smarting and defeated, and Louise triumphant and unscathed. He was the more easily worsted in that his only possible defense would have been a counterattack. He desisted, not from chivalry, but because he could find no objective against which to proceed. He retreated in the face of these assaults to a shelter which did not fail him, and where he found ready healing for these hurts to his vanity. The brilliant malice of Louise made the dullness of Anne seem attractive, and her slovenliness endurable.

But these were wounds of the surface only: pinpricks, nothings. They made Paul wince, but they injured him in no vital spot. For this reason they did not satisfy Louise, who sought an opportunity to inflict on her husband a mortal wound, to injure him as deeply, as incurably, as he had injured her.

To the vow she had made on the night of the old Count's death, that she would not rest until she found Michel, she had since added another: equally, she would not rest, until she had avenged herself, and Michel, on Paul.

The dying words of the old Count had destroyed, with one stroke, the fictitious explanation of Michel's disappearance which had been served to Louise as the truth, and which she had been guileless enough to believe. Those words left her shaken, stunned; knowing that what she had been told was false, but ignorant what the truth was. They dispelled a myth, but replaced it with no facts. She set to work in secret, picking up a thread here, another there; untangling, sorting, arranging; weaving at length another explanation which exactly, she believed, reproduced the truth.

This explanation approached the truth, but still fell short of it. For only second sight could have revealed to her the heart of the matter: the warning Paul had withheld from Michel; and this gift of clairvoyance was denied her.

But the picture, as she reconstructed it, though lacking this detail, nevertheless represented Paul in such light as to fill her with a loathing and contempt for him that could hardly have been greater had her knowledge of his guilt been complete.

For he had lied to her. He had distorted and misrepresented the facts. He knew that, had she so much as suspected what had befallen Michel, neither fire nor floods, nor ice nor snow, nor anything short of death, could have kept her from him. For this reason he made light of Michel's injuries, representing them as of no consequence. He suffered her to be kept by a trifling ailment from Michel in his long agony. He allowed her to believe that Michel, recovered, had left of his own volition, because he had ceased to love her and wished to become a monk.

Now she knew that this was not so. The knowledge was fire and poison, it was bitterness and anguish; but it was also the source of a fierce, hidden joy.

Michel had been done almost to death by the boar. It was a miracle that he lived. He was crippled, and he had lost a hand. Revolted by these defects, his father had dismissed him from Guillemont. Paul had connived at this outrage, seeing in it a chance to better himself; at least, he had done nothing to prevent. By such abominable means he had possessed himself of what was rightfully Michel's — herself, the title, and estate. Of Michel, nothing had since been heard.

This was the outline, as she pieced it together with remarkable accuracy from the scraps of information she was able to gather. But it was an outline merely. There were great gaps in her knowledge, and these she filled in with her imagination.

Where Michel now was, what precisely had befallen him, she could not know; but she could be certain of one thing: he loved her. He would love her always. His love would not waver, or vary, as hers would not. She hugged this knowledge to her heart, and with it nourished her otherwise desolate life.

His injuries were in themselves an explanation of his silence. Maimed, he would not hold her to marriage with him. He would not even wish that she should know what had happened. Without doubt, too, they had lied to him, as to her, telling him that Paul had revived his suit, and that she had listened. This would be all of a piece with the despicable falsehoods woven to separate her from Michel; and since Michel knew that in her folly she had listened once to Paul, what reason would he have to suppose that she had not done so again?

Thus the mists of falsehood rolled away, and the truth was made plain, damning Paul, exonerating Michel, clothing Michel, indeed, with a new beauty, and adding to her love an unendurable intensity, born of her understanding of his pain and his loss. To her knowledge nothing was wanting, save where and how to find him.

This need was now her whole life.

Her first impulse was to set out herself, at once, on foot, where — it did not matter, so long as she converted into action this need which possessed her. But to do this was not only impossible; it was absurd and impractical as well. Such a measure would defeat the purpose of her search. She must be patient. She must wait, she must plan, she must think. Her search must have order and method. She must be secret, and cunning, and determined. None must suspect what she had undertaken, until she and Michel were again united. Then let happen what would: nothing could any longer keep them apart.

There was a sense in which she had already found him. His presence filled her life now as it had in the days when she waited for him at Cançonnet, lending an indifferent attention to Paul, while her heart beat for Michel, ticking off the seconds till the hour of his return. That he should cease to fill her life, it was necessary only that he cease to love her; and when she was told that this was so, and the monstrous report was corroborated by his silence, his absence, his otherwise inexplicable departure, with fierce strength she thrust even his memory from her. Where a light had been that was Michel, and the certainty of his love, all was now darkness and desolation: a stark hunger, a raging want.

At Guillemont, all things cried of Michel, but she was deaf. His image stood all about her, but she was blind. Resolutely she denied herself the pain and joy of memory, for this sorrow is a consolation only where there has been love. A Michel who could cease to love her was a negation. There was, therefore, nothing to remember. There was no Michel.

But now she knew the truth: Michel had not ceased to love her; he loved her still. She flung wide the door behind which she had barred her memory, and all was again Michel.

The Château, the grounds, were filled with his presence. Surely he was coming down the walk; he was in the next room; to turn the corner would be to meet him. She heard his words, his laughter. Looking up quickly, she was certain that she saw him, before the impression vanished, and she knew that her heart and her memory had again tricked her vision. Like an invisible companion of childhood, he was nearer and more real than the creatures of flesh and blood who surrounded her.

But this return of Michel to her memory by no means alleviated her need of him, but rather increased it. Her hunger was not stayed by this substitution, which served only to whet it. To feel him so close that she had but to extend her hand to touch him, and doing so, to find only an absence; to hear him speak, and, listening, find only silence — this could be endured in the case of one dead, of whom on earth only memory remained; but Michel lived. Others, indifferent to him, saw and spoke to him daily; while she, in her desperate want, had only this echo, this dream. Her days marched by, each an emptiness that no memory could fill.

And if her need of him was so fierce and insatiable, what of his need for her? To attempt to answer this question was to invite madness. Such details of the accident and its consequences as flashed through her mind, evoked by her imagination and supplementing her knowledge, she thrust from her as not to be endured. Their effect, however, was to lash her into a fury of impatience. Desperately as she needed him, his need of her was inconceivably more terrible. Therefore, she must lose no time. She must hurry, hurry. She must find Michel.

But where? How?

And to this there was no answer. She did not know where; she did not know how. She did not know what to do.

Frenzied by the need for action, she could not act. She must wait, wait, for action substituting hope, reminding herself that sooner or later she would surely hear some word, however casual, she would find some clue, however slight, that would lead to the discovery of Michel.

But she could not wait in idleness. She must do something, or lose reason. She filled the Château with guests; she entertained them with banquets and balls, carnivals and hunts. This satisfied to some extent her terrible restlessness, and served at the same time a deeper purpose. She assembled these guests from all France, from the relatives and friends of her parents and his: some among them might conceivably have heard rumors of the whereabouts of Michel. This was as near as she could come to instituting a search. She taxed her memory to recall obscure cousins in distant parts, far removed alike in consanguinity and space, who would be pleased to visit Guillemont: from one of these she might ultimately hear that Michel had passed that way. From all this feverish and brilliant hospitality she earned a renown, a prestige, that a duchess might have envied. But for this she cared nothing, since it brought her no nearer Michel.

It is the obvious which is overlooked, the visible which remains unseen. Gossip concerns herself with falsehood, but ignores truth when there is no scandal attached to it. Had Michel fled from the sight of men, seeking to conceal himself in those distant parts where Louise sought news of him, her inquiries would without doubt have brought him to light; but beneath the very shadow of Guillemont his presence remained unsuspected, as effectively hidden as the lost object one seeks in dusty cupboards and dark corners, but fails to find because it is on a table in plain sight.

Meanwhile she gave herself to another purpose which had the advantage of being easier of accomplishment. She determined to make Paul suffer for the wrong he had done Michel and her. She regretted that this must fall something short of her desire, since Paul had no love that she could kill or wound: no love, that is, but himself. And so impenetrable was the armor of his self-esteem that she had little hope of piercing it with a mortal thrust. She wished to level his pride to the earth, to bring it to depths from which it could not hope to rise. And opportunity, which had refused to assist her in her search for Michel by so much as a tap on the door, now knocked, hammered, pounded.

It was impossible that Louise should have remained in ignorance of Paul's connections at Brissac. She was kept informed of developments by a system of domestic espionage both thorough and exact. Marianne, her *femme de chambre,* had a tongue loquacious but not inaccurate. Dressing her mistress' hair, she treated Louise to an unsavory account of Monseigneur's supposedly clandestine alliance that did not far overreach the truth. These relations she punctuated with *ohs* and *ahs,* with vigorous strokes of the brush through Madame's magnificent shining locks.

Louise did not check these narrations, seeing a use to which they could be put.

"And the *children!*" Marianne rolled her eyes upward with an expression more eloquent than any expletive. "To approach them is a penance. They are little pigs. But what would you?" She shrugged. "At Brissac, all are pigs."

Louise turned matters over in her mind, arrived at a decision, and approached Paul.

"You have now," she said, "how many children, Paul?"

The face of Paul flamed, and not his face only, but his neck, his ears, his very scalp. It was the first time she had openly referred to his liaison and its fruits. He knew that she could not fail to be aware of the circumstances, but it was part of her indifference to him that she ignored them. She had not enough regard for him to feel jealousy; she was, he gathered, even relieved that another took a large share of the burden of his attentions from herself. From her insinuations, he could not doubt that she knew all there was to know; from her exact words, he might have supposed that she knew nothing. This forthright question took him off guard. Evasion was not possible. He could only flush crimson, which annoyed him, and answer with the truth, which in any case she must know.

"Two," he said curtly. "Why do you ask?"

"And a third," she continued, "in anticipation: is it not so?"

"Louise!" His flush took on the deeper tinge of anger. "Why must you be so crude?"

"Crude? I?" Her eyes widened; he lowered his before them. "I am crude, merely to speak of what you do? If you wish to be spared the pain of my crude remarks, why do you merit them? I have refrained from alluding to the subject before, not to spare your feelings, but to save my own. The matter bores me. In a life already full of *ennui,* I wish to avoid unnecessary torture of that sort. I ask now, because it occurs to me that I have a duty which I have so far neglected. I assure you it gives me no pleasure, not even to cause you this embarrassment, which, knowing you, I did not anticipate. These children are your heirs: at least, I suppose you will take steps to make them so."

"In due course," said Paul stiffly.

"It has come to my attention that they are not receiving the care and attention which, as your heirs, they deserve. This I can give them, and I propose to do so. I desire that you bring them here."

He felt himself break out in a cold moisture.

"Here? To Guillemont? To the Château?"

"But, of course, to Guillemont. Why not?"

"But that is absurd. Impossible."

"Impossible? Why?"

"I cannot separate them from their mother."

"I do not intend that you shall. Bring her also. It is what I wish. You cannot very well bring the third child without her, since it is not yet born."

"Her parents will not permit."

"Let them come too. There is room at Guillemont for an army. We will establish them in the west wing, and while I see that the education of the children is such as befits your sons, you will be spared those journeys to Brissac, which, though a proof of devotion, you must nevertheless have found very tiring."

Thus Anne had her way and Louise her revenge. Brissac was installed at Guillemont, and the humiliation of Paul was complete.

Anne had her way, but it was a way which she promptly and bitterly regretted. In demanding that Paul remove her to Guillemont, she failed to foresee what position she would necessarily occupy there. Paul would not divorce his wife, he would not make Anne Countess of Guillemont. He would take her and hers there to live, and with that she must be content.

Within two weeks she would have given anything to be able to undo this move which she supposed to be her work, the result of her persuasions. At Guillemont she expected to better herself; to have a certain authority; to order servants about and to be obeyed. She found herself in a situation more abject and contemptible than that of the scullery maids and stable boys; for their position, though one of servitude, was at least in its degree honorable, while hers was not.

She was openly despised, she was treated like dirt, by this red-haired vixen, Paul's wife, who saw to it that nothing should be wanting to make her comfortable in body and miserable in every other way.

Her third child was a son also. Louise took him from her at once, making it plain that the mother's role in regard to him was to be that of wet nurse only. Anne stormed and sulked; she might as well have tried to change the wind or the seasons, as to change Louise.

"I shall die!" she wailed. "I shall become sick! I shall have no milk for him, and then, he will die, too!"

"Do not deceive yourself," said Louise. "I assure you, you deceive no one else. You are distressed, not because I take the child, but because you cannot have your own way. It is a common ill and seldom fatal. I have no fear that it will prove so in your case — not, at least, while your present appetite continues. But should you die as you predict, the loss will not be irreparable. On an estate of this size, there is always an available wet nurse."

Anne screamed with rage.

"These scenes are intolerable," declared Louise. "I do not propose to be annoyed by them. You neglected your children shamefully while you had the care of them. Your love is a pretense and your tears are for effect. Margot, the gardener's wife, has recently borne twins. Yesterday one of them died. If you do not control yourself, and in future hold your peace, I shall not wait for you to die also, but will send your son to Margot at once."

No; the life of Anne at Guillemont was not what she had anticipated, when she demanded to be taken there. She was, however, the only one from Brissac to regret the move. The others profited from it to such an extent that nothing could have persuaded them to return to their former quarters at Brissac — certainly no such paltry consideration as the unhappiness of one of their number.

Chief of those to benefit from the move was Armand Pitou, the young ex-priest with the gift of eloquence and the hands like Michel's.

He made himself thoroughly at home.

The library was his especial province. He was preparing a work which should finally destroy the myth of the Real Presence in the Eucharist, and as a consequence of this, abolish the superstitious practice of Mass. To this end he had dedicated his life. That God had approved it was beyond question. He had already found a printer, pledged to publish and disseminate the work when finished; and now here, at Guillemont, was further evidence of the divine approbation. The library was filled with ecclesiastical writings whose gross superstitions and manifest departures from Truth had but to be pointed out to be recognized, deplored, and abandoned.

He installed himself at the great oak table, elaborately carved and inlaid, which was one of the chief treasures of the Château. Barricaded behind Henri de Guillemont's priceless volumes, whose margins he ruthlessly annotated, he dashed off page after page of script destined to end the tyrannous rule of the Church of Rome on earth.

In the evening he preached to those, convinced or merely curious, who came to hear him. His reputation steadily increased. He trained disciples and sent them out to preach in neighboring villages. Sometimes he undertook these pilgrimages himself, returning with triumphant recitals of success: of souls won from Satan and bondage, to liberty and Truth.

Louise, who did not believe in God, was more contemptuous of the new faith than the old.

She listened indifferently to a few of Armand's discourses, but soon found that they bored her. For these new teachings she had only scorn. They destroyed the beauty of the old faith, and put nothing in its place. For the religion of her childhood she could still feel a sort of bitter regret. She looked back with wistful longing on the days, all golden and happy, when she had been credulous and trusting, when she had believed in God and heaven, in the saints and answered prayer. The old faith was a deception, but it was beautiful; it was a falsehood, but consistent. It had a charm to entice the heart, and, provided one could be first persuaded that there was a God, from this premise there flowed an order and reason to satisfy the mind. One could entertain for it, even while rejecting it, both affection and respect.

But this new religion, as preached by Armand Pitou, was simply an absurdity: a bundle of contradictions and negations without reason or logic, and utterly without beauty. It repelled the mind, it left the heart cold. Armand made converts, not by what he said, but by his manner of saying it. He roused people's emotions by his eloquence, which blinded them to the unreason of his words. Louise could have torn his arguments to shreds. She was tempted, for the sport it would afford her, to do so; but she refrained, because there was no God, and religion did not matter.

Only one thing mattered: that she find Michel.

To everything else she was now indifferent. Her revenge on Paul, if not complete, was at least sufficient. The de Brissac were as insufferable as she had hoped they would be. She had the satisfaction of knowing that among the gentry, whose good opinion he valued, the name of Paul de Guillemont was now an occasion for raised eyebrows, amused glances, and sneers.

And she had the further, the final satisfaction, of knowing that Paul knew it, too.

The care of Paul's children she entrusted to an estimable *bonne,* and thus all her energies were released for this purpose which burned in her with concentrated fierceness; she must find Michel.

And if she did not?

Then she would die; for here was, indeed, that limit of suffering to reach which is death. Again and again she had believed herself close upon it, only to see it fall back before her as she drew near. But now that limit was fixed. She approached, and it did not recede. Her life was a starvation, and the end of starvation is death. If she should be finally persuaded that there was no hope, that she would spend all her days in this desolation, that she would never find Michel, she would not wait for that release to overtake her. She would hasten to meet it. She would end her life.

She was beginning seriously to consider how best to accomplish this solution of her trouble, when her mother anticipated her intention by dying suddenly of one of those affections of the heart which sometimes carry off without warning people otherwise well.

All condoned with Louise on this loss, which was to her a mere cup of sorrow poured into an ocean of grief. How could she feel further loss, when her life was already a total want, an utter desolation? Her father dismissed the servants, and closing all but a single suite, lived on in the Château, a voluntary recluse, giving himself wholeheartedly to the practice of his faith for which he had always entertained such devotion. This retirement he broke only by occasional visits to Louise, who found herself thus stayed in her purpose of self-destruction. The old servingman Baptiste he sent to her at Guillemont because he could not bear to turn him adrift among strangers.

To find occupation for Baptiste was a problem. Time had not sharpened his wits, and she had already a superfluity of servants. At length she hit on the solution of sending him to market at Guillemont, and in this she was truly inspired, though not without some cost to herself. Baptiste returned from market with bread which was unquestionably excellent, and with gossip which bored her to madness. But she did not check his recitations. Though capable of a perfection of cruelty when she chose, in the case of servants, children, and dogs she did not choose; and Baptiste was something of all three.

Heaven witnessed a phenomenon unseen by human eyes, but so extraordinary that the angels, beholding it, must have paused in wonder.

Baptiste hurried.

His mistress called him. In her voice there was a note beyond his powers to analyze, which made his spine crawl. It struck him a blow in the pit of the stomach; it sickened and suffocated him with terror. Above all, it lent speed to those limbs, which in more than fifty years had never hurried.

He sped along the hall, unaware that he was hurrying. All he could think of was that Madame, or someone, was hurt and dying.

Madame was just returned, with Monsieur Paul and a large party, from a hunt. It was at a hunt that misfortune had overtaken the young Seigneur, for whom Baptiste had never ceased to grieve. Every time a party set out for the forest, he was filled with foreboding. Now, hearing the voice of Madame, so strange he hardly knew it for hers, he was certain that his worst fears had been realized.

He found Madame in the antechamber to the library. She was alone and, apparently, unhurt. But something was amiss. She stood by the table in the center of the little room, clutching it for support, trembling visibly. She drew her breath in gasps, like one winded from running. Her eyes glittered with such a brightness as Baptiste had never seen in the eyes of anyone. He was seized himself with weakness and trembling, in anticipation of he knew not what.

"Baptiste," she said, in that same curious voice, shaken and harsh: "Baptiste, answer me. On what days do you go to market for bread?"

The jaw of Baptiste dropped, the power of speech deserted him, he broke out in a cold sweat. His anticipations of disaster had not included the possibility that Madame had lost her mind.

"You heard me!" she cried harshly, striking the table with her clenched hand. "Answer me, Baptiste. On what days do you go to market? Did you go today?"

Baptiste nodded. He found his voice with difficulty.

"But yes, Madame. Today."

"Good." Madame continued, speaking very rapidly, "That bread — it comes from the monastery yonder, does it not?"

"But yes, Madame."

"And it is brought by one of the Brothers?"

"But yes, Madame."

"You have never seen him, Baptiste?"

"No, Madame. The bread is delivered, and he is gone, before I arrive."

"But did you not tell me, Baptiste, some weeks since — that a new Brother came with the bread? One who had not been there before?"

"That is so, Madame."

"And the market people were talking of him, and could talk of nothing else, so that you could bring me no news that day?"

"That also is true, Madame."

"You said, Baptiste, that he suffered some affliction. Did they say — do you recall — what it was?"

Baptiste frowned, then shook his head.

"Deaf, perhaps — or blind — I have forgot."

"Not — not lame, Baptiste? Not crippled?"

Baptiste nodded eagerly, "Ah, yes, Madame, yes. It returns to me. Lame, that was it. And also, Madame, wanting a hand."

"*Oh — !*"

It was a strange sound, half cry, half moan, stifled, choked. Madame bent forward a little over the table, her eyes closed, and biting her lips, as one in pain. Baptiste watched her, in a flutter of alarm, doubtful whether to call help.

"That is all, Baptiste. Thank you. You may go."

The steps of Baptiste retreated down the hall.

Louise stood, clinging to the table, unable to move; stabbed with rapture, with thrust after thrust of agony, deep, fierce, beautiful.

Her search was ended. She had found Michel.

ii

An old priest was brought to Notre Dame des Prés, to die.

This event could not be long delayed. He was utterly broken in health, and consumed besides with a sorrow which weighed more heavily on him as his end drew near.

For it seemed to him that his ministry had come to nothing, and that all his life of labor in the fold of Christ had been in vain.

One after another he had seen his children turn from the faith. These souls whom he had baptized, instructed, nourished with the sacraments, he had watched fall first into indifference, then into open defection. He had pleaded, exhorted, reasoned, argued: to no purpose. Living for pleasure only, they neglected the sacraments, receiving them without devotion, and seldom, if at all. And now the floods of this heresy had rolled down from Germany, that dark land of unreason and unrest, whence disaster had once before overspread the world, and were sweeping them away in its hideous tides. Cut loose by neglect from the rock of faith, none of his children stood against the flood: not one.

One would have done so, but she was dead; and the secret hope the dying priest had so long entertained, that her faith would live on to bear fruit in her son, was, so far as he knew, also in vain.

For this son had disappeared. Where he was gone, and why, the old priest did not know, and could not discover. He inquired long and diligently, but without success. His efforts to arrive at the truth, to obtain exact information, ended in failure. He was, moreover, wasted by severe bouts of sickness, and unable to pursue the matter to a conclusion. He could no longer fulfill his duties; soon he could not leave the house. When it became clear that he was dying, he was removed to Notre Dame des Prés, where every care was given him, that one of so devoted a life might spend his last hours in the tranquillity and peace he so justly merited.

He had made his confession and received the last sacraments; but this could not ease the burden of sorrow that rested on his heart.

For he believed that the defection of his children was his fault. Greater fidelity to duty, more intense devotion on his part, would have held them. He had failed these souls entrusted to him; he was seriously to blame.

Above all, he was guilty of the gravest neglect in abandoning this search which it was now too late to conclude: in omitting to discover, at whatever cost to himself, what fate had overtaken this son for whose future he had entertained such bright hope.

For here was a soul fashioned by God for one purpose: to serve Him at His altar. Of this the old priest had not the least doubt. From this purpose, the devil would strive with all strength and cunning to deflect the one so chosen and appointed. And should he succeed in weaning this soul from the service of God, he would have no difficulty in shaping it thereafter to his own ends, in using it as an instrument of destruction.

And with great and deadly effect.

For this soul was one who could walk no middle way. For him, no life of moderate goodness, of mediocre virtues intermingled with trifling sins, with commonplace defects, would suffice. He must give nothing less than a total allegiance, a fierce and exclusive devotion, to whatever master he chose to serve; he would walk to its uttermost limits the path on which he elected to set his steps. He must be priest or libertine, lost or a saint.

And as he went, so would others go after him, to heaven or to hell.

In fashioning this soul for His service, God had endowed it with no mean gifts. An ardent spirit and keen intellect were here united with comeliness of person and charm of manner. Those so favored cannot live for themselves alone; they cannot remain obscure and ignored. Whether they will or no, they are lodestones to which others turn, after which the crowds are drawn.

Just such a soul as this was even now installed (so the old priest had heard) in the former home of this, his lost and favorite son. Brilliant, handsome, persuasive, an apostate priest used the eloquence given him by God, to turn weak souls from the faith: a purpose to which he had bound himself by the fact of his apostasy, and in which it appeared he was reaping a tragic success.

Dared the old priest hope that it was otherwise with this son of his, whose fate was shrouded in mystery? The very silence was ominous; the circumstances filled him with foreboding. An accident, a disappearance; a body injured, a soul shocked: here was ripe soil for the seeds of bitterness, which planted there by the devil, could hardly fail to bear abundant and poisoned fruit. And the seeds of this fruit would, in their turn, be carried to other souls similarly prepared.

But, in earth so enriched, it was possible for good seed to spring up also, and bear fruit a hundredfold; only, some hand must be present to sow that seed when the soil was turned to receive it. And it was for this that the old priest reproached himself most bitterly: he had not been available to minister to that soul in its need. None knew that soul as he did, none realized its passionate strength, the ardor that would carry it headlong to the limits of good or evil. And if, in its agony, the devil had connived that some malign influence should lure it to its destruction with promises of oblivion, of relief from pain, the old priest shuddered in horror to contemplate the spiritual havoc that could ensue. The loss of tawdry goods is of slight consequence, but the loss of a masterpiece is irreparable. And for this loss the fault would, at least in part, be his.

From the depths of his anguish — his fear for this soul, his reproach for himself — the old priest begged God that if he had not failed miserably in his duty here, if this soul was not in grave danger through his fault, he might know it before he died.

But no word reached him; the mystery remained unbroken.

And now it was too late. News from the outside world could not penetrate here; another day or so would see the end. Only his prayers and his grief could repair this neglect; only a long purgatory could atone for it.

For this he prepared himself, without bitterness and with resignation. He prayed no longer to know what had befallen this soul, but only that God would not permit it to be lost or to suffer hurt through his fault, but would bring it ultimately, through whatever deep waters, to light and peace, to the perfect fulfilling of His holy will.

This prayer brought him some comfort, and he slept.

The dying priest had made his confession to Father Prior, and from him received the last sacraments, without the least suspicion that Father Prior was in full possession of the knowledge he sought.

Father Prior realized that this was the case; and he took measures more effective than any words to ease the burden that rested on his venerable colleague's soul, to assure that he should spend his last hours in holy joy, and die in peace.

Michel knelt in the chapel at that hour which, next after dawn, when Mass was sung, he liked best.

This was the hour when night approaches on soft and beautiful feet, coming first gently and slowly from afar, then swiftly, and with her mantle of silence and darkness covering all things.

It is an hour of magic. Things difficult of accomplishment at other times, are now easy. To walk is to run, and to run, fly. The sharp sights, the hard sounds of day are softened and subdued; all is bathed in glimmering beauty; the heart is lifted to an enchanted world, before darkness hides the real world from sight.

It is an hour of silence, an hour made for prayer. Perhaps here, indeed, is the secret of its enchantment, that all creation at this hour praises God, singing of His beauty and entreating His benediction for the night. At this hour the heart kneels; and did all men with one accord kneel too, the Kingdom of God would without hindrance and without delay be established on earth.

Vespers have been sung; it is not time for Compline. It was at this hour that Michel, stricken by the darkest grief he had yet known, had heard from the depths of his sorrow those words of invitation which determined what his life henceforward should be: *"I seek all those to whom love is a suffering . . ."*

He prayed now, at this same hour, that another might hear and accept this invitation also; for if she did not, she would find on earth neither happiness nor peace.

Since that brief and unexpected meeting, now two weeks past, she had not been absent from his thoughts or from his prayers. What he had seen in her face filled him with anxiety and distress. For she had given him such a look as a starving man might cast upon food, or a man dying of thirst on water, the look of one ravenous, tormented; of terrible eagerness, but without joy.

This look testified to a want and unhappiness which it appalled him to think of; but, what was far worse, it told him plainly that his image had been kept alive in her heart as the cure for that unhappiness, the satisfaction of that want.

And this could not be.

If, therefore, she was ever to find happiness, it must be where he had found it, in the love of God.

For she was one who, like himself, must live in love, or die. Her thirst for love had not been satisfied, nor could it ever be so, by any love on earth; so much was plain. He begged God that she might soon discover this, and be led to the only waters where such thirst as hers could be slaked.

Darkness gathered in the chapel while he prayed.

At this hour it was not difficult to lose oneself in prayer: not difficult, that is, while silence, that sweetest of companions, remained with him undisturbed. But Brother Antoine entered the chapel now, and knelt behind Brother Michel. Brother Michel did not see Brother Antoine, but he had no need to do so in order to recognize him. Like glass broken by a stone, silence was shattered, and lay in pieces at his feet.

Brother Michel reflected that the visits of Brother Antoine were customarily brief. Immediately he reproached himself for taking comfort from this fact. Should he not rather desire that Brother Antoine prolong his visits, that the chapel be filled with a regiment of Brother Antoines, drawn there by love of our Lord than that it remain empty, merely to provide Brother Michel with the blessed privilege of praying in silence?

But the presence of Brother Antoine was a sore trial, nevertheless. The thoughts of Brother Michel bounded away from him, like dogs let loose to run, in so many directions that he could not hope to capture them and reduce them to order.

"It must be that the Brother has hit on a new penance, and wears a suit of mail beneath his habit. I can account for these reverberations in no other way. Plate armor might explain them, at least in part."

To this medley of sounds another had been added. Brother Antoine had contracted a hoarseness apparently chronic; and he cleared his throat at regular intervals, in long raspings, with brief pauses between.

Brother Michel found himself incapable of recollection, of meditation, of praise, of petition — of anything, in short, but anticipation of the next rasping from the throat of Brother Antoine. But he listened in vain for any sound indicating that Brother Antoine had risen from his knees and was about to depart.

Brother Michel had never known Brother Antoine to extend his visits so long.

At length he owned himself defeated.

"When I begin to think murderous thoughts of a Brother, and in chapel," he murmured, "I do not need Brother Etienne to remind me that I have stayed too long. And no doubt I shall be doing Brother Antoine a kindness to leave him in peace. Why should I suppose that I am not an insufferable distraction to him, as I must be a cause of sorrow to Thee for these unholy thoughts? I will therefore try neither Thy patience, nor the Brother's, any further."

He rose, made his genuflection, and left the chapel.

Brother Antoine followed. Outside the chapel, he addressed Brother Michel: "Brother, you, instead of Brother Etienne, are

to take to the sick priest who has just arrived his evening colla-
tion. I waited to tell you till you had ended your prayers, in
order that I might not disturb you."

"I thank you, Brother," murmured Brother Michel.

He limped on down to the kitchen, reflecting that when man
begins to take himself too seriously, giving to his actions an
importance they do not merit, God recalls him to his senses deftly,
with a jest.

The dying priest was roused by a tap on his door. It was the
Brother with his dish of soup. He knew this, and did not open
his eyes.

The Brother was gray-haired, of a forbidding presence, with a
face like a granite cliff. He reminded the dying priest of his
own conscience, of which he had no further need or wish to be
reminded. Therefore, though roused to consciousness, he kept
his eyes closed, pretending to sleep.

The Brother placed the tray on the small table by the bed-
side, but he did not immediately depart.

The priest groaned in spirit. It was no doubt the Brother's
intention to remain and feed him. To be fed by one's conscience
in the guise of a lay Brother is at all times horrible, but especially
so when one is dying. There was, however, no help for it. He
opened his eyes.

Night was come. Except for the candle burning beside his bed,
the cell was in darkness. The priest's first thought was that in
sleep the eventuality he anticipated had overtaken him, but that,
instead of being dragged to purgatory by his conscience, he had,
through some miracle of God's mercy, been led to heaven by
an angel, who now stood regarding him.

Then he saw that the one standing by his bed, bathed in the
light of the candle, whether man or angel, was at any rate not
a stranger.

In all his illness, the dying priest had had no delirium. He had
never seen visions; he was not subject to hallucinations. But he
questioned now whether this figure was not an image evoked by
his desire, rather than a living person.

All doubts were dispelled as the Brother spoke: *"Mon père."*

"Michel! My son — Michel! — It is thou, Michel? I am awake? I do not dream? *C'est bien toi* — it is really thou?"

"It is I, *mon père.*" He knelt by the bed. "It is Michel."

"What do you here, Michel?"

"I bring you soup, *mon père.* By order of Father Prior, who but now informed me that you are come to stay with us."

"To die with you, Michel. But what do you in the monastery? You are in religion, my son?"

"But yes, *mon père.* In religion."

"You are — in orders, Michel?"

"No, *mon père.* I am not in orders. I am a lay Brother."

"A lay Brother, Michel? You?"

"But yes, *mon père.* A lay Brother, who, however, is in orders from Father Prior to assist you to partake of your soup."

"Michel! What need have I for soup? It is enough that I feast my eyes on your face. I fell asleep, not an hour since, in prayer for you. But I do not understand, my son. How is it you are a Brother?"

"It is my vocation, *mon père.* I cannot live, except in religion."

"Ah, yes, Michel. That I comprehend without difficulty. But with your gifts — to remain a lay Brother — when the Church has such need — I baptized you, Michel, and now I am dying. Pardon me if I say what has been in my mind all these years. Have you never thought that you might become a priest?"

There was a brief silence.

"Indeed, *mon père,* I have considered it."

"You have the attributes, my son. What then prevents?"

A trembling seized Michel. He had kept his arms beside him, out of sight. He raised them now, as if to clasp his hands, and placed them before him on the bed.

"There was an accident, *mon père.* I am not as others. This will explain."

There was another and a longer silence. The dying priest extended his hand and placed it over that of Michel.

"This is the reason, my son?"

"It is the reason, *mon père.*" He omitted to mention his lameness, there being no need. "Do not grieve for this, *mon père,*" he continued earnestly. "I assure you, I do not. It keeps me from the altar, and that is a very great sorrow — I will not pretend otherwise — but it is the only sorrow I have. This, which to others would seem such loss, to me has been only gain. But I thought you would have known of it, *mon père*. I thought this news would surely have reached you."

"No, my son. I heard nothing of you, nothing. I knew only that you had fallen upon an accident, and that you had disappeared. The nature of the accident I did not know. I feared the worst for you, Michel. I accused myself that I had not followed you, even to the ends of the earth, to save you from the fate that must overtake you if in your extremity you did not turn to God. I prayed, that if all was well with you, if I had not failed in my duty toward you, I might know it before I died. And now — " The dying priest drew a deep breath, "Oh, Michel! My son! How truly can I say, *Nunc dimittis servum tuum, secundum verbum tuum in pace.* What you tell me fills me with grief for you, but also with the greatest joy. Since you were a child, I have had one prayer for you, and now that prayer is answered."

"And what is that, *mon père?*"

"That you might discover what I knew to be the truth: that God had made you to serve Him as a priest."

Michel regarded his old tutor in astonishment. From the dying priest's face all its look of sorrow had vanished. Of those deep marks it had worn so long, not a trace remained. Shrunken, emaciated, a face which death had indelibly stamped, it was nevertheless filled with shining and with joy.

"But — *mon père* — as you see, it is impossible. I cannot — "

"You may not stand before the altar, Michel, but does that mean that you are not a priest? What injures the body does not change the soul. It may keep you from the altar, but it cannot keep you from the priesthood. For it is Christ who imparts the sacrament, and He ordains whom He wills. Me He has ordained by the hands of the bishop, as is right, and fitting, and necessary for the exercise of the sacred functions — but you He has ordained by His choice, and your consent. This ordination is interior and invisible; God keeps it secret for some holy purpose of His own; but do not doubt that it is real. It may never be recognized on earth, my son, but it is known in heaven. Your mother has great joy in it, Michel. And when we stand before the throne of God to sing the divine praises together — my son, my brother! — it will be seen that there is no difference between us, for we wear the same mark on our souls. In the eyes of men you are a lay Brother, Michel, but in the sight of God you are a priest."

These were the last words of the Abbé Courtot on earth.

iii

Louise made her preparations with the greatest care.

None must suspect what she intended, until she and Michel had taken flight and were beyond reach.

That Michel might not agree to her plans did not occur to her. She fell into the common error of attributing to others the same emotions by which she was driven and possessed. The hungry suppose all are hungry; the malicious see malice in all. Louise assumed without question that the life of Michel, wanting her, had been a long emptiness and desolation, as hers had been, wanting him.

He wore the habit of a Religious, but what did that matter? It changed nothing; it could lessen neither his need, nor hers. It merely meant that he had assumed the only way of life open to him, a way, moreover, that could not but be fraught with heartache, and desolation, and loneliness, from which who would not welcome any opportunity to escape?

She waited only the completion of her preparations to offer him this opportunity, confident that he would accept.

The state of life indicated by the habit was one to which those who assumed it were bound by vows; but for these vows she no longer had any respect. Nor could she imagine that others would regard them seriously, in the face of cogent reasons for relinquishing them.

Let those take refuge in this life who were unfit for any other. Let them bind themselves to celibacy who were incapable of love. Whereas she — and Michel —

In Michel the need for love was fierce and imperious, as in

her. He, like herself, must love or die. And how could either be satisfied, without the other? The sweetness of their love at the beginning, when all was light and promise and spring, was but a foretaste of what that love completed and fulfilled would be.

She had seen Michel for a moment, a second only; but it was enough to show her that the fire which burned in him had been neither quenched by religion nor diminished by time. He stood by the roadside, surrounded by ragamuffins, and as she came abreast of him on horseback, he looked up. What were the comparisons she and her mother had made, so long ago at Cançonnet? *"The robe of Our Lady in the Chapel at Guillemont when the sun is shining. — Those extraordinary eyes of your Michel."*

Extraordinary then, far more so now. To look into the face of Michel was to catch her breath in a shock of pain at its beauty. To meet his eyes was to be stunned by a brilliance surpassing any she remembered. Religion, she thought, must have extinguished that fire. The monotony of monastic life must have dimmed that light. That it had not done so could mean only that his power for love had not lessened, that he was more than ever consumed by a need and a thirst for love, which now, after this long desolation, for both of them would be appeased.

Any scruples he might entertain concerning his vows could be easily dispelled. For he had been tricked into taking them; he had been deceived by the fiction that she no longer loved him into doing what he would not otherwise have done. The knowledge of the truth would release him; if he did not see this at once, she could easily persuade him that it was so; there could be no difficulty here.

The only difficulty was one of time. It would require some weeks for her arrangements to be completed. She must still be patient. She must wait still longer for her love and her happiness; but she could wait now in joy, knowing that the end of waiting was in sight.

Marianne, her garrulous *femme de chambre,* had a brother who was a sea captain. He was setting out from the port of Marseilles, with a party of colonist adventurers bound for the southern Americas, in the spring.

Here, in the New World, mercifully separated by distance as by time from a past which had held only cruel suffering for them both, she and Michel would begin the life they had not yet known, the love that, still untried, awaited them.

Through Marianne she made arrangements with her brother to include among his passengers a Monsieur and Madame de Ravel, of whom, though friends of Madame la Comtesse, Marianne realized with astonishment that she had never heard.

The vessel would not sail until April. Till then she must be content to wait, nursing her secret, drawing from it a fierce joy, counting the weeks, and finally the days, till waiting should be ended, and she would wake from this long and hideous nightmare of her life to find herself restored to Michel, and to love.

iv

Michel kept the words of his dying confessor in his heart, and from them drew great consolation, in spite of the fact that he could not altogether believe them.

That the Abbé believed them there was no doubt. He had spoken with the strength of conviction, with the joy of the knowledge of answered prayer; and surely, at such a time, under such circumstances, he could not be deceived. The certainty granted him in the hour of his death, the reward of his labors and sufferings and prayers, could not, immediately after death, be withdrawn. Such a reversal would be contrary to the nature and goodness of God; hideous and impossible. Therefore, as far as they concerned the Abbé, Michel believed that these words had held only the truth.

At the same time, for himself, he could not accept them as true without reservation. He did not reject them or disbelieve them; he did not even doubt them; he simply was unable to concur in them wholly. The most he could believe was that this answer to the Abbé's prayer was such as would bring joy to both, without being what either had supposed.

He accepted implicitly a previous assurance: *"I would receive you among My ordained priests."* But this secret and hidden ordination of which the Abbé was so confident, for Michel must remain in doubt. If it was true, God would reveal it in His own way and time. No confirmation of the Abbe's words had been vouchsafed him; and lacking such a confirmation, Michel regarded them as a mystery beyond his power to comprehend, until God should make their meaning clear.

Frequently, however, he took them from their hiding place and turned them over in his mind, not because he sought a solution of their mystery, but because to recall them gave him joy. He even discussed them with his companion who, besides his confessor, was the sole recipient of his confidences, and for the same reason: she could be trusted not to betray him.

It was a day in early spring, of intense and unexpected heat. The thick habit of Brother Michel galled him severely, and Marceline found herself overcome by a drowsiness more oppressive than usual. She paid only an indifferent attention to the confidences of her escort, since no answer was expected of her, and she had heard most of them before. Her main concern was how to create some interruption (the children now being left behind) which would provide her with an excuse for at least one nap before reaching home.

"Baptism, Marceline," Michel informed her, as if one reared in a monastery could be ignorant of a truth of faith so elementary, "baptism may be conferred by desire alone, provided other means of obtaining it are wanting. But baptism is necessary for salvation, while ordination, to my sorrow, is not. Other sacraments, too, may be received by desire — by will and consent — lacking the matter of the sacrament and one qualified to administer it. But all are needful in their degree either to assist the soul in its journey toward heaven, or to strengthen it in its battle against sin: to give life, or restore it.

"But Marceline, I have never heard that this is true of Holy Orders, nor do I believe that your information in this matter is more complete than mine. One who desires to be a priest, and cannot, is not in danger thereby of falling into sin, or of losing any help necessary for heaven. Thus it may well be that desire does not confer this sacrament, which is an indispensable source of strength and grace only to those called and qualified to receive it. For this is the aristocrat of sacraments, Marceline. It is reserved for the few — the blessed, the favored few — while the others are for the many, if not for all.

"And in my case, Marceline, is not this deprivation God's will for me? Am I not prevented from ordination, numbered among the disqualified, and for a reason? To know that I had received it would be such joy that I think I could not endure it, and live. It may be that the Abbé spoke the truth: but is it not more likely that — "

Marceline halted. Here at last was an excuse for her nap. She did not consider it a rudeness thus to terminate the discourse of her escort, since it was already familiar to her, and spoken too low to penetrate her excessive drowsiness. And in any case she could not continue. An obstacle prevented. She planted her four feet firmly together, permitted her head to sag, and was lost in instant and blessed oblivion.

Michel, engrossed in his consideration of the sacrament of Orders, did not realize what Marceline was about, until he stumbled into her baskets as she stopped dead before him.

He looked up. The heat of the day and the brilliance of the sun had steadily increased as it drew toward noon, but over all this heat and glare there fell a darkness and a chill.

A horse and rider barred the road. The rider was a woman.

"Michel!" she cried. *"Michel!"*

In her voice was such undisguised joy, such ecstatic rapture, that he recoiled before it, as from a blow.

He stood silent, his eyes lowered.

"Michel!" To the rapture in her voice was added a quivering note of alarm: "You know me — do you not, Michel?"

He inclined his head: "I have that honor, Madame."

"Madame!" she echoed. *"Madame!* But, Michel, I am not Madame — I am Louise! And I have waited so long, Michel — so long — And now I have found you, must you call me *Madame?"*

"Under the circumstances, yes, Madame."

She caught her breath in a deep gasp. He felt his blood turn all to ice, seized with a premonition, a certainty, that the next few moments would be among the most terrible of his life.

The horse pranced, disapproving of Marceline, who slumbered

in happy ignorance of the drama being enacted before her unheeding eyes. Louise dismounted. Michel stiffened, bracing himself to meet what must come.

"Michel!" she cried, in a quivering voice, hurt and pleading: "Michel — look at me!"

"I prefer to spare both of us that pain, Madame."

"Very well, Michel — as you please!" And now she spoke in fury. "Pretend that you do not know me! Pretend that I am Madame and not Louise! Pretend to be aloof, and indifferent — pretend that you are a monk, and not Michel — if you can! But you deceive neither yourself, nor me! You know that it is pretense, and so do I!"

At the last words she swung her riding crop through the air, and would have brought it down on the side of the unwitting Marceline, but the hand of Michel shot out, intercepting the blow.

"I beg you to spare the animal, Madame. She has done you no wrong. Nor, if I may be allowed to plead in my own defense, have I."

"You have done me no wrong, Michel?" she echoed, her voice shrill with anguish. "God in heaven, what are you saying? Are you mad? Do you not know that all this time I have been sick with love for you, and married to your brother, whom I love no more than that horse, or your ass?"

Michel raised his eyes and looked at her, compelled by horror at her words.

"You do not love your husband, Madame?"

She shook her head in furious denial. "No! I hate him! But why do you ask? You know it — you must know it. And for the love of God, Michel, do not call me Madame again. I cannot bear it. It is you I love, and you know that, too. And you love me — you have always loved me. Say it, Michel. Admit it. I know it is true. I shall die unless you tell me it is true!"

She was hysterical, and half sobbing. Michel stood aghast. How to convince her of the truth he did not know, or how to be rid of her.

"I am filled with dismay at what you tell me," he said. "I have prayed that you might find happiness. I shall continue to pray for it. But since you are bound by your marriage vows, as I am by vows of religion, I see no course for you but to accept your cross with what resignation you can. You may even — "

"Cross? Resignation?" she interrupted fiercely, bitterly. "What are you talking about? I was forced to marry your brother by that hideous old man, your father. They lied to me, he and Paul. They did not tell me what had happened to you." Her words poured out in a flood. Michel felt himself beaten into silence by this impassioned torrent, and unable to interrupt. "Do you think I would have remained away from you for a day — an hour — if I had known? They told me you no longer loved me. No doubt they told you the same of me. They wrecked our lives with their greed and malice — yours, and mine. But it is not too late. We are still young. Religion has not killed the fire in you, Michel. It burns fiercer than before. That is why you will not look at me now. You are afraid. But why? Of what? You were tricked into taking your vows, as I was tricked into marriage. It was a stupid and terrible mistake, for you, and for me. But there is still time. We have still a chance for happiness. I have found you, and that is all that matters. We can go away, now, today. I have brought a suit of Paul's. We can hide here, in the woods, till night, and then ride to Marseilles, where a ship awaits us. No one will know." There was a silence. "What is the matter?" she cried. "Why do you hesitate? I bring you freedom, Michel, and love, and happiness. And after all we have suffered, after all this cruel separation, how can you hesitate? What is wrong? What is the matter?"

"Madame," said Michel raising his eyes to hers, "I hesitate only because I do not know how to convince you of the truth. I must be frank with you, though I wound you sorely, and turn what you call your 'love' for me into dislike, or even hatred. Indeed, I hope that this will be the case. It will be much the better way. But the truth, Madame, of which I have little hope of convincing you, is this. If we were dispensed from our vows, or had never taken them; if I were at liberty to go with you, and without sin, nothing could persuade me to such a course. *Nothing,* Madame. On that point I cannot be sufficiently emphatic. If freed from my vows and this habit, I would immediately ask for them again."

There was a long pause. The incredulity in her face hardened into a remote and cruel disdain.

"You mean that, Michel? You *mean* it?" she asked, in a harsh trembling voice.

"There can be no doubt about my meaning, Madame. And that being the case, I should like to be on my way. If I may suggest — "

He looked at her with deep compassion. Beneath its assumed scorn her face was bitter, gray, wretched. She trembled under his gaze.

"Yes — ?"

"I have no right to interfere in your spiritual life, Madame. God gave me neither the will nor the authority. But since the welfare of one of His creatures concerns all, perhaps it is not too presumptuous of me to suggest that you might find help and consolation in your trial were you to tell your confessor all you have told me."

"Confessor!" she repeated with a sudden laugh. She mounted quickly, and looked down from this height at Michel. "Do you then know nothing? Where have you been? Have you not heard that we are all of the new faith now, the old falsehoods being dead, and for your priests, and your confession, and your vows, and you, I give not *that?*"

She cut through the air again with her riding crop, swinging it downward with vicious strength. Michel saw the blow coming, and since it was aimed not at Marceline but at him, made no effort to avoid it or deflect it.

He bowed. "May God be with you," he said.

She uttered a furious exclamation, struck her horse, and galloped past him out of sight. He roused Marceline from her slumbers and they proceeded on their way.

Arrived at the monastery, Michel sought Father Simon.

"Do you recall, Father, how you once told me that you would not fear for the faith until Frenchmen should so far forget their logic as to give corrupt doctrine a hearing?"

Father Simon was laying gold leaf on a capital C. He looked

up in annoyance at the interruption. Seeing Michel, his expression changed to one of astonishment, then to alarm.

"In the name of heaven, Brother, what have you been up to now? Is this some new and extraordinary penance? Have you not suffered mutilation enough already, but you must disfigure your face also? So far it has caused no distress to those who must regard it, and I suggest that you leave it as it is, for their sakes, if not your own."

"My face? Disfigure?"

"Your face! Yes! If you could but see it! Do you mean to say you feel nothing from that gash?"

"It is of no moment. Did you hear what I asked?"

"I wish you would wash that blood from your forehead and get the surgeon to stitch you together and patch you up. You are a sight. It sickens me to look at you. But I see you will not until I answer you. Yes. I remember saying something of the sort."

"That day has come. Frenchmen, Father, are giving the scandalous doctrines of that mad German a hearing."

"Yes, Brother. That is true."

"And not merely in some remote province, but here, Father, in Provence."

"That is true also."

"In that event they crucify Him a second time, before our eyes. What can we do?"

"We can follow Him a second time to Calvary. That is all."

"And if we follow closely — very closely indeed — perhaps," suggested Michel hopefully, "they will crucify us, too."

"I have small doubt," agreed Father Simon, "but that they will."

PART THREE

THE DAY OF FRÈRE MICH'

*Non omnes capiunt
verbum istud, sed
quibus datum est . . .*

9. To Whom It Is Given

i

Armand Pitou threw down his quill, and leaning back in his chair, fetched the deep sigh of one who has spent himself, but in a good cause and to his entire satisfaction, as indeed he had.

The great work was finished.

He clasped his hands behind his head and stretched his legs to their full length beneath the table, strewn with volumes and scribbled pages. Now he had but to sort and arrange these pages, and convey them to the printer whose press had been placed at his disposal; and the end of tyranny was in sight.

It was hot; much too hot for April. The stillness was that of midsummer; the Château might have been deserted. Monseigneur had ridden off some days previously to Arles, where a conference of the Huguenot nobility was in progress. Matters had come to a head between the adherents of the new religion and the old; there were rumors of war. This report Monseigneur would deny or verify on his return.

Armand did not accompany Paul, although invited to be present at this conference. It was more important — it was imperative, rather — that he finish his work. Had it been done in time, it would have averted the calamity of war by persuading all to the true religion.

Even now it was not altogether too late. War might not be prevented, but it would at least be shortened, by his exposition of falsehood and defense of truth. He had brought his arguments to a climax so brilliant as to astonish even himself. None would be able to withstand the force and power of his logic, the persuasive eloquence of his prose. Once printed, this volume would swell the ranks of the Reformers by thousands.

And more. Those who styled themselves "reformed" differed greatly among themselves. All alike claimed to teach truth, but this was clearly impossible. All had, in fact, been in error till now. Here at last, in the work of Armand, was to be found pure truth, so forcefully presented that none could any longer be in doubt. This work would heal the breach between Protestant and Catholic; it would wipe away the differences which separated the reformed from each other; it would accomplish this by sweeping all into a single camp, that of Armand Pitou.

Stretched out in his chair in the library of the Château de Guillemont on this hot April day, his legs extended before him and his hands clasped behind his head, Armand dreamed dreams in which he saw himself as a religious leader with a fame and a following surpassing that of Luther, Calvin, or the Pope.

Unfortunately, there were one or two other matters which cried for his attention. In his eagerness to finish his work, he had allowed his personal affairs to take their course, with results which did not please him. A man who belongs to the world may not permit himself the indiscretions of the obscure; at least, he must not allow himself to be mastered by them. Of this eventuality, Armand realized, he now stood in grave danger. He must take measures to extricate himself while there was yet time, or the consequences might be serious beyond repair.

No sooner had he made this resolution than he postponed the execution of it for at least another day. Quick steps pattered along the hall. His chief indiscretion appeared in the doorway and stood, her hands on her hips, regarding him.

"Ah, Marianne!" He unclasped his hands and extended his arms in a gesture of invitation and welcome. "Enter, my angel! Come, felicitate me!"

She took a step which brought her just within the door.

"Closer!"

She shrugged. "Why should I?"

"Because I wish it."

"And if I do not?"

"Ah, but you do."

"I am not sure."

"But I am. And besides, I need you."

"That is just it. You think only of yourself and of what you need; never of me. I give all, and receive nothing."

She flounced into the room nevertheless, and stood beside him, pouting.

"Do not expect me to take you seriously," said Armand. "It is what all women say and none of them means."

He pushed back his chair and gathered her into his arms. She clasped her hands around his neck, and hiding her face against his shoulder, began to cry.

"Armand, you are so cruel!"

"Cruel? I?" He stroked her hair. "That is impossible. One is cruel to those one hates. And I love you."

"Then why will you not marry me?"

"Since when has marriage been a proof of love? We are happier as we are."

"You, perhaps. But not me. With men it is different. You see the Brissac, how miserable she always is. If you do not marry me, I shall be like her."

"And if I do marry you, then you will be like Madame, whose happiness is obviously unexcelled."

"But Madame does not love her husband."

"Why should she? Husbands are not meant to be loved. To marry is to kill love. I counsel you therefore, marry someone you do not like, and love me."

Marianne permitted her tears to dry. It was a waste of time crying if nothing was to be got out of it.

"Armand, I believe Madame has a lover."

"As why should she not? She is handsome enough to have a dozen."

"Yes. But with this lover I believe she has gone away."

"Impossible!" Armand drew back and stared at her in unfeigned astonishment. She sat upright on his knees, nodding vigorously.

"But yes. Through me she engaged passage on the ship of my brother Jean for a Monsieur and Madame de Ravel. I know no Monsieur and Madame de Ravel, nor does she. This ship will sail presently for the Americas — within a week, if the weather holds. This morning Madame rode off very early, taking with her a second horse. She thought no one observed, but I was awake, and I saw."

"Madame is discreet to leave during the absence of her husband, provided only she does not meet him on the way. At any moment he may return."

She leaned back against his shoulder, sighing deeply.

"Armand, why may we not do likewise? Why may we not go away, you and I, alone, together?"

"But the lover of Madame is free. He may do as he pleases, while I — "

"Yes, Armand?"

"I belong to the world. I may not seek happiness in distant parts, like this so forunate lover of Madame. I must remain at my post, and labor in the cause of true religion."

"And that is what you have been doing with all this writing, Armand?"

"Yes. And now today it is finished. Do you not agree that I have earned a reward?"

"But what does all that writing say? What is true religion, Armand?"

"I will tell you, but I do not expect you to understand. Listen carefully. First, there was the old religion which deceived us all, with its lies about Mass, and sacraments, and confession. From that bondage we are now free. Soon it will be dead and gone, and we must never think of it again. You understand that, do you not?"

She nodded. "Yes."

"Now there is the new religion, but there are many teachers. Each holds an opinion different from the others, though alike in some things. But only two are of any importance. One is a German; his name is Luther, and those who follow him are Lutherans. He teaches that men are so wicked that they can do nothing to please God. Therefore they cannot be saved by any efforts of their own, but only by their faith in the merits of Christ. In this he is right and I agree with him. You follow that also?"

"But yes, Armand."

"Then there is also a Frenchman named Jean Calvin. His followers are Calvinists. He holds that God has already chosen who shall be damned and who saved, and nothing anyone does on earth can change God's will in this matter. The damned may be good as angels, but they will go to hell. The saved may be wicked as devils, but they will go to heaven. And there is some truth in this, too. Both are partly right, but neither is wholly right."

"Who then is right, Armand?"

"I am. For see: we are all damned to begin with, because of the original sin. So much is plain. But, God chooses some to be saved: that is plain, too. Only, it is not enough. After God has chosen us, we must also have faith. If we have faith but are not chosen, it will do us no good; we shall remain among the damned. If God chooses us but we do not have faith, we shall also be lost. In order to be saved, therefore, two things are necessary: God's choice, and our faith. Also, that we believe the true religion, which I am explaining to you."

She stared at him, her eyes big with awe.

"Did you think this up all by yourself, Armand?"

"With the help of Holy Scripture, yes."

"And is that what all this writing says?"

"That, and much more. For I must destroy not only the old falsehoods, but also the new ones of these Lutherans and Calvinists. And then I must point out the truth, as it is to be found in Scripture, so clearly that none hereafter can doubt it or mistake it. And now, today, my angel, that work is finished. Soon it will be printed, and then there will be no more Catholics, or Lutherans, or Calvinists, but only — how shall we say it? — Pitouards."

"Oh, Armand, how wonderful you are! Yes, after such great work, you must have a reward."

She flung her arms about his neck. He held her close and kissed her, groaning inwardly as he did so. Not ten minutes ago he had firmly resolved to simplify his personal affairs; and here he was, embarked on a continuation of the most precarious of them all.

For rumor had it that the pretty and vivacious chambermaid of Madame now rivaled, if she did not supplant, the incredible Brissac in the affections of Monseigneur, a substitution by no means difficult to comprehend.

Armand had no desire to become embroiled with his host in an affair of the heart or any other matter. He cordially disliked Paul and used him to the full. His affair with Marianne he had so far conducted with discretion. He believed that he could at any moment break it off, should it threaten to interfere with his work, or to disrupt the apparent cordiality existing between himself and Monseigneur; he had, in fact, resolved to break it off without delay, as the first step in his program of simplification. If continued, it must sooner or later be known; if known, it would be the end of everything.

And this, then, was how he set about it. Well, it was true: he had earned a reward. And a day more or less did not matter. When Monseigneur returned, he would take his book to the printer, and thus inaugurate his program of simplification in the best possible way, by leaving Guillemont. Meanwhile —

Suddenly the girl stiffened in his arms and freed herself from him with a violent push. "Let me go!" she gasped, and was, in fact, gone as she spoke.

She disappeared into the anteroom as the doors behind Armand, giving onto the balcony, opened, admitting a triple invasion; a blast of heat, glaring sunlight, and Paul.

Shutting the doors, Paul stood blinking. The glare outside had blinded him; for a moment he could see nothing. Then he observed a figure standing by the table: Armand Pitou. He was gathering sheets of manuscript into a pile with his quick, restless hands.

Paul walked into the room and sat down. He mopped his face and neck, crimson from the heat. With him he carried, in his own person, a center from which heat radiated, like a stove. Armand sniffed.

"You smell scorched," he remarked. "Is it then so hot?"

"I have been riding through a furnace," said Paul. "I am a

cinder. It is August, not April. You do not feel it?"

"I am impervious to outward circumstances," replied Armand. "The work has engrossed me completely. Felicitate me, *mon vieux!*" He rubbed his hands together gleefully. "It is finished."

"Finished?" Paul regarded him grimly. "Say rather, begun."

"What is begun?"

"Trouble."

"Trouble? Begun? *Mon vieux,* it will be news when trouble ends."

"War, then, if you prefer. In any case, bloodshed."

"It does not surprise me. Things cannot remain as they are. Who shed the blood of whom, and where?"

"At Vézères some soldiers of our party entered a church and — shall we say? — made themselves at home. The curé objected, unwisely. They shut him up in the church and set fire to it, having first amused themselves with him not a little. The village was in an uproar, but not for long. Soon there was no one left to roar."

"Soldiers will be soldiers." Armand shrugged. "You cannot expect them to show respect for the objects of the idolatrous worship of others. And if these people persist in their superstitions they must take the consequences. But Vézères is far to the west of here."

"The trouble will spread. Coligny, they say, is on his way down from Paris with an invitation to all who are otherwise unoccupied to join him as men-at-arms. The pay will be adequate and the sport good. If he reaches these parts I shall put Brissac at the disposal of his men. It will make an excellent barracks. Certainly it is good for nothing else."

"He will find little sport here," said Armand. "Are not all of his way of thinking? I have seen to that."

"I admit that none can resist your persuasions, but there may be a few who have escaped them." Paul made no attempt to conceal the sarcasm in his voice: at times the ex-priest showed a bland self-conceit which enraged him. "There is a monastery full of monks nearby, whom you have made no effort to convert. And what of Guillemont itself?"

"I have ignored these places purposely, saving them for the last. I threw a wide net, and am narrowing it slowly. And if this had been finished sooner" — he indicated his pile of manuscript — "the sport you anticipate would not be necessary."

"You believe that your arguments will convince all?"

"All who read them, certainly."

"But all cannot read."

"It is their misfortune. All should be taught. Now that books are printed, each could then learn the truth for himself. But for those who cannot read, there are preachers. I have seen to that, also."

"You have seen to everything, it appears. But some are dull of comprehension. Have you converted all to whom you have preached?"

"No. But for those who resist the written and the spoken word, there remain, as you have just told me, the arguments of fire and sword. These, however, should be used only as a last resort. They eliminate, but they do not reform. My purpose is conversion. Therefore I shall take this work immediately to Brocard for printing, and on my return I shall preach at all the towns I have hitherto neglected, so that there will be fewer victims and more followers for Coligny when he arrives."

He gathered up his manuscript and departed.

Paul stared after him, blistering with irritation as well as heat. The ex-priest was a constant, if minor, annoyance to him: not only because of his imperturbable complacency, but also because of a certain resemblance to Michel which for the life of him Paul could not explain. Armand had neither the speech, nor the manner, nor the appearance of Michel. He was handsome, but as vain as a girl; he had, indeed, an almost girlish quality which differentiated him strongly from Michel. The only points of likeness were a certain quickness of motion, and those hands; otherwise, there was no resemblance, but rather contrast.

Nor were his hands as like Michel's as Paul had at first imagined. The hands of Michel, though slim, were strong; what they grasped, they held, and firmly. Whereas these hands of Armand were nervous and wavering; it was plain that they could hold nothing securely, but would let all things slip from them. Here, too, was difference rather than likeness. Nevertheless, in the presence of Armand, Paul found himself haunted by a memory, a ghost, of his brother, whom he had striven so desperately to forget; and he did not like it.

He bit down his annoyance, however, having more pressing matters to engage him. Seating himself at the table, he picked up the quill Armand had discarded. He filled it, drew toward him a blank sheet, and began the composition of a letter to Admiral Coligny.

Brissac he would place at the disposal of the soldiery. To the Huguenot chief personally, he would extend the hospitality of Guillemont, should the Admiral penetrate to these parts in the prosecution of his crusade against those who remained obdurate in their loyalty to the old faith.

ii

Marianne waited in the antechamber, holding her breath, not daring to move. She could not be seen from the library, pressed against the wall as she was; but neither could she leave without being heard, and since she was not given to reading, she could give no explanation of her presence save the real one, which would not do at all. Monseigneur must have smelled more than once, if not a rat, at least a suspicion of perfume about the person of Armand; which did no harm as long as Monseigneur did not associate the source of this fragrance with her.

Marianne was not above enhancing her charms by a discreet use of the perfumes of Madame, when occasion demanded it. These appropriations she did not regard as theft, believing them a just return for the gossip and information she supplied Madame, though it was true that Madame did not permit her services to go unrewarded. She thanked her stars this morning, however, that she had refrained from raiding the dressing table of Madame, although the absence of her mistress provided her with a perfect opportunity for doing so; otherwise Monseigneur could hardly fail to detect her presence now and divine its cause.

Should that happen, Marianne shook in her little boots at the thought of the consequences. Someone's throat would be promptly cut; and not, she would wager, the throat of Monseigneur.

It was not that Marianne was fickle; only, it was so easy to be agreeable, so difficult to say no.

It was so easy to assure each in turn that he was the first, and would be the last; so easy to mean it when one said it, and then to mean it all over again a day, a week later. The words came as readily as if one had learned a part; and at the moment of saying them, one was convinced of their truth; one did not intend to deceive.

In the case of the young preacher, however, Marianne meant them as never before. She meant them not only while saying them, but afterward; this, surely, was a proof of love. She longed to possess him exclusively; to that end she was determined to marry him, in spite of his assurance that marriage meant the death of love. These words were but an excuse, cloaking his reluctance to marry her. She would break down that reluctance; in spite of all obstacles, she would marry Armand Pitou.

The two most formidable obstacles were Monseigneur and Armand himself: that is to say, Monseigneur's devotion to her, and Armand's devotion to his everlasting religion. She must get rid of the one, and surmount the other. How she would contrive this double riddance, she did not know; she was positive only that she would.

She listened: the two men were talking earnestly. Perhaps, if she was very quiet, it would be safe to leave. She slipped off her shoes and tiptoed from the room, unseen and unheard, at least by Monseigneur.

On the landing of the staircase she stopped to put on her shoes. Here a deep casement window overlooked the entrance court to the Château. Looking from the window, she saw Madame ride into the court at a furious gallop, rein her horse up short, and swing to the ground. Leaving the animal as he was, lathered and trembling, with the reins hanging from his neck, Madame ran up the broad stone steps as if in fear of her life, although there was no one in pursuit.

Marianne dragged on her shoes and scurried to the floor above with almost equal speed. She did not wish to be found by Madame, who was plainly distraught beyond reason and measure. What could have befallen Madame passed Marianne's comprehension; but the girl wasted no time in conjecture concerning her mistress' affairs, which sooner or later she must find out anyway.

For the present she was wholly absorbed by her own problem: how to overcome the matrimonial reluctance of Armand Pitou.

iii

Louise knelt by the bed, her head bent, arms outstretched.

It was an attitude of prayer, but she was not praying. She had not prayed for many years. It did not occur to her to pray now.

Like an animal set in frenzied motion by pain, she had run as far and as fast as she could. In this flight she had neither purpose nor direction; she did not know what she was about. Habit turned her feet toward her room; an obstruction halted her in her course. She fell to her knees against it, and there remained, because she could not continue.

She could not have said where she was or how she had come there. She was insensible to everything, but she was by no means unconscious.

She was as one who suffers to the saturation point, but without the grace of oblivion; unconscious of everything save anguish, but fully conscious of that, sodden and limp from pain, and heedless of all else.

Time passed. She did not move. Had the pain she suffered been physical, and of a corresponding intensity, it could not have held her more tightly in its grasp. Brought to her knees, she was kept there by a weight so crushing that she could not even attempt to throw it off. But this immobility was exterior and physical merely. In her soul a storm raged, of which her limp figure, held in the stillness proper to prayer or sleep or death, gave no sign.

Her mad ride home, and headlong flight to her room, had carried her far beyond that limit of endurance to pass which was to die. That limit was now an infinite distance behind her; and yet she lived.

And she would continue to live. To end her life would have demanded action; and she had no power to act. Formerly she had been driven and goaded by pain; now she was held fixed and motionless by it. She could make no move to end her suffering, not even to seek the oblivion of death.

She must live, and without hope. This fact separated all that had been from all that lay ahead. The darkest moments of the past had held some promise of light, however faint, in some future, however remote. Now there was no longer hope, but certainty; and this certainty was loss: final, irreparable.

She had climbed a flimsy scaffold, confident of its support. It gave way beneath her, and she fell from a great height, with nothing to break the fall. She lay now, bleeding, crushed, unable to rise, to move, to call for help; but alive, and conscious: conscious above everything that this fall and this pain were her own doing.

Had she looked, she must have seen how fragile was this structure on which she had undertaken to ascend to happiness. She must have admitted, if not the certainty, at least the possibility, of its collapse. She had closed her eyes, and deliberately. She would not see; she refused to look.

She had found Michel; and finding him, she had lost him, forever.

She had believed him far away, but, once found, attainable. Actually he was closer than the nearest village, and less accessible than the farthest star.

All was spent, and to no end. No new effort she could make would win him now. He was lost, finally, irrevocably, beyond recall. Lost, lost, lost: the word beat a monotonous repetition which would never end, though the cadence might vary: found and lost, found and lost, found and lost. The swinging of this pendulum would not cease until she died.

And with him, she had lost love, forever.

For none could take his place. The time for seeking refuge in substitutions and counterfeits was past. Had the blow been less severe, the wound less deep, she might have rallied from it to seek relief in a perpetual masquerade, in which her want would give to others the face and name of love, but without love. Such deception was now impossible. The reality was a truth so terrible that she could never deceive herself with untruth again.

It was a truth so terrible that she had not considered that it might be. She had made no alternative provision, in case this should happen which had happened. She saw one outcome only: that which she willed. It did not occur to her that there might be another. Rather, she would not permit it to occur to her. Had she faced the situation as it was, she must have seen at least a possibility that her plans might end in ruin. She must have asked herself, as she did now, what, in that case, should she do? What could she do?

Nothing: except live, accept, endure.

This admission brought with it, not the cessation of pain, but a semblance of relief. Doubt at least was ended. She need seek no further: she had found Michel. She need hope no longer: she had lost him. It is doubt which tortures; and nothing could be more certain than her loss.

This certainty was the ground to which she had fallen and on which she lay. She could fall no further; if she did not attempt to rise, she would never fall again.

Thus she was driven to the truth, as a ship which struggles against the storm is driven by it on the rocks. She had fought the truth, and it had conquered her. From this conflict none can emerge victorious. Against the truth it is useless to rebel. Sooner or later truth compels surrender. To surrender early, is to be spared great pain.

Henceforward, she would face the truth, acknowledge the truth, seek the truth, and the truth only. Though the truth should kill her, it was better than deceit. Her life had been woven of falsehood; she would rip that glittering fabric to shreds; cost what it might, she would face the reality beneath.

Falsehood was the structure on which she had attempted her perilous ascent: a lie begotten of her own desire, nourished and fostered by herself. It was this lie which gave way beneath her: from the truth one cannot fall. On the truth she would stand henceforward; nothing should persuade her to depart from it.

This was the truth, hard, and terrible, and safe: she must live without love. She must live without Michel.

Michel lived without love. Could not she?

A trembling seized her. She struggled against it, but could not quiet it. She saw Michel as he stood on the road before her in the sunlight, his eyes lowered. She felt again the pain which stabbed her, sharp and incredibly sweet, as he raised his eyes to hers. In spite of her torment and bewilderment, she had feasted her hunger on his figure and his face. She had devoured his image, fixing it in her memory that she might possess it forever. She saw him now, as clearly in memory as in fact; and this recollection drove her to another truth, which she must face and acknowledge: had Michel the look of one who has ceased to love?

She must answer, and with the truth: the beauty of Michel, which so caught at the heart, what was the source of it, but love?

She had ascribed this brilliance, this beauty, to lack of love, because she willed that it should be so. Of what self-deception had she not been guilty, to satisfy her want and her pride! Those incapable of love, or starved for love, or dead to love, are dead to all things. They have no brightness; they have no life. Though their features are modeled to perfection, they are not beautiful, for beauty is inseparable from love.

Let her pursue the truth to the end, as she was pledged to do. It was love, and not the want of it, which stamped the face of Michel with its beauty. The fire which burned in him was love: deep, strong, and, moreover, satisfied. But, he loved neither her, nor any other woman. Whom, then, or what, did Michel love?

She could not answer. She did not know.

She knew only that she had created a fiction of Michel, compounded of her longing and her pride. To this fiction she had offered herself and her love: it was Michel, and not her fiction, who refused.

Clasping her outstretched hands, she clenched them tightly. In fury at his refusal, she had struck him. Why? Not because he had rejected her, but because he was other than she wished him to be.

She had struck Michel. She killed a myth.

She had not expected the blow to fall. She believed that he would avoid it. The impact brought her teeth together with a jar; it sickened and unnerved her. More than his refusal, it sent her on her headlong flight toward home. More than his rejection, these steps brought her to face and admit the truth.

She had determined that Michel should break his vows, and for her. The Michel of her invention would have done as she wished. He would have exchanged his habit for the suit she had brought; he would have mounted the horse she had provided; he would have ridden away with her as she desired.

To what lengths had her madness gone, that she had believed she could persuade Michel to break his pledged word? Was she out of her mind, to suppose that Michel would enter into obligations he did not intend to keep? Was she insane, that she had seriously proposed to reclothe Michel in a suit of Paul's?

God in heaven, what had she planned to do? What would she have destroyed, had she had her way? She had seen Michel as he now was: could she think of him again as he had been, dressed in the clothes, following the pursuits, of ordinary men? The black monk's habit was cut to him, made for him. It was part of his beauty, it was part of himself. To remove it would be a destruction, a mutilation. To replace it with a suit of Paul's —

Her trembling became a deep shudder. A wave of shame passed over her, burning her with self-loathing, at the recollection that she herself had willed and planned this desecration.

Could she imagine Michel as acquiescing in her demands, as mounting the horse at her request, as riding with her —?

She could not bring herself to finish the question, so violently did her soul recoil from it now. She had seen him only twice; but to the end of her days she would carry his image as she had fixed it in her mind and heart: his beauty surpassing his former comeliness, exceptional as that had been; clothed in the black habit of a Religious, which framed that beauty and enhanced it; filled with a light, a radiance, that could have no source but love; surrounded by a swarm of children, accompanied by a little gray ass.

This was truth. This was Michel.

Thus she was led by a series of truths to face and acknowledge the deepest truth of all. Supposing it to be in her power to exchange this reality for her fiction, would she do so now? The one had refused her love; the other would have accepted it. Which would she choose that Michel should be? Which did she prefer?

Her trembling had increased; she was shaking violently. But she faced this question without fear. Answering it, she felt in her heart a deep stir and quickening, of eagerness, even of joy.

There could be no question. There could be no doubt. The myth of her creating was without truth, without love, without beauty. Whereas Michel, the reality —

She cowered low beside the bed. Hiding her face in her hands, she burst into a flood of impassioned and merciful weeping.

It was the beginning of life, and of hope. It was the birth, not the death, of love.

Alienum autem non
sequuntur . . . quia non
noverunt vocem alienorum

10. The Shepherd and the Stranger

i

Marceline plodded along in the sunlight, certain that something was amiss.

She had no basis for her suspicions save silence, but this was enough. It was, in fact, the reason for her misgivings. She had been the recipient of no confidences for some weeks, and this was unusual. She had assisted at no sung Masses on the way to market, and this was ominous. She recognized her companion by his appearance, which had not altered; she would not have known him by his manner, which had changed beyond recognition, and in a fashion not to her liking. She could only conclude that something was wrong, and seriously so, since he who confided so much to her, refrained from making her a party to this trouble.

Marceline was correct in her conclusions. On a hot April day, now many weeks past, joy had left the heart of Michel, nor could he see that it would ever return. Where peace had been, and beauty, and light, all was now desolation, and darkness, and death. The cup of living waters, at which he had so long quenched his thirst, was turned to bitterness, to gall. Here was grief that sealed the lips, sorrow that could not be spoken, save to Him who permitted, though He did not will, the cause of it.

This cause was twofold, but woven into one sorrow, in which

it was difficult to separate the threads: to determine which grief was intimate and personal, and which extended beyond his own sorrow to include the world: for both were one.

The words of Louise had inflicted on his soul a wound so deep that the blow she actually dealt him passed all unnoticed by comparison. These words received grim confirmation on his next trip to market. He found his friends hysterical. News had been brought which struck terror to their hearts. They crowded about him and demanded to know if what they had heard was true.

"Frère Mich'! Frère Mich'! Tell us — is it true? They say there is war, and soldiers are coming who will kill us all! They are coming from the West, Frère Mich', where already they shut people in churches and burn them! They call themselves by some strange name, Frère Mich', and they do not believe that our Lord lives in our churches! They throw Him in the gutters — they feed Him to horses — and if any tries to defend Him, they cut him to pieces with swords! Oh, Frère Mich'! Is it true? Will they come here? Will they kill us, too?"

"I cannot say, my little ones. But take heart. Do not fear. We must all die some day. Is it not better to die courageously, for Him, than miserably, of some foul sickness, in our beds? And if we suffer for His sake, shall we not be martyrs, and therefore saints? Do we not all hope for heaven? To die for Him is to be sure of it. Can we ask more than that?"

Michel had no hope that these words brought any comfort to his hearers. They wished to learn rather that the soldiers would not come than that they would all die martyrs to the faith and be saints in heaven. To be a martyr is no doubt glorious, but it is also exceedingly uncomfortable. The martyrs lived long ago, and all were dead. They were, moreover, made of different stuff from Paulette Dubois, and Pierre Gapin, and Berthe Masson, who were not saints but the most humble and ordinary of market people. They desired no glory, but only to go on selling their figs and cakes and meats and fish and bread until that remote eventuality called Death should overtake them in its own unpredictable time and manner, of which it was much more agreeable not to think.

One, in fact, was most positive that she would rather be a live market woman than a dead saint; and she made no secret of the fact.

"If God cannot save us from the soldiers, then I will go to those who can. Who will care for my children if their mother is killed? If God wants us to be good Catholics, let Him strike the soldiers dead before they come. If He does not, I will not be so sure but that the soldiers are right and we are wrong." The Widow Douroux shut her thin lips tightly on this pronouncement, and glared at Michel, defying him to answer an argument so incontrovertible.

And Michel had no answer, as He had none to the challenge: "If Thou be the Son of God, come down from the cross."

The cross — It seemed to Michel that never in his life had he known the cross till now. His soul entered into a third night of darkness; and this was like none he had known before. The first night was that which followed the loss of his love, and with her the loss of all that to him meant life; and this, since it included the loss of himself as well, was the very death through which he found life. The second night was that which followed on the knowledge that his heart's desire, that for which he thirsted beyond all desire, could never be his; and from this cross he could not turn, but only carry it with joy, and this God in His grace and mercy had enabled him to do. But the darkness upon which he entered now was a darkness neither of sense (as the first had been, nor of spirit, as the second), in so far as the cause of it related to himself. It was truly night, in that it was beyond him, outside of him, and it included him. Here was the sword which pierced Our Lady's heart, in her helpless anguish for One who was more herself than herself. This is a sword of many blades; it inflicts a wound which has no like. A blade of this sword entered into the heart of Michel; he stood on Calvary, a spectator, and could do nothing.

Every Crucifix was now a living figure. It was no longer necessary to dwell on the Passion of Our Lord as an essential part of his spiritual exercises. The Passion dwelt in him; engulfed him; possessed him with its agony, as the love of Mass had possessed him with its joy; nor were the two separate, but one, wearing only a different aspect, as light and darkness are both of the same day. The agony of the suffering Christ was become the agony of Michel: including him in its power and strength because it was agony of the suffering Church; the dark night, not of Michel, but of the faith itself; the crucifixion of our Lord in His own; Calvary re-enacted, not in an unbloody manner, as in Mass, but in how hideous and bloody a one! And what Resurrection lay beyond this Calvary, who could tell?

Resisting with all his will the temptation to despair, Michel could hardly forbear from crying in his heart, "None!"

Not only at the market, but in the monastery, he heard of terrible things. Reports were brought by guests, by passing strangers, who stopped for an hour, a meal, a night, and were gone. The terror of the market people was well founded; all they had heard was true, and more. The reports hardly varied; they were repeated like a refrain.

"They have a strange name, these people. They call themselves Huguenots. They claim to have a new faith, but as God lives, it is not faith they have, but the want of it. And now we must all believe as they do, or be killed. Down from Paris comes an Admiral of the King. He invites all who will to join him in exterminating the faithful like rats. Thieves and vagabonds, who might get themselves hanged for stealing, will now be paid the King's gold for butchering the subjects of the King. And for what crime? Because they hold the faith of their fathers, and their grandfathers before them, of St. Louis and the great Charlemagne, of the King himself, and of all Frenchmen till now. If that is a crime, then their own mothers and fathers, and all the kings of France, were guilty of it, and deserving of death.

"But there is worse. They stable their horses in the churches, these Huguenots. They break open the tabernacles. They throw the sacrament in the gutters and trample on it; they feed it to their horses. They befoul and desecrate the altars. They use the holy oils to grease their boots; they dress swine and asses in the sacred vestments. If a priest dare protest they kill him with hideous torments. The faithful they dispatch quickly, since there are so many, and they must be done some time with their butchering; for priests they save their cruelties, which pass description. The trouble is still to the West, but it is spreading. It will come."

All this was night, black and hideous; but at the heart of it was darkness more impenetrable still. For Paul, his brother, and Louise, whom he had loved, were of the number of those who did, or who countenanced these things.

During all his life at the monastery, the memory of Louise had shone in the fabric of his past like a thread of pure gold in a tapestry. Till now, this memory had been only joy. That the woman who stopped him on the road was this same Louise passed belief. He would rather have died than be brought to the knowledge that such a change could be.

This woman had borrowed the voice and the features of Louise; but she was not Louise. Louise was beautiful, but here was no beauty. All that his memory had treasured as fair, and worthy of love, was here turned to ugliness, and hardness, and death. The soul of the Louise he had loved was a vessel of purity which the devil had wrested from the hands of angels and filled with his own corruption.

That Louise could be driven by the desolation and hunger of her life to address him as she had done was a bitter tragedy; but it could be understood. The want of love leads to madness, and the victims of madness know not what they do. For that reason they can be objects of neither condemnation nor blame, but only of the uttermost pity. But that Louise should be numbered among the unfaithful, among those who mocked Him on the cross, who crucified Him anew in His children, this was a horror that passed the bounds of truth and entered the dark realm of unreality and nightmare. In the suffering of love there is a certain fitness that gives dignity and even beauty to pain: but here there was none. Here was not only betrayal, but distortion and mockery; it was as if John, and not Judas, had betrayed Our Lord.

Though differing utterly from his former grief, the present sorrow was nevertheless linked to it by the fact that Louise was the source of both. This brought his past before him in a recollection so vivid as to be a resuffering, like the inexplicable recurrence of pain in a wound long since healed, of which there remains not a scar; or like the memory of a grief evoked by a return to the scene of it, though the actual pain is ended.

For that suffering he found now a reason and a use. It had lain hidden all these years, like a treasure buried in days of plenty and since forgotten, but recalled in time of want. Kneeling in the chapel, he gathered out of the past all that sorrow, of which he was now so strangely and vividly reminded, and made a gift of it in her behalf.

"I thank Thee for sending me that pain, and for teaching me now what use I may make of it. I offer it for her return to Thee. Offer? No; I *give* it. An offering Thou mightest refuse; a gift, Thou canst not."

But even from this act he derived no consolation. The gift was given; it could not be refused; at some time, in some manner, it would bear its fruit: this he knew, but the knowledge brought him no joy that he could feel. God is good; but to that goodness the heart of Michel was now insensible. All pain must end; but the promise of the Resurrection did not shorten Calvary, or mitigate its anguish. The light which had shed a radiance upon his ways was extinguished; and although he clung with all his strength to the knowledge that it must shine again, that certainty did not alleviate the present darkness with the faintest perceptible glow.

His gift would not be rejected; Louise would return. Thus he reassured himself, but the words had no meaning. He repeated them without conviction; they were dead. The temptation all but overcame him, to believe that though grace was offered her, she would refuse it, and go her way defiant to the end. God compels none: though He poured His grace in infinite abundance upon her, it yet depended upon her to accept. Against what riches of grace she must have closed her heart, to have changed from the Louise who had been a light in his past, to the hard and bitter woman whose shadow had fallen across his present, turning it all to darkness!

What, short of a miracle, could open her heart again to grace? Dared he hope for miracles? Dared he ask for one? For the salvation of a soul, yes; but he asked with a faith that was of the mind only, not of the heart. It taxed his faith to the utmost to believe that in this matter, desirable above all things though it was, his prayers and his gift would be of the least avail.

And he was assailed by a temptation darker still. Had he not prayed for her daily, during all the years since he had lost her, till now? And was this the answer to his prayer? He thrust this from him with all his strength; he cried to the tempter that the end was not yet. In the end his prayer would be answered; in the end God's goodness would be known. Meanwhile he must walk in darkness and be content; he must pray always, and not despair.

The darkness thickened; the doubts multiplied. More than Louise were concerned in his distress. What of the market people? Were they not likewise in grave danger of defection? Had not God sent him among them that he might be to them a means of help and strength in such travail as any day might come upon them? What certainty had he that he would not betray them in their need? Did he not know his own weakness, and too well? Dared he believe that he himself would stand unshaken in the face of such terrors as had been described to him?

The darkness was alive with devils; and for their jibes and taunts and mockings he had no answer.

And so for many weeks he had kept silence on his way to market. He had refrained even from singing Mass. In his heaviness of heart he could not sing; and the reasons for his sorrow were too many and too grievous to be told, even to the most trustworthy of companions, the most secretive of little gray asses.

Paulette Dubois sat on a log by the roadside, and in fear and trembling awaited the coming of Brother Michel.

Every few seconds she peered down the road: he was not yet in sight. She had come early, to be sure of not missing him. She had taken up her post ahead of the point where the children met him, that she might speak to him undisturbed. In her bosom tumult reigned; she pinned herself to her seat by a resolution firmer than any she had ever taken, or kept, in her life. If he did not come soon, she thought, she would not keep it now; she would flee while there was yet time. Never had she undertaken so drastic an overture as this she contemplated. Prayer was not habitual with Paulette Dubois; but she fortified her wavering resolution with an appeal that was truly prayer, and, for that reason, effective.

"Oh, God, don't let me run away! Make me stay till he comes! Oh, I am so frightened! Oh, what shall I say? Oh, God, I cannot stay! I cannot speak to him — I cannot! I —"

But she had waited just too long. Brother Michel was in sight.

Leaning forward on her log, she watched him approach. The sight of him gave her some courage; she forgot her perturbation in a momentary abstraction.

"How sadly he limps," she murmured. "I had forgotten. Eh, but he is beautiful, Frère Mich'!"

She waited till he was abreast of her, then darted from her place of waiting, and fell to her knees in the dust of the road at his feet.

"Frère Mich' — oh, Frère Mich'!"

Michel stopped dead. In his burdened heart it seemed there was room for no new sorrow; but his first thought was that here was cause of another grief, a new dismay, like one he had already suffered, differing from it only in that the party to it differed. But immediately he knew that he was mistaken.

"Oh, Frère Mich'! You have a moment? You will speak to me?"

Marceline advanced a few paces, and perceiving that she was not accompanied, came to a halt and surrendered herself to sleep.

"My sister, what is wrong? How may I help you?"

"Oh, Frère Mich', it is so hard to say!"

He took her by the elbow; she scrambled to her feet and stood, her eyes lowered, twisting her hands together in agitation and distress. She was half sobbing; her words came between gasping and choking; but in spite of their incoherence, they conveyed a meaning plain beyond doubt. Michel listened in amazement.

"Frère Mich' — it is I, Paulette Dubois, who speak to you. No one thinks well of me, Frère Mich'. If any knew I had stopped you thus, they would say it was for no good. But, Frère Mich', I am not here for any reason they might think, but for another reason — a so different reason! I am frightened, Frère Mich'. If you had not come just now, I would have run away. But now it is too late. I must tell you what I wish to say." She raised her eyes and looked at him. "Is there hope for me, Frère Mich' — for me?"

The heart of Michel quickened its beating. "Hope, my sister? You mean —"

She nodded. "Frère Mich' —" She took a deep breath and poured her words out rapidly. "You said, the other day that if the soldiers should come and kill us, then we would all be saints. I — Paulette Dubois — a saint! I tried to think how that would be, and I could not. It is this way, Frère Mich'. I believed always that to be good, one must be like the Widow Douroux. The Widow Douroux hates me, and she is ugly. Me, I could never hate anyone, and I could not bear to be ugly. She thinks she has no sins, the Widow Douroux; she thinks all she does is right. But she said she would go on the side of the soldiers; she does not wish to be a saint. There was a pain here, Frère Mich'" — she clasped her hands over her bosom — "when she said that. I looked at her, and I thought, why, she is not good. She is ugly, not because she is good, but because she is bad. She does not sin, like me, but she has no love for anyone, and for that reason she is not good. Then I looked at you, Frère Mich', and things came into my head that I have never thought of before. I said to myself, Frère Mich' is not ugly, and he is good. He is always kind. I am a sinner, but he does not hate me. If he should die tonight, he would go to heaven. He will not have to wait for the soldiers to kill him to be a saint. But me, Paulette, if I should die —" She shivered. "Oh, Frère Mich'! You understand? I would not wish to be like the Widow Douroux — but I wish to be like you! Tell me, Frère Mich' — what must I do to be like you?"

She would have fallen to her knees again but he prevented her. In his agitation he could hardly find words to answer.

"Oh, my sister, what is it you say? It is true? You wish — not to be like me — do not say that, my sister, for the love of heaven — but you wish to make your peace with God?"

Tears overflowed her eyes and splashed on the shawl tied across her bosom. She nodded, biting her lips.

"Yes, Frère Mich'. Truly, that is what I wish."

"Oh, my sister, what grace you have received! What joy there is in heaven at what you have just told me! And not only in heaven, but on earth as well. All the saints and angels rejoice, and I with them, my sister."

She sobbed. "But, Frère Mich', what must I do?"

"You must make your confession, my sister. And the priest will tell you what to do."

She nodded, twisting her hands together, choking back her tears.

"I am afraid, Frère Mich'. I wish — you were a priest. I would not be afraid to confess to you."

"My sister, it is God to whom you confess. Remember that, and you will not fear. I cannot hear your confession, but I will do what I can to help you. Go back to the village — you walk faster than I — and wait in the church until I come. I will send word to the curé that you wish to see him, and why; and he will rejoice with all the company of heaven, and with me." He smiled at her. She caught her breath, with a renewed burst of tears. "And, my sister, while you wait, and after you have made your peace with God, do not forget to pray for me."

"For — for you, Frère Mich'?" she gasped. "I — Paulette Dubois — you wish me to pray for you?"

"But assuredly, my sister. Your prayers will have great weight with God. He loves you dearly, to have called you back to Him as He has done. You have listened to Him; you may be certain He will listen to you. Therefore, pray for me, for I need your prayers, and sorely."

"But, Frère Mich', I am a sinner, while you —"

"The sins you are determined to forsake, my sister, are those which God finds it least difficult to forgive, in any who repent of them. Did not la Madeleine become a great friend and lover of our Lord? Is she not one of the very greatest of the saints? But there are other sins far less easy for the sinner to forsake, or for God to forgive. It is from one of these that you have saved me."

She stared at him bewildered.

"I, Frère Mich'? I have saved you — from a sin? What is it you say, Frère Mich'? What sin is that?"

"The sin of Judas, my sister — far worse than that of Madeleine: the sin of despair. Now go, and wait in the church, and pray for me, as I have asked."

She ran along the sunlit road ahead of him. He prodded Marceline into reluctant activity, and followed at his slower pace. A short distance down the road Paulette stopped, turned, and waved her hand. He raised his, returning her salutation. She ran on, blinded by her tears.

Brother Michel broke his long silence.

To the astonishment and relief of Marceline, he began to sing Mass.

ii

"See now, Madame — see! He comes!"

"Who comes, Lucie?"

"He of whom I spoke to Madame: the Brother who brings the bread. From this window Madame may see."

"But will he not observe us staring at him?"

"Ah, no, Madame. He will not look this way. And even should he do so, the shutter will hide us. See now, Madame. Is it not as I said? Did Madame ever see one more beautiful?"

"No, Lucie. You are right. I never did."

"Ah, I thought Madame would agree. It is true, he limps à faire peur, and he has lost a hand. I ask myself, how did that calamity befall? They say before he became a Brother he was a great seigneur, and that he was injured and all but killed in a hunt. Perhaps Madame knows if that is true?"

"How should I know, Lucie? The Brother has not confided in me, I assure you."

"But Madame is so plainly of the gentry. I thought perhaps Madame might have heard. But no matter. See now, he gives the bread, and Jeannot Dubois helps him. They are talking and laughing together. He is a mutilé, but one does not think of it. When one does not see him, one forgets. And then one observes it again, with surprise. Tiens, one says, the poor Brother. How sad it is. But he is not sad."

"No, Lucie. He is not sad. It is easy to see that."

"And for that reason one can hardly pity him. It is strange: to see one so young, and so well favored, and so badly injured, and beyond cure — this surely is pitiful; but one cannot feel sorry for him, not at all."

"His body is crippled, Lucie, but his soul is not. Crippled souls deserve our pity, far more than injured bodies. For that reason the Brother is better off than either you or I."

"Me, I will keep all my hands and my feet, *merci*. See now, the baskets are empty, and he departs."

"Will you please leave the window, Lucie? He is sure to find you staring at him."

"But it pleases the heart to watch him, Madame. And soon he will be gone." She turned from the window nevertheless. "Ah — Madame departs also?"

"I am going into the church, Lucie, to pray for my soul, which needs it. Is the Brother gone?"

Lucie looked again into the square.

"Yes, Madame. He is gone."

Forming an angle with the house of Lucie Marot, *blanchisseuse de fin,* who took lodgers also when any were to be had, was the village church, which, with the home of the curé next to it, filled the west side of the market square. Across the square from the house of Lucie, and at right angles to the church, was the Hôtel de Ville. Under the windows of the *blanchisseuse de fin,* Charles Poulot presided over his stall, receiving and dispensing the monastic bread. Thus Lucie was in a position of excellent advantage to oversee all that went on in the square. It was her especial pleasure to regale her lodgers with detailed accounts of proceedings which, did they wish it, they could very well observe for themselves.

Lucie was somewhat vexed that her new lodger did not seem avid for gossip. Madame was a stranger in these parts, and should have welcomed whatever information concerning Guillemont and its notables Lucie was disposed to share with her. Madame la Comtesse de Guillemont, for example, had disappeared; rumor had it that she had fled to the Americas with a Huguenot lover; this surely was news startling enough to be meat for any stranger. But her lodger had fallen into the silence of a clam at the mention of the subject; one would think she knew where the Countess was, and feared to betray her. Lucie shrugged; she could make allowances when necessary. Madame was very religious, and there was no accounting for the eccentricities of religious people. For this reason, and because she caused no trouble, Lucie could forgive Madame her otherwise inexcusable reserve.

A mystery surrounded her lodger which piqued Lucie sorely, because she knew of no way to arrive at the solution of it. Madame was plainly of the gentry, and a good Catholic; whereas most of the nobility, including the Count and Countess, had gone over to the other side. Monsieur le Curé had brought her to Lucie, explaining that she had recently suffered a great sorrow and desired a quiet place of retirement near the church where she would, for a short time, see no one. Apparently Madame was determined to be deaf and dumb as well as blind. Lucie could induce her neither to listen to her anecdotes, nor to import the least crumb of information concerning herself.

Madame seemed, moreover, fearful of being observed by any. Even on hot days, she wrapped herself in her full cloak, whenever she left the house, pulling the gathered hood over her so magnificent hair. Lucie reflected now that Madame, who was so reluctant to see the Brother from the window, must shortly meet him face to face. The Brother had himself gone into the Church to pray, as he often did, and this but a few moments before Madame: a fact which Lucie had neglected to mention, since Madame had not asked her.

The interior of the church was dark. After the blinding sunlight of the square, to enter it was like walking into night.

Louise knelt in her chosen place, in the rear, a little to one side. At first she could make out nothing but the usual flicker of lights: the sanctuary lamp, and the candles burning before the altar rail. She knew, however, that she was not alone. Somewhere in a side aisle, a woman was making her confession; judging from her agitated sobbing, she was having a hard time of it. Alternating with the distressed voice of the penitent, she heard the soothing murmur of the priest. Gradually the woman's sobs died away; and the church was in silence.

Recalling her own confession, Louise bowed her head in renewed and profound thanksgiving. By what violent means had grace brought her to submission, necessitated by her headstrong will and pride! But, once her submission was made, with what gentle hand had grace led her from that moment on!

The storm of weeping which had followed her recognition of the truth and her submission to it, had left her limp, exhausted, aching as if she had been the victim of physical violence; but utterly at peace.

Peace: how long was it since she had known peace?

She had remained a long time seated on the floor, her head resting against the bed, her hands in her lap. She lacked strength to move or to rise. She was as weak as one who has passed through the crisis of a serious illness. She was capable of nothing but surrender.

After a long while she thought: I must go somewhere. I must do something. I cannot stay here. But where must I go? What must I do?

The answer was immediate: Michel himself had told her what to do.

"— you might find help and consolation in your trial were you to tell your confessor all you have told me."

How gladly would she follow the counsel of Michel! She had had no confessor since her marriage; but was there not always a priest at Guillemont?

She waited till dark; then she quitted the Château, taking with her a few personal belongings, a little money, and some jewels she might sell in case of need. Was she the same woman who had set out that morning, in another century, another life, to turn Michel from his chosen course? Like pain which ceases and cannot even be recalled, the passion which had driven her then was gone as if it had never been.

She went to the curé at Guillemont. She told him her story, as much of it as there was need. He found lodging for her near the church. He heard her confession, and received her back into the home and the refuge she should never have left.

The next morning she was present at Mass. She knelt at the rail with the others. With them, she received the sacrament, for the first time since her Nuptial Mass.

That Mass had been to her a mockery and a farce. The guilt of that Communion, received for the sake of conformity, in bitterness of spirit and without reverence, now weighed heavily on her heart. She had eased it of this burden, along with a hundred others, last night in her confession; she could atone for it now only by the depth of her reverence, the frequency of her Communions, the strength and ardor of her love.

After Mass, she remained in the church a long time, in prayer.

She was surprised to discover that she could pray. She had not prayed for many years, and then only to beg for favors such as a young girl might desire. Now she implored forgiveness for her bitterness, and rebellion, and neglect; she begged to be shown what to do; and she prayed for Michel.

It was easy to pray for Michel. He was a link, binding her to prayer. It was not possible that he should need her prayers; nevertheless, she poured them out for him in an arrears that was long overdue. She should have prayed for him, frequently, daily, during all this time; not once had she done so, to her bitter shame; let her make up now for those black years in which his need had surpassed hers, and she might have helped him with her prayers, and refused to pray: opening her heart to darkness, shutting it to light.

Every day since then she had heard Mass; she had received Holy Communion; and she had prayed. In prayers she quenched the thirst which had tormented her so long; from these waters she could not drink too often or too deeply.

She moved, easing her position. Her eyes, accustomed to the darkness of the church, fell on a figure kneeling to the front, on the opposite side from herself; and her heart all but stopped.

Her first impulse was to leave; then she decided otherwise. Why should she not remain? She was hidden by the shadows, and covered by her cloak; even should he glance in her direction, he could not know her. God had given her this privilege, this blessing, for which she had not asked, and which she did not deserve, of praying in the same church, at the same hour, with

Michel. She would not refuse this gift. She would accept it, with joy and thanks.

She could see only his back, and the partial outline of his face, but there was no doubt that it was he. How could she fail to know him? His cowl was thrown back, his head slightly bent; he knelt straight and motionless, his arms folded in his sleeves.

Her heart reached out to him, in a love which surpassed her former love by as much as it differed from it. She said, to One who heard them both: "I think I have never loved Michel till now. Was it Michel I loved when I sought him, not for his good, but for my pleasure? I did not love Michel: I loved myself. But I love him now — I cannot help it — and I beg that my love may work only for his good. It is because of him that I am here, but he does not know it. Some day it may be I shall tell him. Possibly it will give him joy. He should hate me for my wickedness; if he does not, it is because he is Michel. And because he knows I need it, he may even pray for me."

She bowed her head, drawing her hood over her face. Michel had risen. He made his genuflection and turned to leave the church. Behind the shelter of her hands she watched him, unobserved. He did not see her; he did not, in fact, raise his eyes. She had watched him, as he walked along the road toward her, on that terrible day of her death and rebirth; but then her concern was only for herself; the shadow of her obsession fell between her and Michel. She saw that he limped, but until this moment, she had not remarked how badly. She felt her heart contract, but with something quite other than pity: for it was not possible to pity Michel. Conspicuous as this defect was, she saw further, and without surprise, that it was not incompatible with great dignity, and even with a certain grace.

He passed her, and was gone.

She resumed her prayer: "How can I do better than to pray as Michel prays, to ask what he asks? Let my prayers second his. And if there is any wish, any desire, dearer to his heart than all others, let me entreat that for him, too."

iii

On the broad stone portico of the church, Monsieur le Curé

stood looking over the village square, his heart filled equally with gratitude and with misgivings.

He had just had the happiness of receiving a penitent daughter back into the fold of Christ; and although he rejoiced beyond measure at the miracle of grace which had been wrought in this soul, he was also torn with grief at the knowledge that for one that returned, many left.

He was but newly arrived at Guillemont, appointed to succeed the former curé, who had left the secular priesthood to join a monastic order. He himself was a Parisian. He had traveled from Paris to Guillemont in the company of another priest, formerly of these parts, who was now on his way to Rome, and who had planned to interrupt his journey with a visit to the monastery near Guillemont which had been his home.

Misfortune had overtaken them on the way. They passed through country harassed by civil war. The Huguenot soldiery entered a village where they were spending the night, and they were forced to separate and to flee. Whether or not his companion had escaped with his life, Monsieur le Curé did not know; he had heard nothing from him since.

He looked now over the village square, where the members of his flock, still for the most part unknown to him, were engaged in the wranglings and vituperations proper to their trade; and he wondered how many would stand unshaken, electing to be martyrs rather than traitors, when the day of trial should come.

Not many, he feared in his heart. They were Catholics, yes. They had not yet fallen into heresy. They came to Mass, they received the sacraments, but was this not from habit rather than devotion? Many names were added daily to the list of martyrs written on the walls of heaven; the faith was still strong in many hearts, and the Holy Spirit did not withhold His gift of fortitude from those who asked it; but too many did not ask for it, or desire it, or recognize the need for it. They wore their faith like a cloak, insecurely fastened, which they could drop without effort, should things become too hot.

And there was danger that at any moment things might become very hot indeed. The tide had risen in the West, but was sweeping eastward; that Guillemont would be spared he could not hope. When that day came, what of these sheep of his new flock? Would they suffer themselves to be led to the slaughter rather than buy freedom with defection?

Monsieur le Curé could not answer this question with any certainty, one way or the other. He was still a stranger to them, and they to him; and he felt this strangeness to be a serious handicap in his need to fortify them against the evils and the dangers in the shadow of which they stood. Even their southern tongue was an obstacle; to many he made himself understood with difficulty. In his heart he questioned the wisdom of his appointment to Guillemont; it seemed to him another instance of that grievous mismanagement, that disregard for the welfare of souls, on the part of those in high places, but for which the terrors of these days might never have arisen; but though he questioned, he could not disobey. Accordingly, he was here; and while it seemed to him that another might have been found more suitable for this post than himself, nevertheless he undertook his duties with good will, praying that God would contrive to supply his deficiencies in such manner that his flock would suffer no harm because of him.

"Mon père —"

He turned. Behind him stood a Brother, one from the community of Notre Dame des Prés, to which the companion of his travels had previously belonged.

"Ah, *mon fils!* You are he who directed the penitent to me?"

The Brother inclined his head.

"I had that happiness, *mon père."*

"The curé had not previously seen the Brother. The housekeeper had conveyed to him the message that a woman waited to speak to him, sent by a Brother from the monastery, whom he would find in the church. He discovered the woman without the intermediary of the Brother, whom he had not beheld till now. He looked at him: first casually, then intently.

"Ah, my son, you say well: it is a great happiness — and the greater, alas, because so rare. How many leave, how few return! Of all sorrows, there is none more bitter than this, to see the sheep scattered, and devoured by the wolf, and to know one cannot reach them, to save them in time. And now you have helped to rescue one of his lambs. You say truly, it is a great joy. But, my son, a word of warning." He studied the face of the Brother with quizzical, inquiring eyes. "You are young, very young. You may be tempted by this success to think that your way henceforward is secure. Be on your guard against such presumption, lest, when things become difficult, you fall into the sin of despair. Do not look for an easy road, my son. It may be that God is preparing you for some trial."

He smiled at the young Brother with great kindliness, and extended his hand. The Brother took it. He returned the frank gaze of the curé, and into his eyes, which were of a color and brilliance truly extraordinary, came a look the priest could not for the life of him have defined.

"Ah, *mon père*," said the Brother, rather to himself than to the curé, "I often ask myself, how will we feel at home in heaven, without trials and without pain?"

The curé clasped the Brother's hand, then looked down in sudden surprise.

"Ah, my son!" He touched the hand resting on his palm. "An accident?"

"Yes, *mon père*. An accident." The Brother smiled. "But long ago."

"Treasure this affliction, my son." He clasped the Brother's hand again. "It brings you closer to our Lord. And when future trials come upon you, remember what I say. *A Dieu,* my son. Pray for me."

He vanished into the church.

At the foot of the steps, Marceline dozed in the sunshine. Her nap had already been prolonged far beyond its usual time; she was roused now, not by Michel, but by an unexpected disturbance. She opened her eyes and closed them again. It was out of the question to think of going home; she could not, in fact, have moved had she wanted to. The square was filled with people.

They appeared suddenly, from nowhere, as crowds gather at an accident: as if the heavens had rained them in a flood, or the ground had spewed them forth. There was no slow process of assembling; no gathering by twos and threes. When the curé had addressed Michel, except for the market people and a few scattered customers, the square was empty. Now it was thronged.

Every window, every doorstep, every balcony, was filled. Michel beheld this phenomenon with astonishment, and also with dismay. He should already be on his way home; and now there would be no quitting the square until the reason for this gathering was ended and the crowd dispersed.

At first he was at a loss to account for it. There were no cries or screams, no signs of accident or disaster. The crowd jostled and shoved and pushed, but there was no panic; they were noisy, but not hysterical. Then he saw that the attention of the crowd was directed to the Hôtel de Ville, on the steps of which a young man stood, speaking to the people.

Gradually the noise subsided. The crowd became silent, listening. The speaker was a young man of pleasing appearance, with a personal attraction that was immediately apparent. He spoke with a sort of exalted vehemence that commanded attention. Across the intervening space his words came clearly to Michel:

" — and I bring you happy news; good news; great news. From the bonds of Satan you are free at last! No longer need you fear his domination. You are released from the chains forged by evil men to drag you, slaves, before the Whore of Babylon. Of Babylon, said I? Nay, of Rome!

"I ask you, my friends: how is it possible that men have suffered themselves to be held so long in bondage to this tyrant? Why have we not cast off this slavery long since? Because evil men, mad with lust for power, have deceived us with their lies! They have deceived us; they have betrayed us; they have lured us into slavery with promises of eternal reward, but only that they might trample us beneath their feet and thus exalt themselves. Awake, my friends — awake from sleep! Behold this snare into which you have been led! I, who speak to you, I, too, was once deceived, and therefore I know!

"For they led me in bonds even to the very altar, where as priest I served at their false and idolatrous worship, until my eyes were opened, and I beheld the truth!

"Then I cast off the false trappings of the livery of Satan, which in my blind ignorance I had assumed, and I vowed that

I would not rest until I had broken this yoke beneath which my enslaved brethren still groaned.

"Think, my friends — think of the monstrosity of this lie! What horrible thing is this that you have been taught — that the great and Almighty God should permit Himself to be contained in a piece of bread? Is not this a horror and a blasphemy? Does not Scripture tell us plainly that the heaven of heavens cannot contain Him? But these men will not suffer you to read Scripture, lest you learn the truth, and free yourselves from their bondage. They will interpret Scripture to you, setting themselves up as your masters, and passing on to you only such portions of Holy Writ as may be wrested to fit the meanings they have devised for your destruction!

"Of all the lies they have contrived for your damnation, what can equal this — that a man can change bread into God? Heard you ever such sacrilege, such blasphemy? They bring you to your knees before a piece of bread. They hold this bread on high for you to worship, and they say, 'This is God. Come, eat God. Let me put God on your tongue. Grind God to pieces with your teeth. Swallow God. Receive God in your stomachs and digest God.' Is it possible that God, who made you, can be chewed and swallowed and digested by you? Oh, monstrous deception! Oh, hideous blasphemy! Till now God has suffered this deceit to be held by blind and perverse men, but now the day of His wrath is upon us! And heavy will His hand be upon those who persevere in this idolatry! Turn, my friends — turn while there is yet time, to the truth that will make you free! How terrible is His vengeance upon those who blaspheme His name! Already that vengeance is seeking out its victims! Be warned while there is time! Beware the wrath of God! Turn from your superstitions to the truth!

"In this church also, in the shadow of which you stand, is preserved this blasphemous bread which evil masters have persuaded you is God. But God is even now showing His anger. He wills that in our day this lie shall cease. He would destroy this bread from the face of the earth, that no witness to this falsehood shall remain. He commands that this bread be thrown to horses, and consumed by the very beasts. Here is proof enough of this blasphemous deceit; for if this bread were truly God, as your former masters have declared and taught, what sort of God is it that would suffer Himself to be fed to beasts? Plainly, this — "

"What sort of God is it, you ask, who suffers Himself to be fed to horses? I will answer you!"

All eyes turned from the Hôtel de Ville to the steps of the church. A cry went up, of recognition, and entreaty: "Frère Mich'! Answer him, Frère Mich'! Answer him!"

From the portico of the church, Brother Michel faced Armand Pitou.

"I will answer him, my friends! If God permits Himself to be consumed by beasts, it is to save Himself from men who have sunk below the beasts! Oh, my friends! What horror is here — that men, made to the likeness of God, redeemed by God on the cross, should fall so low that God now chooses to be the food of horses, rather than of men for whom He died!

"But it is not the first time God has made this choice. Was He not born among the beasts? Men shut their doors against the God who came to save them: what refuge had He, but a stable?

"The beasts were present at His birth; but only because men cast Him out. Had one door opened to Him, He would have entered there; He would have chosen that house for His place of birth. For He yearns to make His home with men. He goes from heart to heart, seeking one to welcome and receive Him; but, when all are barred against Him, He finds shelter with the beasts, for He must lodge somewhere. Oh, my friends, let it not be said of us, that He comes to us, desiring to make His home with us, but finds our hearts so miserable a dwelling place, so dark and cold and fouled with sin, that He turns in preference to the very horses, who will give Him a kinder welcome and more fitting shelter!

"Our friend would persuade you, if it were possible, that it is not God who comes to us as bread. In like manner, the men of Bethlehem would not believe that the Child against whom they shut their doors was God. Our friend declares that God, being infinite, cannot be contained in bread. But was not God — the same God, infinite, eternal — contained within the body of a new-born Child?

"How was this possible, my brothers? How could God, the Almighty, the Everlasting, be confined within a human body, man or child? It was possible because He willed it; and God does whatsoever He wills.

"He dwelt among us once as man. He dwells among us now as bread, and for the same reason: because He Himself so chooses.

"They crucified our Lord for blasphemy, because He said that He was God. Is it not rather blasphemy to doubt and mock the word of God, to tell God plainly that He lies? Which of these blasphemed, our Lord who said that He was God or those who spat upon Him, and scourged Him, and slew Him? God Himself took bread, and broke, and said, *'This is My Body.'* Is it blasphemy to believe His words? He said, *'Take, and eat.'* Is it blasphemy to obey Him? He said, *'Do this in commemoration of Me.'* Is it blasphemous to follow His commands?

"Those who killed Our Lord denied that God could become man. Our friend denies that bread can become God. But, are not all things possible to Him? Shall we deny that He can assume the form of bread, or wine, or water — of any creature He may choose? Shall we dictate to the Divine Majesty, telling Him what He may do, and what He may not? May He not dwell among us in whatever guise He wills?

"He could have remained among us in His human form until the end of time, but this was not His will. He must die, and rise again, and ascend to heaven, as man. To remain with us on earth, He has chosen another form, suited to His goodness and our necessity. He became man that He might save men: He dwells with us now as bread and wine, that in this humble form He may nourish the souls of men whom He has saved.

"Our friend says further that it is unthinkable, and blasphemous, that God, as bread, should permit Himself to be consumed by men. But did not God, as man, permit Himself to be crucified by men? And did not they who nailed Him to the cross hurl at Him that selfsame accusation? *'If Thou be the Son of God, come down from the cross!'* As man, He submitted Himself to the hands of those who lashed Him, who crowned Him with thorns, who dragged Him along the road to Calvary, who nailed

Him to the cross. As bread, He submits Himself to the hands of those who cast Him in the gutters, who feed Him to their beasts, who trample Him under their feet, who mock and scourge and crucify Him today, as truly as they did on Calvary.

"He was crucified, not for His pleasure, but for love of us. He takes the form of bread upon our altars, not for His gain, but for our good. Our friend declares it to be impossible that bread should thus be made God at the bidding of sinful men. Oh, my little ones, how sadly he mistakes! For the bread and wine are changed, not at the bidding of men, but at the command of God Himself. *This is My Body — This is My Blood.*' These are not the words of men — what man could have conceived of such a wonder? They are the words of Christ — of Him at whose command the wind ceased, before whom devils fled, and death itself gave way. The priest speaks not his own words, but the words of Christ, in the place of Christ; and the promise of Christ is kept, the will of Christ is done.

" '*This is my Body — This is My Blood.*' Think, my friends — think of these words: the most sublime that have ever been spoken on this earth, the most powerful, the simplest, and the truest. Let none persuade you that Christ did not mean them when He spoke them: for if ever man meant what he said, it was He. When He spoke parables, none understood; when He spoke truth, none believed. You and I, my brothers, who are frail human creatures, we may say one thing and mean another: but He who was God spoke the words of God, the words of Truth. And here He spoke in no parables, no simile, no proverb: He spoke plain. On the night before His death, when He supped with His disciples, had He meant other than He said, would He not have explained it, and clearly?

"Consider, my friends: He, who was God, was on His way to betrayal and to death. Before death, men do not jest. He above all men, at such a time would speak words only of solemn truth, words which all who follow Him are bound to cherish and believe. He said, '*This is My Body, This is My Blood.*' How could He mean, '*This is not My Body, This is not My Blood*'? Of all the words that have ever been spoken in this world since the beginning, let us doubt all others, but be sure of these!

"The bread yields its substance to God; it becomes God. How is this possible? Because God wills that it shall be so, and the bread does not resist. God commands, and the bread obeys.

"Oh, my brothers! What great lesson is hidden in this for ourselves! Bread, the humblest, the most common, the most useful of all God's creatures, becomes God Himself, and for this reason, that it offers no resistance to the will of God!

"Could we but learn, my children, from this lowly creature, bread, to submit our wills to the will of God, we, too, should be transformed into the divine likeness. For that, my little ones, is the will of God for us, that we shall become wholly like to Him. He longs to say of us also, *'This is My Body, This is My Blood';* but unlike the sacramental bread, we oppose the miracle He would work in us. Did we but yield to the divine pleasure, did we but obey the divine command, then we, too, like the bread and wine, should be changed wholly into Him."

Thus far Michel had addressed the people; and to each one it seemed as if the Brother spoke to him alone. All watched him intently; the silence could not have been more profound had he spoken in an empty square. He stood with outstretched arms, pleading with them, by this gesture drawing all eyes to himself, as his words held all hearts.

Armand Pitou listened with the rest. The rapt attention of the crowd constrained him to hold his peace. It was as a hand placed over his mouth, suffocating and smothering him. The words of his rival kept him at bay. He was filled with rage, but until the other had done speaking, he could say nothing.

The Brother turned now, and across the space that intervened between the Hôtel de Ville and the church, he addressed Armand Pitou.

"My friend, your hands have held the Sacred Body of Our Lord. Your hands have consecrated the chalice of His Most Precious Blood. From that chalice you have been privileged to drink. There are those who would pour out their own blood, gladly, could they enjoy that privilege but once.

"And now you deny that He whom your hands have held, He whose Body and Blood have nourished your soul, He whose royal Priesthood you are privileged to share, whose Holy Sacrifice you have offered to the Father in His name — you deny that He is God. Not even Judas was guilty of this infamy. Judas, like yourself, was anointed to His priesthood; like you, he forfeited the dignity and the glory of his sacred calling. Judas betrayed Him to His executioners, but Judas did not say, 'This man is not God.'

"In spite of this betrayal, Christ called Judas friend. In this word, friend, our Lord invited Judas to return to Him. He offered him forgiveness. Judas had but to accept, to be restored to His Priesthood, and to the company of martyrs and of saints.

"Judas repented, but he did not return. He went his way in bitterness, and we know his end.

"Christ calls you friend, no less than Judas. He invites you likewise to return. He will restore you to the Priesthood you have forfeited, the honor you have despised. He offers you the glory of effacing the stain of your denial by mingling your blood with His. Judas went his way, but you — "

Armand Pitou could stand no more.

"Judas! You call me Judas! You dare!" He shouted, hoarse with rage. "I will listen no longer to your insults, your lying and blasphemous deceits!" He turned to the crowd. "My friends, I give you one last chance. I have warned you, the day of vengeance is at hand! I offer you refuge — I offer you escape! Who comes with me will be saved! Who stays will curse the day he was born — for the wrath of God will strike, and spare none! Which do you choose — death with this blasphemer, or life and safety with me?"

A confused murmur arose from the crowd. Michel spoke again:

"My brothers, you have heard him. In this he speaks the truth. Who goes with him will save his life — as Judas saved his. Remember the words of our Lord: *'Who saveth his life shall lose it, and who loseth his life for My sake, the same shall find it.'* God compels no man. The choice is yours." He stepped forward on the portico, and extended his arms in invitation to the people: "You are free to follow him, my brothers, or to stay — with me."

There was no sound. None moved.

Armand ran down the steps of the Hôtel de Ville, and mounted his horse. The crowd gave way in silence before him as he rode from the square, alone.

Omnes enim,
qui acceperint gladium,
gladio peribunt . . .

11. All That Take the Sword . . .

i

Michel returned to Notre Dame des Prés, but not alone.

Among those caught in the crowd, and constrained to listen to the strange preacher, whether they willed or no, was a man-servant who was no longer pink or fat, but a shrunken and faded version of his former self.

This change had overtaken him all at once, following the disappearance of Madame.

Madame was a chain binding him to his past, of which the most grievous sorrow hitherto had been the disappearance of the young Seigneur. Of this old world, only Madame remained; but she maintained him in that world, because she herself had belonged to it. Thus he was spared the necessity of adjusting himself to another, which would have been impossible in any case. A dog is happy in new surroundings, among strangers, provided only he keeps his master; but let that master be taken from him, and what course has he but to pine until he dies?

And now Madame, like the young Seigneur, had vanished; none knew where.

The Château was filled with strangers: hostile, alarming. Standing in the shadow of Madame, Baptiste had not been terrified by them, as a child does not fear in the presence of its mother. But now the protection of Madame was withdrawn. All was fearful and strange; Baptiste was the prey to terrors the more disturbing in that he could not understand them or define them.

He was helpless, lost. None told him what to do, except to order him out of the way. He continued to go to market, because it had become a habit, and none forbade him. While at market, he could almost believe that Madame was at home again, and that on his return he would find matters as they had always been. These trips were therefore the one feeble consolation in the otherwise desolate life of Baptiste.

Caught now in the crowded square, literally pinned against the baker's stall and unable to move, he was seized with panic. This crowd that appeared from nowhere, that jostled and pushed and all but crushed him, was as terrifying as some overwhelming natural calamity, fire or earthquake or flood, before which the hearts of men are brought prostrate in fear. He was helpless until the crowd should disperse.

On the steps of the Hôtel de Ville a young man was speaking. He was not unknown to Baptiste, but this familiarity carried with it no reassurance, but rather the contrary. For the speaker was one of the company of ghouls who peopled the Château, and who had now pursued Baptiste even to the market.

The preacher spoke with a sort of frenzy. He waved his arms; he swayed back and forth on his feet; his voice rose and fell. His words came clearly to the ears of Baptiste, but they carried no meaning. They but added to the confusion in his mind, the terror in his heart. More even than the pushing crowd, they thrust him back against the stall, and held him there, stifling him, crushing him, filling him with darkness and the terror of death.

Like a trapped animal, he knew that he must escape, or die.

To die, was it not to return to the past? To the blessed past, filled with sunlight and contentment, which in the mind of Baptiste was identical with heaven? If that were so, Baptiste had died, though he could not understand how. The people still crowded and pushed upon him. All was still confusion; but, in an instant, fear had left his heart.

It was as if Madame had returned; as if the safe and happy past had taken Baptiste under its protection again. He drew a deep breath, then another, and another. He felt his eyes blinded with tears. He was sobbing, with relief and joy.

He was no longer aware of the market place and the crowding

people. He was back again in the sunlit court of Cançonnet, early on a spring morning, cleaning shoes. He heard the ring of horse's hoofs on the cobblestones; he felt again the joy that moved his heart when, looking up, he saw that the rider was not Monsieur Paul. He remembered how the young Seigneur had swung to the ground, almost before his horse had stopped. He recalled his very words, as the young Seigneur placed his hand on the shoulder of Baptiste, and smiled, and addressed him as an equal: ". . . to lie with skill and conviction is a gift, and we to whom the devil has not given it, can never learn it."

Baptiste heard again the voice of the young Seigneur, so clearly that it seemed to be not a memory, but the voice of one who speaks actually, and close at hand.

The picture of the young Seigneur standing before him in the courtyard faded from his mind, but the voice of the young Seigneur did not. That voice continued, and it spoke words other than those which Baptiste remembered.

Gradually, through the confusion that filled his mind and the tears that dimmed his sight, Baptiste perceived that the young man on the steps of the Hôtel de Ville had ceased talking. He was standing silent, his face dark with anger. He had turned from the crowd, and was looking over the heads of the people toward the church.

The crowd also had turned, and was looking toward the church.

Baptiste permitted his gaze to follow the same direction. On the steps of the church a second speaker stood, addressing the people.

He wore the black habit of a Brother of religion; he was tall, and very slender. His cowl was thrown back on his shoulders; a girdle was clasped about his waist. He stood with arms outstretched, pleading with his hearers. Baptiste uttered a choking cry, and would have fallen to his knees, which could no longer support him, but the crowd prevented.

He who spoke from the steps of the church was the young Seigneur.

Thus it befell that Michel did not return alone, nor did he keep silence on his way home.

Marceline was pleased to hear him speak, but she was surprised, and a little hurt, that his words were not addressed to her.

"Monseigneur — "

"Not Monseigneur, Baptiste: *mon frère*. One is our Lord; we are brothers."

"It is true, Monsieur Michel? It is really you to whom I speak?"

"It is I, Baptiste — who am neither Monseigneur, nor Monsieur, but Brother Michel, to you and to everyone."

"You are not a priest, Monseigneur *mon frère?*"

Michel smiled. "I see that it is of no use to quarrel with your titles for me, Baptiste. This one is original, if not regular. I never heard of a Brother who was at the same time a bishop. And I am not even a priest. There is a great difference, Baptiste, between a Brother and a priest."

"That is true, Monseigneur *mon frère*. Always I wished to be a Brother. I knew I could not be a priest."

"What is it you say, Baptiste? *You* wished to be a Brother?"

"But yes, Monseigneur *mon frère*. Long ago I wished it. And not only then, but always."

"But did you ever make the trial, Baptiste?"

"No, Monseigneur *mon frère*. All told me I was too stupid. I soon abandoned the hope, but not the wish. I have always desired it. Now, seeing you, I desire it more than ever." He looked up at Michel, then lowered his eyes in sudden embarrassment. Some of his former color returned to his faded cheeks. "I — I would like to try if — if you think — if they would permit — that is, if it is not too late — "

Michel regarded the old servant in amazement.

"Baptiste, what you say astonishes me. You are in earnest? You wish truly to be received in the order as a postulant?"

"You said of me yourself, Monseigneur *mon frère,* that I have not the gift of lying."

Michel laughed. "The want of that gift is an excellent qualification in a Religious, Baptiste. When we return, I will tell your story to Father Prior, and it may be he will receive you, as you wish."

"Truly, Monseigneur *mon frère?* You believe he may not send me away?"

"They received me, Baptiste. You will be of more use than I."

"But I am slow, Monseigneur *mon frère.*"

"Ah, that will be a grave hindrance, Baptiste. They receive only postulants who are fleet as the deer, like myself."

"And there is little I can do."

"While I excel at all things — especially at carrying soup."

"Ah, that I can do, Monseigneur *mon frère.* For I am strong in the arms, as always."

"But you have grown very thin, Baptiste."

"I have been filled with such sorrow, Monseigneur *mon frère.* First for you, and now for Madame. And at the Château there are — "

Michel stopped. "For Madame, Baptiste? What are you saying? Has any ill befallen Madame?"

"None knows, Monseigneur *mon frère.* It is as with you. She is gone."

"When was this, Baptiste?"

"Many weeks ago, Monseigneur *mon frère.* In the spring. I remember: it was very hot. Monsieur Paul returned from a journey, and he could not find Madame. She was not in the Château and none has seen her since."

Michel walked on in silence. Whether this was good news or ill he could not know. At length he said,

"Pray for Madame, Baptiste. We can do nothing better, for her or for anyone, than to pray. There were some who grieved for me, not knowing what had befallen me, and thinking I was lost or dead. But there was need rather to rejoice than grieve, for God had given me greater good than I ever asked or dreamed could be. And it may be He will deal thus with Madame, if we ask Him faithfully in prayer."

Baptiste nodded. "But yes, Monseigneur *mon frère.*"

"And what of my brother, Baptiste? Is he gone, too?"

"Monsieur Paul is always there. But he is changed."

"Changed, Baptiste? How?"

"He is fat, and red. One would hardly know him for Monsieur Paul. But you, Monseigneur *mon frère* — " He looked up again at Michel; his eyes swam with sudden tears: "You are not changed. You are the same, only — "

"Only what, Baptiste?"

"It comforts the heart to see you, but there is also a pain. I do not understand."

"It comforts my heart to see you, Baptiste, and there is also a pain. I understand very well indeed. It is always sweet, and also sad, to find again a friend one has lost."

"And now that I have found you, I hope I do not lose you again, Monseigneur *mon frère*. For then I think I should die."

"Ah, no, Baptiste. There is one Friend we can never lose. When we have found Him, whatever happens to any of us on earth, we are never afterward alone. Those only are desolate who have abandoned Him, like my brother Paul, and that wretched man who preached to us against the faith. And for them above all others it is necessary to pray."

"He preached against the faith, Monseigneur *mon frère?*"

"Did you not hear? He preached against the Blessed Sacrament, saying it is not truly the Body of our Lord."

"I heard his words, yes, but I did not understand them."

"I am not surprised at that. He said little that could be understood. He had more rhetoric than logic, and more vehemence than clarity. It is a type of oratory that sways many. If I, Baptiste, should stand in the market place, and invest my voice with the proper cadences — *basso, tremolo, forte, piano* — and cut the air with the prescribed gestures, and pour out my words too fast for any to follow this meaning, or to question if they had a meaning, I, too, could persuade men to any course I chose.

"For example, Baptiste, is not this effective? 'Awake, my friends! Awake from sleep! Consider how evil men have deceived you, for their gain! Are you not made to the image of God? Are you not like Him in all things? Does not Scripture say this, and plainly? Think, then, of this lie you have been taught — that in order to live, you must open a hole in your face, and into it thrust all manner of unseemly things: plants, roots dug from the earth, and even the very flesh of animals! Is this behavior becoming to a man — to the image of God? Does God do so? Are you not His likeness? Why, then, do you permit yourselves to be degraded thus? Because evil masters have persuaded you to this folly, that they may profit from your bondage! They have conspired to keep you in slavery, and for their gain! They will sell you these plants, these roots, these foul creatures from the sea, this flesh of animals, that at your expense they may enrich themselves! But now, at last, I bring you truth! I bring you release from superstition and bondage! God does not eat — why should you? You are His likeness! Assert your freedom! Cast off your shackles! Away with food! Death to those who sell it!'

"Proceeding thus, Baptiste, I could without difficulty launch a crusade to end the tyranny of food on earth. My followers would pledge themselves to destroy food, to kill all who sell it or prepare it. We would burn the harvests and plow under the growing fields. What remained, we would feed to the horses."

"Then all would starve, Monseigneur *mon frère.*"

"Assuredly. And if our friend who preached in the market place could have his way, our souls would starve for want of the food of heaven — which would be far worse."

"I did not comprehend his words, Monseigneur *mon frère.* But I knew that they were evil."

"It is because you have the gift of truth, Baptiste. You smell a lie, even when you do not understand the liar."

"But what will happen, Monseigneur *mon frère?* Will they destroy the sacrament? Will they kill us?"

"It would be difficult, Baptiste, to destroy food from the face of the earth. It is impossible to destroy God. It may be they will kill us, but remember: who dies for Him will live with Him, forever. Whatever happens, we have God always with us. We need not fear."

Again the Community was in an uproar.

Father Prior listened to the story of Baptiste, and greatly to his astonishment, received the old servant as a postulant.

The unwisdom of this decision was immediately apparent to the brotherhood. The strict order which regulated the humbler tasks of the Community was seriously disturbed by the addition of one so little fitted for monastic life as Brother Baptiste, and so incapable of improvement.

Whatever one told him to do, he did the opposite. Plainly, this could not be tolerated. A protest to Father Prior was in order.

But if Brother Baptiste was incapable of learning, his fellow Religious did not share that defect. They at least were able to profit from past experience; and they took good care not to repeat a previous mistake.

Thus, they did not entrust the execution of this commission to another, but Brother Etienne carried the complaints against Brother Baptiste to Father Prior, in person. Father Prior listened, the tips of his long slim fingers placed against each other, his deep-set eyes downcast. Brother Etienne found this position disconcerting in the extreme; he would have preferred that Father Prior look at him direct. It seemed to Brother Etienne that he addressed his complaints to a stone statue, or to one lost in prayer, who nevertheless heard his words and weighed them, unfavorably.

When Brother Etienne had done speaking, Father Prior, after a considerable pause, separated his finger tips, brought them together again, and without raising his eyes, replied.

"I thank you, Brother, for calling my attention to the defects of Brother Baptiste, which try your patience so sorely. I myself was in some doubt as to the wisdom of admitting Brother Baptiste to permanent membership in the Community because of his age, but your words have decided me.

"It is without question desirable that the work of the Community proceed with order and method. But it is even more desirable — it is essential, in fact — that the members of the Community be humble and patient. While you have been enumerating the defects of Brother Baptiste, you have in reality been calling my attention to defects even more serious which I have been in some danger of overlooking, and it is for this that I thank you. It became clear to me as you spoke that the Community is in great need of a model of humility and patience, and that nowhere could I find a better example of these virtues than Brother Baptiste." He raised his eyes and clapped them, as it were, on the eyes of Brother Etienne.

"You have relieved me of the burden of decision, Brother. Brother Baptiste remains."

ii

The departure of Louise left Anne mistress of the Château, in so far as it had a mistress. Thus, Anne again had her way; and again she found it not at all to her liking.

It was one thing to be despised by a Countess, who was also the wife of one's lover. It was quite another thing to be abused by the servant of that Countess, who was herself no better than she should be, but a great deal worse.

However inferior in rank to Paul's wife, Anne at least was not a chambermaid: as she took pains to remind this insolent domestic who presumed to lord it over Paul's mistress in the absence of his wife.

"And I, thank heaven," returned Marianne, "am not ugly and fat."

With her hands she circled her slender waist, staring rudely and meaningly at Anne's uncomely bulk.

Anne burst into tears. She had no protection against such attacks. She could give no answer that the girl would heed.

"How dare you talk to me like that?" she sobbed.

Marianne curtsied in mock respect.

"And how will your Highness prevent?"

"I was born in a Château!" Anne wailed. "I am entitled to some respect!"

"Then why does your Highness not return to her palace?"

Why, indeed?

Brissac, from all reports, was in ruins: not that it had ever been otherwise, as far as Anne could remember. But now it could not be lived in by anything but rats and mice and owls and stray cats and soldiers, who were shortly coming, and would take up their quarters at the abandoned Château. With them was also coming a great general, who would be the guest of Paul at Guillemont: Anne heard this, not from Paul, who told her nothing, but from her brother Pierre, who was planning to join the soldiers when they should arrive. This would at last give him some occupation. The young man suffered from perpetual boredom due to an excess of leisure, which he was neither clever nor humble enough to turn to good account.

Anne's father had died shortly after their removal to Guille-mont, of excesses more substantial and less innocuous than leisure. Her mother still lived, but in a vaporous world of her own imagining, peopled with wraiths and spirits invisible to all but herself, with whom she consorted and whom she daily more resembled. As confidante and adviser, she was of no use whatever to her unhappy daughter, who found herself without help or refuge in her misery. Taunted, ignored, despised by all, Anne had no longer the support even of Paul's favor. He had withdrawn his attentions entirely from her, and it was no secret that the impudent serving wench, formerly the chambermaid of Ma-dame, had now displaced Anne in the affections of Monseigneur.

It was a secret, however — rigorously and hitherto successfully kept by the only two who were party to it — that the chamber-maid did not reserve her affections exclusively for Monseigneur, but shared them with another.

If walls have ears, windows have eyes and doors tongues. Secrets of this sort are never safe. It was inevitable that the liaison between Armand and Marianne should ultimately come to the knowledge of the jealous and embittered woman who was best able and most ready to profit from it.

"*Maman,* what does it mean, to marry?"

Anne stared at her first-born.

"What are you talking about, Paulot? Where did you hear that word?"

"In the temple of *la grand'mère, Maman.* Pierre and Charles and I, we were playing robbers. I was hiding from them. I hid in the temple. I heard a noise, and I thought it was Pierre and Charles, but it was not. It was Armand, and that girl, Marianne. I kept very quiet and they did not see me. They kissed each other a great deal, *Maman,* and Marianne said, 'But, Armand, why don't you marry me? I wish you would marry me.' She said it many times, *Maman,* but he would kiss her and say that he loved her but he would not marry her. Now, to love, I know what that means, but I do not know what the other word means, to marry."

"Shut your mouth," said Anne. "Don't talk nonsense. You will know, soon eonugh."

She was about to slap him when she bethought herself that this information deserved reward rather than punishment. Accordingly, she gave him a bonbon and went in search of Paul.

The plans of Armand Pitou had gone, one after the other, grievously awry. So closely interwoven were these plans that the miscarriage of one affected all the others.

He had lost, or misplaced, his manuscript. This was a disaster of the first magnitude. He could not understand how it had come about.

He remembered concealing his treasure on the shelf in the armoire of his room, to safeguard it against just such a mishap: but he was, he knew, notoriously absent-minded. Without doubt he had removed it to some place safer still, and now could not recall where. He ransacked his own quarters without success. To search the whole Château was clearly impossible, but he explored every corner where he could possibly have laid it, and many where he could not; but to no avail. The manuscript did not come to light.

It occurred to him that it might have been stolen, but for what reason, or by whom, he could not imagine. The sons of Monseigneur were obnoxious beyond belief, and he loathed them; but they were too small to reach the top shelf in the armoire, and this, besides, was not the sort of prank that would amuse them. They would steal any object that took their fancy; but they were not likely to be tempted by mere scribbled pages.

And apart from the children, whom could he suspect? Whatever their personal differences and animosities, in this matter of religion, all at Guillemont were agreed. It was to the interest of all that his book be printed, and as soon as possible. But on the very day on which he had planned to take it to Brocard, he could not find it; he had not found it since.

This was the first reverse he had encountered in his self-appointed mission of freeing the world from the tyranny of Rome. Till now all things had played into his hands: he was not used to reverses. He was therefore utterly at a loss how to deal with this emergency. He stormed; he raged; he fumed in anger and impatience, while realizing that his fury accomplished nothing.

To get his manuscript to the printer was the first step in his plans, on which all else depended. Thwarted in this, he was helpless as to the rest.

He had planned also to break off his affair with Marianne. This depended on his leaving Guillemont, and he could not, or would not, leave Guillemont without his manuscript. His disappointment impelled him to seek the consolations of love more frequently than he might otherwise have done. This intention, therefore, was not only postponed, but might actually be prevented, by delay. To break with Marianne was becoming increasingly difficult; if he did not find his manuscript soon, it would, he feared, be forever impossible.

He stormed through room after room like a hurricane; still the manuscript eluded him. He told himself repeatedly that it must be somewhere; only a conflagration could have destroyed it from the face of the earth; and as long as it was still in existence, he must, he would, find it. At any moment he might come upon it in some unexpected cabinet or drawer, in some corner he had passed a hundred times and overlooked; but meanwhile, precious time, valuable time, was being wasted.

His extended campaign of preaching must also wait till the book was found, but he could turn one at least of these idle days to good account. He could preach at Guillemont.

He selected a market day to assure himself of a sizable audience, and rode to the village confident that his past triumphs would be repeated.

Never, till now, had his words failed of their effect; never had he spoken in vain. Whenever and wherever he preached, he always made converts, few or many. But at Guillemont the devil himself appeared, disguised as a Religious, and answered him. The succession of disasters precipitated by the loss of his manuscript culminated in such a defeat as he had never yet experienced and could not have anticipated.

That it was the devil who answered him, Armand did not doubt. Armand had seen him as he emerged from the church; he watched him talking on the portico with the village priest; he recognized him at once as an enemy of light, and by two infallible signs. He wore the livery of Satan, and he was crippled and maimed as befitted the servants of the fiend, though all were not as plainly branded in the sight of men as this one, and therefore not so easily identified. He broke into the middle of Armand's discourse, and threw over his hearers such a spell that the eloquence of Armand was of no effect.

Riding home in fury, Armand reminded himself that this defeat was not final. There still remained, as he had told Paul, the arguments of fire and sword. These would succeed where persuasion had failed: not to convert, but to punish and destroy. Armand swore that they should be used to their full effect, at Guillemont, and especially at the monastery whence this menial of Satan had emerged to answer him.

Armand attributed his defeat to the diabolic powers enjoyed by his adversary, and also to the anxiety and uncertainty under which he himself had labored of late, and which detracted much from the customary force and power of his words.

This explanation was just and reasonable and Armand told himself that he had no cause to feel humiliated by his failure to convert the village of Guillemont. Nevertheless, he could not bring himself to mention the circumstance to anyone, least of all to Paul.

Nor could he altogether hide from Paul the fact that matters were not falling out entirely as he wished: a circumstance which Paul observed with secret and malicious pleasure.

Marianne turned things over in her mind and decided that the time had come to strike a bargain with her lover.

That the bargain might be concluded on her own terms and to her satisfaction, she laid her plans, simple as they were, with great care.

These plans were based on a strategy which no woman has to be taught, because all are born with the knowledge of it, though all do not use it with equal skill.

Her method was simply to get Armand alone, and then to appear as beguiling and ingenuous as possible, while actually leading him by the nose into a trap which he would not suspect until it had closed upon him.

Marianne had now diverted the essences of Madame, as well as many ribbons and furbelows and articles of finery and apparel, to her own use, and she had no qualms about employing them freely when occasion demanded: as at present.

She put on her prettiest cap and apron. Scented and curled and beribboned, she went in search of Armand. She found him, as on a previous occasion, in the library. Unseen by him, she watched him for a few moments, and nodded, satisfied at what she saw.

His arms were full of books which he had taken from the shelves. He was running through the volumes, shaking the pages, and replacing them, one after the other, in nervous haste. He was plainly agitated and distraught, his hair disheveled, his face flushed. He had the harassed, bewildered look of one who must accomplish the impossible and does not even know how to begin.

Marianne stepped within the door.

"Armand," she said softly.

He turned. Seeing her, he put his books on the table. She approached and stood before him, enveloped in a cloud of fragrance, looking up with assumed shyness from beneath her long lashes. He took her in his arms.

"Armand," she whispered, "you are troubled. Always you are hunting, hunting. What is it you have lost?"

He did not answer, being too occupied with kissing her.

She whispered again, smoothing his untidy hair: "Is it your writing, Armand? Is that what you have lost?"

"But yes." Drawing back, he looked down at her in some surprise. "How did you know?"

"Because I think — I am not sure, Armand, but I think — I have seen it somewhere."

"*You* have seen it?"

She nodded.

"For the love of heaven, where?"

She drew his head gently down toward her again.

"I — I have forgotten. But if you are very nice to me, Armand, perhaps I shall be able to remember."

"In the name of God, what do you mean?" He released her and stepped back, regarding her in astonishment and considerable irritation. "All this time I have been looking for my book, and you knew where it was, and did not tell me?"

She looked down, twisting her hands together, pouting.

"But, Armand, you would not be good to me. You — "

"Do I not give you all the attention I can spare from my work? What more do you want?"

"You know what I want, Armand. I want you to marry me. If you will marry me, it may be I can remember where I have seen your writing."

He stared at her. His face darkened in anger as the full meaning of her words became clear to him.

She returned his gaze, the growing anger in his face answered by increasing bewilderment and terror in hers. She realized, to her dismay, that she had miscalculated, and grievously. The passion of a man for his work can, and often does, far outweigh his passion for a woman, and his jealousy is in proportion to that passion: facts which had hitherto escaped Marianne's attention. This masculine idiosyncrasy was brought to her notice now, all in a moment, and with it the humiliating realization that she was not in his eyes a seductive charmer who had enticed him to her will by a clever trick, but a culprit and a fool who had spoiled everything by a stupid blunder.

Armand stated the same truth bluntly, in unequivocal terms.

"You diabolical little cheating thief!" he shouted. "Marry you! I have a good mind to murder you for this!"

He took a step toward her. She screamed and fled.

He would have followed in pursuit, with what precise intention he himself did not know, but he was detained by an interruption. The doors of the balcony opened, and Paul entered. Armand turned: congratulating himself that again Marianne had escaped, just in time.

But immediately it appeared that this self-congratulation was premature.

Paul was in a towering rage. He wore his sword. His fingers gripped the hilt, and it was plain that he refrained from drawing the weapon with the greatest difficulty.

Armand perceived at once, and to his discomfiture, that the object of Paul's wrath was himself.

Paul made no secret of the fact. He confronted Armand with the reason for his displeasure without hesitation and without subtlety.

"So this is what you have been up to!" he shouted. "Living on my hospitality and seducing my servants while you pretend to work for religion!"

In view of Paul's obvious eagerness to draw his weapon, Armand controlled his temper. Being himself unarmed, he thought it more prudent to placate Paul than to defend his honor.

"I, seduce your servants?" he repeated, in mild surprise. "What are you talking about? What do you mean?"

"You know perfectly well what I mean!" Paul's fingers opened and closed on the hilt of his sword. Armand watched in considerable trepidation. He felt keenly the humiliation of his position: that he, who had just shouted in righteous anger at Marianne, should now be shouted at by Paul. Marianne had fled before him, which was as it should be: but it was not compatible with his dignity that he should now flee before Paul. This sudden reversal of his position smacked of the ludicrous, but he preferred to lose his dignity rather than his life. He moved away from the table to assure himself a free passage to the door in case of need.

Paul continued his shouting: "Because I do not find her in your arms, you think you can deceive me with your lies, but you cannot! She was here not ten minutes ago! The place reeks like a perfumery!"

Armand shrugged. Habit got the better of discretion: "Can I help it if she prefers me?"

"You can leave the place, and at once! I am sick of the sight of you! Get out — unless you want me to throw you out, like a dog!"

"But how can I leave?" replied Armand. "I must first find my book. And things are much too serious for us to become embroiled over some trivial affair of the heart. We are on the threshold of a great victory: the end of darkness and oppression is in sight. We cannot stop now. We must go on, to triumph. When I find my book — "

"Oh, your book, your book!" Paul had drawn his sword halfway from the scabbard. He thrust it back with a clatter which set Armand's teeth on edge. "I am as sick of your book as I am of you! All that writing was an excuse to amuse yourself with my servants while you ate and drank at my expense! Is this the end of all your handsome promises? You said your book would convert the world. You said you would preach to those who could not read. Now there is no book and you have not left the place. Why don't you make good your boasting and bragging? Why don't you show something for all your fine words?"

Armand grew more and more uneasy. He could get the better of any man in an honest argument, but he had never before tried to reason with a roaring bull, whose passion deafened him to persuasion, and who carried a sword and seemed obsessed with the desire to use it. Armand was thus driven to defend himself, even at the cost of admitting his defeat.

"It should not be necessary to tell you that the loss of my manuscript is a bitter disappointment to me," he said stiffly. "And I fail to see how the book can be printed without the manuscript. Nor can I begin my campaign of preaching until I find it. But I have not been idle. I have done what I could. I preached at Guillemont."

"You preached at Guillemont? Where are your converts? Why have I not heard of your success?"

"I had no success. The devil prevented."

"The devil prevented? What do you mean?"

"The devil appeared from nowhere and answered me."

"Ah. I comprehend. Another preacher was present who spoke better than you, so that you could not persuade the people to your views."

"He was the devil himself, I tell you — or one of his arch-fiends. He seduced the people with his lies so that my words had no effect. He was disguised in the habit of a Religious, but it was easy to recognize him for any who had eyes to see. He bore the marks of his master, Satan: he was mutilated and deformed. He limped like the fiend himself, and he had only one hand, while the other — "

It was Armand's purpose merely to convince Paul that his opponent was the devil; he did not intend to evoke the person in question. But Paul stared at him as if his words had had precisely that effect.

"You say — he limped?" Paul repeated, in a harsh, unnatural voice.

"Horribly."

"He had lost a hand?"

"It is what I said."

"And the other was mutilated?"

"It was wanting two fingers."

"Had he — was he?" Paul swallowed. He seemed to put the question with some difficulty: "Was he — well-favored — ? Of a comely appearance?"

Armand shrugged. "In him I saw clear proof of a fact we all know — that the devil can transform himself, when he wills, into an angel of light."

"And — you say — he wore the habit of a Religious?"

Armand was at a loss to account for this questioning, but he was relieved that Paul's anger was diverted from himself. He replied, with something of his old confidence: "A Brother from the monastery yonder, to which I shall direct Coligny and his men as soon as they arrive. I do not understand what delays them; they should be here now. And when that center of idolatrous worship is eliminated, then we — "

Armand's confidence was short lived. Paul cut into his words with vicious fury:

"You will do nothing of the kind — not while I live to prevent it!"

He drew his sword. Armand ran from the room.

Paul overtook him at the top of the stairs and plunged his sword in the ex-priest's back.

Armand threw up his hands with a choking cry and pitched headlong down the stairs.

His body rolled and thudded downward like a sack of meal. It hurtled to the foot of the curving staircase, and lay there, motionless. A dark pool issued from beneath it, and spread over the marble floor.

Paul descended slowly, wiping his sword. He investigated the body. Armand was dead.

Paul stood looking at the man he had killed. He was strangely shaken, but he felt neither compunction nor remorse. His agitation was due, not to the murder, but to the motive for it; and this motive had nothing to do with Marianne.

"So it was the devil who answered you. Well, I have sent you where you can answer him through eternity, my fine preacher! It is gratifying to know that Michel preaches a better sermon than you. And the devil must enjoy this irony, that I have killed a man to protect Michel." A strong shudder seized and shook him; he replaced his sword in the scabbard with a vicious thrust, as if sheathing it a second time in Armand's back. "I will misdirect them — I will kill the lot of them, if I must — but as God lives, I swear they will never find that monastery: never."

A commotion rose in the courtyard: shouts, voices, the ring and clatter of hoofs. Paul stepped over the dead body of Armand and went out to ascertain the cause of it.

It was as he suspected. Coligny, long overue, had arrived.

Thus, the great work of Armand Pitou failed of accomplishing what its author intended, because it was never printed.

It remained for many years in the bottom of a chest of linens where Marianne had hidden it, to which she alone had the key.

Ultimately the chest fell into the hands of an antiquarian who emptied it of its contents and sold them. The pages of writing he placed on a shelf in the back of his shop, as being of interest to no one, where in due course they were devoured by rats and mice.

Whether they would have justified their author's expectations, if printed, it is therefore impossible to say.

Tu es sacerdos
in aeternum secundum
ordinem Melchisedech ...

12. A Priest Forever

i

It was the day of Frère Mich'.

In April it had been hot as August; now, early in December, it was cold as February. The sun was obscured by clouds the color of ice and steel; the water was a dull, cold gray; the wind was that of midwinter, of the north: so vicious and biting that it was impossible to believe that this road, these fields, these vineyards hardly a week since had shimmered in the haze of late autumn, and drowsed beneath a smiling sun.

Michel had much ado to rout Marceline out of her warm stall and persuade her into her harness and on her way, a reluctant and bitterly protesting donkey. Nor was his reluctance far behind hers. He felt the cold sorely, his habit being no protection against the wind which thrust its icy blades between his ribs, and a brutal and living adversary, fought him each step of the way. Marceline trotted along, her ears back, her eyes half closed against the blowing dust, her countenance grim, her whole mien expressive of reproach and indignation; and Michel was tempted as he had never yet been to let her and the weather have their way. He had not gone far before he was conscious of a tightness in his throat and a soreness in his lungs. He debated, seriously, whether it might be the part of wisdom to turn back.

Marceline, sensing his hesitation, looked at him out of the corner of her eye, and indicated plainly that she was more than ready to concur in his decision, should it be the wise and prudent one of return.

In thus anticipating his verdict, and revealing her sentiments too plainly, Marceline like many another woman, defeated her own purpose.

"Marceline, we both alike need discipline. I am ashamed of you, and I hope that you are ashamed of me. Is this the fruit of our monastic life, that we turn tail and run for home at the first touch of cold, giving for excuse that we may have contracted a pleurisy? If we have, it will be a good penance; if we have not, it will be a bad excuse. And to sulk and pout will do us no good. We do not return."

Never had he walked so long a way to the village. Each mile was two, and the last, ten. In this struggle to keep going, he passed the point where the children met him before he realized that there were no children.

He halted and looked about him in surprise. Never yet had they been prevented by heat or cold, rain or snow, wind or storm, from keeping their rendezvous on the day of Frère Mich'.

"What can this mean, Marceline? Where are they?"

Nor was there a living soul in sight. In all his walk, he had, he now realized, met no one: and this was market day. It was cold, yes; but not cold enough to deter the shrewd Gallic bargainer from the pursuit of his livelihood on the day appointed for it. Ordinarily he would have met them, watery of eye and red of nose, hugging themselves in shawls or cloaks, driving their protesting livestock before them with expostulations the more vehement because of their own discomfort; but today there was no one. Michel stood alone in a desert of solitude in which, except for Marceline, no living thing moved, and only the wind spoke.

The icy fingers which had seized his lungs closed now on his heart. This ominous stillness, this absence of all life and activity, could mean only one thing: the Huguenots had come.

He turned Marceline about.

"Go back to the monastery, little one. When they see you coming alone, with your baskets full, they will know all is not well. I will pray to Our Lady, and she will tell them what to do.

She will protect them, and you; and she will put it into the hearts of my Brothers to pray for me." He stood for a moment, stroking the nose of his little companion. "It may be, Marceline, that we have taken our bread to market for the last time; it may be that this is farewell. Go now" — he gave her a light slap on her neat gray flank — "and do not linger, and do not fall asleep on the way."

As if she had understood, the little donkey trotted obediently off down the road. Michel watched until she had disappeared round the bend. Then he went on to the village, alone.

Until he neared the top of the hill, he met no one. All windows were shuttered, all doors barred. The village might have been abandoned, and himself the only living creature in it.

Suddenly, from the heart of this desolation, there rose a shout: "Here is game, comrades! A Monk! A priest!"

Turning a corner, he all but ran into three men lounging in a doorway out of the wind. They wore breastplates and helmets and carried pikes. One of them stepped from his shelter and seized Michel by the arm.

A priest! — The heart of Michel kindled at this designation: his cowl hid the fact that he had no tonsure. But he could not accept without protest that which was not his due.

"Ah, no, my friends. You do me too great an honor. I am not a priest, but only —"

"Not a priest! Ho! ho!" His captor looked Michel up and down. "What are you then — a dancing master?"

"No doubt," said his companion. "How gracefully he steps."

"Come along, priest, and we will teach you to remember your unholy orders. Phoo!" The third man spat at Michel.

They marched him along the narrow cobbled street up the hill, unaware that their words, intended for insult, had filled him with joy.

"A priest: they mistake me for a priest. They could not call me so, if God did not permit. And since God Himself permits —"

Here was a wonder which he could not bring himself to utter, even in the silence of his heart.

Some months before another had called him priest. *"You He has ordained by His choice and your consent."* Beautiful and comforting as those words were, Michel could not accept them as truth, until God should confirm them in some manner of His own which would permit of no doubt. Now again he was called priest, not in love and kindness, but in mockery and contempt: could it be that this was the confirmation of the Abbé's words?

Was it possible, as the Abbé with his last breath had declared, that God had indeed summoned him, Michel, to His priesthood as truly as any who had ever stood before the altar, and had consecrated and ordained him in the sight of heaven, while keeping it secret from all on earth, even from Michel himself?

Had he not offered himself daily, a sacrifice of reparation for the sin of one who, ordained a priest, had despised his sacred office and forfeited its rights?

There was a servant who buried his Lord's talent in the earth, and on the day, of reckoning, the talent was taken from him, and given to another: could it be that God had indeed signed the soul of Michel with the priestly character this other had despised, while decreeing that he should not know it until the consummation of the sacrifice?

Those killed for the faith before baptism, dying as Christians, are by death made Christians. If these men, believing him a priest, should kill him as a priest —?

Joy stabbed him with pain. He would have fallen to his knees in the street, struck helpless by this wonder, pierced through and through with delight, but his captors prevented. They pushed and hurried him along, to the accompaniment of jests which he did not hear; their rude words had lifted his soul to heights of beauty it had never before reached.

The soul finds its fullness of joy in becoming that which it truly is. Michel knew that to be a priest, was to be himself. The deprivation of the priesthood was an interior mutilation as real as that which he had suffered in his body, and far more profound: sent him by God for the accomplishment of His holy purpose, and accepted by Michel with gladness for that reason, but a mutilation none the less.

Deprived of the priesthood, his soul was less than itself, as his body, deprived of its members, was less than itself. However willingly accepted, for however high an end, this deprivation was necessarily a suffering and a loss. To be admitted to the priest-hood would be for Michel to attain his full stature, to be wholly himself; with both hands to lay hold on that which was truly his; to limp no longer, but to stand upright, to leap, to run.

Here was a door through which others passed, but never Michel. *Knock, and it shall be opened unto you:* long ago he had knocked, to be told that this door could not open to him. He sent his heart within, while his body remained outside, in hunger, in longing, in love. Now the key was turning in the lock, the latch was lifting: could it be that this door was about to open, and to him?

Only one step lay beyond this, to reach the summit of beauty and the height of joy: that this door should open wide, this hope be turned to certainty.

But he was not allowed to pursue these reflections in peace. Emerging into the market square, he found himself in the midst of a confusion that brought him rudely back to a knowledge of his whereabouts and a realization of the disaster that had over-taken the village and his friends.

All was in disorder. The market stalls were abandoned. Carts were overturned and the produce dumped in the square. Pigs were running in and out among the empty carts and stalls, squeal-ing with fright. Chickens and ducks and hens squawked and cackled, their wings flapping, their legs tied together; the figs of Paulette, the cabbages of la mère Bigotte, the cakes of Berthe, the bread of Poulot, the sausages of Jean Martin, the shellfish of Pierre Gapin — all were kicked and thrown about the square, as if destined for destruction in such an imaginary crusade against food as Michel had described to Baptiste. A regiment of cats and dogs had assembled and was making short work of the meat and fish.

But this was a minor tragedy, a secondary cause of distress. The square was filled with soldiers, and they were herding the people along singly, and in groups. The protests of the prisoners were added to those of the abandoned and terrified animals, and to as little effect.

Before the Hôtel de Ville two lines of soldiers stood. Past these Michel was escorted, with a conspicuous lack of that reverence due the office to which his captors had insisted on elevating him:

"Comrades, see — here is fun — a priest!"

"And of a strange new sort, who says he is a dancing master."

"And truly I believe he is right. See how he dances: *là-là, là-là.* I wonder, can he sing, too?"

"We will make him sing and dance tomorrow. We will teach him some new steps."

The doors of the Hôtel de Ville were opened and Michel was thrust in.

He found himself in a large paneled room, extending the length of the wing, in which town business was customarily transacted. Along one side, deep windows gave on the inner court. At the end stood a massive carved table and heavy chairs, where, however, no town official now sat. In the room were gathered about fifty prisoners: men, women, even children. At sight of Michel there rose a shout:

"Frère Mich' — it is Frère Mich'!"

Immediately he was surrounded. They threw themselves on him, they knelt at his feet. They clung to him, weeping. They kissed his sleeves, his skirts, his hand. He struggled to shake them off and to free himself, but in vain.

"Oh, my little ones, let me go! I entreat you, let me go! Kneel to God — yes — and beg His mercy for us all — but do not, for the love of heaven, kneel to me!"

He might as easily have silenced the wind.

"Frère Mich' has come — our Frère Mich' has come! Pray for us, Frère Mich', pray for us! God will give us courage, if you ask it, Frère Mich'!"

Paulette Dubois sobbed, wiping her eyes on her shawl. The children had not met him on the road, for they were here. Jeannot attached himself to his sleeve, as of custom, sobbing also, although he did not know precisely why, except that everything was strange, and his mother was crying, which was reason enough why he should cry, too. *La mère* Bigotte clutched his other sleeve in her brown claw and raised it to her lips. Jean Martin scurried toward him like a terrified hare scuttling for its hole. The beady-eyed vendor of shellfish, the enormous pastry artist, the imperturbable cheesemonger, the genial baker who would never again receive the bread of Notre Dame des Prés from the baskets of Marceline — all were here.

All but the Widow Douroux, who had gone on the side of the soldiers, as she said.

Monsieur le Curé also was absent. He was in hiding; word had been brought him in time, and he had escaped.

Recognizing his friends one by one, Michel felt a tightness in his throat which had nothing to do with the cold. For here were martyrs, martyrs all: simple folk, without birth or breeding, lacking the more conspicuous gifts of intellect and spirit, far perhaps from the heights of sanctity in daily life, wrangling and acrimonious in the pursuit of their livelihood, but strong enough in the day of trial to have made this most supreme of all choices: to die for their faith rather than to live without it.

They were, moreover, his people, his own. His place was with them now, to give them what help and encouragement he could. Recalling how nearly he had come to turning back with Marceline, he thanked God who in His mercy had not permitted him, for fear of a pleurisy, to cheat himself of martyrdom. And as God had strengthened him to continue in the face of the wind, so He would strengthen him to continue with these, his children, to the end.

The great doors opened and shut continually, and the soldiers thrust in more victims, of all ages and both sexes. On one such occasion the doors did not immediately shut, but a voice which Michel recognized bawled into the room:

"You, priest! Where is that priest who pretends to be a dancing master?"

Michel looked up. His captor stood in the doorway, silhouetted against the light outside, and holding by the arm a woman. Of her Michel could see nothing, except that she was covered by a long cloak and held her face hidden in her hands.

"Here, you dancing priest! Here is a pupil for you! We have a wager how long your vows will last when you teach this beauty your steps!"

He thrust her violently into the hall. The doors swung shut again behind her.

She stumbled and fell. Michel was unable to reach her to prevent this mishap, but he approached and took her by the elbow, to help her to her feet. She resisted his efforts and remained on her knees, with her face in her hands, sobbing.

"Are you hurt, Mademoiselle? Pay no heed to what they say. They are so many swine, who after all fulfill the will of God in being swine, while these beasts do not. Besides, Mademoiselle, he is quite mistaken. I am not a priest, so that his words which sought to slander the dignity of the priesthood, do not in fact do so at all. I am merely a lay Brother who —"

He stopped short. She had taken her hands from her face and was staring at him, her great dark eyes filled with wonder. The hood of her cloak fell back, revealing a tangle of burnished curls. The amazement in her eyes was reflected in Michel's.

Each stared at the other, transfixed.

"Louise! What does this mean? What do you here?"

She scrambled to her feet, shaking off his assistance. Color flooded her cheeks, and she hid her face in her hands, trembling visibly.

"That man," she gasped. "The things he said — to you —"

"Forget him," said Michel. "He is less than a man, and not worth remembering. Tell me, why are you here? That is what I want to know."

Still she did not answer. She stood tense, her hands tight pressed against her face, struggling to subdue a paroxysm of weeping.

"Come to one side, Louise," said Michel gently.

He led her to one of the deep windows giving on the inner court of the Hôtel. The courtyard was deserted. Looking out on the winter stillness, separated from the others by the length of the great room, they might have been alone.

"Tell me, Louise: are you here because you are one of us? Because you have come home?"

"Yes, Michel — yes." She nodded, catching her breath. "Oh, Michel! Did you pray for me?"

"Have I ever ceased to pray for you, Louise?"

"I knew it." She took a deep breath. "Michel, can you ever forgive me?"

"Forgive you, Louise? What is there to forgive?"

"Oh, Michel — that terrible day, and the things I said! Michel, I do not wish to excuse myself, but it seems to me I was possessed. It was not I who spoke, but a devil."

"I entreat you, Louise, do not think of it again. For I do not. You are right: it was not you, but a devil. And I have too much concern to think of the things of God to remember what is said to me by the devil. Tell me: how is it you are here? How did you come back?"

"Because you prayed for me. Is not that reason enough?"

"I am ashamed, Louise. I prayed with so little faith. I doubted God's goodness to you, because I desired it so ardently. For my distrust I deserve only punishment, but see how His mercy deals with us instead! I begged that you might return, but I did not ask to know it, I did not ask to see or speak to you in my life again. And not only have you returned, but we are here together, and it is precisely the sort of wonder God works for His children, who are base enough to doubt His goodness and ungrateful enough to forget His benefits."

"Oh, Michel! If you say that you deserve punishment for your want of faith, what of me? For I have been guilty of far worse than that — as you know." She looked down, clasping her hands together tightly. "From the time you left, so long ago, my life was a long madness. I wonder that I did not end it, except that God stayed my hand. They told me that you had gone away because you no longer loved me, and I believed it. My love for you was sacred. When that was taken from me, nothing was any longer sacred, neither vows, nor love, nor faith — nothing. I married Paul of my own will, but I married in bitterness, and from spite. Afterward, I learned what really had happened: that you had not gone because you did not love me, but that you had been hurt — cruelly hurt, far worse than I knew — and that your father had sent you away. I discovered that they had lied to you, and to me. I believed that you must still love me, as I loved you, and I vowed that I would not rest until I found you. I no longer believed in God, Michel; nevertheless, I determined to force God to restore to me what He had taken from me. It mattered not to what lengths I went, so long as I had my way.

"And God permitted me to have my way. He permitted me to find you, and to carry out my plans according to my own mad folly. You remember how we passed you on the hunt. Afterwards I inquired — oh, how carefully! I learned where you were, and that you came to Guillemont on market days with the bread. You know the rest. You know what I did, to my everlasting shame."

She paused, hiding her face again.

"Yes? and then?"

"Michel, I struck you. I did not mean to hit you. I thought you would avoid the blow. When you did not" — she shuddered — "it was horrible, Michel, horrible! But it brought me to my senses. With that blow my devil left me. From that moment I began to see things, not as I wanted them to be, but as they really were. I had tried to bend the truth to my liking, and I had broken myself instead. I struck at the truth, Michel, and I killed a lie.

"For I had believed all this time that you loved me, as I loved you. When I saw you, I knew from your habit that you were in religion, but I still believed it; I would not permit myself to believe otherwise. Had you loved me as I thought, you would not have refused what I offered. But you did refuse, and with such finality as to leave me no hope. I knew that I could do nothing to change you, nothing to persuade you differently.

"And at the same time, Michel, I knew that you could not live without love, as I could not. You did not love me, or any other in my place: nevertheless, you loved. I saw that, plainly. Even in my misery I could not mistake it. Your life without me was not desolation, as mine was without you. I had only bitterness, but you had found peace. It shone from you, Michel. It pierced even my darkness, and I could not fail to see it.

"I knew then what I had done. In my blindness I had invented a Michel who did not exist. My invention would have agreed to my plans; you did not. Which did I prefer? Could I have changed you — according to my wishes — would I have done so?

"Michel, I knew there could be no question. Though I should never see you again, I preferred you, yourself, to the falsehood I had set up in your place. I knew, Michel, that if we were free, both of us, to follow the course we had planned to follow so long ago — if you had not entered religion and I had not married Paul — I would choose now — I would a thousand times prefer — that you should do as you have done, rather than seek any lesser happiness with me. I knew without any doubt that you have chosen the better way. I knew what you meant when you said that deprived of your vows and your habit, you would ask for them again, preferring them to the love I had offered you. And Michel, how gladly I would consent to that choice!"

There was a brief silence. "Oh, Louise! — What then?"

"I did what you told me to do."

"What I told you to do?"

"Yes. I went to the curé at Guillemont. He heard my confession. He found a home for me with a woman of the village, and there I have been living since. And, Michel, I never thought to be happy in all my life, but I am happy."

There was another silence.

"Louise, what can I say? I have prayed every day that you might find happiness, and in the love of God. I knew that you would never find it elsewhere. And now you tell me that this is so."

"Michel, I have longed to tell you. I thought perhaps, one day, I would write. I believed you would want to know. But I — I was afraid —"

"Afraid, Louise? Of what? Nothing could give me greater joy than what you tell me — nothing. For your welfare is of first concern to me. You said I did not love you, but you are wrong. In loving God we do not cease to love each other."

She wept, openly. "Yes, Michel. I know that now. But I did not then. I believed that those in religion loved not at all, or with a cold, distant love that is of the mind only."

"It is a common mistake. And some, perhaps, do indeed suffer from this misfortune. But I cannot love like that, nor can you."

"No, Michel. We cannot."

"Nor could the saints. Their love was a conflagration that kindled all it touched. They loved others more, not less, because they loved God. To love all creatures is the sweet burden God imposed on us, and He does not add, to me, 'Excepting only

Louise,' and to you, 'Love everyone, Louise, but do not love Michel.' "

"Ah, Michel! I would be guilty of a great disobedience if God should lay such a charge on me, for I could never fulfill it."

"Nor I. For you are dearer to me than anyone on earth, except, perhaps, the priest who found me, and took me to the monastery, and showed me where this happiness lies that we have been speaking of."

"You should love him best. You owe him most."

"But I have loved you longest. I cannot remember a time when I did not love you."

"Yes. It is a very long time, is it not, Michel?"

"But when I speak to you now it does not seem so. For you have not changed. I would not know that a year has passed since we talked together in your father's garden."

"Save your flatteries, sir, they will do you no good. I have no fortune to bequeath you."

"Nor could I use it if you had. And by that you may know that it is not flattery, but the truth."

"It is you who have not changed, Michel."

"Ah, there you are guilty of a gross prevarication. Nor is it subtle enough to be flattery. For I have been patched and altered like an old garment in the hands of a blundering tailor, and no flattery can persuade me otherwise."

"Michel, the garment is more beautiful than ever — how beautiful you do not know. The alterations have improved it, though I did not think that was possible. And in saying this, I, too, am free from the charge of flattery, having no more to gain from it than you."

"From flattery, perhaps, but not from prejudice: I fear your judgment is not wholly impartial, Louise. But there is no use quarreling with you about so trivial a matter, so I will keep my difference of opinion to myself. Does it occur to you, Louise, that nothing in all our lives has fallen out as we have planned, and yet all our prayers have been answered?"

"Yes, Michel. That is true."

"Even to this, that we might die together. Do you remember?"

"Oh, Michel! Can I forget?"

"I believe that my mother's prayers were always heard: and with good reason, as we now see."

"But, Michel, did you not also ask that — that I might not marry Paul?"

"No, but only that you might prefer me."

"Ah — how easily that was arranged!"

"I omitted to specify marriage as the outcome of this peference, taking it for granted."

"I am thankful for that oversight, Michel."

"Yes. Such a request might have caused some little embarrassment in heaven, seeing it was not God's will for us. For your mother was right, Louise."

"I remember. She filled me with terror. She said God intended you to be a priest."

"No. He did not intend that I should be one, but only that I should desire it."

"How did you find that out, Michel?"

"At the monastery I discovered the most beautiful and perfect thing on earth, and that is Mass."

Louise nodded eagerly.

"Michel, you are right. I have not missed a day since I returned. And now I could not live without Mass."

"And then I knew, Louise, that more than anything I ever wanted in all my life, I longed to be a priest, that I might celebrate Mass."

She looked at him. He returned her gaze. Her eyes filled with understanding and with sorrow.

"Oh — *Michel!*"

He smiled.

"Do not look so distressed, Louise. Did I not say that all my prayers have been answered?"

"But — but not this, Michel. You are not — you could not —"

"It is true, the alterations disqualified me for the priesthood. But God found a use for the garment in spite of them. And that is all that matters."

"Oh, Michel — how thankful I am — at least it was not I — who stood in your way —!"

"Yes, Louise. God gave us nothing we wanted, and better

than we wanted. His will for us was more perfect, more beautiful than anything we planned for ourselves."

"Michel, who would believe this? After all that has happened, we meet thus, and you say to me, 'Louise, I rejoice that I did not marry you,' and I agree with all my heart, and this not from disappointment, or weariness with each other, or because we have ceased to love, but rather because we love more."

"And with a deeper and more perfect love: with the very love of God Himself. It is a love that needs no further purgation, Louise. We love now as we shall love forever: as we shall love tomorrow, please God in heaven."

She pressed her palms against her streaming eyes.

"Forgive me, Michel. It — it is too beautiful. I cannot bear it. In spite of my bitterness and rebellion, my pride and anger, God does not punish me, but sends me instead this beauty and this happiness. Michel! I might never have found it. I might never have known what it was to love like this — in peace, without fear, without jealousy, without torment, without — " She hesitated.

"Without desire," Michel finished for her, "except the desire of loving always more perfectly, of becoming filled to overflowing with the love of God, of becoming ourselves the very love of God. Without His grace, who among us could know it? Neither you, nor I, nor anyone. That is why those who do not know it, deny that it can be. But it is His gift to us, among the very greatest and most beautiful of all His gifts."

"And He gives it to *me*, Michel. I can understand that He should give it to you — but to *me* —!"

"But why to me, Louise, and not to you?"

"Michel, you have suffered, and so cruelly."

"As have you."

"But I rebelled. You did not."

"And for that reason I suffered less than you. Also, I had great help. It is true, God dealt with me harshly once, but sweetly ever since; and I have had such joy as few know on earth, because they never learn what is the truth, that the way of pain is the way to beauty. And for that reason I pity all others, counting them less fortunate than myself, although they might be disposed to pity me."

"It is impossible to pity you, Michel. We pity those who are unhappy; and you are not unhappy. To see you is to know that."

"The saints suffered, and they were happy, because they loved. Suffering is incompatible with happiness only when it is the fruit of bitterness. It is inseparable from happiness when it is the fruit of love. That is why one can suffer, and still be happy, and filled with joy, and even gay, if the suffering is endured for love. Did not our Lord, the day before He suffered, give thanks? And should we not give thanks today? For tomorrow, Louise — tomorrow —"

"Yes, Michel," she whispered. "Tomorrow we die. It is so strange. I say it, but I cannot realize — I cannot even be afraid —"

"Die, Louise? Tomorrow we lay aside these garments we have worn on earth, and in their place, what glory we shall receive! Tomorrow heaven is ours, and beauty, and an end of pain, forever. I cannot think what it will be like to live without pain, but tomorrow it will be as if it had never been. And in proportion as we have suffered on earth, for Love, so much greater will our joy be in heaven. We have great happiness here, it is true; but on earth it is broken and interrupted. Tomorrow we will receive that joy in all its fullness, and it will never end. Tomorrow we do not die, Louise. Tomorrow we live."

The hours passed. The short winter day, heavy with clouds, drew to a close. Unrelieved darkness settled on the room. The prisoners huddled in groups on the floor. Some whispered; some talked in low tones; from time to time there was the sound of sobbing, or of laughter. Some prayed aloud, others knelt motionless. The great doors opened and shut no more; no further victims were added to their number. The cold winter night flooded them with icy blackness. They sank into it, as shipwrecked passengers into a winter sea.

On this night as on all nights, the town clock in the tower struck away the hours till morning; two — three — four — five — six —

After that the curtain of the night began to flutter, and slowly to roll back. Into the room crept a dawn like ashes.

Michel became aware of that unearthly glimmer which is not

so much the coming of light as the yielding of darkness: the sigh of night, realizing that she has had her interlude and must be gone. He had spent the night in prayer so profound that he had lost consciousness of his surroundings and of those about him. Since his meeting with Louise in the spring he had not had such grace in prayer. The darkness he had endured since then was his Gethsemane; and now it was ended. The peace of God flooded his soul; he looked forward without fear to whatever the next few hours might bring.

Pain, yes; but nothing he could not endure; for so God had promised. He must drink the Chalice, of that there could be no doubt; but had he not asked for it? "Since I may not drink it at the altar, grant that I may drink it in whatever form Thou hast prepared it for me, if only I may drink it truly." Had he not meant those words when he prayed them, and with all the strength of his soul? Was not the present hour the very answer to that prayer?

Pain. — It did not seem possible, as he had told Louise, that he was so soon to part from this companion, and forever. Had she not been his sister, his chosen lady, with whom he had lived in closest comradeship, who had not been absent from him in some form for a single day, since their first rude meeting so long ago? Nor had he ever regretted her fidelity; he had not asked to be parted from her. Was he not deeply sensible of her benefits, of the extraordinary blessings she had conferred on him? Had she not led him to the greatest good he had known — to joy, to beauty, to as much of heaven as it is possible to receive on earth? Would she not seize his hand once more, and lead him now to heaven itself? Would he shrink from a last close embrace, before parting from her forever?

"Accipiens et hunc praeclarum Calicem . . . item tibi gratias agens —"

To give thanks in the face of suffering, as He had done, was to exalt it, to crown and clothe it with beauty, to transform it into a sacrifice of praise, holy and acceptable to Him. The coming day would raise His chalice to Michel's lips. Would he not take it, and give thanks, and drink, confident that step by step, God would give him grace in abundance?

Light filtered slowly into the room: a frozen, hostile light, dreary and brittle as ice. It was dawn: the hour of Mass.

But today there would be no Mass.

No Mass? On this day of all days, it was not possible that there should be no Mass.

Michel listened. In the cold and silence an obligation was laid on him, a divine command:

"Have I not placed you here, Michel? Have I not written the words of My Sacrifice in your heart? Have I not filled you with a burning thirst to offer that Sacrifice, before you die? Why have I done so, except that you may offer it now, for yourself, and for My children, in their need? As the priest who stands before the altar represents Me, so you stand before My people in My place. Offer My sacrifice for them, Michel, and for yourself: for that is My desire."

Michel rose, stiff and aching with cold. There was a stirring among the prisoners, as if the dawn had touched them with icy fingers, to waken them. There were sudden exclamations, and bursts of weeping, as they roused to a consciousness of their surroundings, and to the knowledge of what day this was.

Louise knelt beneath the window where they had spoken together, and where Michel had last seen her when darkness swallowed them. Her hands were clasped, her lips moving. As if conscious of his glance, she looked up.

"Michel!" she said. "Michel! This is the day we are to die. God be with us all! Oh, Michel!" Her eyes filled suddenly. "If only it were possible to hear Holy Mass once more before I die. There were years when I could have heard it and did not, and that thought is a sword in my heart. If I might hear it once more, it would make up for all that time, and whatever they did to me, I would remember that I had seen our Lord again on this earth, that He had truly welcomed me back among His own, and I would die happy."

Paulette Dubois sat leaning against the wall, her arms clasped around Jeannot, who still slept. She looked up at Michel, and her eyes were bright with fear.

"Oh, Frère Mich', I am so frightened! But if I could hear Mass, I think I would not be afraid!"

"Last Sunday I was sick in my bed and I did not hear Mass. If I had known it was the last time, I would have crawled on my knees to the Church. Oh, Frère Mich', I would die happy if I could hear Mass!"

It was the longest speech Berthe Masson had made in her life.

"Yes, yes, that is true!" The insignificant treble of Jean Martin rose from the crowd of prisoners, thin and tenuous in the frosty air. "What a pity our Frère Mich is not a priest. Then he could say Mass for us and we should die in peace."

Michel faced the prisoners.

"My friends — my little ones."

All turned toward him. He looked into a sea of faces, on which the light of the cold dawn lay like frost.

"My friends, there are some here who have expressed the holy wish to hear Mass once more before we die. As you know, I am not a priest. But here there is no altar, nor host, nor wine, nor chalice. Lacking these, a hundred priests could not celebrate Mass. All that any priest could do for you now, I can do. The prayers of Holy Mass are written, word for word, in my heart. I will say them — I will chant them for you, as if this hall were a church, and this table an altar, and I a priest. What is lacking, your love will supply. And we will pray to our Lord, and since we desire it so ardently, who are about to die for Him, I believe He will make it a real Mass."

"Yes, Frère Mich'! Yes, yes! Sing Mass for us, Frère Mich'!"

Michel turned, facing the table. The prisoners knelt behind him in rows on the cold floor. He made the sign of the cross.

"In nomine Patris, et Filii, et Spiritus Sancti. Amen."

As he had often done on his way to market, Michel sang Mass.

"Adjutorium nostrum in nomine Domini —"

They understood. Frère Mich' would sing a Mass of Requiem: his, and theirs.

He recited the Confiteor. The response rose in a wave of sound behind him, a plea for mercy more eloquent than he had ever heard, because it was uttered by those who were shortly to submit their final plea for mercy to God Himself: who, indeed, were submitting their final plea on earth to Him now.

"Indulgentiam, absolutionem, et remissionem peccatorum

nostrorum tribuat nobis omnipotens et misericors Dominus. Amen."

The cry for mercy continued: *"Domine, exaudi orationem meam. — Et clamor meus ad te veniat. — Dominus vobiscum. — Et cum spiritu tuo."*

Without hesitation Michel spoke these words, assuming the prerogative, reserved for ordained priests, because he stood before these people in the absence of one who had such a right. He approached the table:

"Aufer a nobis, quaesumus, Domine —"

He was seized with confidence, with assurance. It was as if another acted in him, turning him toward the people, using his lips to speak the sacred words, extending his arms in blessing and in prayer. He himself did nothing.

He sang the Kyrie, the prayers; the Epistle, the Gospel.

Was this his voice which filled the cold hall, flooding it with living and eternal beauty, with the same presence, the same reality that had roused and quickened his dead soul at the chanting of Father André in the chapel of Notre Dame des Prés, so long ago?

"Per omnia saecula saeculorum . . ."

Was it his own voice he now heard, chanting the Preface of the Mass for the Dead, singing these syllables laden with such solemn and angelic beauty that it seemed as if, like the Son of God Himself, they had descended from heaven only to return to it again? Was it in very truth his voice — the voice of Michel — which thus poured forth the beauty of Mass into this bleak and desolate place where he and his companions awaited death? For this beauty which fell on his ears, which enveloped and possessed him, which humbled him with its austere and stately measures, was too great to have its source in him. Arising elsewhere, it flowed through him; he had no part in it, except to lend, to give, himself. His voice? Perhaps; but Another sang. Michel stood, and listened.

"Gratias agamus Domino Deo nostro."

In Mass, space and time are annihilated. In Mass, eternity and infinity are brought to earth. Though Mass is celebrated at a thousand altars, there is but one Mass: one miracle, one coming;

264   THE DAY OF FRÈRE MICH'

one Calvary, one sacrifice, in which all sacrifice is included, of which this offering could not fail to be a part:

"Sanctus, sanctus, sanctus . . ."

Behind him there was no sound. The great room might have been empty. Dawn was fully come by now; the dawn not of sunlight and hope, but of clouds and darkness, of ice and death. Michel entered upon the Canon of the Mass.

"Te igitur, clementissime Pater —"

At the Commemoration of the Living, he prayed for his brother Paul; for those who would put them to death; for his dear friends and Brothers at the monastery; and into the midst of his prayer, across his inner vision, flashed suddenly, to his amazement, the image of the little gray ass, Marceline, as she had trotted away from him the day before, on her way back to the monastery, alone. And why should he not recall her? Was she not one of God's willing and humble creatures, but for whom he would not now be here, and his friend in very truth? For there is none too small, too lowly to be used by God in the furtherance of His divine plan: had not Our Lord Himself chosen to ride just such a little beast, the day before He died?

Before He died. . . . Proceeding, Michel came to the Consecration, to those words which he had hungered and thirsted with unspeakable yearning to say, and now he was saying them:

"Qui pridie quam pateretur, accepit panem in sanctas ac venerabiles manus suas, et elevatis oculis in coelum ad te Deum Patrem suum omnipotentem" — he suited the action to the words — *"tibi gratias agens, benedixit, fregit, deditque discipulis suis, dicens: Accipite, et manducate ex hoc omnes.*

"Hoc est enim Corpus Meum."

Michel bent low over the table, in adoration of his Lord, who, though invisible, was yet present as assuredly, Michel in his heart knew, as if he had held in his hand the host and were endowed with the power of consecrating it. He knelt, rose, lifting his arms, that those behind him, for whom he did this, might with their love supply the image of the Body of Our Lord, though the divine substance was wanting, and knelt again.

Michel did not realize how profound the silence was during his enactment of the holy rite until it was broken.

At the words of Consecration, where usually all sound is hushed, and the silence deepens into mystery itself, there arose now a low, astonished murmur, a deep gasp of amazed wonder, drawn from a hundred throats, rising and swelling into a great cry of exultation and joy:

"*C'est Lui! C'est Notre Seigneur! C'est Lui-Même!* — It is He! It is Our Lord! It is He — Himself!"

For the kneeling prisoners, gazing upward at the genuflection of Michel, saw before the table, not a lay Brother in his dark habit, holding aloft in one mutilated hand an imaginary host. No. The Figure before the table was clothed in white. From it light radiated and poured, so that it stood bathed in a very quiver and stream of light.

Instead of the single maimed hand of Brother Michel, the astonished eyes of the people beheld two hands, and in them a white and luminous disk, the Sacred Host itself. Although not injured as was the hand of Brother Michel, these hands nevertheless showed through each a deep wound, from which streamed, not blood, but light.

"*Hic est enim Calix Sanguinis mei —*"

He at the altar raised aloft the Chalice of His Own Blood.

"*Unde et memores, Domine, nos servi tui — *"

From their profound and awed obeisance, the people looked up again. In the room was no light other than the cold dawn. At the table, Brother Michel, in his dark habit, continued chanting for them the prayers of Holy Mass.

"*Pater Noster, qui es in coelis —*"

It was with the greatest difficulty that they persuaded him of the truth of what they had seen.

"But what are you saying, my people?" he cried. "What is it you say? That our Lord stood at the table in my place? You saw Him — all of you?"

"But yes, Frère Mich'! It is true. It was He — we saw Him, all of us! He was in white, and shining, and He showed us the Host, and the Chalice. In His hands we saw the marks of the nails, and light came from them, Frère Mich', long rays of light!

When we looked again, He was gone, and you were there, where He stood!"

Slowly Michel comprehended that this was so: that all in the room had seen it, not in fancy, but with their bodily eyes, in very truth.

It passed belief, but he believed. It passed comprehension, but he understood. He fell to his knees before the table which had served him as altar, and bowed his head on his arms. In his heart were such singing and rapture as could hardly be endured.

"You He has ordained —"

These words were true. There was no longer any doubt. That had happened which could not happen. That was which could not be. God is good beyond all expectation, and with Him all things are possible.

Michel was a priest, and forever; and on this, the day of his death, he had sung Mass.

News of the massacre at Guillemont, and of the martyrdom of Brother Michel, reached the monastery and surprised none: Marceline, returning alone, with her baskets full, had already informed them of the circumstances as plainly as any spoken or written word could do.

What disposition had been made of the bodies of the martyrs none knew. It was therefore impossible to give the martyred Brother burial; but a Mass of Requiem was sung for him at the Chapel of Notre Dame des Prés.

The celebrant was Father André.

Father André, on his way to Rome, had arrived at Notre Dame des Prés after a long and terrible journey, during which he had been overtaken by the Huguenots and forced to flee and to hide. He reached the monastery on the very day of the massacre at Guillemont. Thus he was too late to see Brother Michel again while he lived, but he was in time to sing a Mass of Requiem for him, as Brother Michel would have wished.

Brother Baptiste begged to be allowed to perform some service in memory of the young Seigneur, whom he had so deeply loved, and for whose death he was inconsolable, in spite of the certainty that Brother Michel, having died for the faith, was now a saint in heaven; and to Brother Baptiste was entrusted the preparation of the catafalque. He asked that none might help him in this task, but that he might be permitted to perform this small labor alone; and his request was granted.

Brother Etienne had grave doubts as to the wisdom of allowing Brother Baptiste to undertake this, or any work, unaided. While conceding that none could be of a better will than Brother Baptiste, Brother Etienne was nevertheless skeptical concerning the latter's ability to carry out instructions with any exactness, no matter how carefully they might be given.

Accordingly, he took it upon himself to inspect the work of Brother Baptiste, to make certain that nothing was amiss, but that all was correctly disposed, and in order.

He went to the chapel early, before the hour of Mass. He perceived at once that it was well he had done so. It was as he suspected: Brother Baptiste, who could be counted on to do everything wrong and nothing right, had not failed to commit his usual blunder.

He had placed the pall on the catafalque with the head of the cross toward the altar.

Brother Baptiste evidently did not know, or did not recall, the significance of this position. Placed thus, the cross indicated that he for whom Mass was celebrated had been a priest.

The chapel was in darkness. Brother Etienne thought himself alone. He did not see Father André, who knelt in the choir stalls, making a long preparation for his Mass.

Filled with grief and unable to rest, Father André had come to the chapel long before daybreak to pray; and he found himself much comforted in his sorrow.

For in the deep silence of the chapel it seemed to him he did not pray alone. His heart spoke as to one not separated from him, but close at hand:

"Michel, my son, why should I grieve for you? You have won the prize we all covet. I know that in heaven you remember me, and will pray that I may win it too. The memory of you will go with me all my life, to comfort and encourage me. You were a flame burning in darkness, and the fire which consumed you was the love of Mass. That fire is all but extinguished in the hearts of men, but you will kindle it again from heaven.

"In heaven nothing is wanting to you, Michel. Your life on earth was a cross, a long and cruel deprivation; but with what joy you bore it, so that none would have thought, to see and speak to you, that you had any longing that had not been satisfied. I knew your thirst and your hunger, for God permitted that you should reveal them to me; and I know now that your longing is satisfied and your thirst quenched. I grieve for myself, that I did not see you, yes; but I cannot grieve for you. For you I can only rejoice."

His attention caught by a sound, Father André looked up. To his surprise, he saw that he was not alone. A Brother was busy at the catafalque. Father André rose from his place and approached the altar rail.

"What do you here, Brother? What is amiss?"

Brother Etienne indicated the cross. "As you see, *mon père,* it is incorrectly placed. I was about to change it."

Father André looked. A deep emotion stirred him as he remarked the position of the cross.

"No," said Father André. "Let it be."

Brother Etienne stared. "But, *mon père,* Brother Baptiste was in error to arrange it in this manner."

"Do not touch it. One so humble as Brother Baptiste can hardly fail to be an instrument of the divine pleasure."

Brother Etienne continued to protest. "But it is a mistake. Brother Michel was not a priest."

"You will obey without question," said Father André sternly. "The divine wisdom transcends our mistakes. God has used the humility of Brother Baptiste to reveal to us a truth known to Him from the beginning, but until now hidden from our sight. The cross shall remain as it is."

Brother Etienne dropped the end of the pall, and murmuring an apology, left the chapel.

If any others observed the mistake of Brother Baptiste, none spoke of it or took measures to correct it.

Thus the cross remained as Brother Baptiste had arranged it, testifying that the Mass of Requiem sung by Father André for Brother Michel was celebrated in memory of a priest.

Translations

CPSIA information can be obtained
at www.ICGtesting.com
Printed in the USA
FFOW03n1340311017
41754FF

9 781621 382904